A STALKER'S PREY

K.D. RICHARDS

COLTON THREAT UNLEASHED

TARA TAYLOR QUINN

MILLS & BOON

First Published in Great Britain 2024
by Mills & Boon, an imprint of HarperCollins*Publishers* Ltd
1 London Bridge Street, London, SE1 9GF

www.harpercollins.co.uk

HarperCollins*Publishers*
Macken House, 39/40 Mayor Street Upper,
Dublin 1, D01 C9W8, Ireland

A Stalker's Prey © 2024 Kia Dennis
Colton Threat Unleashed © 2024 Harlequin Enterprises ULC

Special thanks and acknowledgment are given to Tara Taylor Quinn for her contribution to *The Coltons of Owl Creek* series.

ISBN: 978-0-263-32214-9

0124

This book is produced from independently certified FSC™ paper to ensure responsible forest management.

For more information visit: www.harpercollins.co.uk/green

Printed and Bound in the UK using 100% Renewable Electricity at
CPI Group (UK) Ltd, Croydon, CR0 4YY

A STALKER'S PREY

K.D. RICHARDS

Chapter One

Brianna Baker took a deep breath of crispy, New York morning air and picked up her pace along the Central Park path. There was probably another twenty-five to thirty minutes before dawn broke through the dark skies overhead and Bria wanted to be back at her Upper West Side townhouse before then. The morning air was invigorating and the forty-six-degree temperature was motivating, but the best thing about getting her morning jog in before the sun came up was that there was little chance that anyone would recognize her.

The brief snatches of time where she could be alone, unrecognized and just breathe and be herself, were what had kept her sane since her acting career had taken off and propelled her into celebrity status.

She wasn't complaining, at least not out loud. Acting had been her dream for as long as she could remember. And the fact that people, millions of people, thought she was good enough to spend their hard-earned dollars going to see her movies was thrilling and humbling in equal measure. But that fame had a price. The loss of her privacy for one. And lately, a nearly debilitating insecurity. The third movie in which she starred as Princess Kaleva, warrior princess, sent to Earth from an alien planet to retrieve the five elemental stones needed to save her people from certain death, had broken box office records in the US and overseas. She was officially an international superstar.

She was proud of the Princess Kaleva movies. They were showing little girls everywhere, especially little brown girls, that they were strong, powerful and smart and that they could be anything they wanted to be. But what she really wanted was to be taken seriously as an actress. But ever since she'd taken on the Princess Kaleva role, her agent had found it difficult to convince the Hollywood honchos that she could do the more serious roles.

Which was why she'd lobbied hard for the part of wife and mother, Elizabeth Stewart, in *Loss of Days*, a film about a family in crisis as a result of a child's drug addiction, when it had come up. It was a bonus that the majority of the filming, although on a tight six-week schedule, was going to be done in New York. In her heart, the city was still her hometown, even after fifteen years in California. It had taken some convincing and several auditions, but she'd won the part. And now she was weeks away from finishing the film she felt in her bones would prove to all of Hollywood that she could play serious, dramatic roles and not just be a busty superhero.

Princess Kaleva had pushed her into the ranks of celebrity, but *Loss of Days* was going to earn her the respect as an actress that she really coveted.

She picked up her pace. Although the sun had started to peek over the trees, the portion of the trail she was on remained deserted. She'd been jogging the same loop around the park since she'd come back to New York a little over a month ago to shoot the film. It totaled just over two miles and she wanted to make it the whole way before the park was packed with people.

She pushed through an uphill stretch of the path, her lungs burning. When she got to the top, she stopped, taking a moment to catch her breath.

Footsteps ricocheted off the trees behind her.

Bria glanced over her shoulder.

A figure jogged up the hill in her direction. From the size and gait, she pegged the person as male, but the shadows and a baseball cap pulled down low on the man's head obscured his face.

A bolt of unease shot through her. She began jogging again. She hadn't told anyone on her team about her morning jogs. Mika Reynolds, her agent, would have told her in no uncertain terms she was a fool for venturing out so early, and Eliot Sykes, her public relations manager, would have admonished her for jogging alone. But one thing she hadn't completely adapted to in terms of her recent celebrity was the complete and total lack of privacy that seemed to come along with it. And she wasn't sure she wanted to.

Bria shot another glance over her shoulder. The man was moving quickly, at more of a run than a jog, and with purpose.

She turned and began to sprint, less concerned with pacing herself than she was with getting to a more public space.

He's out for his morning run. He's not chasing you.

She tried convincing herself but survival instincts, honed over thirty-five years of being a woman in the world, pushed her forward.

She could hear the crunch of leaves indicating that the man was still behind her.

A level of fear she hadn't felt for a long time flooded her

body, pushing her forward. She was still a bit of a distance from the entrance to the trail and she hadn't seen anyone other than the man behind her.

Without thinking, she plunged into the trees. Between the noise she was making crashing through the brush and the sound of her heart drumming in her chest, she couldn't tell if the man was still behind her.

She was probably overreacting. The man was most likely just another jogger out for a run, wondering why the weird lady had jumped into the woods.

But a voice inside her head screamed that that wasn't it at all.

She raced through the shadows, branches scraping against her arms and snagging her leggings. Darkness still clung to the dense woods, making her hasty decision seem ever more perilous.

She ran until her lungs threatened to burst, then crouched behind the thick trunk of a tree. She forced herself to listen past her own breathing for sounds that someone else was close.

She didn't hear anything she wouldn't have expected to hear in a thicket, but it was little comfort. If she stayed here and someone really was after her, had she just made it easier for them by darting into the trees? She had even less of a chance now of running into other people.

She couldn't stay cowering behind here forever. She pushed to her feet and plowed forward.

It seemed like it took forever, but finally, she saw the glow of streetlights.

Bria burst through trees, falling onto a walking path in front of a middle-aged man in a suit and carrying a briefcase. He started, freezing for a moment with wide eyes. She could only imagine what she looked like to him.

After a second, he rushed forward, concern plastered over his face for the wild woman who had literally just fallen at his feet. Thankfully, he didn't seem to recognize her. The last thing she needed was to have photos of herself online, leaves clinging to her leggings and twigs sticking out of her hair.

Bria assured the man that she was okay and didn't need an ambulance or the police.

He started away slowly, shooting a glance over his shoulder at her.

She attempted to smile, reassuringly only, but her eyes darted back into the darkness of the trees she'd just burst out of. She couldn't be sure, but it seemed as if the shadows shifted, taking the shape of a head and shoulders.

A car horn honked in the distance, tearing her gaze away from the trees for a moment. When she turned back, there was nothing to see but a solid wall of darkness.

Chapter Two

"I want to hire West Investigations, specifically Xavier Nichols, to provide for my personal protection while I'm here in New York." Brianna Baker sat on the other side of the conference room table at West Security and Investigations headquarters, the hem of her perfectly tailored skirt riding up high enough to reveal a silky smooth, caramel-colored thigh, sufficient to make a man's thoughts wander but not high enough to be tasteless.

Ryan West kept his gaze firmly fixed on her face. Not only was he a happily married husband and father, Ms. Baker was a potential high-profile client.

A potential high-profile client who was apparently familiar with Xavier Nichols, one of West Security and Investigations' best personal-protection operatives. A situation which was, in a word, interesting.

"May I ask who referred you to Xavier?" Ryan asked, not bothering to hide the note of curiosity in his voice.

Ms. Baker hesitated. "Let's just say his reputation precedes him."

It was all he could do to keep himself from laughing in her pretty face at that. If anything Xavier's reputation should have her running for the hills. He was good at what he did, protecting high-priority targets, but he had the people skills of a surly porcupine and communicated mostly in grunts and glances dark enough to turn lesser men to ash.

There was more to multi-award-winning actress Brianna Baker's story, a lot more if Ryan was reading her correctly. And his was a business that required him to be able to read people correctly. "Unfortunately, Xavier has just been placed on a new assignment. But, as I'm sure you are aware, West Investigations is the best in the business. I'm confident that another protection specialist can meet your needs."

"I'm sorry, but that won't work for me." She uncrossed her legs and reached for her handbag. "If Mr. Nichols isn't available, I'll have to find another way to solve my problem."

"One moment, please, Ms. Baker." Ryan held up a hand stopping her before she headed for the door.

She flashed a smile. "Please, call me Bria."

"Bria," he said with a nod. "Xavier happens to be in the office today. Why don't I call him in here and you can explain why you want to hire West Security and Investigations, and Xavier, specifically, to both of us."

She nodded, relief coursing across the delicate features of her face. "Yes, I think that would be a great place to start. Thank you, Mr. West."

"Ryan, please." He reached into his suit pocket for his phone, noticing as he did that some of the tension that she had been holding in her shoulders had faded away.

Brianna Baker was scared. And whatever it was she was afraid of, she believed Xavier was the man who could help her.

BRIA'S ALREADY RACING heart began to thunder once Ryan West declared that Xavier was on his way into the conference room. She was an actress, an award-winning actress no less, but right now, she couldn't find it in her to act as if seeing Xavier for the first time in fifteen years wasn't threatening to completely undo her.

She channeled her character from *Loss of Days*, Elizabeth Stewart, the matriarch of a rich, high-powered family. Elizabeth was always in control. She never let anyone close enough to read her thoughts or pick up on her emotions.

Be Elizabeth.

Bria took in a deep breath and let it out slowly as they waited for Xavier. She realized that Ryan West was studying her. She got the feeling he didn't miss much. That, she was sure, was what made him so good at his job.

She hadn't come to West Security and Investigations just because Xavier worked there, but if she was being honest, she would have at least checked out any private security firm he'd been employed by. Luckily, West was actually one of the best in the country. That was great because she needed the best.

Her stalker had gotten past every security measure she and her people had implemented to date, and if he really had been chasing her on her jog through Central Park earlier that morning that meant he'd followed her across the country as well. She was terrified of what he would do next.

So terrified that she was doing something she'd never thought she'd do. Turning to the man whose heart she'd broken and begging for his help.

Well, maybe not begging, but certainly asking for his help, which required her to swallow a heaping dose of humble pie. But it was worth it if West Investigations found her stalker and stopped the campaign of harassment he'd been on for the past six months.

And if she and Xavier rekindled something in the meantime...

No. Absolutely not. She wasn't there to rekindle anything. Despite the doubt that had crossed Ryan West's face, Xavier's reputation as a personal security specialist, a fancy name for bodyguard, was sterling. She wasn't embarrassed to admit she'd kept tabs on him over the years. He wasn't the kind of guy who had a social media presence, at least not one that she'd been able to find, and she'd deny it to anyone who asked, but she'd tried on more than one occasion.

But she knew he'd gone into the military after she'd broken up with him, become a decorated soldier in the army, then stepped into the private sector working as private security at West Investigations. He'd provided New York-area event security for several actors and actresses she knew. It had been easy to wheedle information about him from there. Actors were notorious for gossiping. And the actresses she knew that he'd worked for previously were more than happy to dish on the tall, dark and handsome bodyguard, even if he was more than a little surly. The surliness only made him sexier.

To that she could attest firsthand.

The conference room door opened behind her and she felt her entire body tense.

Ryan West stood, but Bria remained seated. She wasn't sure she could stand if she'd tried. Her back was to the door, but she could feel Xavier behind her. It had been like that since the first moment they met. Like they were on a special frequency, just the two of them. Whenever they were in proximity of each other, the air pulsated.

Xavier had yet to speak.

"Xavier Nichols, I'd like you to meet Brianna Baker."

Bria turned the chair and stood, facing her first love, hell, the only man she'd ever been in love with, for the first time in fifteen years.

Fear, excitement and desire raced through her.

He'd changed over the years. He'd always been tall and lean, but now he filled out the dark jeans and long-sleeved gray T-shirt he wore. His shoulders were broad, his arms more muscled. His hair was still cut short, but the touch of gray just beginning to crop up around his temples gave him a slightly distinguished air. But the eyes, they were the same. Dark brown, just like his skin, that looked at her as if they could see straight into her soul. Eyes she used to love getting lost in.

Eyes that were gazing back at her now with open surprise and something else she couldn't put a name to.

"Bria." The sound of her name in his dark baritone swept over her like a warm ocean breeze at sunset.

She closed her eyes for a moment, remembering the last time he'd said her name like that. They'd been wrapped around each other in a dump of a rental house they'd gotten with a couple of friends in Atlantic City.

"Brianna." He said her full name this time and she opened her eyes, plunged back into reality. "What…what are you doing here?"

"Xavier, I need your help."

Chapter Three

Xavier stared at the vision in front of him. It took a lot to surprise him. He was a Bronx native, an '80s child who'd bounced from relative to relative and had seen his fair share of messed-up crap while doing it. And then he'd enlisted in the army, which had resulted in a whole new visage of nightmarish events.

But walking into West's conference room and seeing Brianna Baker, in the flesh, not just on a movie poster or in a commercial for whatever new film she was in, shocked him to his core.

He couldn't count the number of times he'd imagined, dreamed of what it would be like to see Bria in real life again. He'd played the meeting in his head thousands of times over the years, but none of those fantasies had prepared him for the moment he found himself looking into her beautiful brown eyes.

"What are you doing here?" He repeated the question. His brain was struggling to do anything other than drink in the woman standing in front of him.

She was gorgeous, even more so than she'd been when they were twenty. The barest hint of makeup accentuated her warm golden-brown complexion and high cheekbones.

Long, beachy waves cascaded over her shoulders. And her figure, a perfect hourglass. High, firm breasts and shapely hips that he longed to pull tightly against his body. Legs that went on for days, ending in the sexiest strappy black heels he'd ever seen. His mind instantly went to a vision of her wearing those heels and nothing else before he shook it loose.

"I need your help." Bria bit her lip, cutting into his fantasy. "West Security and Investigations' help."

He tensed and took a step forward, reaching out for her before letting his hand drop back down to his side. Damn. After all these years, he still wanted to wrap himself around her and protect her from every bad thing in this world. But he didn't have that right. Not anymore. So he went the more professional route. "What's wrong?"

"I have a stalker."

"Why don't we all have a seat and you can give us the details," Ryan said.

Xavier cut his gaze toward Ryan, only then remembering that his boss was in the room.

Bria had always had that effect on him. There was no one but her when she was near.

Bria sat back down, crossing her long legs.

His brain cycled to a memory that had him kissing up the length of those legs.

"Xavier." Ryan's voice pulled him back to the present. Ryan watched him through narrowed eyes.

It would have probably been more appropriate to move to the opposite side of the table and sit next to Ryan, but he slid into the chair next to Bria instead.

Ryan picked up his pen and held it at the ready. Every operative had their own style, but Xavier knew that Ryan felt taking notes by hand was less distracting for their clients during initial interviews. "So Bria, please, tell us how West Security and Investigations can help you."

"As I said, I have a stalker, which given my profession, isn't surprising. However, the stalker's outreach has…intensified over the last week."

Xavier's chest tightened. "Intensified how?"

Fear flashed across Bria's face for a brief moment before it was gone, replaced by what looked to him like rehearsed calm. "He, I say *he* because most stalkers are male, but I don't actually know if it's a man or woman, sent me flowers at my house." She paused for a moment, almost as if she needed to fortify herself before speaking the next words. "I get flowers from fans sometimes, so that's not the issue. It's that the roses were black. And withered. Dead. And the card that was with it was not like the usual fan mail. It scared me." A tiny shudder moved through her body.

Again, he fought the urge to reach out and pull her against his body.

"We'll need to see the note."

She pulled the compact rectangle of a bag hanging from her shoulder onto her lap and extracted a small card.

YOU ARE MINE. AND I'LL BE COMING TO TAKE WHAT'S MINE VERY SOON.

He handed the card across the conference room table to Ryan, looking up at Bria as he did.

She was trying to look calm, unruffled, but she'd never been able to keep anything from him. He could see the fear in her eyes and it ignited fury inside of him.

And terror. Because, even after fifteen years, if anything

was to happen to her, he didn't think he could go on. His heart thudded in his chest.

"Do you have any idea who could be behind this?" he asked.

Bria shook her head. "No. Like I said, I get lots of questionable fan mail. The flowers were delivered to the set and a PA, a production assistant, signed for them and brought them to me. The PA didn't pay attention to the delivery person, and there was nothing with the flowers that indicated what florist they'd come from."

Ryan scribbled something on the notepad in front of him. "We're going to keep this note if you don't mind. Run a few tests on it. They'll probably turn up nothing useful, but you never know."

Bria nodded her assent.

"You said the flowers and this most recent note were a ramping up on the part of the stalker." Xavier rolled his chair a fraction of an inch closer to Bria. He might not be able to touch her, but he was damn sure going to stick close. "When did the stalker first get in touch with you?"

"It started with weird emails about six months ago, as far as we can tell."

"Who is *we*?" Xavier asked.

"I don't actually read my own fan mail, and it became too much after the first Princess Kaleva movie for my assistant to handle along with her other duties. Now I use a public relations firm. They read any fan mail I get and respond appropriately. Most threats are logged and never make it to my attention, but if the threat is deemed credible, I'm notified, as are the police and anyone else who may need to know."

"We'll need the name of the PR firm and whoever handles your fan mail there, as well as your assistant's name and contact information."

"That's not a problem. The PR firm is Eliot Sykes Public Relations. My assistant's name is Karen Gibbs. She stayed in Los Angeles because her mother is ill and she can't be away for six weeks, but I'll let her know she should cooperate and get you whatever you need."

"Thanks," Ryan said. "Now, can you tell us more about these emails?"

"They're anonymous, so it's hard to say for sure that the emails and the flowers are from the same guy. The emails were weird at first but mostly harmless, so my PR team didn't even tell me about them initially."

"Weird how?" Xavier pressed.

A flash of something, hesitation maybe, went across Bria's face before disappearing just as fast. She pulled an envelope out of her purse and handed it to him.

He read each email before passing the printout across the conference table to Ryan. There were over a dozen of them. The first few were all some sort of variation on the same. "Your movies mean everything to me." "We belong together." "I'm your biggest fan." "No one loves you more than me." Pretty typical fan mail. But then the messages progressed to the more personal. Asking Bria out to dinner. To marry him. To have his child.

Hell no. The words screamed through his head. Even though he hadn't said them out loud he hadn't been able to beat back the growl that rumbled in his chest.

He focused on the emails again. Their tone grew even more possessive. "You are mine" and "We belong together" being the most popular themes, it seemed. Then the messages changed, but were somehow even creepier. "I'll keep your secret." "Don't worry. I'll never tell." "Your secret is safe with me, my love."

Not a threat, at least not implicitly, but they made his skin crawl just the same.

He looked up at Bria. "What secret?"

"I have no idea." Bria's gaze slipped away from him.

"This person clearly believes he knows something about you," Ryan said. "Can you think of anything he could be referring to?"

"You have to understand. This person might not even really be thinking about me as me. Lots of fans conflate the character an actor plays on screen with the actor themselves. This secret might be the secret of some character I played who knows how long ago."

Maybe, but Xavier didn't think that was it, and from the look on Ryan's face, he wasn't buying it either. There was something Bria wasn't telling them. But they could circle back to it later.

"The note with the flowers and the emails use slightly different language at times. The note doesn't mention your secret, whatever that may be, and it's an explicit expression of ownership and domination."

"I noticed that, but all the notes came from the same email address, so they must be from the same person. As for the flowers, it's too much for me to contemplate that there are two people out there stalking me at the same time."

It wasn't out of the realm of possibility, given the level of her fame, but there was no need to worry her with that thought at the moment.

"Have you spoken to the LAPD?" Ryan inquired.

Bria's face twisted into a frown. "Yes. They took a report but said there was nothing they could do. No laws have been broken and they didn't think the emails or notes were a direct threat. They suggested I hire private security if I was concerned."

Ryan's brows arched. "There are several excellent private security firms in Los Angeles. Why did you wait until you got to New York to seek private protection?"

A good question and one that Xavier should have thought of the moment she'd started explaining her problem. Bria should have had personal security the minute the tone of the emails had shifted.

He caught her glance in his direction before she focused all her attention back on Ryan.

"I was hesitant to take that step. I didn't want some creep forcing me to change how I live. Until this morning."

Xavier's heart rate ticked up as her voice trailed off. "What happened this morning?"

"I think someone chased me while I was on my morning run in Central Park."

"Why the hell were you running through Central Park when you have a stalker?" Xavier exploded.

Ryan cut him a hard look, but Bria spoke before Ryan could admonish him.

"Because it's how I clear my head," she shot at him angrily. "I won't be held a prisoner. You should know that up front. If West Investigations can't provide protection while letting me maintain my shooting schedule and some semblance of a normal life, I'll find a security firm that can."

Before he had a chance to tell her just that, Ryan held up both hands. "Hang on, both of you. Why don't you tell us about what happened in the park and we can go from there."

Bria explained that she liked to jog in the early morning to clear her head and because there were fewer people out to recognize her. She was out running on one of the paths in Central Park that morning when she'd felt a man coming up quickly behind her. She'd gotten scared enough of the man to cut through trees. She was pretty sure he'd followed her into the woods, but it had been too dark to see his face or any distinguishing features.

Xavier bit his tongue against the urge to admonish her for dodging through the trees. She'd increased her risk, darting into a secluded area. It was one thing to care more about her career than she did about him, but he couldn't believe she'd been so cavalier about her safety. Traipsing around New York alone and unprotected in the wee hours of the morning was just reckless.

"So you aren't absolutely sure you were being chased?" Ryan pressed.

Bria bit her bottom lip. "I'm not 100 percent positive but—"

Ryan held up a hand again. "I'm not doubting you. You did the right thing getting away from someone you thought could be a threat."

Bria's shoulders relaxed.

Unfortunately, every muscle in Xavier's body remained tense. "What about your agent and the producers of your movie? What's their take?"

Bria turned her gaze to him. "Be diligent. Watchful, but they aren't worried."

"But you are worried." Xavier stated the obvious.

"Look, I've been in this industry for over a decade. I've had my fair share of racist fan letters, creepy fan letters and even outright threatening fan letters. This feels different. And frankly, I'm more exposed here in New York, working on location instead of on a studio lot with tons of studio-provided security."

"So you would be paying out of pocket for your security?" Ryan asked.

Xavier shot a glare across the table at his boss. Money? That's what Ryan was thinking about? Who would foot the bill? Well, maybe that was his responsibility as the president of West Security and Investigations, but Xavier didn't care what it cost. Bria was going to have the full weight and protection of West Investigations protecting her 24/7 until they'd caught this sicko stalker, even if he had to pay for it himself. Something he wouldn't have had a hope in Hades of doing when he'd walked away from her fifteen years ago, but now it wouldn't be a problem. He'd done well for himself working in private overseas security after getting out of the army and currently with West Security and Investigations. Not only could he protect Bria now, he could provide for her in the way that he'd only dreamed of when they'd been a couple. The way she deserved.

Bria's back straightened. "Money isn't an issue. A simple Google search will return estimates of my net worth and I assure you even the highest number is an underestimate."

Ryan held up his hands. "I didn't mean to imply you couldn't pay our fee. I only wanted to get a sense of whether we'd be working within the parameters set by a studio or the producers of your movie."

Bria let out a long slow breath. "I'm sorry for jumping to conclusions. No. No, if West Investigations decides it can take me on as a client, you will be working directly for me." Bria cut a glance in Xavier's direction.

"Consider us hired. As of right now," Xavier growled.

Ryan frowned. "Ms. Baker has requested that you be in

charge of her protective detail and I explained that you'd recently been assigned to another protective detail, so that might not be possible, but—"

"It's not only possible, it's done. I'll get Jack to take over my current assignments."

"Xavier." Ryan's voice came low and authoritative.

Xavier met his boss's gaze straight on. He respected Ryan West, and considered him and Ryan's brother Shawn among the few people he'd categorize as friends. But this was Bria. There was nothing he wouldn't do when it came to her safety. If he had to, he'd go it alone, quit his job, take on Bria's protection on his own. He still had a few contacts in the world of foreign private security and mercenaries. He'd pay them whatever it took to establish his own team, but frankly, he knew it wouldn't be the same as having West Investigations on Bria's side.

After what seemed like hours, Ryan gave a faint nod and Xavier started breathing again.

Good. West was the best chance they had of finding Bria's stalker and stopping him before Bria got hurt.

The mere thought of her being hurt had his gut twisting into little knots.

"Well, Ms. Baker, it looks like Xavier is available to head up your protection detail," Ryan said.

Bria exhaled audibly. "There is one other thing. The press hasn't picked up the fact that I've got a stalker. So far. I'd like to keep it that way for as long as possible."

"West Security and Investigations always protects its clients' confidentiality," Xavier responded.

A small smile of relief turned up the corners of her mouth.

An instant yearning to send that smile blooming wider speared him. He shoved it away. She'd made it more than clear fifteen years ago that nothing was more important to her than her career, including him, and he doubted that had changed. She'd come to him for his professional services and that was all.

He'd find the sicko stalking her and neutralize him and then they'd both go back to living their separate lives.

Just like she wanted.

Chapter Four

Ryan had his assistant go over the contract with Bria while he settled Xavier into his office.

"Okay, we don't have a lot of time, so give me the CliffsNotes version."

"We used to date when we were kids. She ended it. The end."

"She ended it."

"I'm over it."

Ryan's brows arched. "I can see that," he said sarcastically.

Xavier frowned. "I'll be fine. Bria's in trouble and I can help her in a professional capacity, so I will."

"And if your prior personal relationship gets in the way, you'll let me know, right?"

Xavier glared. "It won't."

"If it does…" Ryan pushed back.

Xavier nodded, then turned on his heel and went to find Bria. She'd just finished signing the documents that officially made her a client of West Investigations.

"I need to get to the set," she said when Xavier reentered the conference room.

"Your protection detail starts now. I'll take you." He led

her from the room to the secure garage where West parked its small fleet of cars.

If he'd had his way, Xavier would have taken Bria to a safe house and squirreled her away until he came up with a comprehensive plan for her safety. Actually, he wouldn't have minded keeping her hidden until they caught the creep stalking her. But Bria had put the kibosh on any thoughts of a private refuge, temporary or otherwise, while her movie was shooting. So instead of heading for a safe house, he was driving her to the building where the movie was filming most of its interior scenes.

"Princess Kaleva made me a celebrity but *Loss of Days* is going to put me on the map as a serious actress," she explained on the drive to the set.

He made a right onto 42nd Street and drove past Bryant Park.

He shot a glance across the car, but Bria was focused on her phone and didn't seem to have noticed where they were.

They'd been all of nineteen years old when they met in this very park. He'd been heading home from his job as a stock hand at a grocery store in Midtown that no longer existed. Back then, he lived in a tiny studio apartment with a roommate, supplementing his income and picking up whatever side hustles he could to make ends meet. It was a hard life but he had never known anything else.

Cutting through the park, he'd seen Bria sitting on a bench, reading.

She was luminous. He stared at her for far longer than he should have before sliding onto the bench next to her.

She didn't spare him so much as a glance. He finally gathered his courage and asked her how she liked the book.

"It's a play. And I'm in it," she answered, with a smile that made his knees go weak.

"You're an actress."

"Well, I want to be. Someday," she'd responded boldly. "Right now I'm a student at the New York Acting Conservatory downtown." She looked at him expectantly.

He didn't have a clue about the New York Conservatory or any type of school, to be honest. Higher education had been so far out of reach for him he'd never given it a thought. "Sounds fancy."

"Well, it's not Juilliard, but it's a great school and I was lucky to be accepted." There was that brilliant smile again. "My name is Brianna, but you can call me Bria."

He took the hand she extended, and from that moment on, he was a goner. They'd sat on that bench talking, well, she talked and he listened, for another hour. And then he spent the last forty dollars he had to his name, buying her an early dinner at a local café.

They were together for a year. The best year of his life. Bria was kind and outgoing and he was gruff and spoke only when it was necessary, but somehow, they fit. What he felt for her, what they had together was deep, passionate. He'd never known anyone like her before. Never loved anyone like her before.

He'd realized early on that being with her made him want to be a better man. Her ambition had stoked his own, although he hadn't been sure what to do with it. Bria had opened his eyes to the difference between a job and a career that he loved. She made him think about things he'd never contemplated before. About right and wrong. About how to be a good person, a better person. About his future. He hadn't been sure about what he wanted to do for the rest of his life, but he knew he wanted Bria at his side and she deserved more than he'd ever be able to give her on a stock hand's salary.

Then one day, without warning, she'd ended it.

They'd met for lunch at a dingy café not far from her campus, which sold lackluster sandwiches at student-friendly prices. Bria was unusually quiet while they ate and the anxiety encircling her had knotted his stomach until he couldn't take it anymore.

"What is it? I can see something is bothering you," he'd said.

She dragged her gaze from her half-eaten sandwich to his face. "I think we should break up."

The words felt like a sucker punch to his jaw. "Why?"

"I got a part in a pilot. It films in LA. I have to be there right after graduation."

"That's great. But that's no reason to break up."

She reached across the table and grasped his hand. "Xavier, I love you. I do, but this pilot could be my big shot. I need to focus on my career. And your life is here in New York."

He squeezed her hand and pulled her forward so their foreheads met across the table. "If you love me, let's try to make this work. We can do the long-distance thing, and maybe once I've saved a little bit of money, I can move to the West Coast."

Bria closed her eyes. He watched a single tear drop trail down her cheek.

For a moment, he thought she'd agree. That he'd convinced her that their love was strong enough to overcome whatever hurdles life and her career might throw at them.

She stuttered out a breath and pulled away from him. "I'm sorry. I think this is for the best."

Emotions roiled through him, but his pride wouldn't let him beg. He'd stood, taken one last, long look at the woman he loved more than life itself, and walked out of the café.

Three weeks later, he heard that she'd moved to Los Angeles.

FINDING STREET PARKING was out of the question in Midtown, which forced him to park in a garage a block from the film site. He was vigilant in looking for potential threats as he led Bria to the vacant building that the production crew had rented to film the movie. The guard at the door took one look at Bria and waved them both through, much to Xavier's dismay. Lax security. They got a couple of curious glances as they navigated the labyrinth of the people and equipment, but no one questioned his presence.

Finally, Bria stopped in front of a door. "This is my private dressing room."

She reached for the knob and he quickly stepped in front of her.

"Let me go first." He opened the door, noting that it had not been locked. Not that the lock would be much deterrent anyway. A credit card and a good shove would overcome its resistance. The room was small. He could see at a glance there was no one inside.

Bria swept past him into the room.

"The security in this place sucks," he said, turning the flimsy latch. "I want to get you a better lock for this door and I want you to keep it secured. When you're inside and when you're not here."

She gave a brisk nod. "Okay." She turned back to her phone.

He got it. This was awkward. Things between them had not ended on a good note. But as long as she was willing to abide by his rules, they'd get along just fine.

Her dressing room was on a corner on the ground floor, a perk he assumed for the star of the movie. It had windows set high and running along two of the four walls. He tested the latches on the windows and determined they too were a joke. One good yank would be all it took for someone to force one open from the outside.

"The locks on these windows are no good either."

"I know. That's why you're here," Bria said, scrolling through her phone.

"I only saw a couple of security cameras, which isn't nearly enough for a space this large. And flimsy locks on the doors and windows."

Bria shot him an incredulous look. "We have security guards. I don't think it's that bad."

One of Xavier's brows arched. "You don't. I just walked right in, and despite no one knowing the first thing about who I am or what I'm doing here, I wasn't stopped."

Bria shot him a withering look. "You were with me."

His other brow went up. "And? Every single person in here should be wearing a badge identifying them as a member of the cast or crew. If they're here on an authorized visit, they should have a badge that says so. Security cameras should be recording 24/7, at the very least in the public spaces and at the entry and exit doors. I should call Ryan. Have him get our expert out here to work up a full security system." He grabbed his phone from his back pocket.

A laugh burst from Bria. "You're kidding, right? I mean, this building is almost a hundred years old. There's no way the owners are going to let you drill holes in the walls and run the kind of wires you'd need for something like that."

A low rumble tripped from his lips.

Bria smiled wryly. "I see your communication skills haven't improved over the years. Look." She set her phone next to her purse on the vanity and crossed to him.

She stopped close enough that he could smell whatever exotic fragrance she was wearing. Her scent had every cell in his body standing on alert.

"I don't want to tell you how to do your job, but you're not going to be able to approach this the way you usually do," she said, looking up at him with her gorgeous brown eyes.

He frowned. "If we did this how I want to, you'd be safely ensconced in the safe house while I tracked down this scum-bag."

"And I've explained why that won't work for me." She threw her arms out to the side. "Don't you get it? This is it. This is my shot. No more wearing a skintight superhero uniform in movies that are more about my physical assets than my acting chops. This movie is great, and I'm damn great in it. Once the acting world sees that, I'll finally be taken seriously as an actress."

He closed the space between them and curled his hands around her shoulders. "Bria, there is no doubt in my mind that you are brilliant every time you step in front of a camera. You always have been. You have a gift. But it can't come at the cost of your safety."

His gaze was locked on hers. Heat crackled in the space between them. He wanted to kiss her so badly that it was a physical hurt. But he couldn't. Shouldn't. Getting involved now would cloud his judgment. He needed to be clearheaded, focused and—

All remaining thought fled when Bria went up on her toes and pressed her lips to his in a hot, rough kiss. A kiss that sent him hurtling through the past, and returning for a future with the woman in his arms.

Instinctively, he pulled her closer, deepening the kiss.

She made a little mewling sound that sent his manhood straining against the front of his slacks.

A knock sounded at the dressing room door.

Bria jerked back, her hand coming up to cover her kiss-swollen lips. She stared at him for a moment, desire still swimming in her eyes.

The knock came again. "Ms. Baker? Mr. Malloy would like to see everyone on set in five minutes."

Bria licked her lips and looked away. "Yes…o-okay. I'll be there in a moment." Footsteps faded away on the other side of the door. She turned back to him. "That can't happen again."

He was still breathing heavily and, he noted, she was as well. "Why not?" The question came out gruffer than he'd intended, but dammit, there was something still between them. He knew she felt it too. Why not explore it? See where it could lead.

"Because," she straightened to her full five-foot-eight height which was still a good six inches shorter than his six-two, "I'm here to work. I can't be sleeping with my bodyguard if I want people to take me seriously."

Her answer was frustrating in more ways than one, mostly because she was right. After all, he'd been thinking the same thing just moments earlier. But those moments in-between, when his lips were on hers and her body was pressed against his, had sent all rational thoughts fleeing. All rational thoughts but one.

"Why did you come to me?" He asked the question he'd wanted to ask from the moment he'd seen her sitting in the conference room. "Why did you come to West Investigations for your security?"

West was one of the best, sure, but there were other outfits that could have handled her stalker. Firms where he wasn't employed. But she'd sought him out specifically. If not because she still had feelings for him, then why?

"Because I trust you. Despite everything, you may be the one person I trust most in this world. And I'm scared. You once told me you would never let anything happen to me. I'm hoping you really meant that."

He remembered that. They'd taken a day trip to Coney Island. He'd coaxed her onto the roller coaster, not realizing how afraid she'd be. She was shaking as the roller coaster car made its way up the inclined tracks.

"Don't worry," he'd said, wrapping his arms around her. "I'd never let anything happen to you. I promise."

Another, more insistent rap sounded on the door. "Ms. Baker? Please, to the set now!"

"Coming." She started past him.

He caught her arm. "I meant it then. I can back it up now. I won't let this stalker or anyone else hurt you."

Chapter Five

"Cut! That was great, Bria. Just great. I do want to try it one more time," Dane Malloy, the director of the film said.

Dane was a perfectionist. Usually that didn't bother Bria at all since she had more than a little perfectionist in her as well. But she was exhausted, physically and emotionally. Between her stalker, seeing Xavier again for the first time in years and doing the same scene now for nearly an hour, she just wanted to go home, slip into a warm bath and relax. But that was not to be.

They did the scene two more times before Dane was satisfied and let her go for the night. She walked back to her dressing room with Xavier so close on her heels that she could smell his spicy cologne. It sent a zip through her blood, cut through her exhaustion and almost, almost, had her catching a second wind.

She kicked off the four-inch heels she'd been wearing for the scene the moment she entered the trailer and reached around the back of her dress for the zipper.

After a minute of flailing, she finally gave up and turned to Xavier. "Could you help me, please?"

The smirk on his face was equal parts infuriating and

sexy. "I was enjoying watching you, but yes, I will help you. Turn around."

She did as he said. There was nothing intrinsically sexual about what he was doing, but the moment his hands touched her body, she trembled with want. She recalled kissing him earlier and her heart raced.

His touch was featherlight and he lowered the zipper, slowly, much more slowly than was necessary.

She reveled in each simmering second.

After an electrifying, excruciating moment, Xavier's hands stopped moving. He stepped back.

Bria glanced over her shoulder. "Thank you."

Xavier's expression was unreadable. "You're welcome."

She headed for the small bathroom in the corner of the dressing room and quickly changed into her street clothes. After splashing water on her face, she looked at herself in the mirror. "Simmer down. He's here to protect you. Nothing more."

She looked at her reflection again. "Yeah, right."

There had definitely been something between them when they'd kissed. They'd never wanted for desire in their relationship. The overwhelming passion she felt for him was rivaled only by the passion she felt for acting. It's why she'd ultimately broken it off, because she couldn't see a way to sustain both, at least she hadn't thought she'd be able to do it when she was twenty years old.

The industry was hard and grueling. It took everything you had and then some to make it. And she'd wanted to make it. It wouldn't have been fair to Xavier to try to squeeze in a relationship with him between auditions and tapings. She'd done the right thing for both of them back then.

And now?

They were both successful adults. She could be choosy about her projects now. She could afford to take downtime between each film. Maybe they could make it work.

"Are you ready to go?" Xavier called through the bathroom door.

She shook the thought from her head and opened the door. "Ready to go." She slipped oversize sunglasses on even though it was far too dark for them already.

Xavier held her elbow gently and led her from her dressing room.

Between takes, she'd noticed him talking to Dane, several of the other actors, the set security, and one of the producers. She had no doubt they were discussing the lack of cameras and flimsy locks on the doors and windows.

She had no problem footing the bill for a few wireless cameras and latches but even celebrities had to budget. They'd have to discuss his plans later that evening.

The thought gave her pause. Her contract with West was for full-time security. But she wasn't comfortable with a stranger staying in her house. Xavier had been with her all day, but this was a job for him and he'd expect to have some time off. Another thing they needed to discuss.

It was late, but in New York, that just meant a change in uniform for the thousands of people still out and about. Instead of suits and conservative dresses with kitten heels, New Yorkers donned their going-out threads. Sparkly minidresses. Skinny jeans. Crop tops.

Bria kept her head down, hoping not to be recognized while Xavier deftly navigated them through the people.

They stopped at the corner of 42nd Street. It only took a moment for the walk light to begin flashing.

Bria stepped off the curb.

The roar of an engine cut through the normal roar of the city.

She froze. A dark sedan hurtled through the intersection, its grill pointed directly at her.

Almost as suddenly as the car appeared, her feet were off the ground and she was flying through the air. Because she still remembered every inch of his body, she instinctively knew that the brick wall that had slammed into her was Xavier.

He twisted himself so that when they landed he took most of the impact, hitting the pavement on his back and sliding for a fraction of an inch. Quickly, he locked his arms around her as he rolled them both to the far side of the street. Once again she found herself hurtling through the air, this time because Xavier had sprung to his feet, taking her with him and hauling her onto the sidewalk.

"Are you all right?" he asked, running his hands over her arms, his eyes roving over her body, looking for injuries.

Words escaped her and her mind struggled to catch up to everything that had happened.

Was she okay?

As if in answer, a sharp pain stabbed her in the side. Her knees buckled.

Xavier wrapped his arms around her waist, holding her up.

A young man darted up to them. "Oh, man, I saw the whole thing. That guy was crazy."

Xavier focused on the man. "Did you happen to get the license plate number?"

"No, man." The guy shook his head. "I'm sorry. It all happened so fast."

An older man hustled over. "Not so fast. That car was parked there for over an hour," he said with a smoker's rattle.

The younger man frowned at the older man, clearly unhappy with being contradicted. "I don't know about that. I was just walking by."

Xavier's arm tightened around her. "Are you sure?" he asked the older man.

The man nodded. "I'm sure. I own this store." He jerked his head toward the bodega they were standing in front of. "I keep an eye on all the comings and goings around here."

"Did you get the license plate?" Xavier asked.

The man shrugged. "I don't keep that good an eye out. But I'll tell you one thing. That wasn't an accident."

Chapter Six

Xavier insisted on getting Bria off the public street, once he was sure she was unharmed.

"Maybe we should wait for the police," Bria said after they were back in his car and had pulled out of the garage.

"I'll take care of that when I know you're somewhere safe."

"You can take me to my house." Her hands still shook, but she was feeling somewhat steadier than she had in the moments immediately following the car's attempt to hit her and Xavier.

Xavier slanted her a look. "I need to take you somewhere safe."

"It is safe. No one knows I own a place in the city. I own it through a bunch of different LLCs. I even pay for a small suite at the Four Seasons when I'm in town to throw the tabloids off my scent. That's where the paparazzi think I'm staying while I do the movie."

Xavier still looked as if he was ready to argue.

"Please?"

He gave a grunt but said, "Where is this place?"

Bria gave him directions to her Upper West Side townhouse. They drove in silence for several minutes before she could no longer hold back the questions. "The driver could have just been distracted, right? I mean, it might not have been intentional."

"That's possible," Xavier responded in a tone that made it clear he didn't believe the hit-and-run was an accident.

"But you don't think so."

He shot her a glance. "No, I don't. Even if the driver was distracted, there was time to swerve, but he didn't."

"But the stalker, he's been sending me notes, candies, flowers. Then chasing me this morning." Because she was sure now that she had been chased this morning. "And now to try to run me down. That's—" She paused, finding it difficult to get the next words out. "That's a serious escalation. Why would he want to do that now?"

Xavier shifted lanes, going around a slowing cab. "You've made several changes that could have induced the stalker to alter his methods. Leaving Los Angeles for New York, for instance. Hiring private security. The notes that you showed us from this guy are definitely creepy, but the most recent with the flowers was different. More aggressive than the others."

Bria shifted in the passenger seat so she was looking across the interior of the car at him. "More aggressive, how?"

"The 'you are mine' phrase was repeated, but the next line is even more aggressive. 'I'll be coming to take what's mine.' It sounds like there is some anger there. Anger, certainly possessiveness and a host of other things. The forensic psychologist that West Investigations uses may be able to help us there."

Her hands began to shake more violently.

Xavier must have noticed. He reached over and turned the heat on.

The blast of warm air was soothing and she was grateful for it.

Xavier eased the car to a stop at a red light.

"You know as well as anyone how much I've always wanted to be an actress. And yeah, I knew that there would be a downside to becoming a celebrity, but I'm honestly starting to wonder if it's worth it. I mean, how long am I going to have to look over my shoulder? Even if you find this guy, and there's no guarantee you will, there's always the potential that someone else will take his place."

A spark lit in his eyes. She'd always found his protectiveness sexy, and that hadn't changed. If anything she found it that much more seductive now. "And I'll always be there to protect you from whatever threat crops up. You have my word on that."

The light turned green and they began moving forward again.

Xavier navigated the busy evening traffic deftly, but it still took nearly a half hour to make it from the set to her townhouse on West 77th Street. She directed him to the garage at the end of the street. Like most New Yorkers, she didn't have her own car and therefore didn't need one.

He parked, then quickly led her to the townhouse.

Hers was the second unit from the corner, surrounded by a black ornate metal fence. Three stories with stairs that led to a large black door flanked by a series of narrow triple-paned windows on either side of the door. The front yard was small, but instead of paving over it as many of her neighbors had, she'd hired a gardener to maintain the small patch of grass and plant flowers in a miniscule flower bed. Although she owned a two-bedroom penthouse in Los Angeles, she considered the townhouse her true home.

"I'll want to take a look at your security system first thing," Xavier said while Bria worked the series of locks on the front door. She glanced at him, but his eyes were trained on the empty street, scanning it for the hint of a threat.

"Not a problem." Bria pushed the door open and led Xavier into the home's narrow foyer to a cacophony of beeps. She shut the front door behind them and engaged the locks before entering the six-digit code that neutralized the alarm and reengaged the security system. "It's a top-of-the-line system installed by Dustin Home Security Professionals. I spared no expense. I have a service that comes in to check on the house regularly. Since I'm away so much, it seemed prudent."

"Dustin systems are good. It's a brand that West Investigation recommends highly to our clients."

She kicked off her shoes and left her purse on the side table by the door. "Come on, let me show you around."

Xavier made a move to step in front of her. "Maybe I should clear the house first."

"Xavier," she said, unable to keep the exasperation out of her voice, "did you see what I had to go through to get in here? There's no one inside. Come on. You can clear the house as I show you around."

She'd purchased the house out of foreclosure six years ago with the check from the first Princess Kaleva movie. It had been a fixer-upper, but that was the only way she could afford a townhouse on the Upper West Side, even with a multimillion-dollar budget. She'd spent a year renovating, taking down walls wherever it was feasible and opening up the main floor as much as possible. Then she'd spent a small fortune on a designer who'd helped her give the space a clean, modern look while keeping a sense of hominess.

She led him into the living room, which flowed into the formal dining room before opening up to the eat-in kitchen and attached family room. Upstairs there were three bedrooms, one of which she used as a home office, and a bath in addition to the main bedroom and en suite bath. Back on the main floor she pointed to the door leading down to the basement.

"The basement is the only place I haven't gotten around to renovating yet. I want to put a full theater down there someday, but right now, it's unfinished. I keep the door locked."

Xavier tried the handle, but it didn't give.

"I told you. Locked." Bria headed toward the kitchen at the back of the house.

"It's a fairly open flow. You can almost see through the front windows from the kitchen here in the back," Xavier said. "The windows could be a problem. I want you to keep the curtains closed."

"They aren't typical windows. You can see out but you can't see in. I like my privacy."

"Still. Keep the curtains drawn at all times," Xavier said gruffly.

She blew out a sigh. "Sure. Want a glass of wine? I could use a glass of wine." She bent, reaching for the door to the wine cooler tucked under the island.

"I can't drink. I'm on the clock. Do you mind if I take a closer look upstairs and in the basement?"

"Sure, knock yourself out." She grabbed a bottle of white and straightened. "The key to the basement door is in the drawer in the side table in the foyer. I'm going to make mushroom risotto for dinner if that's okay with you."

Xavier's brow went up in surprise. "You cook?"

She laughed. "A lot has changed in the last fifteen years.

I've learned. Eating out isn't as much fun with people asking for your autograph every few minutes."

"I can see how that would put a damper on dinner," he said, giving her a small smile of his own before heading upstairs.

Bria poured herself a large glass of wine, then got cooking. Risotto was fairly easy and quick to make, which was why she always kept the ingredients for it in both her homes. The food that was provided on movie sets could be hit or miss. They only had a few more weeks left of shooting and Dane seemed determined to make the most of them.

She could hear Xavier moving around, first in the basement, then on the second floor above her head while she prepared dinner.

It was surreal to have him in her house. Not that she'd never thought about it. A part of her had always hoped their paths might cross again one day. And that maybe their timing would be better. That some spark of what they'd felt for each other would still be there. At least she knew that part was true. The spark was definitely still there, at least on her side, and she was pretty sure he felt it too. The circumstances were terrible, but she couldn't help hoping that maybe after they'd identified her stalker and neutralized him, they might find a way to start again.

Xavier came back downstairs just as she finished cooking the risotto.

"Perfect timing. I thought we could just eat at the island," Bria said, waving to the bar stools.

"That's fine, but before we do I want to give you this." He pulled a small device from his pocket. It looked like a key fob for a car but with a single button.

She frowned at the device. "What is that?"

"It's a panic button. I want you to keep it on you at all times. If for some reason we get separated, you can hit the button and it will send a signal to West's headquarters that can be followed."

She shot him a bemused look. "You're LoJacking me?"

"No." He tried to hide it, but she caught the slight upturn of his mouth. "It will only send a signal if you hit the button. If you push it by accident, you can hit it again twice, quickly, to turn off the signal. Totally in your control."

She took the device from him, her hand brushing along his. "I do like to be in control." The statement came out sultrier than she'd intended and she could see that Xavier had heard it that way as well. His pupils were dilated and he looked at her with a fiery desire burning in his eyes.

She was on the verge of stepping forward and giving in to the kiss she wanted to press against his lips when he stepped back.

Disappointment flooded through her, but she pushed it away. "Let's eat."

She set the panic button on the counter and busied herself with piling risotto on two separate plates. She slid one in front of Xavier before placing the other in front of the empty stool and sitting down.

She hadn't realized how hungry she was until the earthy aroma of mushrooms and cheese hit her nostrils. She ate hungrily.

"This is good," Xavier said after a few bites.

"Don't sound so surprised," Bria teased back.

He smiled. "It's just that I don't remember you being that good of a cook."

She laughed. "Fair enough. Early on in my career, I did a straight-to-video movie where I played a chef. The movie was forgettable, as in so bad I hope anyone who saw it has already forgotten about it. But the production did hire a real chef to work with me so that I looked like I knew what I was doing. He taught me a few dishes and I found that I enjoyed cooking. It's relaxing."

"*Seasoned with Love.*"

Bria felt her eyes widen with surprise. "You've seen it?"

"I've seen every movie you've been in," Xavier said quietly.

A surprising warmth flooded her at his words. "I doubt that. There were several early on that I wasn't even credited in."

"Every one," Xavier reiterated firmly, his eyes locked on her face.

She didn't know what to say to that. Did it mean something that he'd taken the time to watch all her work? Or was it just one old friend supporting another? And did it even matter?

Questions she wasn't sure she wanted to know the answers to. So instead of pursuing them, she changed the subject.

"Did you find everything you wanted? I mean, is my security up to your standards?"

"Your security system is pretty good. Better than pretty good actually, but there are a few upgrades I'd like to make."

"Whatever you think is best." Bria reached for her wineglass.

"I think it's best if you stay at one of West Investigations' safe houses."

She looked at him over the top of her glass. "Anything but that."

"Even if it compromises your safety?"

"I'm not just being obstinate," she said, setting her glass

down on the countertop. "This is my home. It's one of the only places in the world right now where I can just be me. Bria. Not Princess Kaleva. Not Elizabeth Stewart or whatever other character I might be playing at the moment. It might be hard to understand—"

"I understand. I'm just…concerned."

He covered her hand with his.

A charge shot through her body. She wondered if he felt it too.

"Thank you for being concerned." Her voice was little more than a whisper.

Xavier pulled his hand back.

The loss of his touch felt as if she'd been thrown into a cold bath. She grabbed her empty plate and wineglass and carried them to the sink. "It's been a long day," she said, her back to him. "I'm going to head up to bed. Just leave the dishes. I'll take care of them in the morning."

She hurried toward the stairs without looking at him.

"Bria."

Xavier's voice stopped her before she got out of the kitchen.

She stopped without turning around. "Yes."

"I'm… Good night."

His words seemed weighted and she wondered if he was apologizing for more than just dodging a kiss. But that was a conversation she was in no shape for at the moment.

"Feel free to take whichever of the guest rooms suits you."

Bria hurried upstairs, shutting herself in her bedroom.

There was only one floor between them, but she wasn't sure the distance could ever be overcome.

Chapter Seven

Xavier was no cook, but he could do dishes with the best of them. He cleaned up the dishes from dinner and put away the leftover risotto. When he was done, he checked all the doors and windows in the house one more time. Bria's security was top-notch. He'd have expected nothing less from Dustin security systems, but he was taking no chances with her safety.

It was late, but he still put in a call to update Ryan on the situation with Bria. He'd spoken to one of the movie's producers and gotten the okay to have a security assessment done on the building as long as it didn't interfere with shooting. Ryan agreed to send someone to the set first thing the next morning to do the evaluation and change the locks on Bria's dressing room door and windows.

"How are the two of you getting along?" Ryan asked.

"We're fine. Just like I told you we would be."

Ryan's silence on the other end of the line spoke volumes.

"I need to get some shut-eye," Xavier finally said.

"Sure," Ryan responded. "Let me know when you need me to send relief. I know we argued for you to spend every moment with her."

"I'm not going to leave her until I know she's safe."

Ryan sighed. "I had a feeling you were going to say that."

They ended the call. He climbed the stairs to the second floor and paused outside Bria's bedroom. It was quiet and no light shone from under the door. She must have already gone to sleep.

He turned and crossed the hall, settling into the guest room directly across from Bria's room. He had an emergency go bag in the SUV, but he didn't want to leave Bria to get it. He slid the gun he'd had tucked into the waistband of his jeans under the pillow, shucked his boots and got into the bed, fully clothed.

An hour later he was still staring at the ceiling, wide-awake. The mattress was firmer than he liked, but that wasn't the reason he was finding it so hard to fall asleep. Every time he closed his eyes, he saw Bria step out into the street and the car bearing down on her. He could have lost her today. Lost her again, just hours after she'd walked back into his life.

He couldn't let that happen. He had to find the stalker and put him behind bars before he hurt Bria.

And then? Maybe he'd think about trying to convince Bria to give him a second chance. He'd been a fool at twenty, not to fight for her. Maybe they could have worked things out. But he'd let his pride get the best of him.

The irony of it was, some part of him had always believed they'd find their way back to each other. He'd tried telling himself that he was being a fool, pining for a movie star who had probably forgotten he existed, but the hope had never completely died out in his heart.

But now she'd come to him, needing his help.

A creak sounded in the hall.

His body went on high alert. He bolted upright on the bed

and swung his feet to the floor. Grabbing his gun from under the pillow, he padded quickly to the door.

Pulling it open enough to peer through the crack, he found Bria standing in front of the door. He swung it open, taking in her purple-and-white-striped pajamas and the matching purple eye cover pushed to the top of her head.

"Bria? Are you all right?"

Lines burrowed into her forehead and worry shone in her eyes. "I just got a call from the night guard on the film set. Xavier, the stalker broke into my dressing room. He left another bouquet."

XAVIER PULLED THE SUV to a stop in the alleyway at the rear entrance to the building. Logan DeLong, the head of set security and a former New York City police officer, was waiting for them. Logan was a white man in his midfifties, with thinning red hair and a beer gut. Logan was one of the movie crew that Xavier had spoken to while he'd waited for Bria to finish rehearsals earlier in the day. Logan had given him a feel for the number of staff usually on hand, the security measures, and generally, how the production operated on a day-to-day basis.

"I'm sorry for calling you so late, Ms. Baker, but I thought you'd want to know about the intrusion right away."

Bria reached out and squeezed the man's hand. "You did the right thing."

Xavier scanned the alley. "Let's take this discussion inside." He hustled the guard and Bria into the building. They made their way through a maze of hallways that formed the behind-the-scenes area until finally stopping in front of Bria's dressing room.

The door was open and the lights on. A bouquet of black

roses sat at the center of the dressing table, an envelope with Bria's name spelled out in block letters sticking out of its center.

Bria wobbled when she saw the bouquet.

Xavier reached out a hand to steady her. "You okay? You don't have to be here for this."

She shook her arm free and pressed her hand against her forehead. "I'm fine."

Keeping one eye on Bria, Xavier turned to Logan. "Take me step-by-step through how you found the flowers."

"Well, the cast had left for the night by eight, but a few of the crew hung around to finish some things. Everyone had cleared out by nine. I completed some paperwork and was doing a walk through the premises, like I always do, to make sure everything was locked up tight before the night guard comes on shift."

Xavier nodded.

"That's when I saw the light was on in Ms. Baker's dressing room," DeLong continued. "She doesn't usually leave them on, so I went to check it out. Then I saw the flowers. Most of the deliveries go through my office, but I would have remembered black roses. The whole thing seemed… off. That's why I called you, Ms. Baker."

"Did you touch anything in the room?" Xavier asked.

DeLong shook his head. "No, I didn't even go in."

"Okay. You two stay here." Xavier stepped into the dressing room. Grabbing a scarf that was lying on top of Bria's vanity, he took the envelope from the flowers and opened it.

There was a photo inside but no note this time. The photo was dark and grainy. Obviously, several years old, but it still clearly showed Bria and another man at what looked like a campsite or somewhere in the woods.

He brought the picture to Bria. "Do you recognize this photo?"

Bria's face went sheet white.

"Bria? Do you recognize it?"

"It's from a movie shoot," she whispered. "A long time ago."

"Who's the guy beside you?" Xavier pressed.

"He was my costar. Derek Longwell." She looked at him with an unfocused gaze.

"Do you think he could be the one stalking you?"

Xavier had kept the explanation for his presence vague when he'd spoken to the head of security earlier, but now DeLong's eyes went wide at the mention of a stalker. Xavier ignored him.

Bria looked as if she was barely breathing and he worried that she might pass out.

She shook her head, her gaze finally focusing in on him. "No, it can't be. Derek is dead."

Chapter Eight

Bria woke up to the smell of coffee and bacon the next morning. It took some effort to drag herself out of bed and into the bathroom, and the image she saw in the mirror reflected that. Dark circles rimmed her bloodshot eyes. The makeup people would have their work cut out for them today. She let the water in the shower heat to just shy of scalding, then let it pummel her awake. She dressed and headed downstairs, feeling only slightly more human than she had when she'd awakened.

Pausing at the doorway to the kitchen, she watched Xavier at the stove, dressed in the same tight black T-shirt and blue jeans he'd worn the day before.

Her stomach did a flip-flop. Why was a man in the kitchen always such a turn-on?

Xavier shifted to look at her, his eyes skimming over her from head to toe. He hadn't changed so much that she couldn't read the concern in his eyes. So the shower hadn't helped as much as she'd hoped to make her look human.

"Good morning." Xavier's voice's husky timbre shot through her.

"Good morning."

"Coffee is ready."

"Thank you." She ripped her gaze away and headed for the coffee maker. "You didn't have to cook breakfast. We could have ordered something in."

Xavier spared her an elusive grin. "I may not be able to handle risotto, but I can manage bacon and eggs."

Bria carried her coffee mug to the island and sat.

Xavier slid a plate in front of her, then grabbed a cup of coffee for himself and sat down next to her.

He gave her a few minutes to eat before speaking. "You're going to have to tell me about it."

She swallowed the eggs in her mouth. "Tell you about what?"

After leaving the set last night, she'd shut down Xavier's questions. The shock of finding the photo had thrown her back to a time she'd worked to put out of her mind. She needed time to process, which she'd spent most of the night doing, hence the bags under her eyes. But she'd known Xavier wouldn't be put off forever.

"The photo. I saw how you looked at it in your dressing room last night. You looked afraid."

"How could I be afraid of a photo?"

He looked at her in silence.

"I told you. It's an old photo of me and a former costar."

"What movie?"

"*Murder in Cabin Nine.* It was a cheesy B movie that never got finished."

"Because Derek Longwell died while you were filming it?"

Surprise shot through her.

"I googled his name last night after we got back. Not much about him other than that he mysteriously died on the set of *Murder in Cabin Nine.*"

"Yes, well." She swallowed again even though she hadn't taken a bite. "After Derek's death, the producers decided not to continue with the movie."

"How did he die?" Xavier pressed.

"I... I'm not sure. I think the official ruling was an accident. Derek drank a lot and I think they said he fell and hit his head." She couldn't bring herself to look him in the eye. After fifteen years apart would he still be able to tell when she was lying? But she didn't need to look at him to feel his eyes glued to hers.

"What aren't you telling me?"

The doorbell rang, forestalling her answer. Not that she knew how she was going to answer him. She couldn't tell him the truth. She hadn't spoken the truth to anyone ever and she certainly didn't want to tell Xavier. It would change the way he looked at her forever and she wasn't sure she could stand that.

"I'll get it." She rose.

He waved her back into her chair. "No. Let me. We don't know who it is. You stay here." He stalked toward the front door of the house.

She bristled and followed him into the foyer.

He shot her a look that she ignored.

"It's my agent," she said, glancing out of the front window at the stoop.

Xavier opened the door.

Her agent, Mika Reynolds, jerked back looking stunned. "Who are you?"

Bria shouldered Xavier out of the way before he could answer. "Mika, come in." She turned to Xavier when he still didn't move. "Xavier."

It took another several seconds, but finally, he stepped aside.

Mika made no move to step into the house. "It's fine, Mika. This is Xavier. He's, well, he's my bodyguard."

"A bodyguard?" Mika frowned. "Doesn't look like he's doing that great of a job. You haven't answered any of my calls?"

"Your calls?" Bria grabbed her cell phone from the back pocket of her jeans where she'd slipped it after getting dressed. She had half a dozen missed calls and even more texts from Mika and several of the producers of the film. She'd never turned the phone's ringer back on after leaving the set. "I'm sorry there was an incident last night and I forgot to check my phone."

Mika didn't know the half of it. Bria hadn't even filled her in on the late-night flower delivery yet.

"Yes, I know. We need to form a plan about that actually…"

Movement behind Mika caught Bria's eye. A familiar form jogged up the walkway.

Bria felt Xavier tense beside her. "It's okay. I know him too," she said before turning back to the man making his way up the front steps. "Eliot! I thought you were in LA?"

Eliot Sykes swept her into his arms. "I grabbed a late flight out of LA to JFK."

"And I was already in town, taking meetings on behalf of another client," Mika said.

"You didn't have to come," Bria said, pulling free of Eliot's embrace. "Either of you. It was probably just a distracted driver."

"It wasn't a distracted driver," Xavier grumbled, "and can we take this discussion inside the house, please?"

Eliot kept one arm around Bria's shoulders as they stepped

into the entry. "And you are?" Eliot asked after Xavier had secured the door.

"Her bodyguard," Mika answered from the love seat in the living room where she now sat.

"Bodyguard?" Eliot's arm tightened around her shoulder. "I thought you said you were okay."

"I am okay," Bria said, shrugging free of Eliot's grasp once again and putting some distance between them. "I told you both I was concerned about the notes I've been getting, and the flowers. There have been other incidents since I came to New York to start filming." She filled them in on the most recent notes, being chased on her jog in the park and the flower delivery last night, but left out the photo of her and Derek. As far as she was concerned, the fewer people who knew about that, the less explaining she'd have to do. Or avoid doing, as she currently was with Xavier. "I thought it was best to have personal security, so I went to West Security and Investigations. This is Xavier Nichols. Xavier, this is Mika Reynolds, my agent, and Eliot Sykes. He owns the firm that handles my media and public relations."

Bria walked to the love seat and sat down next to her agent. There wasn't enough space for Eliot to sit too, so he took a seat on the larger sofa in the room. Xavier placed himself at the far end of the living room, leaning against the wall.

Mika's face scrunched as if she'd smelled something foul. "The notes and flowers again. I told you it was nothing to worry about." Mika waved a hand in front of her face as if shooing away a gnat. "All the big stars have exuberant fans. It's almost a rite of passage."

Irritation bubbled in Bria's chest. Mika was one of the best agents in the business because she was laser focused on helping her clients build their careers, but sometimes her focus could be shortsighted. "It's a rite of passage that concerns me, then. We can't be sure whoever is sending them is harmless. My intuition is saying that whoever is doing this is serious, and even though the near hit-and-run could have just been a reckless driver..."

"I think hiring a bodyguard is the right way to go. Especially with this video making the rounds now," Eliot said.

"What video?" Xavier barked, pushing away from the wall and moving back to Bria's side.

Mika already had her phone in her hand. She tapped it twice, then turned the screen so that Bria and Xavier could see it. "Your bodyguard pushing you out of the way, rescuing you from the out-of-control vehicle. It's all over social media." She flicked a glance in Xavier's direction.

Bria watched herself freeze in the middle of the street, trapped in the glare of the white headlights bearing down on her. Her heart rate picked up, remembering the moment, even though there was no way she could be hurt by the vehicle while she was sitting on the sofa in her home. Then Xavier entered the frame, pushing her out of the way. The car roared past them and the recording froze on her and Xavier lying on the sidewalk, Xavier cradling her, staring down at her, his face a mask of concern.

"You can't buy this kind of exposure for the movie." Mika's excited voice cut through the memories.

Bria looked at the woman who'd been her agent for the last decade, who'd taken her on and helped make her into a star. It was as if she was looking at Mika for the first time and she wasn't sure she liked what she was seeing. "We could have been killed."

Mika had the grace to look abashed. "Of course, I'm glad no one was hurt. That goes without saying."

Did it though? Bria couldn't help but feel like it was something that should be said.

"But it is undeniable that this will bring more attention to the film. And that's what we want."

Bria felt the frown she wore deepen.

"I think what Mika is trying to say in her characteristically tactless way is that we can use this incident to get some buzz for the movie." Eliot held his hands up as if to ward off an impending verbal attack. "I know how slimy it sounds, but this is the business. People are talking about your brush with death. We want them talking about *Loss of Days* and how brilliant you are in it and how it is going to make you an even bigger star."

"And maybe even garner some awards buzz." Mika did a little dance on the love seat next to Bria, her face glowing.

Bria glanced at Xavier, but his expression gave nothing away. She really wished she knew whether he was thinking that taking advantage of their near miss was an opportunity or opportunistic. "It sounds like a tasteless move to me."

Eliot slid to the end of the sofa closest to the love seat and reached across the sofa arm for Bria's hand. "It won't be. I promise. Don't I always take care of you? You're my best client and I'd never put you in an uncomfortable situation, but I do think a few strategically granted interviews right now, about the movie of course, wouldn't be a bad idea."

"About the movie? *Loss of Days* won't be out for another year at least. We haven't even finished filming."

"You should know better than that by now," Mika scolded. "It's never too early to start promoting a movie."

"How many interviews?" Bria asked.

"Three or four, tops," Eliot answered. "Just enough to make sure we're in control of the story. We want people to know you didn't suffer any injuries and that you were back at work the next day, ready to go on with this fantastic movie that everyone should see when it comes out."

"Okay," she said resignedly. "Two interviews. That's it, Eliot. I'm still filming, I don't have a lot of spare time."

Eliot beamed. "Great." He sprung from the sofa. "I'm going to get on that right now. It'll give you and Mika some time to discuss a few things."

Eliot strode from the room in the direction of the kitchen, already pulling his phone from his suit pocket.

The show must go on. Wasn't that what they said, she thought wearily. She only wished she wasn't a part of this madman's show.

Chapter Nine

Sykes was on the phone, his back turned when Xavier walked into Bria's kitchen. He studied the man for a moment. Sykes wore a fitted suit in a deep plum shade with a black silk shirt. A goatee dusted his chin and a Rolex watch encircled his wrist.

Finally sensing he wasn't alone, Sykes turned.

Xavier walked nonchalantly to the sink, took a glass from the shelf above it and filled it with water from the tap. He turned, sipping from the glass and watched Sykes.

Sykes's eyes narrowed when he realized that Xavier wasn't going to leave the room. "Excuse me, Ian. I'm going to need to phone you back." Sykes ended the call. "Can I help you with something?"

"You can. You can help by telling me about your relationship with Bria." Xavier leaned back against the counter, effecting a relaxed pose although his muscles were taut and he remained watchful.

"Bria is a client of my public relations firm. And a good friend. A very good friend." Sykes smirked.

Xavier knew Sykes was trying to get under his skin. Unfortunately, it was working. He itched to wipe the smirk off the man's face and tell him how his close friend Bria had pulled him into a smoldering kiss in her dressing room a day earlier or the ripples of desire that moved between them with every look. But letting Sykes get to him would give the man the upper hand.

"That so? Bria never mentioned you, but she always did tend to see the good in everyone. Even those who may not deserve it."

Sykes's eyes narrowed. "Always? So you aren't just some meatheaded bodyguard she hired yesterday?"

"Let's just say we go way back and are also very good friends."

He knew it was petty, but he couldn't help being pleased by Syke's scowl.

"I understand that your firm has taken over handling Bria's fan mail. I need to see everything you have."

"As long as Bria consents, you'll have it."

"How does it work? Does everything come to your firm directly?"

Sykes shrugged. "Most fan interactions occur online nowadays. Email and social media. The case manager assigned to Bria's account responds to the fans and flags the questionable stuff."

"What does the case manager do with the flagged communications?"

"Sometimes nothing. You'd be amazed how much negative stuff comes in. If it doesn't seem like a credible threat, well, we don't have the bandwidth to follow up on everything."

"And when you do get a credible threat?"

"We let the appropriate people know. Mika." Sykes's chin jutted toward the living room. "On-set security if she's working on a movie. And the police, if we deem that necessary."

"Not Bria?"

Sykes nodded. "We let her know too when there is a threatening message, although she has chosen to retain access to all her accounts and does still occasionally respond directly to fans." The expression on Sykes's face made it clear he didn't agree with that choice.

"And you notified the LA police department about the stalker's emails? The ones declaring that Bria was his?" Xavier continued his questioning.

Sykes shifted uncomfortably. "Not at first. I mean, there was no concrete threat. It wasn't the first time Bria got an email from a lovesick fan. No one thought the guy was a stalker. Not at first."

"When did you realize the notes were coming from more than just a lovesick fan?"

"When the black roses arrived at Bria's house. She freaked out and I can't say I blame her."

"And that's when the police were called?"

"Yes." Sykes flipped his phone front to back, back to front nervously in his right hand. "Not that they did anything about it. In fairness, if they followed up on every threat to every Hollywood actor and actress, they wouldn't have time to do anything else."

Maybe. But he didn't care about every actor or actress. He only cared about one.

"Did anyone follow up on how the flowers got to Bria's house?"

Sykes's eyebrows squished together. "What do you mean?"

"Did anyone try tracking down the florist the flowers came from? Look into who delivered the roses?"

"I don't know." Sykes frowned. "I assumed the police would have done that."

"But no one followed up with the LAPD?"

Sykes shrugged again. "I guess not."

Xavier didn't try to hide his annoyance that there'd been so little follow-through initially, but it was something that he'd be sure to remedy, although the trail was probably stone-cold at this point.

"I really wish I could help you more," Sykes said.

"I bet you do," Xavier said without making an attempt to hide his derision.

Sykes frowned. "Look, I want to keep Bria safe as much as you do. Despite what you may think, I'm glad she hired you. Well, maybe not you but that she hired personal security. If there's anything I can do to catch the guy who is stalking her, I'll do it. But at the moment, I need to get back to work. So if you don't have any more questions…"

"I don't for now."

Sykes swept past him. Xavier followed Sykes back into the living room.

Bria looked from one man to the other. "Everything okay?"

"Fine," Sykes assured her.

"I set up the first interview with Ian Cole. I'll send you the details once I've worked them all out. Mika has your shooting schedule?"

"Yes." Bria nodded. "I have some time off coming up, so that would be the best time to do it."

"Great." Sykes smiled. "I'll let you know ASAP."

"Now, speaking of my schedule—" Bria rose from the love seat "—I need to get ready and head to the set. I'm lucky I don't have an early call time today, but I don't want to be late."

Mika and Eliot rose and headed for the door. Mika said

a quick goodbye before pulling out her phone and heading for a black town car idling on the other side of the street.

Xavier bristled when Eliot stopped just outside the door and pulled Bria into another embrace. "I'm going to be in town for a few days staying at my place in Chelsea. Let's have dinner tonight." He shot a look over her shoulder at Xavier. "Alone."

"I don't know, Eliot. I'll have to see how filming goes."

Eliot's mouth turned up in a smile that didn't reach his eyes. "I'll call you later, then." He followed Mika to the town car.

Bria shut the door and turned back to Xavier.

"Nice friends you got there," he said before turning his back to her and heading for the kitchen.

"You don't even know them. They are an important part of my team. Mika is one of the best agents in the business and she's been a good friend to me. And Eliot has gone above and beyond, helping me handle everything with the stalker."

Xavier frowned. "You're right. I don't know them. But maybe you should consider this. Many stalkers know their victims personally. So maybe you should ask yourself how well you really know your team."

THE MOVIE DIRECTOR, Dane Malloy, called, "Action," and Xavier watched Bria become Elizabeth Stewart, matriarch of a not-so-upstanding political dynasty. She took control of the scene and demanded attention. Bria really was a damn good actress. Better than good. She'd been good fifteen years ago when she was a student, but now Xavier couldn't take his eyes off her. Admittedly, her acting chops weren't the sole reason for that. That kiss they'd shared had been brief but soul stirring. And he was determined to do it again. Soon.

"She's good." Ryan's familiar voice came from behind him. Ryan held a tablet Xavier recognized as one they used when they were on-site conducting security reviews for clients.

"I didn't expect you to come out to do the assessment yourself."

Ryan shrugged. "I've never been on a movie set. Couldn't pass up the opportunity."

After Sykes and Mika Reynolds's unexpected visit this morning, he'd forgotten to let Logan DeLong know to expect someone from West Investigations would be coming by to do the security review. "How'd you get on set?" Xavier asked.

"Yeah, security around here is crap. I just told them I was with you and showed my West Investigations employee ID and they let me right through."

Xavier glared at the backs of the security guards, fifty yards or so away, who were supposed to be keeping the set secure. Frustration rumbled in his chest. He'd have to have another chat with Logan DeLong. And maybe get Bria to ask her bulldog of an agent to make a fuss to the producers of the film. After all, if anything was to happen on set, the lax security would be a huge potential liability for them.

He made a mental note, then turned back to Ryan. "Find any fingerprints on the vase of flowers?"

"Nothing," Ryan said. "Guy must have worn gloves. I did get the video from one of the few security cameras. Of course, I'd have twice as many around the set as they do, but at least they do have a couple of cameras. One caught our guy." Ryan pulled out his phone, and moments later, video began playing on screen.

A figure, clearly a man from the shape and size, walked into the frame carrying the vase of flowers he and Bria had found in her dressing room last night. The man kept his head down, and the baseball cap he wore obscured any hope of making out distinguishing features. But the vase of flowers in his hands was clear, as was the fact that he wore gloves. He was in and out of the frame in less than five seconds.

"None of the guards remember letting a delivery guy on set, but..." Ryan let the sentence trail off.

Xavier didn't need him to finish the thought. His tour of the movie set had revealed a number of weak points. Like the fact that there were multiple doors in and out of the building. The official entrance and exit that all cast, crew and visitors were supposed to use were manned. The other doors couldn't be opened from the outside but anyone inside could leave through them. Which meant they could accidentally or intentionally let a stranger on set without going through security, such that it was.

Ryan tapped the phone's screen, and less than a second later, Xavier's phone beeped with an incoming message. "I sent it to you. The techs at West are working on cleaning it up to see if we can get anything more from it, but they aren't hopeful. I've got someone following up with local flower shops here and in Los Angeles, where the first bouquet was delivered, but that's looking for a needle in a haystack."

Xavier wasn't surprised about that. He'd filled Ryan in on the lack of follow-up after the arrival of the first bouquet while Bria got ready to drive over to the set that morning. Neither of them held out much hope this would be a fruitful line of inquiry, but it was legwork that had to be done.

"We'll look anyway." Xavier turned his gaze back to Bria.

Bria chatted with her costar while the crew reset the scene.

"Anything on Derek Longwell?" Xavier asked without taking his eyes off Bria.

"Not a lot. I emailed you what we've got. He was a small-time actor living in LA. Only had a handful of credits when he died on the set of a movie filming in the San Bernardino National Forest a little over ten years ago."

"*Murder in Cabin Nine.* Bria was his costar," Xavier said. "What's the official word on how Longwell died?"

"Cracked skull. He had a blood alcohol level of .17."

"So, sloppy drunk."

"Exactly," Ryan confirmed. "We know he was out with some of the cast members at a local bar. No one remembers him leaving, but everyone agreed Derek was drinking heavily that night. The police theorize that Longwell fell along the path heading back to the hotel and hit his head. He wasn't found until the next morning when he didn't show up to the set."

Xavier turned the information over in his head. "So why would Bria's stalker leave a photo of Bria and Longwell with the flowers?"

Ryan jutted his chin in Bria's direction. "Have you asked Bria?"

"She said she didn't know."

"You don't believe her?"

"She's not telling me something, but if I push her too hard, she might dig in even more. She's got a stubborn streak," he said, thinking about Bria's refusal to go to a safe house.

One of Ryan's brows rose. "You may have to. The stalker left that photo for a reason, which means we need to know everything there is to know about Bria's relationship with Derek Longwell."

The idea that there was a relationship between Bria and Derek Longwell, or anyone else, made him want to punch someone. Maybe several someones. Of course, it was unrealistic to expect that Bria had remained celibate for the last fifteen years. He certainly hadn't. But that didn't mean he wanted to know the specifics of her relationships.

"So, you and Brianna Baker. I knew you were a man who kept his own council, but that's a pretty big secret to keep."

Xavier slid a side long look at his friend. "Wouldn't you keep it to yourself if the best thing that ever happened to you dumped you like a hot potato?"

Ryan nodded sagely. "I probably wouldn't be screaming it from the rafters. I see your point." Ryan was quiet for a beat. "So, the best thing that ever happened to you?"

Xavier grumbled. He considered Ryan a friend, a good one, but that didn't mean he wanted to share his feelings with him. Especially when he wasn't sure about those feelings himself.

Ryan chuckled then sobered. "Look, man, I get it. The right woman can make us go a bit nuts, but Bria, she may be in some real trouble here. Her stalker is getting bolder. Sneaking onto the movie set, even after the shooting had wrapped for the day, was a big risk. Are you sure you can keep your head in the game?"

Xavier turned to look at Ryan head on. "Would you trust anyone other than yourself with Nadia's safety if the situation was reversed?" he asked, referring to Ryan's wife.

Ryan didn't hesitate this time. "No." He sighed. "Just let me know if you need anything. I'm headed back to the office to work on the cost estimate for the upgraded security suggestions." He dropped a set of keys in Xavier's hand. "I took care of the locks on Bria's dressing room door and windows and installed a wireless camera outside the door."

"Thanks, man."

Ryan patted him on the shoulder, then headed for the exit.

Another hour passed before the director finally called for a break for lunch.

A production assistant handed Bria her robe. She wrapped it around herself as she made her way to him.

"Was that Ryan I saw you talking to?"

Xavier fell into step beside her and they headed for her dressing room. "Yes. He did the security assessment, changed your locks and gawked at a real-life movie being filmed."

Bria smiled. "Tell him to let me know when he has some time and I'll give him a proper tour."

They arrived at her dressing room, but Bria hesitated. He read the anxiety in her eyes.

"Hey." He pointed to the camera Ryan had hooked up on the opposite wall from the dressing room door. "No one has been in or out since we left."

Bria took a deep breath and unlocked the door with the key he passed to her.

Inside, she fell onto the sofa. "I hate this. Being scared all the time. Looking over my shoulder."

"I know. I'm sorry you're going through this, but I promise you, we will find this guy."

His words hadn't cleaned any of the concern from her eyes.

"You can't be sure of that. Certainly not sure that you'll catch him before he does something else. Something worse."

His gut clenched because, even though he meant every word, she was right. He couldn't be sure they'd catch the stalker before he lashed out again.

He let out a deep, steadying breath, then sat beside her.

"You're right. I can't promise you this guy won't send another email or more flowers or attempt another hit-and-run.

But I can promise you that I will not let anything happen to you. I will stand between you and any danger. I give you my word on that."

He wasn't sure who initiated it, maybe they both had. But in an instant, he was lowering his head to meet her raised lips. The moment their lips met, an electrical charge flowed through him.

Her lips parted beneath his and he took it as a sign and deepened the kiss. Her hands slid around his neck and he pulled her closer.

He'd known he'd wanted her the moment he'd seen her in Ryan's office, but the kiss just made it crystal clear how deeply he felt for her. He was throbbing with his need to be closer to her. And from the way she was kissing him back, she felt the same.

A ding sounded from the counter where Bria had left her phone while she was on set. She broke off the kiss, rising from the sofa and covering her swollen lips with a hand before turning her back on him.

"That was a mistake. Totally unprofessional of me."

"It might have been unprofessional of both of us, but I don't think for a second it was a mistake. Bria, I think we should talk about what happened between us—" He broke off when her body tensed. "What? What is it?"

He stood and closed the short distance between them.

Bria turned to face him, her face full of fear. She held her phone out to him. "He…he sent me a text. It's you."

Xavier took the phone from Bria's hand. On the screen was a photo of Xavier with his arm around Bria, hustling her from the movie set into his SUV. A red circle with a slash through it had been superimposed over his face. The text underneath the photo read:

GET RID OF HIM. OR I WILL.

Xavier took a screenshot of the text, then sent it to his own phone. Then he pressed the call button on Bria's screen.

Alarm flashed over Bria's face. "You're calling him? You can't call him."

Xavier led her back to the sofa. "Don't worry. I've got this."

The phone rang, but no one picked up. It was a long shot. Just like tracing the number was a long shot. More than likely the stalker was using a burner phone. But that wouldn't stop him from trying.

He ended the call and started another. "We might be able to trace this."

Ryan wouldn't have made it back to West's headquarters yet, so Xavier tried Shawn, Ryan's younger brother and co-owner of West Security and Investigations.

Shawn picked up on the second ring, and after a brief explanation, set out to trace the number that had just sent the text to Bria's phone.

"Shawn is on it," he said, punching off the call, "but it could take a while. Are you finished with filming for the day?"

Bria shook her head. "No, I've got another scene to shoot."

Damn. He'd hoped to be able to take her home, but he knew she wouldn't leave the cast and crew in the lurch.

"Xavier, I'm scared." Fear pulsed off her.

He reached out and pulled her into his arms. He dropped a kiss on the top of her head. "I know, but we're going to find this guy and stop him. I promise you that."

Chapter Ten

For the next three hours, Xavier prowled the edges of the set, never taking his eyes off Bria and the people around her. He'd always known how talented she was, but now he was getting a glimpse at just how much of a dedicated professional she was as well. The text message had clearly upset her, but she pulled herself together and headed back to the movie set when the production assistant called for her. She acted the scene over and over, never missing a line.

Over the course of the next several hours, she filmed scene after scene without letting on how shaken she was. Of course, he could see it. In the nervous glances around the set between takes and in the way her eyes sought him out the moment the director called cut. He made sure to stick as close to her as he could, both so that he could keep an eye on her at all times and to give her the sense of security that she seemed to need at the moment.

The notes and flowers were terrorizing for Bria, but until now, the stalker hadn't exhibited a direct desire to physically harm her or anyone else. But the text message with his photo, along with the attempted hit-and-run, couldn't be taken as anything other than a direct threat against them. An escalation in the stalker's MO. He wasn't scared for himself, he was scared for Bria. Because there was no way he was leaving Bria's side, which meant the stalker might escalate even further. And there was no way to guess what he might do next.

While Bria worked, Shawn called to fill him in on the attempt to trace the text message. The techs at West had done their best to locate a name or location for the call, but not surprisingly, the message had come from a burner phone. The device was currently off or disabled, so unless the stalker used it again, they were at a dead end with regards to tracing the text back to the sender.

The director finally called a wrap on the day's shooting just after eight that night. It took Bria another half hour to get out of her wardrobe and makeup, then they drove back to her townhouse on the Upper West Side.

West had secured several parking spaces in the garage across from Bria's townhouse and gotten permission, via a hefty fee, to install cameras so that the spaces could be monitored from the West offices at all times. It was the best they could do for the moment, since Bria continued to refuse to go to a safe house.

Xavier scanned the street as he hustled Bria toward her townhouse, wishing she'd agreed to stay somewhere that at least had an attached garage. They made it to the sidewalk in front of Bria's home when he noticed movement several yards ahead of them. A man huddled behind one of the lampposts that lined the sidewalk. The man's head popped out from behind the post, and the light from the yellow bulb overhead glinted off something in the man's hand.

Xavier propelled Bria through the gate surrounding her property. "Go inside and lock the door. Don't open it for anyone."

He didn't wait to see if she followed his direction before he took off down the sidewalk.

The man looked around the post again, his eyes going wide. He turned, darted between two cars parked at the curb and then dashed across the street.

Xavier caught him by the collar as he made it onto the opposite sidewalk and slammed him face forward against the side of a parked SUV.

"Who are you?" Xavier barked.

"What the hell!" the man stammered, trying to wrench himself out of Xavier's grasp.

Holding him in place with one hand, Xavier patted him down, ripping the man's wallet from his back pocket.

His California driver's license gave his name as Bernard Steele and listed an address in Los Angeles.

"Let me go! I'm going to call the cops," Bernard wailed.

"What are you doing here skulking on this street?"

"Hey, man. It's a free country!"

Xavier gave the man a shake. "Do you feel free right now?" he growled into the man's ear.

The click of fast-moving footsteps had both men turning their heads.

Bria appeared around the side of the SUV Xavier held Steele against.

"I told you to go inside and lock the door," Xavier barked, frustration lining his voice. "Stay back."

"Bria, get this jerk off of me," Steele stuttered.

Xavier pressed the man against the car a little harder.

"Xavier, he's not here to hurt me. Bernie is a photographer. Part of the paparazzi, to be exact."

Xavier hesitated before taking a step back and allowing Bernie to turn to face him.

"Paparazzi?" No one was supposed to know that Bria owned a home on this block. He was sure they hadn't been followed from the set when he'd driven her here, so how did the photographer know where to wait for Bria?

"Your man is crazy!" Steele glared at Bria. "He broke my camera."

Xavier scanned the asphalt. A black digital camera lay on its side next to the SUV's tire.

"I'm going to sue the hell out of you, Brianna Baker."

Xavier bent, picking up the camera. The screen was black and had a spiderweb of cracks running through it now.

Bria stepped closer and Xavier angled his body so that he was between her and Steele.

She frowned at him before turning her attention back to the photographer. "Let's just everyone calm down. My body-guard may have overreacted a bit, but you were lurking, and there was no way to know you weren't actually a threat. How about I buy you a new camera and we can forget about this whole misunderstanding."

"Misunderstanding," Steele sputtered. "He assaulted me. I'm calling the cops."

Bria fisted a hand on her hip. "And how many times have you pushed and bumped and prodded me, trying to get that million-dollar picture? Maybe I should start calling the cops. As a matter of fact, I'm pretty sure New York has laws against stalking. Surely hiding in the trees outside someone's home in order to get a photo of them qualifies."

"I wasn't hiding in the trees or stalking you," Steele said unconvincingly.

Bria tilted her head and gave a saccharine smile. "Oh no? Well, that's how I'm going to tell the story. And we all know how convincingly I can tell a story, don't we, Bernie?"

Steele swore under his breath. "A new camera tomorrow."

"Tomorrow," Bria agreed.

"Fine," Steele acquiesced, taking a small step forward and finding Xavier blocking his getaway.

"Do you mind," Bernie spat, gesturing for Xavier to step back.

Xavier didn't move.

"Xavier," Bria said, exasperated.

"I have some questions for this guy, first." Now that he was more or less certain that Steele wasn't a real threat to Bria, he shifted so that he was at her back and she was less exposed to anyone else who might come along. He'd have liked to take his interrogation of the photographer inside, but having this man in Bria's house wasn't happening.

"What questions?" Steele crossed his arms over his chest.

"How did you know to wait for Bria on this street?"

Steele scoffed. "I'm not telling you that."

Xavier took a menacing step forward and was gratified to see fear leap into Steele's eyes.

"Xavier." Bria rested a hand on his bicep and a tantalizing heat flushed through his body despite the circumstances. "Bernie, I could still call the cops."

Steele let out a pained sigh. "Look, I can't go burning my sources. They'll stop talking to me if I do."

"Give me a break," Bria laughed. "You're not exactly Bob Woodward breaking Watergate. You sneak up on celebrities to catch them in an awkward photo."

"Way to minimize my life's work." Steele sniffed. "Really makes me want to help you guys."

"Steele!" Xavier bellowed. "You're testing my patience here." He leaned closer, crowding into the man's personal space.

Steele held his hands up in a surrender pose. "Okay, whatever, it's not even worth it. I got an anonymous tip. A call from a burner phone, saying Bria had a place on this block. I've been scoping it out for a few hours now. I was almost ready to give up when I saw you guys heading for the house."

Xavier held his hand out. "Let me see your phone."

Steele must have realized it wasn't a request.

He took his cell from his jacket pocket and slapped it into Xavier's hand. "The call came in earlier today. Around noon."

Xavier scrolled through the list until he got to the blocked number. There wasn't a lot of information to be had other than the time the call had come in and the length of the message, but he noted that the number was the same as the one that had accompanied the photo and threat against him to Bria earlier in the day. So their guy knew where Bria lived. Not good. He had to talk her into staying at a safe house whether she liked it or not. In the meantime, Steele might be their best lead when it came to finding the stalker.

"Was the caller a man or a woman?" Xavier asked Steele.

Steele shook his head. "Couldn't tell. It sounded like they were using one of those digital voice-changing apps or something."

Another dead end. Xavier fought against frustration. "Do you usually believe tips from random, anonymous callers?"

"Man, I get tips from all kinds of people. You wouldn't believe it. This one seemed like it might be credible. I knew Bria was filming in the city and she is from New York, so it seemed plausible she had a secret love shack somewhere in town." Bernie smirked.

Xavier itched to smack the smirk off the man's face, but that was likely to end the cooperation he was currently getting. "Notice anything unusual about the call? Background noise? A car horn? Anything?"

"Nah, man. It was a short call. The person gave me an address for Bria and said she was staying there while she was filming. Then they hung up."

A gust of wind blew down the street and Bria shivered next to him. He needed to wrap this up and get her inside where it was not only warm but safer than standing out in the open.

"Have you been taking photos on the movie set?"

"Not on set, because I haven't found a way in. Yet," Steele said, obviously put out about that fact. Given the pathetic nature of the building's security, Xavier could only surmise that Bernie was lazy or bad at his job. "But I have gotten some good shots from hanging just outside the perimeter."

"Have you noticed anyone suspicious lurking around or asking about Bria?"

Steele grinned. "Man, there's always someone asking about Brianna. She's Princess Kaleva. Hollywood's It Girl of the moment."

The man was working on Xavier's last nerve, but he gathered what was left of his patience and tried again. "Anyone who struck you as a little too much of a fan? Maybe a little bit obsessed."

Steele cocked his head, thinking about the question. "Not really."

"No or not really?" Xavier growled.

Steele held his hands out in surrender pose. "No, okay, I mean there are just the usual lookie-loos, fans and whatever, you know."

Xavier held his frustration in check. Taking a step forward, he made sure to crowd into Steele's personal space again. "It's in your best interest to keep Bria's address to yourself. And I'm only going to tell you this once. If I catch you hanging around here again, you won't have to worry about calling the cops, understand?"

Steele tried for an unaffected stare, but Xavier was good at reading people. The man was scared. Good.

After a moment, Steele looked at Bria. "I better get that camera tomorrow."

"I said you would and you will," Bria shot back. "I'll have it sent to your office first thing."

Xavier handed over the broken camera but not before taking out the memory card.

"Hey!" Steele exclaimed.

"I'll hold on to this to help keep you honest," Xavier said. There wasn't much he could do if Steele had already backed up the photos and videos he'd taken of Bria to the cloud, but at least he'd have the originals. Maybe he'd caught something that could help them find the stalker, even if he didn't realize it.

"That wasn't part of the deal," Steele grumbled.

"It is now," Xavier barked back.

Bria gave Steele a what-can-you-do shrug and a movie star smile. "You'll have your new camera tomorrow, Bernie. The best model on the market." Bria held up three fingers in the Girl Scout salute. "I promise."

Steele took his broken camera and shot another glare at Xavier before stepping away.

"Bernie," Xavier called out, stopping the paparazzo before he got far. "Remember what I said, Steele. If I see you on this street again, I won't be nearly as friendly."

Chapter Eleven

Once they'd gotten inside and were safe behind a locked door and the alarm system, Xavier read her the riot act for not following his earlier instructions. Or what amounted to the riot act for him, which meant bluntly telling her how stupid it was not to have thought about her safety first. Then he'd started pressing again to take her to a safe house. She was too exhausted to argue with him, so she didn't. Instead, she shot off an email to her assistant about purchasing a camera for Bernie and grabbed a wine cooler and the leftover risotto from the fridge and took it to her room to eat alone and in peace.

The texted threat against Xavier had rattled her to her core. Xavier had always made her feel safe. He was the epitome of the strong, protective type, but the threat against him reminded her that he could be hurt just like anyone else. Tonight it had only been Bernie lurking in the shadows, but what if some night soon it was someone far more dangerous? She couldn't handle it if Xavier was hurt because of her.

Tomorrow she was going to tell Ryan West she wanted a different bodyguard. Or better yet, she'd fire West Investigations altogether. Ryan was right, there were other security firms just as good as West Investigations. Security firms that didn't employ the man whom she had feelings for. Feelings she knew had grown deeper in the years they'd been apart.

And then she wouldn't have to tell Xavier what she'd done during the *Murder in Cabin Nine* filming and watch as he realized the kind of person she was. She knew the photo of her and Derek was the stalker's way of telling her he knew her secret. But how? She'd never told anyone. It was her deepest, darkest secret. Did the stalker intend to expose her? Or was it a prelude to blackmail? She spent hours in her bedroom, her mind shifting between concern for Xavier's safety and fear that her terrible secret was on the verge of being publicly exposed.

She wasn't sure when she fell asleep. It felt as if she'd only been dozing for a moment when a loud noise jolted Bria awake. Her bedside clock read 3:58 a.m. She sat up in bed and the sound came again. A thud against the front door.

She climbed out of bed and went to the window, careful to stay to the side, even though she knew she couldn't be seen from outside. She peeked out.

She caught sight of the tail end of a black sedan before it sped out of sight. An Uber dropping someone off, maybe? But she didn't see anyone making their way to any of the neighboring houses. She scanned the street until her gaze fell on what looked to be a bundle of clothes lying in front of the black iron gate surrounding her front lawn.

Her heart hitched at the sudden realization that what she was looking at wasn't a bundle of clothes at all. It was a person and they appeared to be hurt.

A knock sounded at her bedroom door and she pulled it open to find Xavier standing on the other side. He wore his pajama bottoms and a wrinkled white T-shirt. In his hand was a menacing-looking black gun.

"Are you okay?" he asked, his gaze panning past her to scan the room.

"Yes. But I think there's someone outside who needs help." She waved him to the window and they both looked out together.

Xavier cursed. "Stay here. Lock the door and don't open it to anyone but me."

He glided down the stairs. She turned back into the room and grabbed her robe from the foot of her bed, shrugging into it before following him down the stairs.

He had the front door open and was making his way down the steps carefully, toward the person lying on the sidewalk in front of her home.

Xavier knelt next to the body of a man, feeling for a pulse.

She hurried to his side, then mentally kicked herself when she realized her phone was still in the house charging on her bedside table. A moment later, shock gripped her as she focused in on the face of the man lying in front of her, realization setting in.

Bernie Steele.

They'd just spoken to him only hours ago and now he was... She wouldn't let herself think what her eyes were telling her.

"I'll go back in and call an ambulance," she said, making a move to turn back to the house.

"Ask for the police." Xavier pulled his hand away from Bernie's neck and looked up at her from his crouched position. "He doesn't need an ambulance. He's dead."

Chapter Twelve

The street outside Bria's home swarmed with police and emergency services vehicles. The first officer to arrive on scene had separated him from Bria and now they were each being questioned by detectives separately. Thankfully, they'd deferred to Bria's celebrity, and the implied threat of a host of lawyers keeping them from their two best witnesses, and consented to doing their questioning in Bria's house. Bria was in the living room being questioned and he sat at the kitchen counter with Detective Oliver Roslak. Roslak had a mop of brown hair and wore a wrinkled black suit over an equally wrinkled blue shirt. Despite his slightly disheveled appearance, his gaze was sharp and intelligent.

"Okay, walk me through it again, if you don't mind," Detective Roslak said, casually looking down at his notebook.

"No."

Roslak looked up, startled by his matter-of-fact refusal.

He had already walked Roslak through everything that had happened from the time he and Bria returned to her house until the moment the first officers arrived. Roslak had tried to act nonchalant, but he knew enough about police work to realize that he'd be a suspect, at least for a while, given the encounter he'd had with Bernie right before his death. Bria and the security system in the townhouse would provide him an alibi of sorts, but he was a security specialist. He knew there wasn't a system in existence that couldn't be manipulated, and given his past and maybe current relationship with Bria, he wasn't sure how inclined the detectives would be to believe her.

Nope. He'd told his story and he wasn't going to give the man the opportunity to twist his words.

Roslak forced a smile, but his eyes were narrowed to slits. The combined effect made him look like a lizard. "This is just routine questioning. I just need to make sure I got the details right."

"I'm sure you do, Detective. But I'm not going to sit here and go through rounds and rounds of questioning. I told you what transpired tonight. We'll make the home's security information available to you and your medical examiner will tell you that Bernie was dead before his body hit the sidewalk. That should be enough to clear Miss Baker and myself."

"You think?" Roslak growled.

Xavier just smiled.

"Mr. Nichols, this is a serious matter. Now, I'm sure you don't want it to get out that you're not cooperating with a homicide investigation."

He folded his hands on his lap. "I'm sure I don't care. I've told you what I know."

Roslak slammed his notebook closed. "Okay, I'll tell you what I know. By your own admission, you and the victim got into a heated argument last night in which you put your hands on him. That's assault. I could arrest you for that right now."

Xavier held his wrists out. "Do it. You and I both know the charges won't stick, and after I've been charged, you won't be able to talk to me without counsel present. No lawyer worth their salt will let their client talk to the cops after a charge has been laid against them. And trust me, my lawyer will be worth his salt."

Brandon West, Ryan and Shawn's older brother, was a top-notch attorney, as was Shawn's wife, Addy. Both lawyers were used to swooping in and getting West Investigations' employees out of stickier jams that the one Roslak was proposing. They'd both probably read him the riot act for talking to Roslak without one of them present now, but he had nothing to hide, despite Roslak's unabashed suspicion.

Roslak swore. "Let me pose a hypothetical for you, then. You don't have to talk since you're so shy," he said with a derisive snort. "You and the victim got into it earlier in the evening. You're enraged because he's been following you. You rough him up a little bit and tell him to get lost, but he doesn't do that. You find him poking around later that night. Maybe he's even peeping in the windows, catching a glimpse of you and the woman playing slap and tickle."

Xavier clenched his fists and reminded himself that Roslak was trying to get a rise out of him. An arrest for assault when the propertied victim couldn't press charges would be thrown out in a heartbeat. But an arrest for assaulting a police detective would be much harder to make disappear.

"Or maybe he's just peeping on her," Roslak added, after taking a beat to see if his goading was working. "I hear nudie pics of the right celebrity can bring in real money."

"I wouldn't know," Xavier shot back. "You clearly hang out with a lower-brow crowd than I do."

Roslak scowled and continued. "You lash out at the victim. Stab him, and realizing that now you have to do something with the body, make up this ridiculous story about finding him on the front stoop."

"On the sidewalk in front of the house. And the only thing ridiculous here is your story. Bria allowed you to search the house. You didn't find a knife. There's no blood anywhere in or around the house, including out on the sidewalk where the body was found, which confirms that the murder happened elsewhere. Your hypothetical doesn't match up with the facts, Detective."

Roslak huffed but didn't say anything more.

"So, are we through here?" Xavier stood.

"For the moment." Roslak rose. "Stay available, Mr. Nichols."

"Always, Detective Roslak."

BERNIE WAS DEAD. From the snatch of conversation she'd overheard between the paramedics, who had arrived shortly after she'd called, he was dead before he landed on the sidewalk in front of her townhouse. He'd been stabbed in the chest, then transported to her front door.

A shudder snaked through her.

"Take me over the events of the evening one more time." Detective Ivy Morris held her pen poised over the small notebook in her hands. She crossed her thin brown legs at the ankle. Her boxy suit was ill fitting but didn't hide the curvy figure beneath.

Bria massaged her temples. "Do I have to? I already told you everything I know, which isn't much."

Detective Morris smiled sympathetically. "I know it's been a long night. Just one more time so I know I have everything straight in my head."

Bria sighed heavily and leaned against the arm of the

sofa she was sitting on. Morris's partner was taking Xavier's statement in the kitchen. Bria glanced toward the back of the house, but she wasn't able to make out Xavier or the detective.

"Something, a sound, woke me up just before four this morning. I didn't know exactly what it was, but it happened again and it sounded like it was coming from outside."

"Did you have any idea what the noise was?" Detective Morris asked.

Bria shook her head. "No. It just sounded like a thud. Maybe like someone falling, but I can't be sure."

"It appears that someone threw two rocks at your front door. We found them on the porch and there's a bit of damage to the door."

Bria pressed her palms together. She hadn't noticed any rocks, but she took the woman at her word. So someone wanted to make sure that she and Xavier were the ones to find Bernie's body and not some passerby. And Bria was sure that someone was her stalker.

"Can you tell me what happened next?" Detective Morris prodded.

"I got out of the bed and peered through the window. I saw something that looked like a pile of clothes on the sidewalk in front of my house." She continued retelling the events of the night.

Detective Morris scratched out notes and nodded for her to go on.

"There was a knock on the bedroom door and Xavier asked if I was okay. I took him to the window to show him what was outside. He told me to stay inside, but I followed him out of the front door." She took a steadying breath for what came next. "I didn't realize it was Bernie at first, but

I could see that it was a person, a man. I'd left my phone in the house, so I started to turn back to go call for an ambulance when I realized I knew the person in front of me."

"And by Bernie you are referring to Bernard Steele?" Morris scribbled notes.

Bria nodded. "Yes."

"And you knew him, how?"

"He's a paparazzo. He's followed me for years now, taking my picture."

"You live in Los Angeles, correct?" Detective Morris looked at her with more than a hint of suspicion. "He followed you all the way across the country for a picture?"

"Celebrity photographs are big business, Detective. The paparazzi will follow an actor or actress all over the world for the chance to get a million-dollar photo."

The woman looked at her with open skepticism. "Million dollar?"

"It's a figure of speech, but the right shot can sell for anywhere from one thousand to ten thousand dollars. Or more, if the photo is an exclusive."

Morris let out a low whistle. "That's a lot for a picture."

"Exactly. Bernie has made taking my photo a significant part of his business model."

"So you knew him well?" Morris was back to scribbling in her notebook.

"Knew him? Not really. We weren't friends. He wasn't the worst of the paparazzi though."

"I understand there was an argument between Mr. Nichols and the victim earlier in the evening." Morris kept her tone light, but Bria got the hint.

"I wouldn't describe it as an argument. Xavier was escorting me home when he spotted someone he believed might be a threat. He approached and we discovered it was Bernie. Xavier asked him some questions and then advised him not to loiter on the street in front of my home."

Detective Morris's brow went up. "That's not how one of your neighbors described it. They heard the victim yelling about a camera, that he'd been assaulted and threatening to call the police."

Bria shrugged. "Bernie dropped his camera. He was upset, and not unexpectedly given his line of work, he tends... tended—" she corrected herself "—toward the dramatic. I offered to buy him a new camera and he calmed down." Bria guessed she'd have to cancel that order now.

"That's a very different story than the one your neighbor told us."

She shrugged. "I don't know what my neighbor told you, but I was standing right there. That's what happened." Or close enough. There was no way she was going to give Detective Morris grounds to suspect Xavier any more than she already did. Her version of events was close enough since there was no way that Xavier had anything to do with Bernie's murder. She'd told her about the text message threatening Xavier, and about the other emails, notes and flowers she'd received from her stalker. Detective Morris had listened but didn't appear to be putting much stock into the idea that her stalker had progressed to murder, much to Bria's chagrin. It was obvious who could have killed Bernie, but Morris was far more interested in the confrontation between Xavier and Bernie than she was in hearing about the stalker.

"Okay, so after the...discussion between Mr. Nichols and Mr. Steele, what happened?"

"Nothing. Bernie drove off and Xavier and I went into my house."

She eyed her warily. "And then…"

"It was late and I was exhausted. I went up to bed."

"By yourself?"

Her face heated further. "Xavier is staying in the guest room if that's what you're asking."

Detective Morris gave an apologetic smile. "I'm not trying to pry into your personal life. I'm just trying to ascertain whether the two of you were together for the whole evening."

"I went upstairs to my room and he went up to his a few minutes after me."

"And about what time did you go to sleep?"

"I'm not sure exactly. I went to my room around nine fifteen, but I didn't go to sleep right away."

"So you can't vouch for Mr. Nichols's whereabouts after you went to bed at 9:15 p.m. Is that correct?"

Bria's back straightened. "Xavier didn't kill Bernie."

Detective Morris pressed her lips together tightly. "Ms. Baker, after 9:15 p.m., you can't say exactly where Mr. Nichols was, correct?"

Bria ignored the question for a second time. "Xavier didn't do this. He doesn't have a motive, but more importantly, if he'd left the house the alarm would have sounded."

"He's been staying here, but he doesn't know the alarm code?" Morris shot back.

"He does, of course," Bria gritted out. "But when the alarm is deactivated, even with the code, it beeps. It would have woken me, I'm sure of it."

Detective Morris didn't look convinced. She wrote something in her notebook. "Is there anything else you can tell me?"

"Would you listen if I did?" Bria said.

The detective closed her notebook. "Ms. Baker, I'm just

trying to do my job here. A man has been killed and I intend to find out who did it."

Footsteps approached from the hall. Xavier and Roslak appeared.

"I've finished taking Mr. Nichols's statement," Roslak said.

Detective Morris rose. "And I've just finished up with Ms. Baker." Roslak looked from Bria to Xavier. "Neither of you have any plans to leave town in the near future, do you?"

"I'm shooting a movie here for the next month," Bria responded. "And I'm pretty hard to lose track of. Just open any tabloid and there I am."

"I've no plans to leave town at the moment," Xavier answered far less sarcastically.

"Good. Good. Well, then we will be in touch."

Bria walked the detectives to the foyer. With the door open, she could see the ambulance and most of the police cruisers had left while she'd been giving her statement. The street was almost back to normal except for the unmarked sedan double-parked a few feet from her home. Still, she couldn't help but see Bernie's lifeless body lying on the pavement.

She closed the door quickly and turned, pulling up short when she found Xavier waiting only inches away.

"We need to talk," he said.

Bria stifled a groan. "Xavier, I'm really not up for it."

She moved to go past him, but he stepped in front of her.

"Too bad. It's no longer safe for you to stay here. Bernie knew you owned this place and apparently so did whoever killed him. And I'm sure that in a matter of hours, so will the entirety of the New York paparazzi, if they don't already."

This time she didn't try to stifle the groan that escaped from her lips.

He placed his hands on her shoulders. "More importantly, it's time for you to tell me everything."

"What are you talking about?"

"This secret of yours that the stalker thinks he knows. And the photo of you and your former costar. What is going on, Bria? Do you know who's stalking you?"

Chapter Thirteen

"Of course not." Bria stalked past him into the kitchen.

"Then, what are you keeping from me?" Xavier followed her.

She programmed the coffee maker and contemplated how loaded his question was. A lot had happened in the fifteen years since she'd broken up with him, but she knew that wasn't what he was asking.

He wanted to know about the photo of her and Derek Longwell. Why the stalker had left it for her.

She couldn't be sure, but she had a good hunch. And if she was right, if her stalker knew her deepest, darkest secret, her career was over. And most likely her freedom as well. But she also knew that Xavier wouldn't give up. He'd keep asking until he wore her down or he'd go out and investigate himself. And that, she didn't want.

If he had to know her secret, she wanted to be the one to tell him. Even if it meant he'd never see her the same way again. She took her mug from the coffee dispenser and carried it to the island.

Xavier hopped onto the stool next to her.

Bria wrapped her hands around the mug, soaking in its warmth and taking a sip to fortify herself before she said the words that could change her life forever. "Derek Longwell was the star of a C-list indie film that I got cast in about three years after I'd moved to Los Angeles. The budget wasn't big, but we all had visions of the film becoming a breakout indie hit like *The Blair Witch Project* and other indie films around that time period." She gripped the sides of her coffee mug. "The entire cast and crew was young and mostly just happy to have a paying job on a real movie."

"What happened?"

Bria slowly let out a deep breath. "I killed Derek Longwell."

Xavier looked at her impassively. "Start at the beginning."

Bria's hands shook just going back to that night in her memory. "The film's shoot was scheduled to take a little over a month. We were about two weeks, maybe a little more into it and shooting was going well. The cast and crew would often hang out at a bar about a few blocks from the motel where we were staying. Most of us were at the bar one night, celebrating after having spent two days shooting a pivotal scene. There was lots of drinking. Some drugs, although I never partook in that. The rest of the cast and crew was still going strong around midnight, but I was ready to call it a night, so I headed out to walk back to the motel. It wasn't far."

The trembling in her hands became more pronounced. She'd never told anyone what had happened that night, for good reason, but somehow telling Xavier was harder than she'd ever imagined. It wasn't just that telling him her secret could be the end of the career, the life, she'd worked so hard to build. It mattered to her that he believed her, and the possibility that he might not, that he might turn against her,

was more terrifying than any of the other possible consequences of her confession.

He reached out and took her hand, the simple gesture giving her enough hope to continue telling her story.

"I didn't make it out of the parking lot before Derek caught
up to me. He said it wouldn't be right to let me walk home
alone at night. There was a path through a wooded area that
you had to use to get back to the motel, so I was more than
happy to have company. He was drunk, a little unsteady on
his feet, but I'd seen him in much worse conditions since
we'd started filming. We were on the path when he suddenly
grabbed me and kissed me. I pushed him away, tried to make
light of it but also let him know that I wasn't interested. But
he didn't care what I wanted. He grabbed me again, pulled
me into the trees and his hands were all over me. I fought
back, but he hit me."

His grip on her hand tightened, not to the point of hurting her, but she could tell by the hard set of his jaw and the
fire in his eyes that he was teetering on the edge of rage.

"I fell and he was on top of me." The memory slammed
into her. She took a steadying breath before continuing. "I
knew he wasn't going to stop, and as hard as I was fighting
him, he was much stronger than I was. I don't even remember
picking up the rock, but it was in my hands and I smashed
it against the side of Derek's head. He screamed and rolled
off of me. I didn't wait around to see if he needed help, I just
got up and ran back to my room at the motel."

"You didn't call the police? Report his assault?" His words
were little more than a growl, but she knew the anger wasn't
directed at her. She could hear the pain in them.

Bria shook her head, the terror of that night as real at that
moment as it had been twelve years earlier. "I think I was

in shock or something. Derek was the star—" she made air quotes "—of the movie. His stepfather had put up most of the money that was being used to produce the film. Even if the director and crew believed me, their jobs were dependent on Derek, not me. I was expendable."

"You have never been expendable," Xavier said fiercely.

"I spent the whole night huddled in my room, waiting for Derek to break down the door and try to finish what he'd started or for the police to come and arrest me for assaulting him."

"But neither happened."

She shook her head. "No. The next morning everyone returned to set. Everyone except Derek. It wasn't unusual for him to be late, so no one was worried at first. I just tried to act like everything was normal. Like nothing had happened. I hoped Derek would be embarrassed enough by his behavior that he'd just make up some story about the injury to his head and let it go." She shuddered out a breath. "Eventually, we got word that a couple on an early morning hike had found Derek's body. I was terrified and sure that I was going to jail."

"Did the police question you?" Xavier asked softly, and although she could still hear the fury in the words, he seemed to have wrested it under control.

She nodded. "They questioned all of us. Maybe I should have told them the truth, but I was still a nobody then. Derek's stepfather was some bigwig hedge fund or investment banker or something. He had connections. I didn't know what he'd do to protect his stepson, even in death."

"The truth is Derek Longwell was a creep who assaulted you and you defended yourself. The truth is his death was an accident brought on by his own actions."

How many people were in jail who had told the truth believing the system would work? "I told the cops that Derek had walked me back to my room and said he was going to go back to the bar. He was drunk, everyone at the bar could attest to that. I don't think the police in that town had the wherewithal to conduct a real investigation. A few days later, they officially ruled Derek's death an accident. It was March, but we were in a densely wooded area and the temperature at night was consistently in the thirties or lower. They concluded he was drunk, fell and hit his head. I think the official ruling was a combination of blood loss and hypothermia from the cold. I've carried the guilt with me ever since."

"You have nothing to feel guilty about."

She wished she could believe him. "I could have called for help. Sent someone to check on him."

"You said it yourself. You were in shock. You'd just been victimized yourself and you weren't sure that summoning help was going to do anything other than open you up to further trauma. Your actions are understandable."

Bria rose and stalked across the kitchen, putting her now-empty mug in the sink. "My actions might be the reason the stalker is terrorizing me now."

"I will find whoever is doing this."

Bria kept her back to Xavier, her hands gripping the countertop on either side of the sink. So many thoughts had swirled in her head since finding that photo with the flowers, but there was one she just couldn't seem to shake no matter how ludicrous it seemed.

She turned to face Xavier, still using her hands to brace herself against the countertop. "I've been thinking that maybe, I don't know how, but maybe Derek is the one doing this."

Xavier cocked an eyebrow. "Maybe he isn't really dead?"

"I'm not sure, but no one else was aware what happened that night."

"We aren't certain that anyone does know about Derek's assault on you."

Bria shot him an incredulous look. "What other possible message could the stalker mean to convey by that photo and all the references to 'my secret'? Hitting Derek and not owning up to the truth of that is by far the worst thing I've ever done. Maybe—" She paused, swallowing hard before forcing the next words out of her mouth. "Maybe I should go to the police and confess everything? Then the stalker wouldn't have anything to hold over me and he wouldn't have any reason to go after you."

Her resolve to fire West Investigations to keep Xavier out of harm's way had faltered with the light of day and finding Bernie's body. She wanted Xavier safe, but she wanted him at her side too.

Xavier rose and crossed the tile floor. He cupped her face in his hands. "I can take care of myself. Confessing to a crime you didn't commit isn't going to get this guy to stop. That's not how stalkers operate. We are going to figure this out. The photo, the stalking, everything, but you have to trust me. Can you do that?"

She let go of the countertop and wove her hands around his waist, keeping her eyes trained on his. "The answer to that is easy. I already trust you. I always have."

Chapter Fourteen

Xavier stalked into the West Investigations headquarters. His emotions were still in upheaval from Bria's revelation. She'd been attacked and may have killed a man.

And I wasn't there to protect her.

He knew it was a waste of time to blame himself for something he had no control over, but he couldn't seem to stop himself. Bria thought she'd taken a life and he knew firsthand how that weighed on a person. He'd had no choice, that someone was likely to die at your hand was a fact of life for a soldier at war, but that didn't mean he felt the significance of that act any less acutely. He often felt it was the exact opposite.

He should have been there, but he was here now. And he would move heaven and earth to protect her.

Bria wasn't on the shooting schedule for the next two days and he needed to talk to Ryan about their next steps in person. He'd enlisted another West Investigations employee, Gideon Wright, to stay with Bria while he was at West headquarters.

Ryan was in his office. He waved Xavier into a chair in front of his desk and set the report he'd been reading aside.

"Xavier, I'm glad you're here. Seems you had one hell of a morning."

He'd called Ryan before the police arrived at Bria's house and had given him a quick heads-up on having found the paparazzo's body in front of Bria's townhouse. Now he gave a more fulsome description of the morning's events.

"I don't like this one bit," Ryan said. "This is a huge escalation if the stalker is our killer."

"It is, and we know that Bria's stalker is motivated. He followed her across the country."

"And we know that a changed situation can push a stalker to act out." Ryan jutted his chin in Xavier's direction. "You're a new element in Bria's life and he issued a threat to you with that text message. It's possible that he saw the photographer as a threat too."

"And it would be a whole lot easier to get to him than it would be to get to me."

"Exactly," Ryan agreed. "If this guy wants to show Bria just how serious he is about making her his, killing a man who is, for all intents and purposes, also stalking Bria is one way to do it."

Xavier drew in a breath. "There's more I need to tell you."

Ryan shot him a weary look but gestured for him to go on. Xavier recounted what Bria told him about the night Derek Longwell attacked her.

As Ryan listened, his expression reflected increasing concern. "So Bria's stalker could be connected somehow to this actor Derek Longwell's death."

"It's possible," Xavier conceded.

"You know this information makes West's association with Bria much more complicated. She confessed to killing a man."

Xavier felt his body tense. "It was self-defense."

"I'm not saying it wasn't, but it doesn't change the fact that a man is dead and Bria didn't tell the authorities the whole truth concerning the incident," Ryan shot back.

"We're not turning her in."

Ryan sighed. "I have to think about this firm."

"Fine. I quit." Xavier stood. "I'll handle Bria's security myself, and if you go to the authorities, I'll deny I told you anything."

"Just slow down." Ryan held up his hands. "I'm not going to the police." The unspoken *yet* hung in the air between them. "I suggest we look into Derek Longwell's life and death ourselves. See if we can't pinpoint our stalker and maybe drum up some evidence that might support Bria's claim of self-defense."

Xavier held his hands fisted at his sides. "I'm never going to agree to turn her in to the cops."

"I gathered that. But it might not be up to you. If her stalker really does know about what she did to Longwell, he could reveal it at any time. It will be better for Bria if we're already prepared when and if that happens."

Xavier hesitated for a moment before giving a terse nod. Everything Ryan said made sense even if he didn't like it.

"I need to talk to Bria. Without you in the room," Ryan said.

"Why? I've already told you what she said."

Ryan gave him a hard look. "You are too close to this situation. You don't just want to protect Bria, you want to save her and that's clouding your ability to be objective."

"I can be objective," he growled.

Ryan snorted.

"Fine, I'm not objective. I'm breaking the cardinal rule of

private protection. I have feelings for the woman I'm supposed to be protecting. But you ought to know better than anyone how that feels. How it can make you crazy but also sharpen your instincts because you have something to lose if you make the wrong decision."

It was well-known among those who worked for West Security and Investigations that Ryan's wife Nadia was a client when the two of them met and fell in love. Nadia's brother had gotten himself, and by extension her, into a heap of trouble with organized crime. Ryan had thrown every resource West had at protecting Nadia and helping her out of the jam her brother had created, despite warnings from his brother Shawn and several other people.

Ryan held his hands up in surrender. "Fine. I'm a hypocrite. I'd do... I did the same thing you're doing. But that's how I know it can go disastrously bad. I did end up in the hospital and Nadia was kidnapped."

"I remember you were fine and you saved Nadia's life. All I'm asking is the chance to do the same for the woman I..." Xavier caught himself before he said what he'd been thinking. What he'd been feeling since he'd walked into the conference room days earlier and seen Bria sitting there. Hell, if he was honest, it was what he'd felt since the moment he saw her sitting on that park bench in Bryant Park fifteen years earlier.

He loved her. He'd never stopped loving her despite her having given him the heave-ho fourteen years ago.

"The woman you what?" Ryan said, his mouth upturning ever so slightly.

He was sure Ryan knew what he'd been about to say, but he wasn't ready to profess his love for Bria to Ryan out loud. "The woman I've been charged with protecting."

Ryan shook his head. "You've got your head so far up your..." he mumbled, letting the thought trail off. "Look, I'll concede that, despite your emotional involvement, you are the best person to watch over Bria. But I need you to trust me. I need to talk to Bria if West Investigations is going to help her."

I need you to trust me. Hadn't he asked the same of Bria only hours earlier? He did trust Ryan. He'd trusted Ryan, Shawn, Gideon and all of the other operatives at West literally with his life on more than one occasion, but somehow it was harder to trust them with Bria's life.

Because she means more to you than your life does, the voice inside his head intoned.

And that was the heart of it. He'd willingly give his own life for Bria's, but of course, he couldn't expect the same of anyone else at West Investigations. Still, despite his earlier threat to quit and protect her alone, he knew that having Ryan and the West team on his side was the best chance they had of figuring out the connection between Derek Longwell's death and Bria's stalker.

"Fine."

"Good." Ryan was all business. "Gideon's with her now?"

Xavier nodded.

"I'll have him bring her into the office. While I speak to her, you should pull everything you can find on Derek Longwell and the *Murder in Cabin Nine* movie."

"Bria said the film was shelved after Derek's death. His stepfather was one of the major funders and apparently after Derek was gone, he didn't see any reason to continue financing the venture."

"Still, at the very least we need to try to dig up a list of the cast and crew of the film. Occam's razor. The most obvious answer to the identity of our stalker is that he or she worked on *Murder in Cabin Nine* or was close to someone who worked on the movie. If nothing else, it's the logical place to start given the photograph that was left with the flowers in Bria's trailer."

"I'll get started on that." Xavier rose and headed for the door.

"Xavier." Ryan's voice stopped him before he left the office.

Xavier turned back to face his boss and friend.

"Be careful. You may be right that your feelings for Bria are an asset now, but they could just as easily turn into a liability. And that could be dangerous for you both."

"I DON'T APPRECIATE being interrogated, especially by people I'm paying to protect me," Bria said, marching into the conference room where Xavier had spread out all the information he and West's researchers had pulled so far on the people closest to Bria. Eliot Sykes. Mika Reynolds. Bria's assistant, Karen Gibbs, who they'd confirmed was still in Los Angeles. They'd also pulled background reports on her costars on *Loss of Days* and her last two films.

The possibilities were quickly becoming overwhelming. Bria literally came into contact with hundreds of people while she was filming a movie and those number swelled into the thousands once they took into account promoting the movies, fans, reporters and any other number of events and award ceremonies she attended in a given year. The stalker could be among these people or completely removed from them. Someone whose connection to Bria was entirely in his or her head, making them virtually impossible to find.

He was currently focusing on the cast and crew from

Murder in Cabin Nine given the photograph and what Bria had told him, but he really had no way of knowing if he was looking in the right place. *Murder in Cabin Nine* had been a relatively low budget film with a small cast and crew by Hollywood standards, but there were still more than twenty names on the list, including the director and producers.

Xavier rubbed his temples and tried to keep his frustration from bubbling over. "It was necessary. We need to know everything you know."

Bria fell into a chair on the opposite side of the conference room table. "And you didn't believe that I'd told you everything. Is that why you sicced Ryan West on me?"

The vein in his neck jumped. "I didn't sic anyone on you. And I believe you. But Ryan is right. I'm emotionally involved. I'm sure he was better at pressing you, getting you to remember things you didn't even know that you've forgotten, than I would be."

"You didn't trust me to tell you the truth," she said, hurt shining in her eyes.

"I didn't trust me. I didn't trust my feelings for you would let me be as objective as I needed to be to question you properly."

Bria looked away.

Neither of them was happy about the current situation, but deep down, he knew that Ryan was right to have questioned her himself. Now they had to move on and focus on what needed to be done.

"I'd like you to take a look at this list." He pushed the paper indicating the names of the cast and crew of *Murder in Cabin Nine* across the table.

She studied the paper for a moment before looking back

up at him. "These are all the people who worked on *Murder in Cabin Nine*."

"Yes. Right now we're working under the theory that the stalker is connected to that film."

Bria shook her head. "I can't imagine anyone I've worked with doing this."

"Someone is, and right now we don't have a lot to go on."

Bria looked at the list again. "Honestly, I can't even remember most of these people." She pointed to one of the names on the paper and smiled. "Rob, I remember though. He was a sweet kid. Everybody's friend."

"Robert Gindry?" Xavier pulled up the information West had compiled so far on Gindry. It wasn't a lot. Gindry wasn't in show business anymore. He'd gotten out of the industry more than ten years before and was now an insurance salesman. And a pretty successful one, based on his address, which Xavier noticed was not that far from Manhattan. "He's not acting anymore and he lives in Connecticut. Just outside of the city."

Bria shook her head. "No way. I know it's been more than ten years since I've spoken a word to him, but Rob was the kindest, sweetest soul you'll ever meet. Everyone loved him. He was everyone's friend. You'll never convince me he's my stalker."

Xavier frowned. That was just the kind of sentiment a lot of predators relied on. Instead, he pressed on. "Anyone else on the list you can tell me something about?"

"The name Morgan Ryder is kind of familiar, but I can't quite grasp why."

He searched for information on Ryder in the files they'd pulled already, but came up empty. "Morgan Ryder. The name is pretty androgynous. Was Ryder male or female?"

Bria shook her head. "I honestly can't remember. I can't pull up a face to go with the name, but there's something about it. It's probably nothing. Maybe he or she is still in the business and we've crossed paths since filming *Murder in Cabin Nine*. Or maybe the name is just reminding me of a character in some script I've read. It could be nothing."

Or it could be something. There was no point in pushing her now though if she couldn't remember. "If you remember what it is, let me know."

"Of course I will."

"There are only two people on this list, that we know of, who live within driving distance. Robert Gindry and Tate Harwood, the director of *Murder in Cabin Nine*."

Bria's brow rose in surprise. "Tate is on the East Coast? I wouldn't have thought he'd ever leave Los Angeles."

"He works for a production company headquartered here in Manhattan. The home address we have for him is in Brooklyn."

"I take it you think we should pay Rob and Tate visits."

"I should pay Gindry and Harwood visits. You should stay safely ensconced in a safe house until your stalker is locked behind bars."

Bria shook her head. "No way. If you go to talk to Rob and Tate, I go with you."

"Bria."

"I'm not some shrinking violet who's just going to cower behind the big strong man while he protects her. And you'll have a much easier time getting Rob and Tate to talk if I'm with you."

"I've never had difficulty getting anyone to talk to me," Xavier growled.

Bria smiled. "I'm sure brute force has its place, but I don't think this is it. Especially when it comes to getting Tate to meet with you. You can't do anything for him, so he's not going to be inclined to give you any of his time."

"And you think he'll talk to you?"

She laughed. "Oh, I know he will."

Chapter Fifteen

The research West Investigations had compiled on Tate Harwood was thorough. His cell phone number was listed among the contact information. It took a moment to convince Tate that the call wasn't a joke or crank call, but just as she'd predicted, once she'd convinced Tate she was who she said she was, he agreed to meet with her. They agreed to a time the next morning and Bria ended the call just as Ryan led Detectives Roslak and Morris into the conference room.

Their arrival seemed to suck all the air out of the room.

Bria glanced from Xavier to Ryan. The two men shared a look, conveying information only the two of them were privy to. What was clear, however, was the tension in both their bodies and the hardness in their expressions.

Detective Roslak stepped in front of Xavier. "We have a few more questions about the night you found Bernard Steele, Mr. Nichols."

"Why don't you and Detective Morris have a seat, then?" Xavier gestured to the chairs surrounding the conference room table. "I'll be happy to answer whatever questions you have."

Morris's smile was feral. "Actually, we'd like you to answer them down at the station if you don't mind."

Xavier's expression remained unchanged. "And if I do mind?"

"Then we'll have to change this from a request to something more formal," Detective Roslak answered.

Bria took a step closer to Xavier. "Wait a minute—" Her voice came out high-pitched and laced with all the fear for Xavier she felt at that moment. "What the hell is going on here? Xavier didn't even know Bernie."

Ryan laid a hand on her shoulders. "Let's stay calm here. Xavier, you go with the detectives. I'll have Brandon meet you at the station."

Detective Morris glared at Ryan. "An attorney isn't necessary. As we said, we just have a few more questions for Mr. Nichols."

"Let's not be cute, Detective," Xavier growled. "You're not really giving me a choice. Answer your questions voluntarily or you'll arrest me, right?"

Both remained silent.

"I'd say an attorney is most definitely in order," Ryan said.

Bria grasped Xavier's hand and squeezed. "I'm going with you."

She wasn't exactly sure why the detectives wanted to talk to Xavier, but it was clear from the expressions on his and Ryan's faces that they thought the situation was serious. Whatever was going on, she wanted Xavier to know that he had her support.

He returned her squeeze and gave her a thin smile. "There's no need. Brandon West is one of the best lawyers in the city and there will be nothing for you to do at the police station but wait. Stay here where Ryan can look out for you."

She opened her mouth to object. "Please. It will be easier on me if I know you're safe. And if I'm not back in time to take you, Ryan or someone else from West Investigations can accompany you to your interview this afternoon."

She'd forgotten about the interview. Eliot had sent her the details last night and she'd forwarded it along to Xavier. She was to meet the reporter, Ian Cole, that afternoon at the Ritz Carlton.

She didn't like leaving Xavier to deal with the police alone. Every fiber of her being urged her to stay with him and fight whatever misinformed theory had led the detectives to drag Xavier down to the station. But she trusted him, more and more with each passing day. If he said it was best that she stay here at the West Investigations offices, that's what she'd do.

"Okay," she said reluctantly.

She watched Xavier leave flanked by the two police detectives, more scared in that moment than she'd ever been before.

THE DETECTIVES HAD led Xavier into a small interrogation room when they arrived at the police station and left him there saying they'd be back in a moment. He'd been staring straight ahead, body relaxed, breathing even, for the past half hour. The light on the camera in the upper-left corner was dark, but he knew better than to think that the camera wasn't on and recording. The stark gray cinder block walls of the interrogation room were intended to remind people of the inside of a prison cell, a not-so-subtle intimidation tactic used by the cops in order to get criminals to loosen up. The long absence and drab surroundings no doubt worked to induce most people to talk. He wasn't most people.

The door to the interrogation room finally opened. Brandon West strode in, laying his briefcase on the table before opening it and taking out a leather portfolio. Brandon took the seat next to Xavier while Roslak and Morris slid into the chairs on the opposite side of the table.

"Detectives, does one of you want to tell me why you dragged my client down here to ask him questions you surely could have asked him in a less...coercive environment?" Brandon snapped at them.

"I wouldn't call this a coercive environment for a former decorated soldier such as your client. He's deployed to Iraq and Afghanistan, so I'm sure he's been in much more difficult situations," Detective Morris said in a measured tone.

"I'm sure he has, although I do find your likening this situation to literal war zones interesting." Brandon flashed a smile.

Morris's lips thinned.

Detective Roslak cleared his throat. "As we told your client, there was really no need for you to come to the station, counselor. We just have some routine questions we wanted to ask him."

Brandon leaned forward and pinned Roslak with a look. "You and I both know there is no such thing as routine questions, so let's cut the crap. You ask your questions and I'll decide if my client is going to answer them."

Xavier held back a smirk.

Brandon West may wear five-thousand-dollar suits and spend more on one haircut than Xavier spent all year on shape-ups, but he was a damned good lawyer. Especially, when it came to keeping his brothers and their friends and employees out of the line of police fire. There'd been some talk among the rank and file at West regarding whether they should continue to call on Brandon on the rare occasions they ran afoul of the cops, given that he'd started dating one himself. But it didn't appear that his feelings for Silver Hill detective Yara Thomas had dulled his sharp edges at all. If anything they seemed to have been sharpened to a deadly point.

Roslak and Morris glared back across the table for a long moment before Roslak turned his gaze on Xavier. "Could you go over what happened last night again for us? Starting with your arrival at Ms. Baker's townhome and the confrontation with Bernard Steele."

Brandon tapped one finger against the table, his signal not to answer. "As I understand it, Mr. Nichols has already given you a statement, Detective."

"He has," Roslak gritted out. "We just want to make sure we got everything down correctly."

Brandon's smile was cool. "Why don't you tell us what you're confused about and we'll see if we can help you understand things a little better."

Roslak scowled. "Mr. Nichols, you stated that you had an argument with Mr. Steele. We were able to get the video Mr. Steele took with his camera in front of Ms. Baker's townhome from his online storage, and it seems as if you and Mr. Steele had more than just an argument."

"Is there a question in there somewhere?" Brandon asked in a tone that hinted at boredom.

"Did you put your hands on Mr. Steele?" Detective Morris asked.

Brandon tapped the table once. "If you have the video as you say, you already know the answer to that question."

"I did, and I told you I did in my initial statement," Xavier answered the question, drawing a look of rebuke from Brandon. He appreciated Brandon being here, but it wasn't his style to hide behind a lawyer.

"Yes, well, your statement made it seem as if it was a little skirmish," Morris continued, "but the video shows that it was a bit more than that. You threw the victim against a car, not once but twice and broke his camera, did you not?"

Brandon tapped the table. "Again, a question answered by the video. I don't see why you've brought my client in, detectives."

"We're getting to that, counselor," Roslak growled.

"I pushed Steele against a nearby SUV when I thought he was a danger to the client I was hired to protect. He dropped his camera when I did so. I don't know if it was broken but it couldn't have been too bad if you have video from it."

"Ms. Baker offered to buy Mr. Steele a new camera, did she not?"

"She did," Xavier answered before Brandon could tap.

Brandon sent him another look.

"In fact, Ms. Baker offered the new camera as something of a bribe, correct? To keep Mr. Steele from calling the police and having you arrested for assault."

"He's not answering that question. You're asking my client to speculate on not one but two people's motivations."

"Not a problem." Roslak waved the question off as if it was nothing. "How about this one? Mr. Nichols, you and Ms. Baker aren't just employer and employee or bodyguard and protectee, are you? You've had a long-standing relationship with her, haven't you?"

"Long-standing, no. Bria and I knew each other when we were younger. It's part of the reason she felt comfortable hiring West Investigations when she realized she had a stalker.

But before she contacted West Investigations two days ago, we hadn't spoken in fourteen years."

"But if you hadn't spoken to her in well over a decade, why would she seek you out?"

"That sounds like a question that should be directed at Ms. Baker," Brandon shot back.

This time it was Xavier who shot Brandon a hard glare. The last thing he wanted was for the detectives to get the idea that they should drag Bria down to the station and start questioning her.

"You've been staying at Ms. Baker's townhouse for the last few nights. Protecting her." Roslak smirked. "Is that correct?"

It took work to keep his expression neutral and not allow the detective to see his disdain. "That's correct."

"And Ms. Baker indicated in her statement that she told you the code to shut on and off her security system. Is that also correct?"

"It is."

Xavier watched a hint of concern flare in Brandon's eyes. "Get to the point, Detective."

"The point, counselor, is that I've been thinking about this case long and hard." Roslak folded his hands behind his head and leaned back in his chair. "Ms. Baker thinks she has a stalker. She's filming in New York and seeks out an old flame. Someone she thinks might still have the hots for her. Someone who she could maybe manipulate with stories of old times and promises of new ones." Roslak let the insinuation hang in the air for a moment before plowing forward. "Mr. Steele traveled over three thousand miles to take pictures of Ms. Baker. That sounds pretty stalker-y to me. Maybe you, or Ms. Baker, thought he was your guy. Maybe you decided to take matters into your own hands. You use your firm's considerable resources to find the rental Mr. Steele is staying in and you eliminate Ms. Baker's stalker problem."

"Sounds like all you have is a whole bunch of speculation, Detective Roslak, and unless you have more than that, we're done here." Brandon stood.

Xavier followed his lead and stood as well.

"If you want to speak to my client again, call me first." Brandon nodded at each of the detectives, who remained seated. "Detectives." He gestured to Xavier to head for the interrogation room door.

They strode through the halls of the police station and out the front doors in silence.

Neither spoke until they were safely ensconced in Brandon's BMW and on the road back to West Investigations headquarters.

"So what do you think about all that back there?" Xavier finally asked.

Brandon shot a glance across the car. "They're grasping."

"That's good, right? Like you said, it means they don't really have anything."

"Maybe," Brandon said. "Our problem is that people who are grasping tend to be desperate, and desperate people will grab on to anything that looks like it could help them. And right now, it seems as if they're reaching for you."

Chapter Sixteen

Xavier had left with the police detectives more than three hours earlier and Bria spent most of that time pacing the conference room. Ryan had offered to have someone drive her home but she'd insisted on waiting for Xavier to return.

She'd wanted to call in the top New York criminal defense attorney, but Ryan had suggested she wait. His brother Brandon wasn't directly employed by West Security and Investigation, but he had plenty of experience dealing with the NYPD.

Waiting for Xavier to get back to West Investigations headquarters was like torture. They couldn't possibly think that Xavier had something to do with Bernie's death. She'd made it clear in her statement that Xavier had come to her room only moments after the sound outside had roused her from sleep. He couldn't possibly have gotten inside and upstairs that quickly. Not to mention she'd seen a car speeding away. Whoever killed Bernie had to have been in that car, and it wasn't Xavier.

She was on the verge of marching down to the police station and demanding they let Xavier go when he walked into the room.

She rushed toward him and into his arms without pausing to think. "Oh, thank goodness. I was starting to think they'd arrested you or something."

She felt some of the anxiety she'd been carrying since Xavier had left with the detectives seep out of her body as he wrapped his arms around her waist.

"Not quite," the man who'd walked into the room behind Xavier said.

Bria looked over Xavier's shoulder at the man with him. He looked enough like Ryan and Shawn West that she didn't need to guess that he was their older brother Brandon.

"Ryan said I had nothing to worry about since he was sending you to represent Xavier. I guess he was right."

Brandon West shot her a dazzling smile. All the West brothers were attractive enough to have solid careers in the entertainment industry, but she could immediately tell that Brandon West had that extra something, the "it" factor that was necessary to make star status. And he was a lawyer. There was probably some sort of irony in that, but she was too worried about Xavier at that moment to ponder it.

She turned to Xavier now. "Are you all right?"

"I'm fine." His arm was still around her waist. "It was just a few questions."

Bria studied Xavier's face. It had been fourteen years since they'd been truly close but she could still read him. It hadn't just been questions.

"This is where I take my leave of you," Brandon said, stretching a hand out to Xavier. "Call if you need me."

The two men shook and Brandon left them alone.

"What did they ask you?" Bria asked as soon as the conference room door closed.

"It was just some more routine questions about finding Bernie."

Bria pointed a finger at him. "No, don't do that. The cops don't show up at your job and take you to the station just to ask routine questions."

Xavier was silent for a moment, considering.

She crossed her arms and waited.

"They think I might have had something to do with Bernie's death."

"That's ridiculous!" The words exploded from her.

"Don't worry about it. It will be fine."

Bria began pacing again. "This is my fault. I dragged you into this, and now the police consider you a suspect in a murder."

"Hey." Xavier stepped in front of her, stopping her pacing. He took both her hands in his. "You are not at fault for any of this. The stalker or whoever killed Bernie is the only one at fault here. What we need to do is focus and find that person."

The feel of his hands in hers steadied her.

She nodded. "Okay."

Xavier let her hands fall to her side. "We're going to talk to Tate Harwood tomorrow morning. We still have a little time before you have to be at your interview with Ian Cole. What do you say we go try and speak with Robert Gindry now."

Bria agreed, and minutes later, they were on the road to Connecticut. They spoke very little, both of them lost in their own thoughts. So much had happened in such a short period of time, and no matter what Xavier said, she couldn't help feeling guilty about having pulled him into the mess that was currently her life.

Xavier pulled the car to a stop at the curb in front of a yellow brick colonial with black shutters. The lawn had been recently mowed, as evidenced by the neat vertical rows still visible in the grass, and the hedges on either side of the front door were trimmed to exactly the same height. The house was the picture of the quintessential American home.

"I'm stating, again, for the record, I don't like you being here," Xavier growled.

"And I'm stating, again, for the record, that I don't care. Now, are you ready?" Bria unlatched her seat belt and reached for the door handle.

"Wait. Let me come around first."

She rolled her eyes, but waited for Xavier to open the door for her. "Thank you."

Xavier closed the car door behind her and started up the walkway. "If I say we're leaving, we're leaving, okay?"

"Fine, but I'm telling you, Rob is not my stalker. He was the nicest guy ever."

Xavier slanted her a look as she reached out to press the doorbell.

"People change," he said.

"You've never met Rob."

A moment later, the door opened and a girl of thirteen or fourteen stood in front of them. Her head was down, her gaze focused on the cell phone in her hand.

"Hi. I was hoping to speak to Rob Gindry. Is this his residence?" Bria asked.

"Yeah. May I ask who's—" The girl's head came up and she choked on the remainder of her sentence. She stared in shocked silence for a long moment before letting out an excited ear-piercing squeal. "Dad!"

Bria wasn't unaccustomed to this sort of greeting from some people when they realized who she was, but the girl's voice reached an octave that made her flinch all the same.

She felt Xavier tense next to her. She reached out and

placed her hand on his arm. The teenager wasn't a threat to anything other than their eardrums.

A crash sounded from the second floor of the house and then footsteps thundered down the stairs. Rob came into view, a baseball bat clutched in his hand just as a brunette woman careened around the corner, a rolling pin in one hand and a cell phone in the other. Both parents were ready to fight to the death in defense of their offspring.

Xavier pulled her back several steps, positioning his body between Bria, Rob and the woman Bria assumed was Rob's wife.

He needn't have worried.

"It's Brianna Baker. Princess Kaleva, at our door." The girl jumped up and down, yanking on her mother's arm as she did. The woman looked confused, unsure of exactly what was going on. It didn't escape Bria's notice that she still held on to the rolling pin as if ready to smack someone in the head with it any second.

"Brianna Baker?" Rob let the baseball bat fall to his side, a wide grin blooming across his face. He turned to his family. "I told you I knew her!"

He leaned the bat against a wall, then stepped out of the house, sweeping Bria into a crushing hug. He pulled back after a long moment. "I can't believe you're standing on my porch. Come in. Come in."

Rob swept them into the house. "This is my wife, Alexandria." He motioned to the woman, who set the rolling pin on a side table and extended her hand.

"Nice to meet you," Alexandria said, her eyes still clouded with questions.

"And this is my daughter, Cleo, who I will be talking to

about not screaming as if she's under attack unless she is actually under attack later today."

"OMG, Bria. I love you. Like, Princess Kaleva is such an empowering female character. All my friends love her. We've seen every one of the movies. I mean, I've seen all of your movies. Dad makes us watch them. He said he knew you from his acting days, but, like, I would have never imagined you'd show up at our house. I have to call Tiffany."

"No." Bria reached out and touched the teenager's hand, looking from her to her parents. "I am sorry to drop in on you like this, unannounced, but it would be better if no one knew I was here."

Cleo's face fell. "But my friends will never believe I met you if they don't see you for themselves."

Bria smiled at the girl. "How about I take as many self-ies with you as you want, enough so that no one could ever doubt I was here, but you can't post them or show them to anyone until after I've left?"

Cleo considered it for a moment. "Deal."

Alexandria smiled and hooked an arm over her daughter's shoulder. "How about we go get refreshments for Bri-anna and...?"

"Oh, please excuse my poor manners. This is my friend, Xavier Nichols."

Rob, Xavier and Alexandria said their hellos. Cleo barely acknowledged his presence, her eyes were still full of stars and glued on Bria.

"Okay," Alexandria said, turning her daughter toward the back of the house. "Let's get those refreshments started."

Cleo reluctantly let her mother lead her away.

"Come, please, have a seat." Rob led them into a sunny living room with two well-worn sofas facing each other.

Xavier followed them but didn't sit down. "Do you mind if I take a quick look around the house?"

Rob's brows went up to his receding hairline.

"Xavier is my friend, but he's also my bodyguard."

Rob's eyes swept over Xavier. "That makes sense." He shrugged. "Sure. Go ahead."

Xavier walked through the attached formal dining room and disappeared around a corner.

"Cleo isn't exaggerating, you know," Rob said sitting on the sofa across from Bria. "I do take the family to every one of your movies. I'm so happy you're doing so well."

"Thank you, Rob. And it looks like you're doing well too." Bria gestured, indicating the home around them.

Rob smiled, waving away the compliment. "I gave up on acting, which I'm sure you know. To be perfectly honest with you, I never had the talent to make a real go of it, and once I met Alexandria, I wanted to be able to build the life she deserved. We moved to Connecticut, where Alex is from, after we had Cleo. I sell insurance now."

"Well, your family and your home are beautiful. It looks like you made the right choice."

"I did. And look at you. You've definitely been making the right career choices. Princess Kaleva. Maybe I should have curtsied instead of hugging you."

Bria laughed. "No need for that."

"So, what brings you to see me? Don't get me wrong. I think you just earned me the father-of-the-century award, but I doubt you've sought me out just to raise my stature in my daughter's eyes."

Xavier returned to the living room. She waited until he sat to answer Rob's question.

"I don't know if you've seen the papers recently, but I'm having trouble with a stalker."

Rob leaned forward. "I hadn't seen that. I make sure to keep up with your movies, but I can't say that I read the gossip rags."

Bria smiled. "You're better off for avoiding them." Her smile fell away. "But this stalker, he's been sending me emails for a few months now and recently started sending flowers. With the last bouquet he sent a photo of me and Derek Longwell on the set of *Murder in Cabin Nine*."

Rob let out a slow breath. "Derek. I haven't thought about him in years. He was talented. His accident was such a shame."

"We're looking into whether the stalker's motivation might have something to do with the film or Derek Longwell's death," Xavier interjected. "We're hoping you can help us."

Rob leaned his elbows against his thighs. "I'll help in whatever way I can."

"Bria said you were close to Longwell back then. Was there anyone else who he was close to?"

"Derek wasn't the easiest person to be friends with," Rob said pointedly. "He had a huge ego. I mean, we were all struggling actors for the most part, but he came from money. Even though he wasn't a name, he'd never had to worry about how he was going to feed himself or make the rent. He was one of us, but the money also separated him from us, if you remember."

"I do," Bria said. "I remember we all stayed in that crappy motel close to the area where we filmed but Derek had a car so he stayed a couple towns over in a nicer hotel."

Rob pointed at her. "Exactly. He'd buy everyone's drinks

for the night, but he wouldn't go back to the motel with us. One of us but not really one of us, you know."

"So how did you and Longwell become so close, then?" Xavier asked.

"I don't know if I'd say we became close. My wife says I've never met a person who wasn't a friend, and that's true to a point. I do find it easy to befriend people, but a lot of that is that I'm a good listener and I don't judge, at least not outwardly." Rob chuckled. "People like to tell me their problems. Derek was like that. Our friendship was based largely on his complaining to me about how horrible his stepfather and mother were."

"The stepfather who was bankrolling the movie he was in?"

Rob nodded. "Derek could be a lot of fun, but he was a spoiled brat. Constantly complaining about his parents, but he always took the money they gave him." Rob shrugged. "We were young."

Xavier cut a glance at Bria. They'd discussed how they were going to approach Derek's assault on her on the drive over. They needed to know if Rob could possibly be the stalker. If somehow he knew that Derek had planned to attack her or if he'd figured it out and this was his way of getting revenge for his friend. Bria hadn't bought into the possibility when Xavier floated it, and she was even surer that Rob had nothing to do with the stalking now. Still, she knew Xavier wouldn't be satisfied without asking Rob directly.

"Rob, I have to ask you something. It's about our time on the film." She'd agreed with Xavier that they wouldn't give specifics about Derek's assault. The last thing Xavier would want her to do was to give Rob the idea that she might have had something to do with Derek's death.

"Sure. Shoot," Rob said.

"Did you know that Derek tried to force himself on me?"

The stunned expression on Rob's face was more than enough to convince Bria that he'd had no idea.

Rob pushed to his feet. "No. Absolutely not. When?"

"I was able to fight him off and get away," Bria said, ignoring his question, "but it occurred to me recently that I might not have been the first woman he tried that with. Or the only woman he tried to assault on the set of the film. And as you said, people talked to you."

Rob paced a short line in front of his chair. "Bria, I promise you, if I'd known he'd attacked you, attacked anyone, I would have turned him in to the cops myself. Derek never said anything to me and neither did anyone else."

Bria believed him. They asked a few more questions but Rob didn't know anything that would help them.

She kept her promise and took several selfies with Rob's daughter and wife before saying goodbye to the family, apologizing for leaving without partaking of Alexandria's homemade scones, and promising to keep in touch with Rob.

"Rob was no help at all," she said, frustrated, when she and Xavier were back in the car.

"Hey, that's the nature of investigations. We just have to keep talking to people until we find someone who can help." Xavier reached across the console and pressed a kiss to her palm.

She tried to let his reasonableness soothe her, but as he pulled away from the curb, she couldn't help feeling things were going to get a lot worse.

Chapter Seventeen

A little over an hour after leaving Rob and his family, they were nearly at the Ritz. Xavier's phone rang. Ryan's name rolled across the in-dash screen. He accepted the call using the buttons on the SUV's steering wheel. "Bria and I just left Robert Gindry's place. I've got to get her to the hotel for her three o'clock interview, but I'd planned to call you while she did her thing and brief you on what we learned or, rather, didn't learn from him."

"I'm not calling about that." Ryan's voice came through the car's speakers. "The press has gotten wind that someone was killed at Bria's townhouse last night."

He glanced over at Bria. Her eyes were wide with shock.

He swore. "Bernie wasn't killed at Bria's house. He was killed somewhere else and his body was left in front of Bria's house."

"You wanna make that distinction for TMZ?" Ryan shot back. "Bottom line is there's a horde of media in front of Bria's place right now."

Bria's phone rang. She snatched it from her purse and looked at the screen. "Mika. Probably calling to tell me exactly the same thing Ryan is saying right now." She declined the call.

Xavier swore again. "So the whole world knows where Bria lives now."

A breath whooshed out of Bria's lungs. He reached across the gearshift and took her hand, giving it what he hoped was a reassuring squeeze.

Bria's phone rang again. "Eliot. They are going to keep calling until I answer," she said before declining that call as well.

"It's not safe for her to go back to her place," Ryan said, stating the obvious.

"Copy that. We'll head into the office now. We can game plan our next steps when Bria and I get there."

"No." Bria shook her head. "I have to go to my interview."

Xavier glanced at her. "You can't still want to do that?"

"I didn't want to do the interview in the first place, but Eliot was right about the importance of controlling the narrative. It will be even more important now. And with the interview already set up, I can actually get a jump on framing the story."

A ball of frustration knotted in his chest. More Hollywood shenanigans.

Bria's phone rang again.

"It's Eliot. I'm going to take it and tell him the interview is still a go. If you can't drive me to the hotel, I'll call a car." Bria didn't make the statement as a threat but as a matter of fact.

He swore for a third time, but made the right turn at the next light that would take them to the Ritz-Carlton, where the interview was scheduled to take place.

"Thank you," she mouthed before punching the button on her phone to connect.

Xavier switched Ryan's call from the car's speakers to the Bluetooth headset in his ear. "You caught that?"

"Yeah." Ryan sighed. "You're on your way to the Ritz Carlton now?"

"Yes. We're about an hour away if traffic isn't too bad."

"Okay. I'm sending Gideon and Shawn to back you up. We know that the reporter who is meeting with Bria knows where she'll be. It seems unlikely that they'd have tipped off their colleagues to the location of the interview. They'd probably want to keep their exclusive to themselves, but I'm not taking any chances with Bria's safety."

"I agree. We checked out this reporter right?"

"Yeah. Bria's PR guy sent the name to us yesterday. He's clean."

"Be safe and keep your eyes open."

"Copy that." Xavier punched off the call with Ryan and a minute later Bria ended hers.

"Eliot has arranged for us to enter through the back of the hotel to avoid the other guests. He also spoke to the reporter interviewing me, who assured him that he hasn't shared the fact that he's doing the interview or the location with anyone other than his editor."

"Ryan's sending Shawn and Gideon to back me up. I'll tell them to meet us at the rear of the hotel."

He made the call.

They spent the rest of the ride in a flurry of text messages and phone calls. Mika and Eliot had already arrived and were waiting with a change of clothes for Bria in the suite where the interview would take place. The reporter hadn't arrived yet.

Shawn and Gideon were standing at the staff entrance of the hotel when Xavier pulled the SUV to a stop. Shawn opened the door for Bria while Gideon jogged around to the driver's side door as Xavier climbed from the car.

"I've got a secure spot to park. Then I'm going to scout the perimeter and set up a lookout point in the lobby," Gideon said.

"Good. We're in suite 1248. Stay on coms. I'm hoping this interview doesn't take too long." Xavier looked across the hood of the SUV. Shawn was leading Bria inside the hotel. His gut clenched as she disappeared behind staff entrance doors. He trusted Shawn, but he didn't want to let Bria out of his sight.

"Got it." Gideon climbed into the SUV and Xavier hustled toward the doors Shawn and Bria had disappeared through.

He caught up to them getting into the freight elevator. The elevator jerked them upward.

"Not exactly how I imagined an A-list movie star traveled," Shawn joked.

"You'd be surprised how many freight elevators I've been in," Bria shot back. "A lot of my glamorous lifestyle is nothing more than its own form of Hollywood magic."

"A bit of Hollywood magic a lot of people would love to experience."

Xavier was more concerned with reality than playing make-believe. "Did you check out the suite?" he said, focusing Shawn back on the task at hand.

"Yes. The suite and the eleventh, twelfth and thirteenth floors. No suspicious activity. Once we get Bria settled, I'll walk you through the paths of exit I've identified."

Xavier gave a terse nod. "Good."

"Guys, this is not a military mission. It's just an interview with an entertainment reporter. I've done a million of these things." She took his hand. "Everything will be fine. I'll be fine."

The elevator doors opened on the twelfth floor and Shawn took the lead, Xavier falling in behind Bria so that she was sandwiched between the two of them. They made their way quickly to suite 1248.

Sykes and Mika rushed to Bria the moment she stepped inside.

"Don't you worry about a thing," Mika said, pulling Bria into the suite's living room. "Eliot and I are handling the vultures in front of your house as we speak."

Mika pulled Bria onto the sofa and she and Sykes fell down on either side of her.

"I've been on the phone for hours now, making sure that it's clear that you are the victim in this horrid situation," Sykes said.

Bria frowned. "I'm not sure that's accurate, given that Bernie is the one who was killed."

Something flashed over Sykes's face. Xavier didn't know him well enough to know whether it was anger or hurt, maybe both. But his features smoothed almost immediately. "Of course the dead man is the true victim of this crime. I just meant that I'm doing everything I can to make sure the press keeps the focus on that fact and acknowledges that you had absolutely nothing to do with this man's death."

Bria covered her agent's hand with her left hand and rested her right hand on Sykes's leg.

Xavier clenched his teeth against the jealousy that swelled in his chest.

"Thank you, both of you, for everything you've done for me. I know it's been a chaotic few days."

Sykes leaned over and pressed a kiss on Bria's cheek.

"That's what we're here for. Anything you need, you just let me know."

"What I need right now is to get ready for this interview." Bria gave Sykes's leg a pat and rose.

Mika stood too, gesturing toward the closed doors of the suite's bedroom. "I got a couple of options from Alexander McQueen or, if you're feeling a bit riskier today, there's a Versace dress in the mix as well."

"I'm sure I'll find something that will work."

Bria disappeared into the bedroom to change.

Shawn ran Xavier through the exit scenarios he'd worked through in case they needed to get Bria out of the hotel quickly. Xavier would like to walk the planned escape routes himself, but there was no way he was leaving Bria's side.

The reporter showed as they were going through the plan.

Xavier left the greeting and setting up to Sykes and Mika, but that didn't stop him from studying the man who'd shown up.

Ian Cole was tall, blond and blue-eyed, and fit. He'd be no match for either he or Shawn if he did try something, but Ryan had said his background check had come up clean, so there was no reason to expect anything to go wrong.

Then, why was his gut churning?

Bria was right, she'd done tons of these interviews. The likelihood that the stalker would show up here was slim. Between Xavier, Shawn, Gideon, hotel security and all the many, many cameras throughout the hotel, attempting something here would be risky to the point of foolishness.

Which didn't mean the stalker wouldn't try. It might even make it more likely he would. Killing Bernard Steele had been risky and foolish and he'd done it anyway. It was clear the stalker was escalating and maybe even losing his grip on reality. Who knows what that might lead him to try.

The doors to the bedroom in the suite opened and Bria swept into the living room.

He had no idea whether she was wearing Alexander McQueen or whatever other designer outfit her agent had bought for her, but he knew she was breathtaking.

She'd chosen to wear a dark green jumpsuit with gold heels and matching gold jewelry. She'd pinned her long straight hair back and added large bouncy curls to the ends. She stepped out of the bedroom, her eyes sweeping over everyone in the room. Her gaze lingered on him for a moment before she crossed the room to greet the reporter.

His fingers ached with the need to touch her, but he hung back.

Just as Bria said, she was a pro at this. She handled the interview deftly, wrapping the reporter around her finger, exhibiting genuine grief over Bernie Steele's death and imploring whoever had a hand in it to come forward and turn themselves over to the police. The interview ended and Bria saw Ian Cole to the door. It was clear from the sappy look on Ian's face that the man was more than a little smitten with Bria.

Get in line, pal, he thought. Then, on second thought, *No, don't get in line. Bria is mine.*

He heard the words in his head, how they were almost exactly the same ones that the stalker had used in his note, and shuddered.

He wouldn't put himself in the same category as her stalker, no way. But thinking about Bria as his, that was objectifying her, thinking of her as something that could belong to him. Bria was and always had been her own person.

She belonged to no one but herself and he wouldn't have it any other way.

As if she knew he was thinking about her, Bria looked over at him and winked.

No, she couldn't belong to anyone, but that didn't mean they couldn't be a team. Lifelong partners.

It was something he wanted to think about more but not now. Now his priority had to be Bria's safety. She couldn't go back to her townhouse. While she'd been doing the interview, he and Shawn had discussed the best place for her to stay.

They'd come up with an answer, but Xavier wasn't sure Bria would like it.

Bria closed the door behind the reporter and turned back to the room.

"You did amazing," Eliot said, crossing the room and pulling Bria into a hug that sent Xavier's jaw hardening.

"You did a wonderful job, darling," Mika said. "You had that reporter eating out of your hand. I'm sure the article will be very sympathetic toward you and everything you've been going through. Good news, since I hear that things haven't been going as smoothly as we might have liked on set." Mika's brows arched.

Bria frowned at her agent. "No movie ever runs smoothly. Things are just fine."

"Good." Mika gave Bria's shoulder a pat.

Someone knocked on the room's door.

Bria was closest to it, but Xavier stepped forward quickly, gently stopping her from reaching for the latch. He motioned for her to move back and looked out of the peephole.

A bellhop dressed in the uniform of the hotel stood in the hall. He held a long white box with a red bow.

Xavier opened the door.

"Hello, sir. A package arrived for Ms. Reynolds." The bellhop thrust the box at Xavier and waited expectantly.

After a moment, Sykes stepped up next to Xavier and thrust a wad of bills into the bellhop's hand before shutting the door.

Xavier turned to Mika. "This is for you."

Mika looked at him with an expression of surprise. "Me? I can't imagine who'd be sending me something here."

Xavier sent a pointed look in Shawn's direction. "Do you mind if I open it?"

Mika waved a hand. "Go right ahead."

Xavier placed the box on the round table in the corner of the living room. Shawn came to stand to his right with Bria, Sykes and Mika standing on the other side of the table.

The fleeting thought that the package might be an incendiary device floated through his head, but that seemed unlikely, given the hands that the box had probably passed through on its way to the room.

Still, he lifted the top slowly, expending a small breath of relief when nothing exploded.

Relief quickly turned to anger as he processed what he was seeing inside the box.

Half a dozen black roses and a photo of him leading Bria into her townhouse. His face had been scratched out with a bloodred marker, and the word "die" scrawled across the bottom of the photo.

Chapter Eighteen

Bria leaned against the passenger door exhausted, thankful that no one could see her through the heavily tinted windows. Shawn, Xavier and Gideon had questioned the bellhop and every other hotel staff member who had handled the flowers, but no one knew anything helpful. Or at least, they weren't willing to share the information if they did. The only thing anyone could tell them was that the flowers had been delivered by a man in dark clothing and a ball cap pulled low over his forehead and eyes. The hotel security feed had confirmed that, but the man had been careful to keep his head down. The camera hadn't captured an image of him that was clear enough to be recognized. He carried a clipboard and looked like every other delivery person in New York City, according to the concierge who'd signed for the box. They'd gleaned one ominous clue from the concierge, however. The man had expressly stated that the package was for Ms. Reynolds in suite 1248, which meant he knew that Mika had reserved the room.

She hadn't wanted to believe someone close to her could be her stalker when Xavier suggested it, but now? Mika had insisted that, aside from Ian Cole, only she, her assistant and Eliot knew which hotel and room the interview would be taking place in. Xavier was having Ryan confirm with Ian that he hadn't let the meeting place and time slip to someone, but she knew he hadn't. In her experience, reporters were compulsive about protecting information regarding an exclusive interview. No way would a reporter have risked the competition finding out about the meeting and crashing it.

Which made it all the more likely that somehow, someone she trusted was betraying her in a terrifyingly upsetting way.

Bria opened her eyes and glanced across the car at Xavier. Not for the first time since this whole ordeal began, she was thankful that she'd gone to him for help. Even after their breakup and the years that had passed, he was the one person in the world she knew she could count on, no matter what. And at the moment, he was the only person she trusted completely.

And that made her wonder about the choices she'd made in her life up until now. Sure, she had fame and fortune. She'd achieved her goal of becoming an actress, and not just one who could pay the bills but one who'd never have to worry about paying the bills again. An actress with influence in the industry. A role model for other little Black girls to look up to and know they could achieve their dreams too if they were willing to work hard for it.

But she was also isolated. Surrounded by studio executives, agents, PR people and fans but very much alone when she bore down to the root of it all. When she'd needed help the most, she'd had to reach back fifteen years to get it. What did that say about the life she'd chosen for herself?

She knew what it said about the man she'd left behind for that life. It said that he was caring and generous beyond what she likely deserved.

It said that she'd made a mistake leaving him all those years ago.

She shook the thought from her head. She wouldn't have the career she had if she had stayed.

But what about now?

She had the career. The influence. The money. Maybe now she could have the man too.

"What?" Xavier said, breaking into her reverie.

"What, what?"

"Why are you looking at me like that? If you're worried, don't be. I'm not going to let anything happen to you."

"I know that." She sighed. "Do you think that the police will be able to find the delivery guy?"

At Ryan West's insistence, Xavier had called the police and they'd filed a report after he and Shawn had questioned the hotel staff. With Bernie being killed and left in front of her house not long after the confrontation with Xavier, Ryan felt that it was in Xavier's best interest to have everything on the record. There were too many innocent men in prison for Bria to be sure he was right about that, but Xavier had agreed with his boss.

"No. I don't think they'll look too hard either. No crime was committed. But filing a report puts on the record that you are being stalked."

"Yippee."

Xavier made a left turn and took the ramp for the Holland Tunnel.

"Where are we going?"

He shot a glance at her before focusing back on the road in front of him. "Your place isn't safe. Too many people know about it now, and the press are probably still lurking if they aren't just camping out there."

"I agree." As much as she hated it, her beloved townhouse just wasn't safe for her at the moment. "But you didn't answer my question."

"I'm taking you to my place."

Her stomach did a flip-flop. She wanted to see Xavier's place. To see how he lived. But spending the night at his place felt...emotionally dangerous. On some level, she knew it wasn't all that different from him staying at hers, but at her townhouse, she was on her own home turf.

"I don't have a change of clothes."

"I can have a female operative at West Investigations pick up some things for you."

"That would be great. Thank you." She smiled, relieved that one thing was easily handled, since there was so much else in her life at the moment that couldn't be.

"I'll make the call now. While I'm at it I'll also order us something for dinner. Anything in my fridge is well past its best-by date. Is Chinese food good for you?"

"Perfect."

He made the calls.

"Are you sure it's safe? I mean, people have seen you and I together. The stalker or the press might think I'd be hiding out at your place and look up your address."

Xavier arched an eyebrow. "They could look, but they won't find it. I own it through a private company."

"Ah." She smiled. "I totally get that." She'd had to purchase her townhouse in a similarly circumspect manner.

"Trust me. I have a top-of-the-line security system, my neighbors mind their own business and I have a friend across the street who is former Special Forces. It's unlikely anyone would find you here, but if they somehow do, they're in for a surprise. You can relax."

Relax. She was starting to forget what that felt like. But if she was going to relax with anyone, it would be with Xavier.

Her body heated at the thought of just how relaxed he used to make her.

Forty-five minutes later, Xavier pulled into the driveway of a small bungalow in a New Jersey suburb and hit a button on his sun visor that sent the garage door opening. He pulled the car in, shut off the engine and closed the door before getting out and leading her into a mud room off the kitchen.

The open space living room/dining room/kitchen felt more like a loft than a single family home. The peaked ceiling was lined with dark wood beams and a stone fireplace climbed the far wall. A brown leather sectional sofa was positioned so it faced a flat screen television but also took advantage of a large bay window looking out on the backyard. A wood-topped table that matched the beams overhead anchored the dining space, and the kitchen looked as if it had been newly remodeled with light granite countertops and stainless steel appliances.

"Your home is gorgeous."

"Thanks," Xavier said, flipping on the lights in the living room. "It didn't look so gorgeous when I bought it five years ago. I did a lot of work to whip it into shape."

"Well, it definitely paid off. It's very warm and comfortable."

"I'm glad you think so." He smiled. "And you should. You know, make yourself comfortable. Here, let me show you to the guest room."

He pointed out his bedroom as he led her down a short hall off the main room. Xavier kept walking but she paused at his door. Just as with the main living area, his room was masculine but lived-in. A king-size mahogany bed sat against the longest wall in the room flanked by matching, round bed-side tables. A five-drawer dresser completed the set. From the doorway she could see into the small en suite bathroom, which also looked as if it had been recently updated with white marble flooring and a glass-enclosed shower.

Her mind jumped to an image of falling into the bed with Xavier, the soft linens at her back, his lust-covered face looming over her. Desire ran through her core.

"You're welcome to sleep here if you prefer it to the guest room."

She jumped at the sound of Xavier's husky baritone in her ear.

Heat flooded her face. There was no hiding what she'd been thinking. "I was just taking a look."

"Look all you want."

She moved toward him, going onto her toes and pressing her lips against his, softly at first, but when he responded, she deepened the kiss. His hands roamed down her sides, to her hips to cup her butt. She didn't want him to stop. She was edging them into the bedroom when the doorbell rang.

Xavier managed to pull back.

"That's dinner."

Another delivery person with terrible timing. She sighed internally. This was one time she wouldn't have minded having dessert before dinner.

She waited until Xavier had paid for the food and shut the door firmly before stepping out of the hallway. He didn't need to tell her that it was important that as few people as possible knew where she was staying.

He grabbed plates, silverware and cups while she took the food from the bags and peeked into the cartons to see what he'd gotten. She hadn't paid much attention while he was ordering the food, but she wasn't surprised to see that he remembered her favorite dishes. Peking duck. Scallion pancakes. Dumplings. It was all here. More food than they could probably eat in two nights.

The smell hit her, reminding her it had been several hours since her last meal. Her stomach growled in anticipation and they both spent the next several minutes eating in comfortable silence.

"Thank you for letting me stay in your home," Bria said once she'd had enough food to take the edge off her hunger. She reached for the bottle of red wine Xavier had opened and poured herself a half glass.

"You're welcome. You're always welcome here."

She studied his face but found nothing there except honesty. "You really mean that, don't you?"

"Of course I do."

"Even after how things ended between us?"

He let out a long breath. "That was a long time ago. I admit, seeing you again brought some of those old feelings, that old resentment up again. But you did what was best for you at the time, and obviously, it paid off."

She traced the ridge of her wineglass with her index finger. "I don't regret choosing my career then. At the time, I couldn't have managed acting and having a relationship. It was never about you though. It was always about what I had the capacity to handle at one time back then."

And now she wanted both. The thought raced through her head. She wanted him and her career. But she knew it might be too late for that.

"I get it. In a very real way, your decision was the best thing for both of us. I wouldn't have gone into the military if you hadn't dumped me."

"Really? I've been meaning to ask you how you ended up enlisting. I don't remember you mentioning wanting to join the army."

As much as her breaking up with him had hurt, the one silver lining was that it had led to his enlisting in the army. He'd never be sorry about that. "Because I hadn't even considered it until the night you broke up with me."

Her mouth formed a shocked O.

"I somehow found myself in Bryant Park that night, after you gave me my walking papers. I don't even remember getting off the subway, but I was sitting in the park, well after midnight, when a police officer found me."

"The park closes at night."

"That's exactly what he said. But he also saw that something was wrong. To this day, I don't know why but I just unloaded everything on him. My dead-end job. My girl breaking up with me. Everything. And Officer Jarell Hurt, who'd only gotten out of the army a few years prior, suggested that if I was looking for something to take my mind off a broken heart and a new career path that the army could be for me. Turned out it was one of the best decisions I've ever made."

"Wow, that's some story."

"Jarell is a good man. He's retired now, but we still get together regularly for a beer or to watch the game on television."

"Does he know Brianna Baker is the girl who broke your heart?"

Xavier looked away. "I told him." He picked up his empty plate and carried it to the kitchen sink.

She grabbed her plate and followed him. She reached across him and set her plate on top of his in the sink. Turning so there were only inches between them, she looked up at him. "And now? Are you going to tell him I'm back in your life?"

His hands fell onto her shoulders. "Are you back in my life?"

Chapter Nineteen

Bria stood pressed against him, her heart pounding against his chest. The need to sweep her off the ground and carry her to his bedroom was nearly overwhelming. He'd had sexual partners other than her, but he'd only ever experienced a need so palpably strong with her. From the look in her eyes, she felt it too.

Somewhere in the back of his mind, he realized becoming intimate with Bria again could be a bad idea. It would most likely lead to him alone with a broken heart just as it had before. But drowning in her beautiful brown eyes, heartbreak seemed a small price to pay to have her in his bed once more. Then she drew even closer, pressing her pelvis against his already stiff length and all reason flew out the window.

"I want you, Xavier." The way she said his name made him long to hear her say it again, but this time, as he thrust himself inside of her. "Tell me you want me too."

It wasn't a profession of love, but it was enough for him right now. More than enough.

He held her tightly against him. "You can feel how much I want you." He rested his forehead against hers. "But there's no going back if we do this."

"There's been no going back from the moment I saw you again. At least not for me."

That was all he needed to hear. "It's always been you, Bri. Always." He dipped his head down and claimed her mouth. She tasted like heaven.

Her hands traveled down his chest and across his hips until she gripped his backside. He grabbed the hem of her sweater and pulled it over her head, letting it fall to the kitchen floor. She wore a sheer, lacy black bra and when he dipped his hand under the material and cupped her breast, massaging her nipple with his thumb, she let her head fall back and moaned.

It was the most erotic and beautiful thing he'd ever seen.

"You are so damn gorgeous. Do you know that?"

She looked at him. "I missed this. I missed you."

Something inside of him melted at her words.

He swept her into his arms, taking her mouth in a hot, heavy kiss and carried her to his bedroom. He set her down in front of his bed. "I missed you too, sweetheart. So much more than I can say. But I plan to show you just how much."

He found her mouth again while her hands worked at the button of his jeans. Moments later, their clothes were littered across his bedroom floor and he finally had her where he wanted her. In his bed.

He took his time, his hands exploring. He brought his mouth to one breast and then the other, lavishing her nipples with the adoration they deserved. She was all curves and softness, a contrast to his hard edges, but somehow, they fit. At that moment, he would give anything to know that she would be in his bed every night for the rest of his life. But if all they had was tonight, he was determined to make it memorable.

He kissed his way down her body and then back up again until he worked his way to the sensitive flesh on the inside of her thigh. He felt her shudder in anticipation and his already painfully tight groin pulsed with need.

"Xavier, please. I need you now." Her face was flushed with desire.

He was determined that she should have her pleasure before he took his, so he focused on her luscious body.

He slid his hands beneath her bottom and tilted her up, bringing his mouth to her core. She was more than ready for him and it didn't take long for her to find her release. Her muscles clenched and her body vibrated as she tipped over the edge, screaming his name.

BRIA WAS STILL coming down from the climax Xavier had sent shooting through her body when he reached over to the nightstand and took out a condom. Watching him sheath himself renewed the never-ending desire she seemed to have for him. She hadn't been exaggerating when she'd told him she'd wanted him from the moment she'd seen him again. If she was being totally honest, she'd never stopped wanting him.

Now here he was, crawling up her body, seating himself at her opening. And she craved nothing more than to feel him inside of her, tipping her over the edge with desire again, and again, and again.

She reached out for him, guiding him to where she wanted him, opening her legs to accommodate his size. Her gaze was locked on his face, not wanting to miss his expression the moment he entered her for the first time in far too long.

He gave a guttural moan as he thrust himself inside of her. She opened wider, taking him in fully, adjusting for his girth and length. He felt amazing. So much better than she could have ever imagined.

And then he began to move inside of her, and all thought fled. All she could do was feel. And it felt so damned good.

Far too soon, she felt her body tensing again.

Xavier smiled down at her as a second orgasm rocketed through her body. And then his smile faded as he thrust into her harder, faster, deeper, barreling toward his own release.

She thrust her hips in time with him, wanting to give him as much pleasure as he'd given her, riding a third wave building inside of her.

Their bodies exploded in time with each other. She felt him pulsing inside of her even as the walls of her core clenched around him.

Xavier rolled onto his side, breathing hard and pulling her in close to him. Her heart raced along with his and she pressed a kiss to his chest. She lay in his arms, wanting to share with him what she was feeling at that moment. Wanting to say those three little words she should have said fifteen years ago.

But she didn't. Because those three little words weren't all that mattered.

They'd both built lives for themselves far away from each other, and at some point, they'd have to return to those lives. But maybe they could figure out a way. Other people did it. Why couldn't they?

But she didn't have to think about that now.

She wrapped her arms around Xavier and held him tightly. For now she could pretend that this, the two of them right here, would never end.

Chapter Twenty

Bria was still asleep in his arms when Xavier woke. Part of him wished he could stay where he was, holding her. He knew waking up next to her was temporary, but he couldn't help wishing that it wasn't.

Instead of dreaming dreams that couldn't be, he got out of the bed, taking care not to wake Bria, and headed for the bathroom. Showered and dressed, he reentered the bedroom, only to find the bed empty.

He found Bria in the kitchen, sipping freshly brewed coffee from one of his favorite mugs. She was barefoot and wearing the shirt he'd shed in a hurry before taking her to bed the evening before.

"I hope you don't mind," she said, a hint of hesitation in her tone. "I made coffee."

He crossed the kitchen and bent to place a kiss on her lips. "I don't mind at all."

He poured a mug for himself. "Tess, one of my coworkers, is going to bring you some clothes to wear. She should be here soon. Hopefully, the press mob has moved on and we can get back into your place sometime today."

"To stay? Or just for me to pick up a few things?"

"I think it's best if you stay here for the time being. Even if the press has backed off, your address is out in the public now. I want West to do a full security sweep and assessment. Your security was good, but you'll probably have to level up now."

Bria rubbed her temple with the hand that wasn't holding her mug. "Whatever you need to do."

He shot off a quick text to Ryan asking him to take care of the sweep.

Bria sat her mug on the counter. "I missed a call from Tate Harwood last night."

The slight smile on her lips told him she was thinking about what they'd been doing when the call must have come in. The memory put a matching grin on his face.

"Is that so?"

She swatted at him and he dodged out of the way.

"Tate says he's available to see us anytime today."

He couldn't keep the surprise off his face. "Really? It was that easy."

Bria's smile grew wider. "I told you he'd be falling all over himself to take the meeting. It probably helped that I hinted at maybe having a project I was interested in talking to him about."

"Okay, and how is he going to react when he finds out there is no project?"

Bria shrugged. "He won't be happy, but he'll get over it."

The doorbell rang.

"That's Tess."

Bria headed for the hallway leading to the bedrooms. "I'll call Tate back and set up a meeting for this morning. I have to be on set by two today." She disappeared down the hall.

He went to the front door, and after checking that it was in fact Tess standing on his porch, he let her in.

Tess's gaze moved around his home in a practiced, efficient scan. "Nice. We should have a company happy hour or two here."

He arched an eyebrow. "I don't think so."

Tess laughed and handed him the shopping bags she held in her hands. "Not a lot open this early in the morning. Had to hit the big box store. Nowhere near as nice as the stuff that Bria is used to wearing, but it'll do until she can get her own things."

"Thanks. I know she appreciates it."

Tess cocked her head to one side. "Huh. So."

He didn't like the way she was looking at him. "Huh. So. What?"

"The two of you are hitting the sheets. Honestly, I saw it coming a mile away, but Ryan won't be happy."

Xavier turned his back to her. He'd never been the kind of man to kiss and tell and he wasn't going to start now. "You don't know what you're talking about."

Tess laughed. "Okay, but I'll give you some advice. If you want to have a chance that Ryan doesn't pick up on the fact that you're doing the midnight rumba with a client, you should tap into your growly side some more. You are far too chill, for you, to convince anyone you haven't recently gotten laid."

He turned back to Tess with a scowl on his face.

"There he is. That's what I'm talking about." She laughed again.

"Thanks for the clothes. Now, get out."

Tess left, still laughing.

He carried the bags into the bedroom, catching Bria still on the phone with Harwood.

Even though she didn't have the call on speakerphone,

Xavier could clearly hear Harwood's excitement on the other side of the line. He agreed to meet with Bria in his office in an hour.

"The power of being an A-list celebrity," Bria said after ending the call.

"An A-list ego to match," he teased.

"Gotta have something to balance out the self-doubt."

"Just make sure you use the power for good and not evil."

"Always," Bria shot back with a sexy smile that made his insides melt.

He left her to shower and change while he again read through the background information they'd compiled on Harwood.

Bria reappeared in the living room forty-five minutes later in skinny jeans, a fancy off the shoulder shirt and black pumps. Her hair was up in a complicated twist and her makeup looked expertly applied. It was simple, classic, but she still looked like a million bucks.

"Wow, you look great."

She beamed. "Tate's online bio with Panthergate Productions lists him as a producer. But based on my experience, that could mean anything from he's a glorified coffee boy to he's the brains of the operations. In either case, he'll undoubtedly want to exploit our renewed relationship to up his clout within the company."

"Tough business," Xavier said, taking the oversize sweater she carried in her arms from her and holding it open so she could shrug into it.

He wrapped the material around her shoulders and she turned slightly, leaning back against him and looking up at him with a wink. "Thanks."

He pressed a kiss to her neck and she sank back farther.

"What do you say to going back to bed?"

He pressed a kiss to the other side of her neck.

"I don't think we have time for what you're thinking," Bria said teasingly.

"You know you're thinking about it too," he teased.

She giggled. "Maybe, but we still don't have time now. Later."

He sighed and stepped back, letting his hands fall from her shoulders.

Bria turned and faced him. "When we get to Tate's office, let me do the talking, okay? He's bound to be a little put out when he realizes the project I mentioned to him on the phone is looking into Derek's murder, but he won't want to jeopardize our renewed acquaintance."

Xavier quirked an eyebrow. "So I'm to act like nothing more than your obviously lethal, devastatingly handsome bodyguard?"

She grinned. "Whose ego is showing now?"

He grinned. "Is madam ready to go?"

Bria grabbed her handbag and slid it onto her wrist. "She is."

The Panthergate Productions offices were on the east side of Manhattan, but they weren't far. Traffic was merciful and they arrived only fifteen minutes late. The building offered valet parking, and Xavier slipped the valet a fifty to keep the car in front of the building although he was pretty sure the young man would have done it for nothing more than the smile Bria shot him as she'd gotten out of the SUV.

Xavier strode into the building at Bria's side. It was as if she was a magnet, compelling all of the heads in the lobby to turn toward her. An excited buzz hummed through the air.

He swept his gaze over the mostly suit-clad people, most

likely employees of the production company coming or going to lunch or meetings. None of the faces held a threat. They mostly reflected excitement.

A heavyset, middle-aged man in a light brown suit hurried through the security gate toward them. Xavier recognized him as Tate Harwood. The face was the same as the photo he'd seen in the background check Ryan had pulled, even if the man was now thirty pounds heavier and ten years older. His hair was almost completely gray with only a few stray patches of dark brown pushing through. The crow's feet around his eyes were the bigger indicator of his age, which Xavier knew was fifty-two.

"Brianna Baker," Harwood boomed in a voice just a touch louder than it needed to be. "How are you? How long has it been? Too long, much too long."

It wasn't at all subtle, but a glance at the faces watching them revealed that it was working. The gazes of the people in the lobby moved between Brianna and Harwood, alight with curiosity about the man who somehow knew Brianna Baker personally.

"Tate." Brianna air-kissed Harwood on either cheek without actually touching him. "You are so right. It has been too long. When I learned you were back in New York and working at a production company, I just knew I had to reach out to you."

Harwood folded her arm around his and began to lead her toward the bank of elevators. "And I am so glad you did." He sent a glance over his shoulder, taking in Xavier, who had fallen into step behind them.

"Oh, I hope you don't mind. Xavier goes everywhere with me. Personal security. You know how it is." Bria tapped Harwood's arm lightly. "Such a pain, but I trust him implicitly."

"Of course," Harwood said, sparing Xavier one more look before focusing all his attention on Bria. "And this is my assistant, Mary Beth." Harwood gestured to the woman who was holding the elevator doors open and waving off anyone who tried to enter.

They stepped onto the elevator and the doors slid closed before the elevator car started its smooth climb upwards.

"I've had Mary Beth order in refreshments from Pâtisserie la Reine. I remembered how much you like dessert," Harwood said.

"Oh, that is so sweet of you. Of course, I have to watch what I eat so closely now, I'm not allowed to eat half of what I really want to." Bria laughed the tinkling laugh he recognized from her interviews.

"The price of fame." Harwood joined in laughing with her.

The elevator stopped at the twenty-third floor, and Harwood led them into a glass-walled conference room. He clearly wasn't going to let a drop of reflected importance go unnoticed.

Bria seemed to be taking it all in stride. She may have been used to living in a fishbowl, but Xavier wasn't. Even though Harwood had firmly closed the door after they'd entered the conference room, Xavier remained uncomfortable with the number of people strolling down the hall and gawking from the other side of the glass.

Harwood's assistant bought in coffee and the pastries. Bria accepted the coffee and demurred on the pastry.

No one offered him refreshments at all. He did as Bria asked and took up a position in a corner of the room, faced the glass wall and faded into the background.

After several minutes of small talk and catching up, Bria got down to why they were there.

"Tate, I'm sure you're wondering why I called you out of the blue today."

"Well, I am a little curious, yes."

"The truth is the project I'm working on involves *Murder in Cabin Nine* and Derek Longwell's untimely death."

Harwood flinched.

"I know it's a tragedy that those of us who knew Derek were all affected so deeply by. Especially those of us working on *Murder in Cabin Nine* with him. I mean, you know how the cast and crew on a film can become family. We were the people closest to him in his last days and moments."

"Yes, well, the industry lost a great up-and-coming talent in Derek," Harwood said unconvincingly.

Bria leaned forward across the table. "I've been thinking about starting a production company. You know how brutal this business is, especially to women, and a Black woman, well, I've got—what? Maybe five to seven more years left as a lead actress."

Harwood nodded. "Your talent and skill as a performer is timeless and boundless. But I can't argue with the fact that this business favors youth over talent."

"Exactly." Bria slapped a hand against the lacquered tabletop. "I want to plant my feet firmly in the industry soil. Producing my own content would do that."

Harwood cocked his head, a look of confusion coming over his face. "Are you thinking about reviving *Murder in Cabin Nine?*"

"Heavens no. The script was terrible. I'm thinking about telling Derek's story. The up-and-coming actor whose career and life were ended in a haze of mystery far too early. Audiences love what-could-have-been stories. I mean, we are still seeing massive audiences for biopics about Marilyn Monroe decades after her death."

"Derek was no Marilyn Monroe."

"No, of course, he never had a chance to achieve what she did, but ten years ago, he was probably the equivalent of Tom Holland or Harry Styles. He could have been, at least, and that's all that's needed to make a compelling story. What could have been?"

"Maybe." Harwood's eyes darted around the room. He smoothed his tie. "I'm not sure what I can do to help you," he said, his tone decidedly chillier than it had been moments earlier.

"As much potential as Derek had, I think you and I both know that he wasn't perfect, and if I want to do this biopic right, I have to tell a balanced story. The good and the bad."

"I… I still don't see where you're going…"

Bria sucked in a deep breath and then let it out slowly. "I never told anyone this at the time, but Derek attempted to force himself on me. I was able to fight off his attack."

Harwood's back straightened. "I didn't know anything about it. I hope you know that if I had I would have fired him immediately. Father producer or no father producer."

Bria waved a hand. "As I said, I never told anyone. Times were very different then. But that's why I'm sure that I wasn't the only woman Derek pulled that crap with. You worked with Derek several times on several different films. I figured you might know of other women who had similar experiences."

Harwood pulled at his tie again and didn't look Bria in the eye. "I did work with Derek on a number of films, but I wouldn't have tolerated such behavior if I'd known…"

"Of course, you would have." Bria cut him off sharply.

"Derek was your bread and butter. But I have no plans to use the biopic to focus on what you did or didn't do years ago. At least, not at the moment."

Xavier smirked internally at Bria's interrogation technique.

Harwood swallowed hard, his Adam's apple bobbing. "What do you want to know?"

"Was there anyone you can remember who might have known that Derek attacked me? Anyone he was close to on set?"

Harwood scoffed. "You were there. Derek wasn't close to anyone. He didn't have friends. Thought he was too good for everyone."

"He could be full of himself," Bria agreed.

"That's a kind way of putting it. He was a class-A jerk." Harwood sighed. "Look, I'll admit I'd heard rumors about Derek's heavy-handedness with women, but I knew nothing about him attacking you. And as far as friends who might have known, I can't help you. Hell, Derek's own stepfather didn't like him. Talked about him like he was something he'd scraped off his shoe. That's probably where Derek learned it from. Do you remember how he treated that one guy who worked on the film with us?"

Xavier's ears perked up.

Bria's brow furrowed. "What guy?"

"Oh, you must remember him. He had a small part, only a couple of lines. What was his name? Now, him I did have to talk to Derek about, get him to back off a little at least. Nice guy but very awkward, kind of quiet. The kind of guy bullies love because he's not going to fight back."

Everyone eventually fought back, that was one thing that Xavier learned. Some people just had a greater tolerance, but they also tended to be the people most likely to explode when they finally reached their limit.

"What was his name?" Harwood looked at the ceiling, thinking. After a moment, he snapped his fingers and grinned. "Morgan Ryder. I'm surprised you don't remember him, Brianna. Now that you've stirred up all these memories from the movie set, the one thing I remember about Morgan in addition to how badly Derek treated him is how big a crush Morgan had on you."

Bria shot a glance across the room at Xavier. "I don't remember him."

Harwood shrugged. "He was that kind of guy. Forgettable, I mean. It's funny though. I ran into him a few years back when I was still living in Los Angeles. He'd completely changed. Slick suit. Two-hundred-dollar haircut. Nice ride. A real poor-guy-makes-it-big transformation."

"I guess that's good for him," Bria said.

"Sure. It's great. Like I said, nice guy. Totally deserves it. I almost didn't recognize him and he seemed surprised when I did. He'd even changed his name or I guess stopped using his stage name. Morgan Ryder." Harwood guffawed. "He's still in the business, kind of. Owns his own PR firm. Eliot Sykes Public Relations."

Chapter Twenty-One

Xavier threw the door to Ryan's office open, pausing long enough to allow Bria to enter first before he strode inside with purpose. "Eliot Sykes is the stalker."

"We don't know that for sure." Ryan sat behind his desk, working on his computer.

Shawn was also in the office, tapping away on a laptop on the sofa.

"I'm sure," Xavier growled.

He'd called Ryan on the drive from Tate Harwood's office and briefed him on his and Bria's meeting with Harwood. Ryan had apparently briefed Shawn.

"I'm working on tracking down this Morgan Ryder. So far, no luck. I've got Tansy working on it also. She's better at scouring the bowels of the internet."

Tansy Carlson was the best computer tech and researcher that West Investigations had. If anyone could dig up proof that Eliot Sykes and Morgan Ryder were one and the same person, it was Tansy.

"I've tried calling Eliot," Bria said. "He's not picking up his cell phone."

"And his office says he hasn't been in contact for the last two days."

Shawn's head snapped up. "Two days. That means he's been off the grid since the paparazzo was dumped outside of Bria's house."

"Oh my..." Bria pressed her hand against her stomach as if keeping the contents from coming up. "I hadn't even thought about what it means if Eliot really is my stalker. He must have killed Bernie." She sat down hard in one of Ryan's visitors' chairs.

Ryan looked across his desk at her with sympathy in his eyes. "We will find him. And until then, we will keep you safe from him."

Xavier felt every one of Ryan's words right down to his bones.

Tansy burst into the office. "I've got it." She had a wide grin across her face and held a printout above her head triumphantly.

"You found Sykes?" Xavier advanced on her.

Tansy took a step back, confusion coloring her face. "What? No, sorry. I meant I found the proof that Sykes and Ryder are the same person." She held out the printout.

Xavier took it. It was a copy of a very old web page that appeared to have been focused on discussing Hollywood celebrities. The sheet of paper was full of comments about Morgan Ryder. A small, grainy, indecipherable thumbnail photo was in the top left corner, but when he flipped to the second page he found Tansy had managed to blow the picture up and print it out. It was still grainy, but it was without a doubt Eliot Sykes, aka Morgan Ryder.

"I bookmarked the site so we could get back to it whenever we needed to," Tansy said.

Xavier passed the sheets of paper to Ryan. "This has to be enough to take to the cops."

Ryan scanned the papers. "It proves Sykes is Ryder, but it doesn't prove that Sykes is the stalker. We need more before the police will do anything."

Xavier hissed out a breath. He knew Ryan was right.

"He lied to me," Bria said. "If nothing else, by omission. He must have known we'd worked together on *Murder in Cabin Nine* and he said nothing for nearly two years. That's something."

"Fire him. In fact, I strongly suggest you do, but it's not illegal to lie to your employer."

"I'd hold off on firing him." Shawn rose and joined them at Ryan's desk. "We don't know if he knows we suspect him. We may be able to use that."

"He's not answering Bria's calls," Xavier pointed out.

Shawn's mouth twisted into a grimace. "I said 'may be able to use that.' It looks like Bernie's murder has pushed Sykes past the point of playing the good guy PR rep. He may be fully engulfed in his own decisions about being with Bria and has completely jettisoned his outward life."

"Oh…" Bria pressed a hand over her mouth.

Ryan shot Shawn a hard look.

"Sorry," Shawn mouthed back.

"I think I need to freshen up." Bria rose.

"I'll show you where the ladies' room is." Shawn hurried to extend his arm to Bria and she took it with a small smile of thanks.

When they were gone, Xavier turned back to Ryan. "We have to do something now."

Ryan stood, came around his desk and faced Xavier. "We are doing something. We're protecting Bria. We're searching for Eliot. We're staying diligent. That's all we can do at the moment."

"It's not enough," Xavier growled.

"I didn't say it was. It's what we have." Ryan hesitated. "Remember when I said that you were too close to Bria to be responsible for her security?"

Xavier didn't respond. There was no way he was going to desert Bria now.

"I know you're not going to leave her protection to anyone else," Ryan said, reading his mind. "I'm just reminding you that if you let your emotions do the thinking, you aren't going to be as effective as Bria needs you to be."

"I can separate my emotions from my job."

Ryan scoffed. "Right. Like you've been doing? Everyone can see what you feel for Bria. And I can tell it's affecting you."

He wanted to deny it, but he couldn't. He wasn't thinking as clearly as he would be if he was protecting anyone other than Bria. All he could think about was what he'd do if she got hurt or worse. He'd survived fifteen years without her, in part because he believed they were both doing what they were supposed to be doing with their lives. If they couldn't do it together, well, at least they were happy-ish apart.

But the thought of a world without Bria in it… He was sure he couldn't make it through an hour in that world. So he'd give his life to make sure that was a world that never existed.

"I can't deny I have feelings for Bria. Always have, always will. But we had our chance and she chose her career over me. We can't change that and I doubt she wants to. She'll go back to Hollywood when this is all over and I'll still be here. So whatever is going on between us now, it can't last."

Ryan's gaze moved to the office door.

Xavier turned even though he already knew what he'd find.

Bria stood there, Shawn behind her. Her back was ramrod straight, hurt shining in her eyes. She'd clearly heard every word he'd just said.

Damn. He hadn't meant to hurt her, but he'd only said out loud what they both knew to be true. Hadn't he?

The moment of silence seemed to go on forever before Bria spoke. "There's been a change in the shooting schedule. They need me on the set."

Shawn cleared his throat, nodding at Xavier. "If you want to stay here and keep searching for Sykes, I can take her."

"No. I'll do it," Xavier said.

"Thank you." Bria's response was icy enough to skate on. She turned, sending Shawn scurrying to move out of her way.

"I'd have thought it was impossible to make this protection detail worse," Shawn said, keeping his voice low as Xavier passed by him, "but you always have been good at achieving the impossible."

Xavier growled before hurrying to catch up with Bria.

Chapter Twenty-Two

Whatever is going on between us now, it can't last.

Stupid. Stupid. Stupid. That's exactly what she was for entertaining the idea that somehow she and Xavier could find their way back to each other. For thinking that he'd even want to. He saw the night they'd spent in bed together as nothing more than fun rolls in the hay for old times' sake and she'd been envisioning white picket fences. It sounded like the kind of script she'd toss in the garbage bin after the first five pages.

At least now she knew how he felt. It was ironic when she thought about it. She'd pushed him away fifteen years ago to pursue her dreams, and now he was pushing her away. Karma really was something else.

Well, she hadn't been voted People's Choice Awards' best actress twice in a row for nothing. She pushed her shoulders back farther and kept her eyes trained on the streets of Manhattan. She might have been heartbroken on the inside, nearly falling apart with grief for the future she'd already begun spinning in her head, but she wasn't about to show it on the outside.

Xavier pulled into a space in the small parking lot next to the set.

"Bria, I'm sorry about what I said back at the office. I was just—"

She held up a hand, cutting him off. "No need to apologize. I totally understand." She opened the passenger door and stepped out.

Xavier got out and hurried to her side, a frown on his face. "You're supposed to wait until I come around the car."

"I'm sorry. I forgot. I'm running a little late though, so could we hurry?"

She moved past him toward her dressing room. She stopped at the door. The room was big as far as dressing rooms went, but way too small for her and Xavier and all the emotions she had swirling inside. If he came in with her, there was no way she wasn't going to erupt and she had too much pride to let him see her fall apart over him.

She turned to face him. "The scene we're shooting this afternoon is important. I need to concentrate and prepare. Would you mind waiting out here?"

A part of her felt like a heel for even asking. A diva too special to let the hired help inside her precious space. The other side of her screamed to get away from Xavier if only for a little while. The screams won out.

The frown on his face deepened. "Fine," he spat. "I'll need to check out the interior first though."

She stepped aside to let him pass into the dressing room. He was back in less than a minute. "It's clean."

"Thank you."

She showered and headed over to wardrobe and makeup with Xavier's words still echoing in her head. The fact that he trailed behind her the whole time made the words that much louder in her mind. But she pushed them aside when she was called to set and did her job. She'd always had the ability to get outside herself and into the role she was playing. It was one of the reasons she was so good at what she did. She was happy to see that her personal drama with Xavier hadn't changed that.

She managed to complete the scene in only three takes and headed back to wardrobe to change. Once again, Xavier waited outside her dressing room as she gathered her things. She took her time. It was hard enough riding in the same car with Xavier after hearing what he thought of their relationship. Or lack thereof. Spending another night under the same roof… She didn't think her heart could stand it.

He'd offered to take her to a safe house when she initially hired West Investigations and that seemed like the best option now, given the changed circumstances. Maybe Shawn or one of the other operatives could stay with her. She knew Xavier would resist the suggestion, but she was the client. If she insisted, Ryan West would have no choice but to go along with her desires.

Now she just had to tell Xavier.

She steeled herself and stepped out of the dressing room.

Xavier fell in step beside her after she locked the door and headed for the parking lot.

"I think it would be best if Ryan assigned someone else to my protection detail."

"No."

"You don't get to decide. I'm the client."

"You aren't just a client and you know it. I'm sorry about what I said. I didn't intend for you to hear it."

"That, I got," she scoffed.

"That's not what I meant," he growled.

They passed the security checkpoint and entered the parking lot. There were several more vehicles in the makeshift area now than there had been when they'd arrived.

"It doesn't matter. You can't control how you feel. I get that. But neither can I. Seeing you again, being with you again, it's brought up a lot of emotions I thought I'd dealt with a long time ago. But that's not your problem. If you don't feel the same way, then you don't."

Xavier laid a hand on her arm, gently stopping her from moving forward. "I didn't say I didn't feel something for you."

"But not enough." She turned her face away from him so he couldn't see the tears that were threatening to fall although her voice was thick with them.

"I—"

The rest of his words were caught in the sound of an explosion that rocked the light blue sedan parked several spaces away.

Not far enough away to keep the blast from lifting her and Xavier from their feet and flinging them backward, across the parking lot.

Bria landed on the asphalt, pain reverberating throughout her entire body. Darkness swelled behind her eyes and she knew she was only seconds away from losing consciousness.

She turned her head, looking for Xavier, her fear for him palpable despite the pain she was in.

What she saw sent terror shooting through her alongside the pain.

Eliot.

He was beside her, lifting her into his arms.

"You're mine. Everything is going to be okay now."

Those were the last words she heard before the darkness claimed her.

Chapter Twenty-Three

"I need to get out of here. Now," Xavier said, struggling into a sitting position in the hospital bed.

He reached for his IV line but the nurse grabbed his hand before he could rip it out of his arm. "Mr. Nichols, you can't leave yet. You were unconscious for several minutes. The doctor has ordered a CT scan."

"I don't care what the doctor ordered. I'm leaving." He'd awoken in the back of an ambulance on the way to the hospital. If he could have, he'd have forced them to turn around and take him back to the movie set. He didn't have time for a hospital visit. He needed to find Bria.

"Xavier, listen to the lady." A voice boomed from the door.

Ryan strode into the room, followed closely by Shawn. The brothers wore matching expressions of concern on their faces.

"Sykes has Bria. Do you have a line on where he's taken her?" Xavier shot the question at Ryan.

"Not yet. But the police have put out a BOLO on Eliot and his vehicle, and West has employed all of our resources. We will find them."

"The panic button," he said, desperation lacing each word.

Shawn shook his head. "She hasn't hit the button."

Xavier's heart leaped with fear. He had no doubt that West and the police were doing everything they could, but would it be enough?

The brothers shared a glance.

"What? What aren't you saying?" Xavier demanded.

"The cops also went to Sykes's apartment. The doorman said Sykes hasn't been there in a couple days and the building's management wouldn't let them into the place."

"Okay, so they need to get a warrant."

Ryan and Shawn glanced at each other again.

"Spit it out," Xavier growled through his teeth.

"There's only your word that Sykes took Bria and you were half-unconscious," Ryan said. "The police say they don't have enough to formally open an investigation into Sykes for kidnapping, and without it, they can't get a warrant to search his apartment."

He squelched the urge to bellow. Instead, he pointed to the IV and trained his gaze on the nurse. "Take it out now or I will pull it out."

The nurse studied him, ostensibly gauging just how serious he was. He reached for the line again.

"Okay, okay." She went to work taking the line out of his arm. "But if you are going to leave, you'll have to sign a paper saying you left against medical advice."

"I'll sign whatever you want, but you better bring it now. I've got work to do."

"Dude, you aren't going to be any help to anyone if you pass out," Shawn said. "Do what the doctors say and let us handle finding Sykes."

Xavier glared at the two men. "Would you, if it was Addy out there somewhere with a deranged man?" He looked at Ryan. "Or Nadia?"

His friends stayed silent.

"Exactly."

The nurse finished removing the IV. "Stay here. I'll be right back with the AMA form."

He was itching to get out of the hospital and start searching for Bria, but he nodded. Two minutes. That was all he was giving her before he took off. Long enough to put on his shoes, if he could find them.

He rose as the nurse left the room and headed for the closet. Luckily, he'd come to before they'd taken his clothes off him so he didn't have to worry about walking out of the hospital in a gown.

"What do we know so far?" He opened the closet door and found his shoes, watch, wallet and cell phone on the shelf inside in a large clear plastic bag.

He reached up, stifling a groan and fighting back dizziness.

Shawn gently nudged him out of the way and grabbed the bag. "The camera facing the parking lot caught the explosion, but we can't see you or Bria." Shawn carried the bag with his things back to the bed while Xavier followed at a slightly slower pace.

"Did anyone on set see anything? Which direction Sykes took off in, maybe? The make and model of the car? Anything?"

Ryan shook his head. "At the moment, it looks like you and Bria were the only ones in or around the parking area. The cops are questioning everyone on set at the time of the explosion."

Xavier sat much more slowly than he'd have liked and put on his shoes. "The cops aren't going to tell us anything even if they happen to get something from a witness."

"I know that." Ryan frowned. "Which is why I've also got people asking questions. We have to be discreet though, given we don't have any power or jurisdiction. But everyone on set knows that you were protecting Bria and so far people have been forthcoming."

"They just don't know anything," Xavier snapped, the frustration and fear bubbling in his chest.

"I sent Gideon to keep an eye on Sykes's place in case he shows up."

"Fine." Xavier finally finished lacing his boots and stood. "He can help me search Sykes's apartment when I get there."

"Let's just slow down a minute," Ryan said, stepping in front of Xavier.

"Let's not slow down," Xavier barked. "We don't know what that maniac is doing to her right now." He paused to swallow back the emotion that had swelled in his chest and throat. "I'm not waiting another minute before doing everything I can to find her. Now help me or get the hell out of my way."

Ryan blew out a deep breath before stepping aside. He and Shawn fell into step beside Xavier as they made their way down the hospital corridor, only stopping briefly at the nurses' station so that Xavier could sign himself out of the hospital against doctors' orders.

Shawn drove and they made good time getting from the hospital to Sykes's Chelsea apartment. Shawn illegally parked the SUV a block from the building and they walked back.

Gideon met them in front of the building's revolving glass doors. "The doorman agreed to let you go up to Sykes's apartment. You only have five minutes."

Shawn's eyebrows rose. "How did you manage that?"

A ghost of a smile crossed Gideon's lips. "The old-fashioned way. A bribe."

Gideon resumed his post outside the apartment, keeping an eye out in case Sykes showed up while the rest of them marched into the lobby and past the doorman who barely spared them a glance. They were silent on the elevator up to the eleventh floor.

Shawn picked the lock on the door and they were inside Sykes's apartment within a minute of stepping out of the elevator.

"Careful," Ryan warned. "If the cops ever do get a warrant, we don't want them to know we were here."

The apartment wasn't large and the decor was minimal. The four of them split up with Shawn taking the living/dining/kitchen combination, Ryan taking the second bedroom, and Xavier heading for the main suite.

A king-size bed with a leather headboard sat against one wall, facing a sleek, black wall-mounted television. The bedside tables were empty and the closet and single dresser in the room held nothing other than clothing.

Xavier crossed the room into the adjoining bathroom. Another door on the other side of the room opened into the hallway. He found cleaners and a sponge under the sink but nothing that would lead them to where Sykes might be holding Bria.

"Xavier, Shawn," Ryan called. "In here."

Xavier entered the room behind Shawn and pulled up short. Ryan had the closet doors open. The walls inside were covered in photos of Bria. Some of them were of her in Los Angeles, while others had been taken more recently in New York. There were even a few of him and Bria together.

The pictures made his blood boil, but he tried to focus

on what they might tell them about Sykes and where he could be.

"He's obsessed with her," Xavier whispered.

He stepped forward, examining the photos more closely. A knot formed in his stomach. Several had been taken through the windows of Bria's townhouse, likely with a long-range lens but still too close for his comfort.

"Nothing here tells us where Sykes has taken Bria." Xavier slammed his palm against the open closet door.

"Maybe there is. Look at this." Shawn held a notebook open, flipping through the pages. "I found it under the bed."

Ryan and Xavier each took a side and looked over Shawn's shoulder.

The notebook was full of Sykes's fantasies about the life he and Bria would live together.

"Here." Shawn turned the page and pointed. A photograph of a farmhouse had been taped onto one page above more ramblings about Sykes and Bria going somewhere where it would be just the two of them.

"Doesn't look like there's an address visible."

Xavier reached over Shawn's shoulder and pulled the photo out of the book, hoping to find an address or some writing on the back that would tell them where to find the house. There was nothing.

It took all his strength not to rip the photo into tiny pieces.

"If Sykes owns this place, it's not under his own name," Shawn said.

"Look under the name Morgan Ryder. He may have inherited it, so we should also look under his parents' names and any siblings' or any other family members'."

"I'll call into the office as soon as we're back in the car,"

Ryan said. "We should get out of here. We've already spent more than the five minutes Gideon paid for." He laid a hand on Xavier's shoulder. "We will find her."

Chapter Twenty-Four

Bria woke on an unfamiliar sofa, in an unfamiliar room. She had no idea how long she'd been unconscious, but she could see through the large window in front of the sofa that she was lying on that it was dark outside. The moon was bright though, so she could see that there was nothing beyond the window but a large lawn that ended where a copse of trees began.

Her head throbbed. She lifted her hands to her head and found that they'd been tied.

Xavier.

He'd been beside her when the car exploded. Where was he now? And was he okay?

He had to be. There was so much she hadn't said. So much time they'd wasted.

She pushed herself into a sitting position. Someone groaned. It took a moment before she realized that someone was her. Her entire body ached, almost enough to outweigh the fear coursing through her. Almost.

Eliot stepped into her sight line. "You're awake. Good." The smile she'd once found charming looked grotesque now. "I made us a romantic dinner to celebrate the first night of our new life together."

Fear clouded her already foggy brain. Eliot was her stalker. He was delusional. Dangerous.

She had to break through his delusions. Get him to let her go.

"Eliot, I think I need a doctor. I need you to take me to the hospital."

Eliot went to his knees in front of the sofa. "You bumped your head. I got you two aspirin. I'll take care of you." He reached out and pushed a lock of hair off her forehead.

She fought against the desire to shrink away from his touch. Swallowing her revulsion, she said, "I think I need a doctor. Please, Eliot."

He pushed to his feet as if he hadn't heard her at all. "After you've taken your pills, I'll help you to the dining room. Everything is ready."

There was no way she was going to swallow any pills he was offering her. Her head was pounding, but right now what she needed more than anything was for it to clear. "I don't think I need aspirin. My head is feeling better."

Eliot grinned. "That's great. Let's eat, then."

He reached for her arm and helped her get to her feet. She wobbled but found her footing quickly. Eliot didn't let go of her arm. They moved into the formal dining room. Eliot had set the table with two elaborate place settings complete with salad and bread plates and crystal. Her eyes glanced over the silverware. He'd set a fork by her place setting, but only his had a knife. Of course, it would be a lot easier to use them to defend herself if her hands weren't tied.

She hoped it wouldn't come to that. Eliot was clearly not in his right mind, but maybe she could talk him back into his senses. Make him see that this was not the way to win her love.

He pulled out a chair for her at the table and she sat.

The change in position drew her attention to something in her pocket.

Her panic button.

If she could get her hand into her pocket and hit the button without Eliot seeing, Xavier would know exactly where she was.

She held her still tied hands out in front of her. "I can't eat with my hands tied."

Eliot had already placed the food, in covered dishes, at the center of the table.

"Yes, you can." Eliot reached for the open bottle of red wine on the table between them and poured them each a glass. "I'll help you. It will be romantic. I can feed you."

Her stomach turned. So he wasn't going to untie her. Fine. She could still hit the button. Maybe without even reaching into her pockets. The fabric of her slacks wasn't that heavy.

She shifted her hands back into her lap in what she hoped was a pose that looked casual to Eliot. He didn't seem to be watching her closely at all, lost in what he imagined was some sort of romantic dinner. And where did he think this romantic dinner would lead?

The thought sent a shudder through her. She moved her hands toward her left pocket.

Eliot stood. He whipped the covers off the platters on the table with a flourish, revealing a roast and vegetables. He sliced the roast, then doled out food onto each of their plates before sitting down again.

"Now, isn't this lovely? I can't tell you how long I've waited for us to be together like this. No agents, no fans, no costars. Just the two of us, the way it should have been since

Murder in Cabin Nine." Eliot reached across the table and used his knife to cut her meat.

She recoiled, not wanting him near her with a knife in his hand. Or at all.

Eliot frowned.

She plastered a smile on her face and tried to look as if she'd moved just to give him more room to slice her food. It seemed to work. In more ways than one.

Eliot returned her smile, but she was more concerned with the fact that the shift in her body allowed her easier access to the panic button. She pressed the button through the material of her slacks, feeling the small fob pressing into her leg.

Please work. Please work.

"I know you had a part in *Murder in Cabin Nine.*"

"You were so nice to me. I've never forgotten that, although I know you didn't remember who I was."

"I'm sorry I didn't remember you. Is that why you've done all this? Because I didn't remember you?"

The look he gave her reflected genuine shock. "Of course not! I mean, I've loved you since we met on set, but I totally understood you had to focus on your career. I don't hold your ambition against you."

The way he spoke, as if they'd had some type of relationship that didn't solely exist in his mind, sent a shiver through her. But she wanted to keep him talking. It might be the only way to bring him back to reality.

"I think we should spend some time together, just the two of us, laying a strong foundation for our relationship going forward, but after a few years, I wouldn't have any problem with you going back to work. I mean, it would be a shame to let everything I've done to further your career go to waste."

Eliot giggled as if he was in on a secret that she wasn't.

A sinking feeling in her gut said he wasn't just talking about the public relations work he'd done for her. "Are you talking about your PR work?"

He giggled again. "That's just the little stuff." He leaned across the table, all wide grin and wild eyes. "I killed Derek Longwell."

Bria sucked in a sharp breath, but Eliot didn't seem to notice.

"I saw what he did to you. Well, I saw him on top of you in the woods and you hit him with a rock. Good girl." His smile was grotesque. "You ran away, but Derek was stunned. When he saw me approaching he barked at me to help him. I helped him all right. I picked up the rock you'd hit him with and hit him again. It only took one blow."

Bile rose in Bria's throat despite her empty stomach.

"And Bernie? Did you kill him too?" She knew the answer, but something compelled her to hear it directly from Eliot.

He nodded, spearing a bit of potato and meat with his fork and popping it into his mouth. "He was easy." Eliot spoke around the food in his mouth. "I'd been keeping tabs on your place. I saw that bodyguard of yours get into it with Bernie. Bernie had no right to follow you like that," Eliot said with a frown and no hint of irony. "Taking pictures of you everywhere you went. Invading your privacy."

"Why did you leave Bernie's body in front of my house?"

Eliot's head dipped and he looked at her out of the side of his eye, shyly. "I wanted you to know what I was willing to do for you. How much I loved you. I didn't tell you about Derek and that was a mistake. I wasn't going to make that mistake again."

He'd let his delusions get the best of him, but this was not the moment to tell him that.

"So everything...the emails, the flowers. You killed Bernie. You did it all?"

"For you," he said. "I followed you to New York to keep an eye on you while you were filming. I wanted to be close to you. I always want to be close to you."

How had she missed it? Eliot had lost all connection with reality.

"Eliot, you know I care for you and respect you as a friend."

He kept cutting as if he hadn't heard her.

"This isn't the way to get me to fall in love with you. You need to let me go."

"Why? So you can run into the arms of that bodyguard of yours? Do you really think I don't know that you're sleeping with him?"

She sucked in a deep breath. She hadn't thought twice about having Eliot over to her apartment in Los Angeles or the townhouse in New York. Had he planted some kind of listening or video devices? No, no, he couldn't have. And even if he had, she and Xavier had been together at his house not hers. Still, the thought of Eliot somehow watching them, even if he hadn't had a view inside their homes, was sickening.

A deep scowl twisted his lips. "I see I hit the nail on the head." He stuttered out a deep breath. "It's okay. I can forgive you one indiscretion. As long as it never happens again, of course."

"That's why you sent me that photograph and the threats against Xavier. You wanted to frighten him away from me."

He scoffed. "I should have known better. A meathead like

him. All brawn and no brains. I should have just killed him like I killed Bernie."

Eliot sawed her meat faster.

The words coming out of his mouth were terrifying but not nearly as much as the knife in his hand. "Eliot," she said in a voice she hoped was soothing. "We can work this out. Just untie me."

The knife slid off the plate, and Eliot's hand hit her wineglass sending it toppling over. Red wine spread across the white lace tablecloth.

Eliot surged to his feet, throwing the fork and knife down on the table. "Look what you made me do! I wanted our first dinner as a couple to be perfect." His eyes flashed with anger.

Terror swelled in Bria's chest. She cut her gaze up at him.

He reached down and yanked her to her feet, pulling her to his chest. "Now you'll have to pay for that."

Chapter Twenty-Five

Xavier's heart hadn't stopped beating as if it would pop out of his chest at any moment since he regained consciousness and realized Bria was gone. It had already been nearly four hours, and with each passing moment, he found it harder to breathe. Sykes could have taken her anywhere in four hours.

Focus.

He, Shaw and Ryan returned to West Investigations' headquarters while Gideon remained at Sykes's building, keeping lookout. Now they sat in the conference room, awash in the information that West's researchers had been able to find on Eliot Sykes, aka Morgan Ryder. In his early twenties, Sykes had embarked on a middling acting career that included only one credit for a deodorant commercial. They'd been able to turn up a couple of Morgan Ryder's headshots. The man in the photograph was definitely a younger Eliot Sykes. Tate Harwood had also been able to dig up a thin file on Sykes from his work on *Murder in Cabin Nine*, which had included Sykes's application for the production assistant's job. He'd listed his older brother, Joseph, as his emergency contact, and Ryan was working on finding contact information for him now, but he was apparently doing a stint with Doctors Without Borders so it was slow going.

The police weren't telling them anything officially, but Brandon was using his police contacts to funnel information to them unofficially. Unfortunately, the cops hadn't made any more progress on finding Bria than he had. Where was she?

Xavier pushed the file he was reading away and let his head fall into his hands.

"Hey, why don't you take a break?" Shawn dropped a hand on his shoulder and squeezed.

"I can't." Xavier reached for the background report on Sykes again. "There has to be something in here that gives us a clue to where he's taken Bria."

Excited voices mingled with hurried footsteps in the hall. Ryan and Tess burst into the room.

"Bria activated her panic button," Ryan said.

Xavier pushed to his feet and dashed around to the other side of the table where Tess had sat the laptop she'd carried into the room.

"She's too far away to get an exact location but we can tell the general area. She's, or at least the panic button's signal, is in Putnam County about an hour and ten minutes away," Tess said.

"I've already got Gideon on his way and we'll let the cops know when we're en route," Ryan said, falling in step beside Xavier as he headed from the room. "The signal should get more precise as we get closer to the button's location."

"Good," Xavier said, forgoing the elevators and pushing through the door to the stairwell.

Ryan grabbed his arm, forcing him to stop. "Are you sure you're up for this? I can't have you running on pure emotion. I need to know your head is on straight."

He understood where Ryan was coming from. He'd be no good to Bria and a potential danger to Ryan and whoever else was at his back if he couldn't rein in his emotions and think rationally.

He took a deep breath and let it out. "I can do this."

Ryan nodded, but Xavier read hesitancy in his eyes.

Xavier was able to cut the hour-and-ten-minute drive down to something closer to forty minutes. They kept Tess on the speaker, giving them updates on the panic button's location.

"Damn," Tess's anxious voice carried through the SUV's speakers.

"What is it, Tess?" Ryan said.

"The GPS in the panic button just went offline."

Xavier's heart thundered. "What does that mean?"

"We lost the signal."

Ryan swore.

Xavier was too terrified to react. If they couldn't follow the panic button's signal, they had no idea where to look for Bria.

"Have we found any connection between Sykes and a house, a business, a shed, anything out here in Putnam County?" Ryan barked.

"Nothing yet. We're still looking though," Tess responded.

Xavier wracked his brain. There had to be a way to locate Bria. He couldn't get this close and fail her. "I've got the photo of the farmhouse on my phone," he said, an idea blossoming in his head.

He navigated the SUV into a hard right turn, bouncing into the parking lot of a combination convenience store and gas station.

Ryan slanted a glance across the car at him. "What are you doing?"

"We need to know where that farmhouse is. That's the best lead we have to where Sykes might be holding Bria and since the panic button's GPS leads us to this area, it stands to reason it's located somewhere near here."

Xavier swung into a parking space and slammed the car into park. "When you're lost you ask for directions. We show the photo around and ask if anyone can direct us to it."

He hopped out of the car with Ryan on his heels.

The man behind the counter inside the convenience store looked up as they entered. "Hello, can I help you find something?"

"I'm hoping you can." Ryan took the lead. He pulled the photo of the house up on his phone. "We're trying to get to this house, but our GPS has died and we don't have the exact address. Do you recognize it?"

The man's eyes narrowed with suspicion. "I'm not sure."

Xavier reigned in his frustration. "Sir, a woman has been kidnapped. She's being held in this house." He tapped the phone's screen. "If you know where this house is, please help us find her."

The man studied them for a long moment. "Are you cops?"

Xavier and Ryan shared a glance.

"No," Ryan answered. "We're private investigators and friends of the woman who has been kidnapped."

"PIs." The man's expression morphed from suspicion to eagerness. "I always wondered what it was like to be a PI. Like that *Magnum PI*, you remember the old show?"

"Sir, please," Xavier pressed. "The house. Do you know where it is?"

The man sighed. "It looks like the old Dobrinsky place although no Dobrinsky has owned it for more than thirty years. People around here still call it that though."

"Do you know who owns it now?" Ryan pressed.

"Um...some doctor and his family bought it way back when."

Xavier shot a look at Ryan. Sykes's father and brother were doctors.

"No one has lived in the house for years now though. Not since the old doctor died. I guess his wife, if she's still alive, or his kids own it now."

"How do we get to the house from here?" Xavier asked, impatiently.

The man frowned but gave them the address for the house and sketched a map out on a napkin.

Ryan threw a hurried thank-you over his shoulder as they ran back to the car.

Xavier gunned the SUV in the direction the man had told them to go, while Ryan called Gideon and Tess to give them the house's location.

Since Xavier wasn't about to allow the fact that they had no legal authority to go after Sykes stop them, he, Ryan and Tess decided on the drive up that Tess would call the local police once they'd safely rescued Bria.

Xavier spied the semi-obscured driveway that the convenience store clerk said led to the farmhouse. He could see how they could have had trouble with the GPS tracker in Bria's panic button. The house was almost completely obscured by trees. There was no way they'd have seen the structure simply driving by. From the looks of it, the property encompassed several acres. Which also meant that there could be other buildings on the property where Sykes was holding Bria. Buildings it would take time to find and clear. Time Bria might not have.

Xavier stopped the car and cut the engine as soon as the

house came into view. He and Ryan stepped out of the SUV just as Gideon pulled to a stop behind them.

They met in the space between the two vehicles.

"Gideon, you go around the back," Ryan said, pulling his gun from its holster. "Xavier and I will enter through the front."

They crept toward the farmhouse. The exterior confirmed the convenience store clerk's statements about the home having been sitting vacant for an extended period. The lawn was overgrown and the siding needed to be replaced in several places. The stairs leading to the porch were crumbling and several shutters were missing from the front windows.

Gideon cut across the lawn and headed for the back of the house.

Xavier and Ryan waited several moments, giving Gideon the opportunity to get into place before they moved up the crumbling stairs to take position on either side of the front door.

"Ready?" Ryan whispered.

Xavier said a quick prayer that they'd find Bria inside and safe, then nodded.

"On three," Ryan said. "One, two, three!"

Chapter Twenty-Six

"You need to understand that you are mine!" Eliot's face twisted with rage. "I love you."

"You killed two people. You blew up a car and kidnapped me. That's not love."

Eliot's eyes darkened. He let out a scream that felt as if it shook the foundation of the house.

Bria's heart thundered in her chest. There was no reasoning with Eliot. He was lost in the delusion he'd created for himself.

Her hands were still bound, but she lunged for the table and grabbed the knife. In one quick motion, she turned back to Eliot and slashed it across his face.

Blood spilled from the wound and Eliot howled, hitting her across the cheek and sending her tumbling into the back of her chair. The knife fell from her hand and slid under the table, out of reach. Luckily, she managed to stay on her feet.

"You bitch!" Eliot pressed the palm of his hand to the wound on his face and glared at her. "I'll kill you."

He took a step toward her, but she lowered her head and drove her body into his chest, sending him reeling backward.

Bria kept moving forward, past him and out of the dining room.

The layout of the house was a mystery to her, but she'd seen a set of stairs from the living room sofa when she'd regained consciousness and she headed that way now.

The hallway was pitch-black, which was a double-edged sword. On the one hand, it made it harder for Eliot to see, but it also made it harder for her to see. Presumably Eliot knew the layout of the house so the advantage went to him. The hallway was long and curved. She tried the doors lining it, finding the first two locked.

She ran for the third door, as the sound of Eliot's footsteps trailed down the corridor. The door opened without a sound and she darted into the room, turning the flimsy lock, despite knowing it wouldn't stop Eliot if he really wanted in.

"Bria. Oh, Briiiiiiaaaaa." Eliot called out her name in a singsong voice. She could hear what sounded like the handle on one of the other bedroom doors being jiggled and then footsteps moving again.

She worked her wrists in hopes of loosening the ropes enough to slip them free, as her eyes darted over the room searching for something to use as a weapon. There was nothing in the room except a bed, stripped down to the bare mattress, and a dresser. She considered for a moment, searching in the dresser drawers, but rejected the idea as the footsteps in the hall drew louder and closer. It didn't seem like Eliot was forcing the locked bedroom doors open. Not yet, at least. And as long as he wasn't, she had time to come up with a plan.

"Come out, come out, wherever you are," Eliot sang. "Really, Bria, I'm tired of this game. Why don't you come on out here and we can talk about this like adults. I can be reasonable."

The handle on the door to the room she was hiding in

moved up and down. There was nothing but a thin piece of wood separating her from Eliot and she was terrified he could hear her thundering heart.

After what seemed like an eternity, she heard his footsteps continue down the hall, away from the door. She let out the breath she'd been holding. She couldn't hide in this room forever. Eventually, Eliot would start forcing the locks and there wasn't even a closet in the room that she could hide inside of.

She was finally able to loosen the knot on the rope Eliot had tied her hands with enough to slip one of her hands, and then the other, free. Ugly red marks marred her skin, but at least now she'd be able to fight back.

She had to move. Back toward the living room and presumably a door. She didn't know where they were exactly, but Eliot had to have driven her here, so there must be a road somewhere nearby. She just had to get to it and hitch a ride with a passerby to a nearby town or police station. And all while avoiding Eliot. It wouldn't be easy but the alternative...

She shuddered.

More footsteps and the squeak of the floorboards sounded faintly from down the hall. And then another sound, rusted door hinges being forced open. Apparently, Eliot had found an unlocked room. There wasn't likely to be a better time.

Bria eased the door open and peeked into the hall. It was empty but a door at the far end stood open. It was now or never.

She slipped from the bedroom and ran as quickly and quietly as she could back toward the front of the house. But not quietly enough. She threw a glance over her shoulder just in time to see Eliot step into the hallway.

Their eyes met as she turned the corner and raced out of the hall.

Eliot bounded after her.

Bria fled down the stairs and past the dining room and through the living room, past the sofa that she'd woken up on. Just beyond the living room was another hallway that split in two different directions. She had no idea which way led to the door and no time to figure it out.

She lurched to the right.

"Bria!" Eliot thundered behind her.

Her lungs burned, but hope swelled in her chest when the large front door came into view. She grabbed the handle and pulled, but it didn't budge. She flicked the lock and still nothing happened.

Eliot must have done something to keep it from opening.

She turned, looking for another exit.

Eliot stood at the fork in the hallway.

His gaze sent ice through her veins. There was no doubt in her mind he was going to kill her.

Unfortunately, there was only one direction to go in, and it required heading back toward the stairs. Well, she wasn't going to go without a fight.

Bria gave a primal scream and raced at him. A look of surprise colored Eliot's face as she threw herself into him and they both hit the floor hard.

She'd trained six days a week, weights, cardio and some martial arts, while she was filming the Princess Kaleva movies. She reached for that training now, throwing punch after punch to Eliot's face and neck. She heard a crunch as one of her blows made contact. A satisfying gush of blood flowed from his nose.

She scrambled to her feet.

But Eliot recovered fast. He pushed to his feet, driving his shoulder into her stomach as he rose.

The attack stole the breath from her lungs, sending her wobbling on her feet.

Eliot's arm whipped out and around in a circular motion, connecting with Bria's jaw. Tears swam in her eyes and she fell to her knees.

Don't lose consciousness. She fought against the desire to go to sleep. Every instinct in her body said that if she did, she'd likely never wake up. She shook the drowsiness off in time to see Eliot's foot kick out.

Surprising herself she caught his leg before it made contact with her ribs.

Shock flashed across his face when she yanked with all the strength she had. Shock turned to surprise as he realized he was losing his balance.

She scrambled to her feet as he hit the floor on his back and ran for the dining room. There had to be a kitchen in the house. Hopefully, it led to a back door, and if not, she'd at least be able to grab a weapon to defend herself.

She made it to the living room before Eliot tackled her from behind. She landed on the hardwood floors hard enough to rattle her teeth.

He flung her onto her back.

She reached for the wound on his face, scratching at it, his eyes, wherever she could reach. He yelled in pain, then grabbed her by the hair, slamming her head into the floor.

Bria's ears rang and her vision swam. She tried to focus, to make her body move, but the signals weren't getting from her terrified brain to her limbs. She couldn't just lie there. She had to keep trying. She needed to stay alive until Xavier found her.

It took every bit of strength she had, but she managed to flip onto her stomach and begin crawling away from Eliot. The room spun, but she could make out the long hallway she'd been headed for when he'd tackled her.

"I thought you were the one." Eliot's voice came from behind her. She glanced over her shoulder and saw that he was standing in the middle of the room, watching her, tears falling from his eyes. The sight was equal parts pitiful and petrifying.

She moved faster and the front door of the house came into view.

Eliot's footfalls sounded behind her.

He yanked her to her feet just as the door crashed open.

Xavier stood in the doorway, his gun held outstretched.

Eliot's arm came around Bria's throat, cutting off most of her air supply.

"Let her go," Xavier demanded.

"No! She's mine. We belong together." Eliot took several steps back, dragging her along with him.

Xavier stepped farther into the house, followed by Ryan West. Both men had their guns pointed at her and Eliot. But she knew they wouldn't shoot. She was in the way.

She heard a door burst open somewhere behind her.

"You've got nowhere to go, Eliot. We've got you surrounded. Let her go and we can talk about all of this. If you hurt her, you're a dead man."

Eliot's arm tightened around her neck and he dragged her back several more steps.

Xavier and his men hadn't heard Eliot earlier. They didn't know that there was no chance that he'd give up. He'd see them both killed first.

Bria could feel herself getting light-headed. She didn't

have long before she passed out, and who knew what Eliot would do then. She needed to do something to get herself out of the line of fire.

She lowered her head and bit down on Eliot's forearm.

He yowled and loosened his grip enough that she could slip under it. She launched herself away from Eliot.

Xavier and Ryan thundered forward, barking at Eliot to get onto his knees, while Gideon rounded on Eliot from the kitchen. It must have been him she'd heard bursting into the house from the back door.

Eliot reached behind him and a shard of light glinted off the knife as he whipped it forward toward Xavier.

The gunshot thundered through the room.

Eliot froze, the knife still outstretched. He looked down at his stomach where blood had already begun blooming over his shirt. He stumbled, then collapsed.

Ryan rushed forward, grabbing Eliot's hands and placing them in cuffs while the third man kept his gun trained on Eliot.

Xavier hurried to Bria's side and pulled her into his arms. "Baby, are you okay?"

She looked into his eyes and told the truth. "No." Her hands trembled, adrenaline still surging through her body. "Is he dead?" She tried to peer over Xavier's shoulder to get a look at Eliot, but he shifted, making it impossible for her to see past him.

She could hear Ryan on the phone with 9-1-1, asking for an ambulance immediately. Eliot must still be alive. She wasn't sure if she was relieved or not.

She wrapped her arms around Xavier, pulling him close and burying her face in his chest.

"It's over. You're safe now."

And for the first time in months, she actually felt like that might be the truth.

Chapter Twenty-Seven

Bria watched through the tinted windows as Xavier made his way over to the SUV from the front of the police cruiser where he'd been speaking to the Putnam County police detectives. They had not been happy to discover that Xavier and his men had taken it upon themselves to rescue her instead of alerting their department. The detectives still weren't happy, but her statement describing her kidnapping and Eliot's loud and unhinged ravings that she was his, had done a lot to neutralize the tempers of the local cops. It had also helped that West Investigations had implied that they'd let the Putnam County chief of police take credit for having saved Hollywood's darling from the stalker who'd kidnapped her.

Xavier opened the back door of the SUV and slid in beside Bria. She had the heat cranked up and a blanket wrapped around her shoulders, but she didn't begin to feel warm until he wrapped his arms around her.

They held each other for several minutes before pulling away.

"Is everything okay? Are you and your guys in trouble?" she asked.

Xavier shook his head. "I don't think so. At least, nothing major anyway. The chief is too busy dreaming about all the press he's going to get."

She let out a deep breath. "That's good, I guess."

"I don't like that he's trading on you being kidnapped to advance his career."

"I'm used to it. It's not just Hollywood that's cutthroat. If that's all it takes to keep you, Shawn and Gideon out of jail, I'm happy to let the cops have their fifteen minutes at my expense."

"Are you really okay?" Concern shone in Xavier's eyes.

He ran a finger over the bruise that was forming on her cheek. She had several other bumps and bruises from her fight with Eliot. They would take a few weeks to heal completely, but no permanent damage had been done, which was what she told the EMTs who had tried to take her to get checked out at the local hospital.

She didn't want to leave Xavier, and the police hadn't been through questioning him so she'd declined the offer.

She leaned her forehead against his. "I was terrified in that house with Eliot. But one thing I knew for sure was that you were looking for me and that you would move heaven and earth to find me. And you did."

"I will always be there for you when you need me. Always." He kissed her softly.

She was still struggling to process that Eliot, a man she'd considered a friend and trusted confidant, was her stalker. Xavier was right. She hadn't known Eliot at all. His delusions had run deep. The police had already discovered that Eliot had followed her to New York a few days after she'd crossed the country to start filming *Loss of Days*. He'd been the one delivering the flowers, and feeling threatened by

Xavier's presence and the obvious feelings she had for him, he'd escalated his stalking.

"There's something I need to tell you." She'd promised herself that when she got out of that house and away from Eliot, she'd tell Xavier how she felt about him and she wasn't going to waste another moment before keeping that promise to herself.

"I let you go fifteen years ago without telling you how much you mean to me. I loved you then and I love you now. And I'm hoping it is not too late for us. I don't know exactly how we'd make it work, but I know I want to make it work with you and I'll do whatever it takes. Move to New York and commute back and forth to Los Angeles when I have to. Or I'll focus my career on projects that film on the East Coast. Whatever it takes. I just know that as hard as I've worked to become Brianna Baker, movie star, that's how hard I'm willing to work to build a relationship with you that lasts," she said pointedly, remembering what he'd told Ryan about their relationship not being meant to last.

"Bria, about what you overheard me say—"

She held up a hand. "I don't want to look back. Let's start from here. Committed to making us work. What do you say?"

She waited anxiously for what felt like hours until a wide grin began spreading across Xavier's face.

"I love you too."

She grinned. "You do?"

"I do." He grinned back. "And you don't have to change a thing."

Her heart beat fast. She was having trouble processing what he was saying beyond the joy she felt at hearing he loved her as much as she loved him. "Why? What do you mean I don't have to change a thing?"

"Ryan and Shawn have been planning to open a West Coast office for a while now and they offered me the job of heading it up some time ago."

"You mean you'd be willing to move to Los Angeles?" She could barely believe what she was hearing. She hadn't even considered that he'd move to be with her.

His smile grew wider. "I'd be more than willing. I don't care where I live as long as you're there too."

Love swelled in Bria's chest. She threw her arms around Xavier and kissed him with all the passion and yearning that had laid dormant in her heart for him over the last fifteen years and all the hope she had for the years to come.

Chapter Twenty-Eight

"I could get used to this life." Xavier stretched his arms over his head and burrowed further into the oversize deck chair next to her.

The Pacific Ocean stretched out in front of them as far as the eye could see. The breeze off the ocean cooled the sun's warm rays. She understood where Xavier was coming from, but a few days was all they could manage, budget wise and time wise.

Bria laughed. "I suggest you don't. Renting a yacht is okay for a couple days for our honeymoon, but we both have to go back to work eventually."

He reached across the short space separating their chairs and took her hand, turning it over and kissing her palm. Love tugged at his heart every time he saw his ring on her finger. It had been such a long road for them getting here. But here they were. Together, forever.

"I guess I'll just have to be content with a long weekend with my wife and the wide open sea."

"It's not so bad." She smiled at him and his heart fluttered.

"It's not bad at all."

And it wasn't, especially after everything they'd gone through in the last eight months. Eliot had insisted on going to trial on the stalking and murder charges. The case was a slam dunk for the prosecution. The cops had found the knife that had killed Bernie Steele in Eliot's apartment and they'd been able to find traces of Bernie's blood under the handle, even though the knife had been cleaned. He and Bria had been called to the stand as witnesses. Testifying had been especially difficult on Bria, who'd had to relive her kidnapping and being held captive by a man she'd thought of as her friend. They'd both been relieved when the jury had come back with guilty verdicts for Bria's kidnapping, Bernie's murder and a host of other charges. It wasn't clear that he'd ever be charged for Derek Longwell's murder, unfortunately. Eliot had insisted that Bria was lying about his having confessed to that murder, and given the years long lag and the shoddy police work that had been done back then, it was unlikely the prosecutors could get a conviction. Still, Eliot would be in jail for a very long time for the crimes he'd been convicted of, which was exactly where he belonged.

Xavier had wasted no time in asking Bria to marry him after the trial was officially over. He'd taken her out for a romantic dinner the very next day and proposed. And she'd accepted.

He'd have married her that night, but Bria had wanted a wedding, nothing big and definitely something private, but she'd wanted all their friends and family to know how much they loved each other. Their schedules had kept them too busy to plan a wedding. He'd moved across the country to California and had opened West Investigations' West Coast office. He was happy to say the new office was taking off, but it had been a lot of work in a short time.

And Bria had been traveling a lot promoting *Loss of Days*. The audiences and critics loved the movie and her performance in particular. She'd already been nominated for several awards and there were even whispers that she'd be nominated for an Oscar next year. They'd been ships passing in the night to some extent, but they'd made the most of the time they'd been able to spend together over the last several months.

Then, two days earlier, she'd surprised him by renting the yacht and proposing they have the boat's captain, who was also a justice of the peace, marry them at sea.

They'd exchanged vows the night before, under a setting sun, the first mate and the yacht chef acting as their witnesses.

It was perfect. Just like his wife.

"What are you thinking right now?" Bria asked.

He leaned over and kissed his bride. "How much I love you and how lucky we are to have found our way back to each other."

"I couldn't agree with you more."

* * * * *

COLTON THREAT
UNLEASHED

TARA TAYLOR QUINN

To the Colton readers, who are the most important and cherished members of the family.

Chapter One

He'd had sex with her. What in the hell had he been thinking?

Clearly, he hadn't been thinking. Sitting in his office, Sebastian watched her through his window. Weeks had passed and still he watched with too much interest as the beautiful veterinarian left the kennel where she'd been seeing to a pregnant dog after her regular office hours at her clinic in town and headed toward his house. That messy bun—did she always have to wear it looking so bedroom-like?

The long blond hair had been down by the time she'd left his bed. Had she loosened it? Had he? Things had been so intense that night, with Oscar being injured by shrapnel from gunfire. Him calling Ruby in the middle of the night, afraid the heavily bleeding canine was going to die on him.

As if sensing his current unrest, the golden retriever mix—and Sebastian Cross's personal canine companion—grabbed a stuffed octopus and brought it over to shove it in Sebastian's hand. He and Oscar had started Crosswinds together, training search-and-rescue dogs, like Oscar, for people all over the country.

Oscar didn't seem at all fazed by that night two months before. But Sebastian, thinking he'd lost his only family member—pacing in his home while Dr. Ruby Colton worked on Oscar—had been thrown back a few years. He'd thought he'd left the panic behind. And the vet—she'd finished with Oscar that night and had come upon Sebastian in a particularly low moment.

One no other human had witnessed before.

How it had gone from there to…sex…

Wiping a hand down his face, he turned from the window in his office—chosen because of the view of his property—and headed toward the back door off the kitchen. The door Ruby used every time she came to check on Oscar.

He grabbed another quick glance out the kitchen window. When it was light outside, the vastness of his land, the lake at the edge of it, soothed him.

Anytime of the day or night, sight of the kennels did the same.

Neither was enough that evening as he heard the knock on his door.

In the two months since "the night," as he'd come to think of it, neither he nor Ruby had mentioned what had happened. They'd both pretended nothing had. They had to, right? Owl Creek was a small town. And she not only tended to the search-and-rescue animals that he trained, but she also gave free medical treatment to the PTSD dogs he provided to veterans who needed them.

Still…if nothing else, he had to apologize.

To her. To someone.

She was his best friend's little sister, for God's sake.

Wade Colton was the closest thing he'd ever had to a brother. And he'd gone and…

The knock came a second time.

He hadn't been himself that night. A reminder to never,

for any reason, allow himself to be around another human being when he was sinking.

Oscar stood at the door, staring at him. With a nod, Sebastian opened it.

And, while the dog gave his doctor an enthusiastic greeting, Sebastian took the few seconds that Oscar gave him to find an easy smile and paste it on.

SHAMELESSLY USING OSCAR as a distraction, Ruby spoke with real joy to the boy wagging his tail and licking her chin, avoiding the big mountain man with his shaggy dark blond hair and beard. She related to animals so much better than she did to people. Understood them. Fully accepted and embraced their unconditional love as her top need in life.

Steadying the dog with her tone of voice as she told him, "Good boy, stay," she checked his left hindquarter and left shoulder—both areas from which she'd had to remove shrapnel that fateful night two months before. Thankfully, neither had suffered muscle damage.

"He's healed nicely," she said to Sebastian, still running her fingers lightly over the dog's fur. "You're such a good boy," she told Oscar. "No bad guy's going to slow you down, huh?"

She stood then. The next thing on her agenda not quite as easy as telling the man his dog was well. It had to happen eventually. The longer she put it off, the less chance she'd seem at all natural as she met the blue eyes of the man she'd known most of her life as her older brother's friend.

A boy they'd seen only during the summers he'd spent at his family's cabin in Owl Creek—the home in which he now lived.

She remembered quite clearly how he'd left one year in August as a boy and had returned the following June as a man. He'd grown what had seemed like a foot, had a mustache and shoulders that blocked out the sunlight when he'd stood in front of her, teasing her about her crooked pigtails. She'd developed a bit of a crush on him.

Something that had faded as she, too, had changed, grown, become a woman.

So why had she, how could she have...?

Her gaze met his. Neither said a word.

They had to talk about it, didn't they?

At some point?

If for no other reason than to verify that they weren't telling another soul, ever, what had happened. Most particularly not Wade.

Big-brother hassles, she did not need.

Sebastian's smile wobbled a little. She opened her mouth...

And jumped, clutching Sebastian as a painfully loud crack sounded, followed immediately by a crash, and then a squeal and deep growl from Oscar. The canine was on point, staring at the door.

"Was that a gunshot?" The words burst out of Ruby, followed by a frantic "I'm calling 911."

Sebastian was already at the door.

"Wait, Sebastian! Are you kidding? Don't go alone. Wait for the—"

He was out the door before she'd finished her sentence.

WITH RUBY AND Oscar in the house, and all the dogs on the premises at risk, no way Sebastian could wait the ten minutes it would take the police to get from town to his five acres on the lake. He had a woman—and dogs—to protect. Grabbing his gun from the metal cabinet on his way out, he kept his back to the cabin as he rounded the corner.

The unsolved shooting in the middle of the night two months before still weighed heavily on his mind. He was in full United States Marine Corps mode as he moved with supreme precision, darting his head out for only a second, focusing in that second and pulling back as the second came to a close.

With the sun starting to set, his vision was somewhat compromised, but he got the job done.

As soon as he knew all four sides of the house were secure, he darted behind the small medical building to get closer to the kennel. His biggest concerns were the outside stalls and large, fenced-in, play-and-training area. His four employees—a full-time trainer and three part-time assistants who cared for and cleaned up after the dogs—were gone for the day. But a dozen dogs were there. One pregnant and another with a litter of new puppies.

At the back corner of the medical building, he repeated his earlier process, shot his head out, pulled it back.

And, adrenaline pumping with a dose of anger, he flattened himself against the wall. Someone had completely shot out Ruby's windshield. A red glare blinked on and off in the glistening mess and Sebastian turned to see flashing lights coming up Cross Road—the private drive leading to his cabin. He wasn't fool enough to go after a shooter on his own with the professionals arriving. He just kept watch over the kennels until several officers spread out around the entire training facility, and then, with his same military precision, made it back into the house with his bad news.

"YOU HAD NO business going out there alone!" Ruby's tone was sharp, instigated by the fear raging through her, as Sebastian came back inside the house.

Sitting on the floor with an arm around Oscar, who was half in her lap, she flushed as she saw the displeased expression on the man's face. "I'm sorry. I have no business speaking to you like that," she amended, embarrassed.

And scared.

And so thankful that he was standing, unharmed, in front of her.

His shrug made her want to hug him. "You're probably right," he said. "Military training doesn't preclude sitting around and waiting for others to save you." He was still frowning, though.

"What?" she asked, standing, fear returning in full force.

"Your windshield's been shot out."

Hers? But…

Brow creased in a hard line, she stared at him. The shots two months before—she hadn't been anywhere near the place. She'd assumed whoever had been responsible then was attacking again…

"*My* windshield?" she asked.

Even if the shooter wasn't one of Owl Creek's citizens, who all pretty much knew her SUV, both front doors had been painted with the emblem and name of her veterinary clinic.

Did someone have a problem with Colton Veterinary Clinic?

Or with her personally?

Mind spinning, she couldn't come up with any viable explanation.

It's not like she had any exes. There was no one whose heart she'd broken who could want revenge. No new girl-friend who could be jealous.

And at the clinic?

She drew a total blank.

Shivered.

Sebastian, hands in his pockets, was squirming a bit on his feet, as though he was having a hard time keeping his distance.

At least, that's the way her mind was currently translating his actions.

Because she was afraid, she knew. Felt uncharacteristically vulnerable.

"I'll need to have it towed," she said then, unnerved by her unusual reaction to the burly man as well. They'd had sex. She didn't want, or need, any complications from the one-night mistake.

Of that, she was certain.

She was a doctor. Had built a hugely successful practice and was only thirty.

No room in her life for the prepubescent girl who'd once had a crush on the kid Sebastian had been back then—in spite of the fact that as a grown woman, she noticed that the inches and muscles and facial hair he'd sprouted were attention getting.

No room, ever, for any full-time romantic relationship. It just wasn't what she wanted.

"As soon as we get the all-clear from the police, I'll help you clean out any personal stuff and drive you back to town." The man had found his voice.

She nodded. Smiled at him. "Thank you."

And felt a niggle in her lower belly when he smiled back.

AS IT TURNED OUT, Sebastian didn't get a chance to assist Ruby with her vehicle clean-out, or to drive her back to town. As soon as word got out that Ruby Colton had called the police after being present at Crosswinds Training when there'd been gunfire—and, of course, it had gotten out, since she was daughter to the man who owned half the town—her brothers had shown up in full protective mode.

Chase and Wade were at Sebastian's door within half an hour of the police showing up. Fletcher, the middle of her three older brothers, a detective with the Salt Lake City police force, seven hours away, was on the phone, demanding answers.

Chase, the oldest at thirty-six and vice president of Colton Properties, went straight to Ruby. Within seconds, while Wade still had Fletcher on the phone, Chase had her on his cell with their mom and dad, assuring Jenny and Robert that she was absolutely fine. She'd heard a shot was all.

She'd been safe inside the house, checking over Oscar, the entire time.

Sebastian heard it all peripherally. Wade, the youngest brother, fellow marine and as a kid, best friend to Sebastian, made a very determined beeline for Sebastian, demanding to know every detail of what had happened. And when the police came in, saying there was no sign of a shooter anywhere on Crosswinds' five acres, all three men had been ready with questions.

It turned out there was a fresh set of what appeared to be male shoe prints, size ten to eleven, out by the main road. It was likely the shooter used a scope, and never actually set foot on Sebastian's land.

Which set off more conversations between those in the

room and those still on the phone. Did that mean Ruby had been targeted?

Or was this more seemingly random violence aimed at Crosswinds? And hitting Ruby's car would be more impact-ful than the previous shot into brick that had sent shrapnel into Oscar, who'd woken up Sebastian in the middle of the night to go out.

Oscar had heard someone outside that night. Sebastian couldn't prove it but was certain of the fact. And he told Wade so when his friend asked again about the previous shooting event.

The February ground had been clear at that time, but with the wind chill, they'd been looking at below-zero tempera-tures and everything had been too hard for footprints. By morning, the land had been covered with a couple inches of snow. Investigators had never found a shell casing.

And they hadn't yet in this instance, but they intended to keep looking.

While Sebastian was still answering Wade's questions, in between Wade talking to Fletcher, Chase was escorting Ruby out of the cabin. Wanting her off the property as soon as possible.

Sebastian watched her go, saw her look back at him, or at least at Wade and him, with something like regret in her eyes. He felt it, too. Had wanted to be the one to help her. Since the damage had happened on his land.

But when he glanced over and saw the way his friend, who was ending the call with Fletcher, was watching his older brother and younger sister leave, the look of resignation on his face, Sebastian made a sharp return to reason.

Ruby hadn't been looking at him. She'd been watching over her big brother. The sorrow had been for Wade—not due to some ridiculous desire to have Sebastian be the one to take her home.

He welcomed the return to reality.

"How you doing?" Sebastian asked Wade then, a question that, a few years before, would have been completely in line with their friendship.

In the past few years, after Sebastian had left the Marines—they'd joined together, but Wade had stayed in—they'd naturally grown apart.

"Not you, too," Wade said with disgust, turning so that Sebastian's view was of the left side of Wade's face only.

The move, more than the words, spoke to Sebastian. He'd received his share of pity since he'd been back in Owl Creek. Had hated it every bit as much as Wade must. "You think you're less than you were?" he asked quietly. Wade hadn't been back long, but the man hadn't come to see Sebastian yet, or accepted any invitations to meet for a beer.

Anger filled Wade's one good blue eye with such intensity that Sebastian took a step back. And heaved an inner sigh of relief.

"Hell no. I can still take your ass. You want to give me a try?" Wade half growled, and Sebastian fully understood the note of real frustration in Wade's half-teasing invitation. Growing up, the two of them had taken on each other more than once. Wrestled. Tried to prove who was stronger.

No one had ever been seriously hurt, but they'd each landed bruises a time or two.

"Lead with both fists, man, just like always," Sebastian said then. "You know what you know. That there's nothing less about the man you are or the power you wield with one seeing eye instead of two. It's up to you to show the rest of the world."

Wade grunted. Clearly not looking for any warm feelings at the moment.

Sebastian got that, too. A hundred percent.

"People only know what you show them," he said, anyway. Because he'd learned the lesson himself after his stint in the Marines had ended so abruptly.

And because Wade Colton had picked him up, out of his insecurities, and set him straight every single summer his parents had deserted him at the cabin. Leaving Sebastian with a nanny to watch over him rather than a family to have fun with.

"You told me once that my value was whatever I thought myself worth," Sebastian murmured, remembering.

The words had been with him ever since.

Chapter Two

Ruby was not happy about her vehicle being shot at. She'd been shaken up by being present during the potentially danger-filled episode.

She wasn't buying in to any theories that the violence had anything to do with her in particular. Simply a matter of wrong place, wrong time.

There'd be vandalism at her clinic, or her home, if she was the target. Threatening notes or texts. Some kind of altercation.

She'd lived in Owl Creek her entire life. Had never been in a long-term relationship. Wasn't involved in anything controversial, anywhere. Nor had she ever lost an otherwise healthy patient on her operating table. She'd had to deliver some sad diagnoses. None of them brought any anger toward her to mind.

Even online, her clinic had only good ratings. Not a single one-star anywhere.

She'd spent the evening going over the facts, multiple times, with her brothers and sisters and parents. She answered texts from her uncle Buck, whose ranch Wade had recently started working and living on, and from her cousins, too.

And had eventually given in to the pressure and agreed to spend the night at her folks' well-secured home.

"You're a Colton," her mother, Jenny, told Ruby as she peeked into the room Ruby had picked for the night, one of the four upstairs guest bedrooms in her parents' newest home. The bed faced a wall of windows overlooking the lake. "Being a Colton makes you prey to anyone who could want to hurt any of us. Your father's built an empire. You don't do that without making enemies. Even if it's just someone who is jealous."

Her mother was right, of course.

But that didn't change the fact that, with the shooting of Ruby's windshield, Crosswinds was the logical target. Which meant that Sebastian and his dogs, out there all alone, could be in danger.

She told herself, as she was lying in bed worrying about him, that having been there, hearing the gunshot, was what was keeping her awake.

That and the fact that his programs—both search-and-rescue, and the pets he trained to help veterans with PTSD— were vastly important to her, too.

Plus…he'd been a peripheral part of her summers growing up.

And she'd had sex with him.

No. That wasn't it. And she wasn't going to think about it.

She just needed to make sure that he agreed that they'd never, ever talk about it or tell anyone. Ever.

Then she wouldn't have to worry, every time she saw him, that he'd bring it up. Or she would. That it would somehow show up and stand there between them.

She needed it done.

She reminded herself of this fact when, three days later,

Sebastian called to tell her that Jasmine, the German shepherd she'd been checking on the night of the shooting, was having her babies. With three other veterinarians working full-time at the clinic, she was able to take a break and head out to Crosswinds.

Ruby had counted ten puppies on the X-ray she'd done earlier in the pregnancy. Sebastian said she'd only had seven and was straining. Ruby made the ten-minute drive in eight. Pulled up with her brand-new windshield, parked on the opposite side of the little dark green medical building, her own little Crosswinds mini clinic, and ran inside.

Sebastian stepped aside as soon as he saw her, and she went to work. Saw the sack of fluid blocking the birth canal, a situation made worse by the fact that the eighth puppy Jasmine was trying to push out was a breech. Ruby handled both issues without pause, and half an hour later, she stood over the litter, telling the big mountain man, with his shaggy hair and beard, and who was clearly worried about both Jasmine and her newborns, "You've got ten healthy pups there."

She cleaned up. Grabbed her shoulder bag, intending to leave Sebastian with the newborns he was perfectly capable of looking after. "I'll send the bill over," she told him. The search-and-rescue portion of Crosswinds was funded by the individuals and organizations that needed the dogs and paid for her services. Usually, she took the time to make out the charges on the computer that was set on the counter for that purpose.

For all he knew, she was pressed to get back to the clinic. Truth was, she wasn't feeling like herself around him.

"I'll walk you out."

She nodded, though being alone around him was what she was trying to avoid. At least until the jitters from the gunshot the other night dissipated a bit. But he was probably right. The conversation had to happen.

Since he clearly had a plan in accompanying her to her vehicle, she waited for him to start.

"I want to pay for your windshield."

What? Not at all what she'd been expecting.

"Insurance covered it. And no. It wasn't your fault."

"The police are looking into Crosswinds being targeted," he told her what she'd assumed all along. And yet, her insides tightened uncomfortably at the news. For Sebastian. And the dogs. "I guess there've been a couple of anonymous complaints about the noise. When one dog barks, they all think they have to get their two cents in." He shrugged.

"Anonymous noise complaints?" she asked, slowing her steps as she frowned up at him. "You're on five acres, ten minutes outside of town. Who's close enough to hear anything?"

His nod didn't feel like a good thing. "That's what I said. And what everyone else seems to get. Which apparently points more to the fact that I'm being deliberately targeted for some reason. They're looking into that now. They didn't find a shell casing the other night, either, so right now, all they have to go on is a size-ten shoe print. It's not like there are traffic cams out here. And we have no way of knowing if the guy came from town or the opposite direction altogether."

The tension in her grew. Sebastian, the dogs, his programs—they helped so many people. And after burning herself out at the clinic, on call 24/7 for years, she'd hired more people and had been finding her own personal energy and joy return as she volunteered for Crosswinds's PTSD dog-placement program.

"Have you had any disgruntled customers?" she asked.

"Someone whose dog didn't perform as they thought it would?"

He shook his head. As she'd known he would. Sebastian personally guaranteed the satisfaction of his clients. His dogs served as they were trained, or he took them back and found them good homes as pets. In all the years he'd been in business, it had only happened once that she knew of.

"I've opened my life up to the police," he said then. "We've had multiple interviews and they're following up on everyone I can ever remember knowing..."

"What about back in Boise?" she asked then. Sebastian had grown up in the city, two hours away from Owl Creek, summering at the cabin on the five acres that was now his permanent home. Property that had been in his family for decades. "Your father was a doctor, right? Maybe something to do with one of his patients?" She was grasping, she knew. Just needed him to have the answers that would bring his nightmare to an end.

"Again, the police are investigating every possibility..."

"What about cousins?" She knew he'd been an only child, but... "Is there someone who felt cheated by you getting the family property?"

He shook his head. "I'm it, in terms of family."

The words were like a punch to her solar plexus.

She couldn't imagine...with five siblings and four cousins right there in town, all growing up together—sometimes all ten in the same house—the idea of having no one...

"What do the police say?" she asked, caring much more than she wanted to. He was a friend of her brother. Not her own intimate concern. Peripheral. Not personal. No matter how many times she'd repeated the words in the past two months, her heart was not getting the distinction.

But Ruby knew she had to.

She'd had enough friction in her home growing up. Her parents, while respectful of each other, weren't close. So she'd basically had two different authoritative sources to deal with on her own, going back and forth between the two, to get any sense of what was expected from her. Then, being one of six growing kids, with bright minds and a ton of energy, and add in her aunt and uncle's broken marriage and her mother trying to compensate for her own twin leaving her husband's brother by taking care of his four kids...

She had enough family to last her a lifetime. And an aversion to sharing her home on a permanent basis. Except with the various animals she fostered.

Which meant that any personal feelings she might think she was experiencing for a man with whom she'd had sex were just going to have to go away.

She didn't want them.

SEBASTIAN WATCHED THE expressions flit across Ruby's face as he told her the current police theory was that the culprit was exhibiting behavior that was escalating. Going from bogus complaints to random gunshots.

He couldn't read her. She'd always been such a curious mixture of compassion and aloofness...and not just with him. Growing up, Ruby had been the one who didn't join in. Who preferred to make her own entertainment—reading a lot of the time—rather than jumping in a boat with the rest of them and shooting out across the water.

Didn't much matter what she was thinking. His missive was going to be the same.

"You have to stop coming out here until we get this resolved." He put it right out there. The other night...if she'd been in her SUV when the bullet had hit...

No.

"I've got puppies to watch over," she told him, chin high, as she stood up to him. She didn't even give him so much as a shake of her head, to let him know she was disregarding his wishes. "Fletcher told my parents that if this guy was out to hurt someone, he'd have done so," she continued. "Oscar's injury aside," she added. Then just kept talking. "This person had no way of knowing that Oscar was even out there. That was an anomaly."

The police had said the same. And Ruby Colton was acting as though if she just kept on talking, not giving him a chance to get a word in, she'd change his mind.

"This is my property," he butted in when she took a breath. "All that matters here is what I say. And I'm not going to take a risk with your life..." He'd been up all night that first night after her car had been shot. Dealing with cold sweats and a mind filled with images of what could have happened.

"So you're going to let all the people relying on search-and-rescue dogs miss out? And all the veterans needing dogs to help them live normal lives...they just go without?"

She had spunk. It got his ire up.

And his appreciation, too. In spite of himself.

"Believe it or not, Dr. Colton, we raise a lot of healthy dogs here who will get along just fine without your services for the time it takes the police to find this guy." He was smiling. Crosswinds needed her. She knew how grateful he was for her help—most particularly with the volunteer veteran program. But his gaze bored into hers, as well. Her safety was nonnegotiable.

"Like today?" She upped her chin another notch. "You confident you'd have ten healthy puppies right now?"

"I only called you because I knew you were coming out to check on Jasmine, anyway," he told her. "And the police say that the perp's pattern, based on the shootings and the complaints, is to hit weeks apart. But this is it. Now. Today. No more until whoever is out to get me is in jail."

"My parents still think the shooter could be after me. With all of the public fundraising I've been helping with, everyone knows how much the work out here, the services Crosswinds provides, means to me."

He hadn't thought of that. If the police had, they hadn't said so.

He wanted to fire her on the spot.

And knew it wouldn't do any good if someone was already after her.

"I don't buy it," she told him. "If someone wanted to hurt me, they'd be going after my clinic. Putting up bad reviews. Accusing me of letting an animal die. Flattening my tire while I was at work…"

She stopped as he cocked his head, frowning, but half smiling, too.

"What?" she asked.

"You sure you aren't the perp?" he teased, even knowing it was in no way a joking matter. Just…someone had to ease the tension.

"I've…given this a lot of thought over the past few days. Having my windshield wiped out, and then dealing with each member of my family—every one of them a know-it-all, mind you—I've had to shore up my defenses. My car was shot at while I wasn't in it. And it wasn't even on my property. That does not mean I need to go into hiding."

He opened his mouth to argue with her, but she got the next word in first. "What about you?" she blurted. "You're right here, going on with your life, running your business, and every single one of the occurrences has to do with this place. Yet, you aren't shutting down."

"I can't shut down. Too many people rely on—"

"Exactly," she interrupted. "So what makes my life more valuable than yours?"

He had an answer for that. But the challenge shooting at him from those unrelenting green eyes kept his mouth shut.

For the time being.

She climbed into her SUV. Shut the door on him. Started the engine.

But he and Ruby Colton weren't done talking about the matter.

And when they were, he intended the last words to be his.

Chapter Three

Ruby had no cause to visit Crosswinds that next week. Sebastian emailed photos of the puppies feeding, telling her that Jasmine and the gang were doing great.

She'd already released Oscar from her care.

He had no new dogs arrive.

And she knew he was deliberately trying not to need her.

There also hadn't been any other signs of unrest in her life, or, according to Wade, Sebastian's, either. Things at Crosswinds had been running smoothly, with no upsets all week.

And yet, she was still feeling...jittery.

Because she needed to talk to him. To get things back on an even keel. Before Wade noticed the tension between them. The last person she'd ever want to know about her fantastical mistake with Sebastian Cross was her overprotective brother. Wade was a strong adversary on a good day. But with having his entire life upended after being blinded in one eye, with his career in the Marines no longer an option, he wasn't in a good place mentally.

Sitting in her office on the second Thursday in April, waiting for her two younger sisters, who'd called to say they were bringing lunch to share with her, she wondered if she should drive out to Crosswinds after work. Just get everything with Sebastian out in the open. It was not her way to let things linger, or fester, unless doing so let them slowly evaporate into the ether.

Having sex with a client, who was also her brother's close friend, didn't seem to be something that would fade away quietly.

She wasn't acting like herself.

Hence, her sisters bringing lunch to share with her in the middle of their busy weekday schedules. Checking up on her. Or just wanting her to know they cared.

Either way, after the shooting ordeal at Crosswinds, she wasn't going to convince her family that she was fine—her usual, untroubled, independent self—until she started to feel that way again.

She had to talk to Sebastian.

Hannah and Frannie, twenty-eight and twenty-six, respectively, came in together. Hannah was carrying a reusable insulated bag bearing the logo of her catering business, and Frannie had a cardboard holder with three cups of coffee from her bookshop café.

Unusually happy to see them both, she stood to help divvy up the goodies they'd brought, taking a foil-wrapped package out of Hannah's bag, hoping for her sister's signature grape-laden chicken-salad wrap, and caught the scent of coffee when Frannie removed the lid and set a cup in front of her.

One whiff, and the jitters she'd been feeling turned into cold sweats. Her head swam.

And she opened her eyes to see both sisters staring at her with panicked gazes.

One on each side of her chair. A hand each on the arms of her chair.

Her chair.

She'd been standing.

"What's going on?" she asked, hearing the weakness in her tone.

"You passed out, that's what!" Hannah, the no-nonsense Colton, stated emphatically. "We need to get you to the ER."

"I'm fine," Ruby said, sitting up. Waiting for the light-headedness to return. "Seriously," she added, when it didn't.

"Come on, Ruby," Frannie, the quiet bookworm, and baby of the family, said, her hazel eyes imploring. "You don't just pass out for no reason."

"You're a doctor," Hannah added, her green-eyed gaze no less impactful. Because looking into Hannah's eyes was like looking in a mirror. Colton eyes. Similar to their dad's eyes, and exact replicas of Uncle Buck's. "You know this isn't normal or fine."

She was a doctor of veterinary medicine. Not a doctor for humans.

But because Hannah's point was valid, she agreed to let them drive her to the clinic in town. Just to get her vitals and fluids checked. It made good sense.

And would reassure her little sisters so that they didn't go running to their mother with the news of Ruby's little mishap.

"It's the stress," she told them as they waited for results of the urine and basic blood tests, which would, she was sure, show no infection. "I haven't had much of an appetite."

"I knew you weren't fine," Hannah said, sitting on her right, leaving the chair on the left to Frannie. "You could have been in that car for all the shooter knew. If he shot from as far away as the cops said he did. Of course, you're overwrought."

"The stress from everyone watching over me," Ruby said

dryly. "I love you all so much, you know that, but eleven of you, twelve including Uncle Buck, texting me at least once a day..."

Hannah glanced at Frannie, across Ruby's perfectly healthy frame. "Yeah," she said. "We should have been better organized about that." Her middle sister's tone held definite I-told-you-so isms.

"Hannah wanted us on a schedule, so there'd be a timeline," Frannie allowed. "Fletcher said it was better, since you live alone, if we each just check in throughout the day."

Her words dropped off. And Ruby didn't know whether to laugh or groan.

As it turned out, she didn't have a chance to do either as the physician's assistant who'd seen her entered the small exam room.

The first thing the woman did was glance at Hannah and Frannie, then her gaze landed on Ruby. "Is it okay to talk in front of your sisters?"

Frannie gasped, clutching Ruby's left hand so tight that she felt her baby sister's nails digging into her skin. "Of course it is," Hannah said, covering Ruby's other hand with her own.

Just laying her palm there. Warm. Supportive.

She met the medical professional's gaze. "Yes," she said calmly. There was nothing a simple urine or basic blood test was going to show in such a short period of time. Her vitals had been fine. But then she'd been certain of that before she'd come in.

The PA looked only at her and said, "You're pregnant."

She couldn't be.

It had to be a mistake.

As soon as she got to her own transportation, she was going to get a home pregnancy test—out of town, so no one would see her buying it—and prove the PA wrong.

Sitting in the front passenger seat of Hannah's car, Ruby continued to feel the weight of her sister's open-mouthed, disbelieving stares—just as when they'd been in that tiny room at the clinic.

A room that was now forever ingrained in her brain and would probably give her nightmares in the years to come.

Huh. Her, pregnant?

The woman who knew one thing about herself for certain.

She couldn't ever see herself wanting a husband.

Let alone raising a family.

She could not be pregnant.

"Who is he?" Hannah's question came the second she closed her driver's door.

"There is no *he*."

"You had yourself inseminated?" Frannie asked from the seat directly behind Hannah.

"Of course not. Either of you see me as the mothering type?"

"Yes," they answered in unison. Shocking her so much, she turned to stare at each of them in turn.

"You know the last thing I want is to get married and have a family."

"I know that's what you say, but you'll make a great mother, sis." Hannah's tone was unusually soft. Compassionate. The woman was so in love with little Lucy, she figured everyone would feel the same after giving birth. "Now, who's the father?"

No way. Uh-uh.

"No one."

Sebastian Cross wasn't even her lover. He most definitely was not the father of the child. Even the one that only existed in one PA's words and on a chart.

Charts could be corrected.

Words, maybe not forgotten, but the mistake could be forgiven.

Yes, that was it.

There'd been a mistake. Picking up her phone, she dialed the clinic. Asked to speak to the doctor. Insisted on holding, was still holding when Hannah pulled up at Colton Veterinary Clinic, parked and turned off her ignition.

"I didn't even know you were dating anyone," Frannie said, as they all just sat there.

"I'm *not* dating anyone." She didn't even try to keep the exasperation out of her tone. And then, as reality hit her, she filled with total panic.

Her sisters thought she was...

Turning in her seat, phone still to her ear, she stared them both down. Hard. A big-sister, I'm-seriously-going-to-tell-every-secret-you've-ever-had stare. "Do not breathe a word of this to anyone," she said then. "I mean it. Not Mom. Not anyone."

There was no compromise on that one.

She saw the glance Frannie and Hannah shared. It didn't bode well and did nothing to calm Ruby.

"I'm serious," she said. "My medical information is private."

Frannie shook her head. "But, Ruby...a baby..."

Ruby cut her off with a glare. "It's a mistake," she said. "Which is why I'm waiting to speak to the doctor in charge today. And even if it wasn't, this is my business to share or not, to handle how I see fit, not yours."

She was dead serious.

Hannah, the only mother among them, sighed. And Ruby drew her first easy breath since the PA had made her ridiculous announcement. "Just tell me that you weren't... forced, or..."

In light of the recent happenings at Crosswinds—her car being shot at, all the worry her family had shared on her behalf—she felt Hannah's concern to the bone. "I swear to you, sweetie, no one has ever touched me, like that, without my full cooperation."

"So you did sleep with someone," Frannie said softly. "Who is he?"

"No one," she said again, calmer now. "It's a mistake."

Hannah still sat, door closed. She was the one Ruby knew she had to contend with if she wanted her secret kept. Frannie was naturally quiet. Reserved.

"I won't say anything about the baby," Hannah said then. "You're absolutely right, it's your secret, your business. But if you are pregnant, your secret's going to start showing itself before too long."

Hannah had been there and done that.

Ruby nodded, looked at Frannie. "You'll keep this to yourself?"

"Of course, I won't say anything." Frannie looked as though she wanted to say a lot, though.

"Say it wasn't a mistake...would you have it?" Hannah asked.

Ruby knew what Hannah was really asking. And was fairly certain her sister wouldn't judge. Whether Hannah agreed with Ruby's decisions or not, she would want to be supportive. "I wouldn't *not* have it," she said softly.

And had to escape the car before she threw up all over her sister's upholstery.

A WEEK HAD gone by since the shooting of Ruby Colton's windshield and her subsequent visit to deliver Jasmine's last three puppies.

A week without seeing her.

Sebastian was still on edge. Someone had shot up his property. Twice. Causing damage both times. First the shrapnel hit Oscar—though, arguably, that had likely been collateral damage, not intentional—and then Ruby's windshield had been shattered.

And the complaints…

Who was out to get him? When would they hit next?

The not knowing was getting to him—maybe that was the perpetrator's goal?

Give him an enemy to fight, and he'd get the job done. Sitting around waiting for an attack from an unknown source that could come without warning?

All the Marine training in the world wasn't going to prepare him for that.

Not well enough to suit him, at any rate.

So he focused on the training he excelled in—search-and-rescue. Each dog generally took two years of weekly training before being ready for a search-and-rescue mission. At Crosswinds, he had canines at every level of training, all the time. Those just starting out. Those almost ready to go to work. Some had handlers who came to Owl Creek, stayed at one of the motels in town that gave Crosswinds a special rate and came out to the facility to work with the dog before taking them home.

Search-and-rescue wasn't an easy business. Or a cheap one. He ran a highly accredited, elite organization. Yet, a lot of handlers were volunteers. Sebastian did what he could to keep his costs down for them. His property, while outfitted as well as the best training facilities, was all basic brick and wood buildings—all painted one color. The military green he preferred.

And he did as much of the training himself as he possibly could.

The second Thursday in April, he'd spent the morning and midafternoon at Buck Colton's ranch. One of the golden retrievers, Elise, a relative of Oscar, was at the tail end of avalanche training. He'd needed to take her to an unfamiliar site, with another dog and avalanche tools—spikes and shovels—lying around.

Malcolm Colton—Wade's cousin—and Malcolm's SAR dog, Pacer, had helped with this particular session many times.

They had ridges dug out for that purpose. Sebastian would bury Malcolm in one, under a couple of inches of dirt with full breathing capability, and give his trainee—that day, Elise—Malcolm's scent, while Pacer was given a different smell to follow and went off for his prey. The idea was for Elise to ignore Pacer and all other distractions to follow Malcom's scent, and then be willing to dig to get to him. For which she'd get a treat.

The girl performed in record time. Every single time they repeated the exercise. Getting to Malcolm, and then racing straight to Sebastian to lead him to her find.

At one point, when the burial point was on a steep incline, she stayed with the uncovered body and barked until Sebastian came to her.

Sebastian was just heading back to his truck, with Elise trotting, head high, at his side, when Wade came out of the barn. He called out to Sebastian.

In jeans, a long-sleeved denim shirt and cowboy boots,

Wade walked with the same sense of command he'd displayed in his US Marine Special Forces uniform, black eye patch and all.

"Quick question for you," Wade said, petting Elise's head as he reached them. "My sister Hannah just called. She says that Ruby's been dating someone, has some boyfriend, but won't say who. Hannah thinks this might be the guy who shot out Ruby's windshield. Said she was really odd, to the point of angry, when Hannah asked her about him. None of us had any idea she was dating anyone. Did you?"

Sebastian shook his head immediately.

Ruby had a boyfriend?

A development he'd never even considered.

Relief didn't flood him, as he'd expected it to.

She might have mentioned that detail.

Sleeping with another guy's woman was not his way.

And could cause unforeseen complications—like a guy targeting her at Sebastian's place.

"Anyone who's been at the kennels that she might have had contact with?" Wade continued to grill him. "She's been spending so much more time out there, and with the handlers you have coming in..."

He thought over the people who'd been in and out of Crosswinds, when Ruby might have been there, who might have taken exception to Sebastian's friendship with her, from before Oscar was shot.

That's when the violence had started. With Oscar's injury.

But the complaints had started before then.

And had continued.

She'd slept with Sebastian while she'd been seeing someone else?

Gut clenched tight, he had to admit it made sense. They

could have taken offense at how much time Ruby spent with Sebastian's dogs. Maybe not believing she was just seeing the dogs. The jealous boyfriend...shooting up his place in the middle of the night. Complaining about noise. Then still seeing his girlfriend's vehicle there until dawn?

Maybe she'd explained she'd just been there for Oscar. Had sworn that nothing else had happened. She'd sure been eager to pretend that it hadn't.

Maybe the guy had seen her with Sebastian again.

Made sense that the violence would have escalated.

And most definitely fit shooting out Ruby's windshield while she was parked there.

"I can't think of anyone," he told his friend honestly. Sebastian was reeling from the sudden turn of events. Did the guy know Ruby had slept with him?

How could she not have at least told him she had a boyfriend?

If the perp was this violent without knowing the full story, how much further would he go if he found out they had slept together?

"How sure is Hannah that she has one?" Sebastian asked, careful to keep his question completely casual. Curious. But, because of the violence, concerned, too.

"She's positive. She wouldn't say how she knew but she told me that her proof was one hundred percent positive. She's worried sick."

Sebastian didn't blame her. After that news, he was, too.

Worried about the potential for more violence, worried about Ruby's safety. And a bit concerned about the incredible disappointment coursing through him.

He'd never have taken Ruby Colton for one to screw around on her boyfriend.

Or to have sex with Sebastian and not tell him she was in a relationship.

Not that the sex meant anything.

But with the violence, her windshield... They'd talked about possible threats. About any potential enemies.

Why hadn't she at least told him about her secret possibility?

For that matter, why did she have to keep it secret at all?

That question led to an unpalatable, and yet possible answer.

The guy was married.

And Sebastian's day had just gone down the toilet.

Chapter Four

Ruby talked to the doctor at the clinic.

And after work, she went back to the medical facility on her own for a second urinalysis.

She'd had a period since she'd slept with Sebastian. Granted, it had been light, but that happened occasionally, based on her workload and stress level.

And since making the hellacious mistake of having sex with her older brother's friend, she'd been fairly stressed.

Besides, they'd used a condom.

She hadn't been kidding, or doubting herself, when she'd been so adamant with her sisters regarding her test results.

She'd known they couldn't be right.

And being a doctor, she also knew that sometimes test results were skewed. A faulty test strip. Or technician. Both happened, even in the best hospitals and clinics.

Then she'd thrown up.

Something she hadn't done since she was a kid.

And she'd gone into full doctor mode. Symptoms. Tests. Results.

When symptoms contradicted each other, test a second time, just to be sure.

And there she was, walking out of the clinic, just after

seven, having watched the test being run, and the results appear, right along with the doctor.

She, Dr. Ruby Colton, DVM, was pregnant.

And in two years' time, there was only one man she'd had sex with.

Once.

She had to talk to Sebastian.

Thought about calling him.

A charged conversation like the one they were bound to have...might be better over the phone.

Easier, at least.

In her car, she glanced at the second set of test results. And knew she had to drive out to see Sebastian. He deserved to see the results, both sets of them.

She stopped by her office and made copies of both test forms she'd received that day, put her own in a folder and folded his and put them in her satchel. She lifted the leather bag up to her shoulder, and, with a "have a good evening" to the evening staff, she left.

On a mission.

A distasteful one.

The best way to handle those were to get them done immediately. No overthinking.

Just complete the task.

Keeping her mind on her meeting with Sebastian, trying to find words for the conversation that would result in the least drama, she felt like the ten-minute trip out of town to his place lasted for hours. She found no words.

Every sentence her mind started sent her into panic mode and she had to abort the effort.

Abort.

She wasn't going to do that.

She'd told Hannah she wouldn't even before she'd been pregnant.

Before she'd known she was.

I've got this paperwork I feel I should show you, Sebastian, out of courtesy, but it doesn't require any involvement from you at all. Not even a name.

The sentence appeared as she pulled up Cross Drive.

No one knew she'd slept with him.

No one ever had to know.

Yes. That thought worked better than any other one she'd had since throwing up in her own clinic's parking lot.

Drawing up by Sebastian's back door—because coming from the medical building or the kennels, the back entrance was the one she always used, not because she was afraid to leave her car in view of the road—she pulled open the screen door to administer her customary two short knocks.

The mission was underway. Would soon be complete.

"Eeoowooah!" The male holler rent the air, filled with anger. With gut-wrenching pain. Sending shivers up and down her spine. Instinctively pulling the screen to her body, crouching up against the wooden door keeping her from the house, she glanced at the yard around her.

And toward the kennels.

The sound came again. Animalistic.

Clearly coming from the house. Heart pounding, thinking only of the pain inherent in the sound, she turned the doorknob. Felt it give. Hurried inside, already reaching for her phone.

And saw Sebastian sprawled back in a recliner, eyes closed, with an open laptop on its side on the floor.

"Yaawwwah!"

She jumped back as the horrible sound came from his throat, just before he threw a heavy fist at…nothing.

And it hit her.

Sebastian. In the Marines, just like Wade.

Early discharge.

His head was still, his cheeks and lips skewed right, then left, the muscles scrunching one way, then the other, like he was cringing from one side of his face at a time. All of it hiding beneath the light beard.

She'd taken a training class on PTSD before Wade came home. Mostly for herself. She'd needed to know what her adored older brother might be going through.

Sitting at attention, Oscar watched Sebastian. Glanced at her. And back at his owner. The retriever was a search-and-rescue dog, not one trained for the veterans Crosswinds also served.

She couldn't get close or risk being hit. But Oscar could. She'd seen the dogs in training. Had helped train some over the past few months.

Moving behind Sebastian's chair, she motioned for the dog, pointing for him to sit beside the chair. The big mountain man was striking up, out, with the movements he was making. Oscar's head was below the arm of the chair. Oscar knew to nudge Sebastian's hand for a treat. She waited.

And felt tears fill her eyes as, less than a minute later, the dog, hearing Sebastian cry out, nudged his owner's hand.

Sebastian woke up, his eyes glazed at first, and then crystal clear as he focused on Ruby, moving out in front of him.

She'd never felt less welcome anywhere in her life.

"WHAT IN THE hell are you doing in here?" Sebastian heard the accusation in his tone, wasn't sure he had the where-withal to withhold it.

Wasn't sure he wanted to try.

"You have no business being here," he said, angry. With her, yes. Because she was there. Because she'd slept with him without telling him she had a boyfriend.

Because, with everyone working so hard to find out who was behind the attacks at and on Crosswinds, she hadn't said a word.

But most of his anger was aimed at himself.

He'd been gone again—had slipped into the hell that was the part of his life no one ever saw. Or knew about.

"I wanted to talk to you," she said, sounding like some doctor, not the compassionate woman, the friend, who'd been offering so much of her time to Crosswinds. "I heard you holler out…"

Seeing his computer lying sideways on the floor, he snatched it up. Closed it. Stood. "How long have you been here?"

"Long enough."

And didn't that just put the plunger on anything good about the day.

"Yeah, well, I'm fine—you can go now." Oscar nudged his hand and Sebastian went to get the dog the treat he'd already asked for once.

Wait. Oscar nudging his hand…had woken him. He looked at Ruby.

"I made him sit by you," she said. "I didn't know what else to do…"

She cared.

That mattered.

Not for any reason he could come up with.

But it did.

And it hit him why he couldn't seem to get by what had happened between them two months before. It wasn't the sex calling to him, although it had been—yeah—but...she knew.

She'd sat with him, held conversation like any other time, making no mention of the panic attack he'd been suffering. She'd just...brought him down. By being herself.

She knew.

And he wasn't sure he was sorry.

He had no idea what to do with that.

"Oscar's a search-and-rescue dog," she said then, as if his dog was the issue at hand.

He nodded.

"Because you don't want anyone to know you need one trained for..."

"I don't need one," he said gruffly. Then leaned on the corner of the wall, one ankle crossed over the other, as if entertaining in the near dark, while standing, was a normal thing.

Ruby turned on the light by his chair.

Sat down in the one just like it a few feet away.

"How often do you have them?"

He sat, too.

Why not. The day couldn't get any worse.

"I hadn't had one in more than a year." He'd told her the truth, was glaring at her again. "Until the night Oscar was shot. Or rather, the night after that."

He'd had the panic attack first, the night of the shooting.

And sex. He'd had sex that night, too.

With a woman who had a boyfriend. Possibly a dangerously jealous one.

How could she not have told him?

Not only because his place was being attacked, but also… to protect herself? Why wasn't she telling anyone? Didn't make sense to him.

But then, he wasn't at his best.

Not even half best.

"But you had them when you first came home?" Her softly uttered question hit him in a weak spot.

He needed to get rid of those.

All done. No more.

"I was called home to deal with the deaths of both of my parents, who'd been killed in a car accident, what do you think?" he asked, not kindly.

He had to get rid of her before he did another thing he'd regret. Like telling her how someone else knowing, having *her* know, seemed to lighten his load some. Even while it made him feel weak.

His anger didn't seem to reach her. She didn't tense. Didn't stand to go.

The woman didn't even frown at him.

He deserved some kind of facial disapproval, at least.

"What memory does the sound of gunfire trigger for you?"

He nodded. Reminded himself that he was not happy with her. The boyfriend, and all. And said, "Wade and I joined the Marines together, but, as you know, we ultimately served separately." What the hell. If he had to get it out, might as well get it done with.

Better that then get into some wimpy-feeling personal conversation about her having sex with him while she was involved with another man.

Or having sex with him at all.

"I ended up in Afghanistan, along with a buddy, Thane,

I'd met at boot camp. Like me, he was an only child. Had no other family. One night we were drinking. A lot. Too much. We were shipping out the next day and he asks me what's the single most painful thing I could ever remember dealing with to date. You know, like he was thinking about the pain we might be walking into."

Her eyes aglow with warmth Ruby sat up straight. Like her shoulders weren't going to bow, no matter what he said.

Like she could take it.

Maybe even wanted to take it.

And it struck him… She could be using him to better understand her brother who'd just returned, seemingly broken. He'd like that.

To help Ruby help Wade.

"I told Thane about Jerry."

"That spaniel you had when we were kids?"

"I had him until I was seventeen," he told her. "He was a rescue dog, and sometimes I felt like he'd rescued me, not the other way around. I was home alone a lot growing up. A lot. But when Jerry came, it was different. I had someone to greet me at the door. Someone who was as happy to see me as I was to see him."

He stopped. Helping Wade was one thing. Becoming a sap…not.

"Jerry had been abused. All he wanted was someone to be kind to him. He was the most gentle living being I've ever known." *Move on.* "So I told Thane about the night Jerry died," he said, finishing.

The End.

"What did Thane say to that?"

Right. The point he'd been getting at. "He told me about the night his dog, Bear, died. It gave us something in common. An understanding of what we could be walking into," he explained, completely serious as he met her gaze. "We never mentioned our dogs, or that night again, but it was like we knew. And the knowing, the accepting that life could hurt like hell, gave us strength to get the job done. To do what we had to do to try to prevent, or stop, others suffering so much worse."

Her gaze was glued to him. He wasn't sorry.

Until he remembered that she had a boyfriend. That Hannah Colton had irrefutable proof of a man in Ruby's life.

What was it about the woman that sucked him in? Made him someone he was not? He didn't want to connect.

Not with her, definitely. But not with any other human being, either. Not like that.

"You're about to tell me that Thane died over there, aren't you?" Her words fell like cotton balls around him. Over him. Soft. Tender. Until there were so many of them he knew he could suffocate.

"I was about to not tell you that he died lying right next to me in a dirt-filled cove we'd dug out of the side of a mountain," he said, standing.

Time for her to go.

She didn't take his hint. Didn't get to her feet and head to the door. Instead, looking up at him, she said, "You can cross-train Oscar. I'll help if you'd like. No one has to know..."

Cross-train... Oscar nudging his hand...

"He can help stop the nightmare at its onset," she said, telling him something he knew better than she did. He just hadn't figured himself for needing the help.

He lived alone. There was no one to protect from his very private, very personal struggles. It wasn't like he dozed off on the job.

Or out to eat.

She was getting too close, pushing herself way too far in.

Hands firmly on his hips, Sebastian did what he had to do. Shoved her right back out again with an accusatory tone that left no room for doubt. "Why didn't you tell me you have a boyfriend?"

Chapter Five

"Excuse me?" Ruby stood straight, completely affronted at first, and then just worried about him. Was he still in the clutches of his nightmare? Thinking she was someone else?

It was the only thing that made sense.

"That night we had sex, you were seeing someone else." His words would have been her worst nightmare if she'd ever gone off the rails far enough to have dreamed it.

Completely shocked, she stood there with her mouth open. Couldn't think of a single thing to say.

"Wade told me," he continued.

Wade? It was like she'd walked into the twilight zone.

"My brother Wade?" She'd gotten the words out. That was a start.

"Of course, your brother Wade," Sebastian said, still standing there, all burly mountain man. His hands, which had been on his hips, had dropped to his side.

She didn't know what that meant, either.

"It's not like what we did meant something," he said then. "It was a reaction, I get that. Something that happened in the moment without thought. And I get that you didn't owe me anything. The anonymous complaints, even the gunshot that caught Oscar... It could have been him, if he's the jealous type and didn't like the time you were spending out here. But still, we hadn't done it yet, so I can even get your silence until that point. But when the shot went directly through your windshield. That night everyone thought it was personal. The way Chase whisked you out of here, insisting you stay at your parents'. And Fletcher was all over the case. Even the police were asking about everyone we knew, or had known. You didn't think to mention this guy? Just in case?"

She had to go. Get out.

He was out of his mind. Slamming her.

She headed for the door.

And... *Wade*?

Sebastian had to be hallucinating.

She got herself outside. Door shut behind her. Was peripherally aware that Sebastian wasn't following her. And slowed her pace long enough to take a full deep breath.

All of the reading she'd done on PTSD, and she hadn't seen a thing about waking hallucinations that were set in real time.

But there was paranoia...

He had to still be in the throes of the demons that ate at him. Lying next to his best friend as he was shot, watching him die. And immediately following, to be called home to the sudden deaths of his parents—his only living relatives.

She couldn't leave. Not until she was sure he'd climbed his way out of the personal hell she'd found him in the night of the first gunshot. She'd thought his panic then had been induced by Oscar's being shot.

She should have known it was more than that.

And Wade.

Did her brother know that Sebastian was struggling with PTSD-like symptoms?

Was that why Wade's name had entered into Sebastian's rant?

Her having a boyfriend was just ludicrous. No way anyone in her family would spread around that claim.

And...the baby.

For a few minutes there, she'd forgotten.

She was pregnant.

From one night that, in Sebastian's own words, meant nothing.

She couldn't even get a one-night stand right, and he thought she had a boyfriend?

She stumbled on the way to her car.

She had to tell Sebastian about the baby. But not right now. Not until his mind was clear.

But she couldn't just leave him like he was, either.

Heading to the only place she felt welcome at the moment, she entered the medical building with the key Sebastian had given her long ago. Was greeted by Jasmine, who, instead of wagging her tail, whined from inside her large, round two-foot-high fencing, and stared up at Ruby.

Her first thought was that the dog knew, too. That Sebastian had told her canine patients that she had some secret jealous man who was shooting up the place. Jasmine had walked over to the blanket-covered matting where her puppies slept.

Was nudging at a makeshift bed.

All personal thoughts fleeing, Ruby stepped over the fencing and kneeled next to Jasmine. "What's the matter, girl? What are you telling me?" she asked. She'd come in to check on the puppies—or just to play with them for a second, to get her equilibrium back.

And maybe to have a heart-to-heart with the new mama, feeling a bond with Jasmine.

But as she started to check over the puppies, her heart began to pound. Three of them weren't well. At first, she thought it was the last three she'd birthed, but looking at the markings, she knew it wasn't. Which made no sense.

Phone out of her pocket, she dialed Sebastian immediately.

"I'm sorry, Ruby. So sorry. I had no right to come at you like that—"

"Come down to the clinic," she said, breaking in on him. "Three of the puppies have weak heart rates, raised temperatures and they're panting hard. We need to get them into town, where I have everything I need..."

Where she could do blood work. Run urinalysis. Start IVs.

After dropping the phone, she was already gathering up the babies. Grabbing a box filled with supplies, dumping them onto the floor, to use the box as a carrying bed for them. Had them settled, had picked up her phone, her satchel and was at the door, when Sebastian appeared.

Taking the box from her, he didn't speak. Didn't even look at her.

She didn't look at him, either.

At the moment, their drama didn't matter.

There were lives at stake.

SEBASTIAN DROVE.

Ruby wanted to be able to watch over the puppies, and he was glad to have her do so. Was thankful that she'd been there.

That, even after his supreme rudeness, she'd gone down to check on the puppies.

"You think they're going to make it?" he asked.

"It's too soon to tell. They aren't convulsing. That's a good sign." She hadn't taken her eyes off the puppies since she'd climbed into the back seat of his truck, right after he'd loaded their box there.

None of them were spoken for yet. He didn't even know if they'd have the characteristics necessary to be search-and-rescue trained.

But if they weren't suited to SAR, they could still make great service dogs for the too many veterans who needed them. Or companions to kids who might need an extra friend.

Like himself?

He'd like to blame his harsh words to Ruby on the nightmare she'd helped pull him out of. She'd calmed him, and he couldn't explain that to himself in any way that didn't set him on edge.

He'd been fighting the effect she had on him as much as he'd been reeling from the news that she had some secret guy in the wings.

Whether the guy was the one vandalizing his place or not.

And that's where his defenses flew sky-high. Why on earth—other than as the possible source of the violence—should Ruby not telling him about her boyfriend matter to him at all?

The only thing that needed to matter right now was the health of the puppies she was tending to. He'd called one of his employees, Andy Martin, to head to his place and sit with Jasmine and the other puppies, to watch over them just in case any of the others started exhibiting signs of unconsciousness, rather than mere sleep. If they couldn't be woken up.

He pulled up to the back entrance of the clinic as Ruby instructed, was out of his seat the second he'd turned off the truck, flinging open the back door and reaching for the box, while Ruby climbed out her side.

She hadn't said what she thought was wrong. He didn't ask. Didn't want to distract her.

He just assisted, following all her instructions to the letter, as she checked vitals, drew blood, looked in noses and mouths.

He knew enough about dogs to write a book. About breeding them. Raising them. Training them.

Medically, he only had enough knowledge to be deeply concerned. Three lives... In all his years at Crosswinds, he hadn't lost one.

She'd told him to stay with the puppies while she went to the lab. Was back sooner than he'd expected.

"They've been poisoned," she said, as she worked over all three dogs with an efficiency that left him in the dust. "It's some kind of petroleum-based something," she explained, no longer asking for his help. "Maria, one of my most experienced techs, is on her way in. We need to get IVs started, but first, I'm administering an absorbent demulcent. We don't want them to vomit. Petroleum-based poisons can do permanent damage to the lungs..."

He held up his hand. "Hold that thought," he said, and then, phone in hand, dialed Crosswinds to check on Jasmine and the other puppies, only hanging up after being assured that all were breathing fine, had normal temperatures and heart rates.

As he hung up, he heard the back door open and shut.

"It might be best if you wait in my office," Ruby said then.

She had other help. Didn't want him around.

He got it.

Knew he deserved her rejection.

Headed to the door.

"Sebastian?"

He turned back in time to see her glance up at him. "If we caught it in time, their chances are good. Only one in one hundred healthy dogs die of poisoning that's caught in time. We should know within a couple of hours, at the most..."

Their chances were good, not great. They were dealing with less-than-two-week-old puppies. Not healthy grown dogs.

And petroleum-based poison? Like paint thinner?

The puppies were in a secure crate. No way they could get into anything.

If Ruby hadn't driven out to check on them, if she hadn't continued on to her task after he'd been such a jerk to her, those puppies would have died.

After turning on the light as he entered Ruby's office, he sat on the edge of the desk and called the detective who'd been assigned to his case. He'd been given a number to use, day or night. Glen Steele, the detective who picked up, said he'd send a team out to Crosswinds immediately.

After hanging up, Sebastian called Andy to let him know the police were coming.

And then, with too much pent-up energy coursing through him, he stood again, knocking a folder he hadn't even seen to the floor. He was going to do as she instructed, wait for her in her office. But cooped up in one room when someone had been on his property? Poisoned puppies?

Who did that?

It took a special kind of sickness to attack babies of any kind.

He picked up the folder, telling himself not to let his thoughts venture back to Ruby dating such an individual.

Whether the perp was someone she knew or not, Sebastian's property had been invaded again. Someone had actually been inside a locked building. Purposely attacked innocent puppies.

His employees had all checked out already, as he'd known they would.

Who else had been at Crosswinds since he'd stopped to see the puppies after dropping Elise back at the kennels upon returning from Colton Ranch?

A piece of paper had half slipped out of the folder. Sebastian opened the folder to right it.

The police would once again interview each of the four Crosswinds employees. Get an accounting of anyone they'd seen on the property.

And...

What was that?

Express Medical Clinic.

Ruby's name typed clearly on the first line.

He noticed that part last.

After he'd seen the result marked positive.

She was positive for something.

He closed the folder quickly. Put it back on the desk.

Didn't want to process what his one accidental glance had seen first.

Pregnancy test.

Chapter Six

It was almost eleven that night before Ruby walked into her office. She'd called Sebastian earlier. Told him he could go. Maria had offered to drive her out to pick up her SUV when they were through, but she'd declined. She could call any one of her brothers or sisters to take her, yet that night, or, she finally decided, in the morning.

She wasn't eager to have another conversation with Sebastian Cross that night. Whatever he'd been going through, whether it had been real or the result of an episode triggered from his past, she'd felt as though she'd been stabbed by his words.

Hurt beyond one friend speaking harshly to another.

She'd been hurt like a woman got hurt by a man she'd slept with. As though there'd been something romantic between them.

Because she was pregnant?

The knowledge had surfaced to taunt her any time her head hadn't been filled with medical thoughts over the past couple of hours of monitoring puppies. And waiting.

She was pregnant.

Couldn't wrap her mind around the test results, the fact

that they said what they did. Let alone get any further along than that.

The doctor at the clinic had told her to make an appointment with her ob-gyn sooner rather than later. At two months, there were many things they could determine already.

And she needed to be on vitamins.

Some of it she'd remembered from going through Hannah's pregnancy with her.

Nothing that felt at all real to her.

Or as if the information was part of her own life.

The three puppies were showing marked signs of improvement. She expected them to be just fine.

And wanted to just go home to bed with that victory the last thing on her mind for the day.

Instead, she was going to her office to sleep on the couch. The pillow and blanket she kept in the closet for that purpose would do just fine. She'd already set the alarm on her phone to wake her every two hours.

She opened her office door, ready to give up her concerns and rest, and stopped. The one person in the world she absolutely did not want to talk to that night was still there. Sitting on what was supposed to be her bed in about five minutes.

"I thought you went home." Over an hour before. She'd told him to go.

He'd never actually said he would. He'd just asked after his puppies.

"You said the little ones would need two-hour checks throughout the night." He didn't stand, or grab keys from wherever he'd stashed them, or make a single move to vacate what was soon to be her bedroom.

"That's right." She stood in the doorway. No way she was

going to be in a bedroom with the man. Not ever again. "I've already set my alarm."

"You can't be getting up every two hours. You need your rest."

What was he? The veterinarian police? As well as the dating general?

"You need to go."

"I need to apologize," he said instead, his hands on his jean-clad thighs as he met her gaze straight on. His beard was like a picture frame to the straight line of his mouth.

Drawing attention to his lack of smile.

"I want to tell you why I overreacted as I did tonight, except that I have no idea how to do that. But I know I was one hundred percent wrong and I'm truly sorry."

She wasn't in the mood to be forgiving.

She was tired. Hurt. And apparently pregnant, too.

"I just want you to know, if you need anything... I know your family gets a little overwhelming for you sometimes, and, you can, you know... If you need someone to spout off to..."

What the hell? He couldn't still be hallucinating?

Was she?

She moved into the room far enough to drop down to her chair. With the desk in between them. An office, not a bedroom. "What on earth are you talking about?"

"You were there for me that night Oscar was hurt. And then again tonight. You've seen me at my worst—at least more of it than anyone else has ever seen. And... I'm hoping that... We're friends..."

"Sure. I guess we're friends," she said, truly confused. And too tired to figure things out. "What's going on, Sebastian? Are you sick or something?" Were his struggles more than residue from his past? Was it something physical? Something that was going to get worse?

Her heart pounded and her stomach felt sick.

"I know," he said.

She frowned. Tears of frustration pushed at her. She held them back and asked, "Know what?"

"I was on the phone, leaned on your desk. I accidently knocked the file off, Ruby. I saw the test results."

The file. Results.

Her gaze landed on the only such item on her desk. The one she'd left when she'd folded up Sebastian's copies of the paperwork and put them in her satchel.

Cold, hot, nervous as hell, panicking, she stared at him. He was so calm.

And offering to be there for her?

"You know?" she asked. Was this something he wanted, then? Something he'd welcome?

She hadn't, for one second, considered that possibility.

They'd never even been on a date.

He was Wade's friend.

His nod was slow. Seemed to be filled with compassion. "Does the father know yet?"

She blinked. Shook her head. Wanted to stamp her feet. Or kick something.

"What do you mean 'does the father know?'" she asked, her tone low. Filled with warning.

He shrugged the big strong shoulders she'd run her tongue all over. "About the test results. They're dated today. And you were at my place shortly after you'd have finished here." With a sideways nod of his head, he kept right on talking. "This boyfriend… I figure, since you're keeping him a secret from your family…there might be some challenges, and in spite of my earlier words tonight, I just want you to know that I'm here to support you in..."

"Stop it." She bit out the words. Stood. Everything he'd thrown at her earlier cascaded down on her. Along with the boatloads of hurt his words had generated. "How could you think that of me?" She raised her voice. Didn't care. "Aside from the fact that we owe each other nothing in the dating department, how could you possibly think that I'd have some secret guy and, in the light of ongoing events, not tell anyone?" *Or, in light of the fact that we had sex, not tell you?* The words were there, wanting to be said. She stifled them for all she was worth.

"Hey, I'm just an innocent bystander here. My earlier outburst aside. I still take full responsibility for that."

"Move on, then. Tell me how you've drawn such a demeaning conclusion about my private life."

"I was at Colton Ranch today," he said, looking as weary as she felt. "With Elise."

He'd been avalanche training, she translated, with a definite lack of patience.

"Wade came up to me and asked me if I knew who the guy was. He thought maybe it was someone you'd met through Crosswinds. Like a handler who'd come in for training, or something."

"What?" The scream filled the hallway of the vacant clinic as she sank back down to her chair. "Has the whole world gone mad?" Or was it just her small part in it?

Pregnant? Her brother claiming she had a secret boyfriend? Sebastian accusing her of putting everyone at risk by not exposing the guy to the police investigation?

"Wade said Hannah came to him today. She was apparently really upset. Which, for Hannah..."

Ruby slumped back, every bit of energy draining out of her. Hannah had promised not to mention the baby.

"According to Wade, Hannah had irrefutable proof that you've got a secret boyfriend, and they both think that he might be the one after you. They're afraid your secret is putting you in danger."

Which was why Sebastian had been so upset earlier.

At least one thing in the world made sense.

Until she thought about telling the man sitting on her couch, who was being so kind to her, that the baby he thought belonged to someone else was his own.

Her stomach jumbling with nerves, she waved toward the lone folder on her desk. "That was her proof," she told him, slowly. Hoping maybe he'd figure things out on his own and need some space as badly as she did.

That he'd just go and leave her alone.

Because alone was how she was going to have to handle the next phase of her life. Even without thinking ahead, she'd known from the instant she'd heard the second results that she was going to be doing it by herself.

Maybe she was hoping they were going to point at folders, then talk around the issue and leave it at that.

When he sat there, looking at her expectantly, she said, "I fainted this afternoon. Hannah was..."

Sebastian sat forward, frowning, his gaze creased with concern. "You fainted? Are you okay? And you've been standing out there all night tending to my dogs? You should have said something."

He was a compassionate man. She'd known that about him...always. The way he was with dogs—he got them, just like she did. Accepted, and gave the unconditional love without reservation.

"I'm fine," she said, looking at the folder then, not at the man across the room. Thankfully, Sebastian was taking his seat again. Him towering over her was not a good thing for her equilibrium, either.

"Apparently the smell of coffee is going to be off my list for a while," she said inanely. Something she'd only just realized. "Hannah and Frannie were here having lunch," she continued, buying herself time because she was too tired to just take charge and get what was coming, over with. "They insisted we head over to Express Medical, and I did so just to quiet their fears."

"You didn't know?" More of that compassion was showing from his eyes. She hadn't realized how much she'd noticed that about him.

Because it was always focused on his dogs. Or people his dogs rescued. Or the veterans who needed his dogs.

She shook her head. "I was sure it a mistake, and told them both so. And forbade them from telling anyone about the false result. I went back for a second test after work. To prove myself right."

Would he piece it together now? She'd had the test and then driven out to his place.

Sitting forward, Sebastian rubbed his hands together, lightly, as though uncomfortable. "So...who is he, Ruby? Why the need for secrecy?"

He still didn't get it.

"It's you, Sebastian."

IT'S YOU, SEBASTIAN. He couldn't have heard her right.

No way did his name have anything to do with this one. Coming at her with accusation in his tone—yes. But...being a secret boyfriend?

Because he sure as hell couldn't be what she was trying to tell him he was.

No matter what.

He was going to live without human beings in his home for the rest of his life. That decision had been made years ago.

His dogs were his family.

Being a secret boyfriend, one who still lived alone... He could, perhaps, in the future, wrap his mind around that one, but...

He shook his head.

There was just no way.

"I used a condom," he said quietly. Careful to be respectful of any emotional state her news would have flung her into. "A fresh one. All three times."

Three times in one night.

What a night that had been.

"I know." Ruby nodded, seeming far calmer than the situation warranted. "That's one reason I was so certain the test had produced false results."

One reason. There were others? He waited to hear them. Needed to hear them. To build his case against what she was trying to make him out to be. It wasn't happening.

When she didn't elaborate, he pushed. "What were the other reasons?"

"My cycle. I've had it."

Oh. Maybe a bit too much information there. For a friend trying to be supportive. That was maybe better left to the secret boyfriend.

If there was one. The thought hit like a brick to the face. He was generally an intelligent man. Quick to grasp what was in front of him. "Hannah was there to hear the test results," he said slowly, piecing it all together. "She couldn't tell anyone about the diagnosis, and so she did the next best thing. She went to find out who the father was."

"That's my guess. It sounds like Hannah. Definitely my no-nonsense little sister."

Ruby looked tired. More than tired. She looked...lost.

He had to go.

It's you, Sebastian. Even if he'd heard her right—which he wasn't sure he had, but he wasn't asking—she had to have confused him with someone else.

Maybe if he wasn't there, she'd call the father.

Maybe she couldn't call him. If he was married. Was at home with his wife. Maybe he even had other children. Clearly, if she could tell the father, expose their relationship, she wouldn't be sitting here talking to Sebastian.

She trusted him. The knowledge felt...good.

But no way could he take on this problem. He couldn't be what she was trying to make him out to be. And trusted that she'd see that. She'd just received the news. Was still in shock.

Remembering both times she'd come upon him when emotional unrest had him at his worst, he leaned forward, elbows on his knees, and said, "Are there any more reasons?" For him, rational talking helped. Focusing on the reality right in front of him, little pieces at a time.

"I've only had sex once in two years. The odds are just too incredulous to believe."

Once. In two years.

She'd meant two months, right? Only once since him?

He stared at her. She was staring right back at him. Gaze clear. Not happy. But clear.

It's you, Sebastian.

He stood up and strode out.

Chapter Seven

Ruby hadn't given Sebastian's potential reaction a whole lot of thought. She hadn't even been able to land on one of her own, let alone imagine his.

However, him calmly walking out on her, without a word, was a complete surprise.

Sitting there at her desk, at nearly midnight, with most of the city outside asleep, she'd never felt more alone in her life.

Hannah, damn her, had been worried, trying to watch out for Ruby, to help her deal with a situation she'd clearly not been tending to well herself. And Ruby loved her for it. But her sister had just put the weight of twelve Coltons on her shoulders, when she wasn't even handling the tiny weight of one growing inside her.

Denial was the first stage of grief.

Was it a stage of life, too?

Was she grieving the loss of the life she wanted?

Or just giving herself time to process?

She heard steps in the hallway. Grabbed the gun her father had made her learn how to use and keep in her desk drawer, because she was a Colton and you never knew...

And saw Sebastian standing in her doorway, the box of puppies in his arms.

She didn't say a word. The little ones were his. And out of imminent danger. Being with their mother would be a good thing. And Sebastian would remain with them all night. She didn't have a doubt about that.

Instead of saying whatever goodbye she'd figured he'd come to say, he walked into the office. He glanced at the gun she held, but didn't hesitate as he stood directly in front of her desk.

"These are the babies in my life," he told her. "The only babies I can ever have."

After sliding the gun back into its place, she locked the drawer with the switch on the underside of her desk. "I'm not asking anything from you, Sebastian," she said, feeling steady with the words.

She hadn't consciously thought about it, but there it was. Sitting right with her.

"Like you, I didn't expect or want this, but I knew this afternoon that if the positive result was accurate, I was going to have the baby. My choice. Made completely without you. We—you and I together—don't have to do anything differently, change anything about our relationship. We work well together, and… I hope, as you said tonight, we're friends, too…"

He shook his head. Opened his mouth and, not ready for his rejection, she blurted out more words. "I can do this alone. As we've already established, I have a huge, nosy, caring family who will butt in all the time and help me. Even when I don't need it." She smiled. It hurt her cheeks.

Everything she was saying hurt, too.

She'd drawn a metaphorical picture of the way she'd wanted her life to look. She was in the middle, a spinster. The cacophony of growing up in such a large family, the tension between her parents, her mother's hurt feelings, the distance…and then Aunt Jessie and Uncle Buck… The idea of bringing any chance of any of that into her own home…

In the picture, Hannah's sweet Lucy had been the little love of her life. Being an aunt fulfilled her motherly instincts just fine. And her practice, the animals who consumed her days and a lot of her nights, too, took up most of the rest of the space. With just enough room left over to fit every member of her family and Owl Creek's citizens. The town was her picture frame. The pieces of wood that supported her, kept her together.

Sebastian seemed to shrink as he stood there, silently holding his box. The puppies were sleeping. She'd noticed that immediately. And were breathing normally.

"You deserve a stable, loving husband. Your children, as much or more so." When he finally spoke, the words carried calmness. Truth. "As you witnessed for yourself earlier tonight, I can't provide that. Not because I don't want to, or because I'm not willing to. Not because I wouldn't give my all to try, but because it's out of my control."

If Oscar was PTSD-trained…or Sebastian got a second dog that was…

She stopped the thought short. No wishing for stars in the sky on a sunny day.

"It's okay," she told him. "I don't want a husband, Sebastian. I've never had a long-term relationship because I didn't want one. I'm thirty and single by choice." The words came easily. There was a new catch in her heart as she said them, though.

And a hose filled with panic blowing a gasket inside her. How did a strong-minded, independent woman like herself accept the fact that she'd had no choice in the biggest matter in her life? Keeping the baby was a choice.

But getting pregnant? She'd taken precautions and...

"That night..." Sebastian said, as though reading her thoughts. Her gaze darted to him as he continued, "If it hadn't been for my panic attack, we'd never have..."

No, they wouldn't have. But... "I wanted to." He had to know that she hadn't been completely selfless that night. Sex asked too much from her to just be a distraction.

For a second there, his eyes lit up and he grinned. Her lower belly responded.

Then he sobered. "That panic attack is precisely why I can't offer you..."

"I wouldn't accept it if you did," she told him quietly. She didn't want any marriage. Let alone one born out of pity or obligation—which was what her parents' marriage had been. Or had become, by the time Ruby was old enough to be aware of such things.

Maybe all marriages became that, inside a home's walls. How did anyone really know?

"I'll be that friend I spoke about a little bit ago. When I was thinking there was a boyfriend..."

She nodded. A little smile flowered inside her. "I'd like that."

And now, he should go. Since he was taking the puppies back to Jasmine, she could go home and get some rest.

Except that her car was at his place.

She most definitely was not going back there. Not this late at night. Without an emergency to tend to.

Besides, her little two-bedroom house on the lake was calling to her. It was all hers. And only hers.

Sebastian wasn't leaving. "I should be there when you tell your family I'm the father."

Her family and Sebastian—her father and Wade and Sebastian—in the same room when she announced that she'd gotten knocked up by mistake and was going to be a single mother?

She could feel the tension all the way up to her ears. The pressure...

"Can we leave that thought for another day?" she asked him. "Let's wait at least until after I've had my first appointment before we tell anyone anything..." There could be something that would prevent the pregnancy from continuing. She was still in her first trimester. Could miscarry.

And did not want to.

A strange sense of grief had hit as soon as she'd thought of the possibility of losing the baby. So much so that she issued a quick, silent and very fervent prayer to the fates that her fetus was healthy.

The sensation took over her entire being. That need for the little raspberry-sized being growing inside her to be well.

Not understanding herself, or life in general, she settled for a "thank you" to Sebastian when he agreed to her request.

Him being the father of her baby would be their secret.

For the moment.

"Would you mind giving me a ride home?" she asked him then, thinking his ready acceptance would be a given. After all, she was carrying their mutual result of the choice they'd made together to have sex. He could provide some transportation.

Didn't mean she needed him. Or wanted his help.

It was just the way the math added up.

SEBASTIAN WAS SO far out of his element that he couldn't find himself. He saw the immediate steps in front of him and took them.

He got the box of sleeping puppies settled in his truck, waited for Ruby to climb in and started the engine.

Looking out the windshield, the future hung before him. Drive off the lot and down the mile or so to Ruby's little house on the lake. He'd been by it countless times. Had never been inside.

His child would be living there.

The thought came and he sat with it.

He wasn't going to be a husband, or a live-in father, but he was going to have a biological child in the world.

It didn't compute.

He'd made his decisions. Set his course.

But sometimes, as had happened with the tragic deaths of his parents, life went off course. He was going to have to adjust.

He couldn't change what he couldn't change. His occasional panic attacks. The unpredictable nightmares. His need to live alone.

But he had a lot of rerouting to do.

The child would come first. What was best for the life he and Ruby had created.

And Ruby was his responsibility, too. In part. Since she was housing the child—over the next seven months, but after that, too.

He'd call his banker in the morning. Start the work on a new financial plan.

And someone was out to get him...and possibly her. A vision of the completely shattered windshield—one bullet in the exact right spot—on her vehicle, not his, shot through his mind as he pulled into Ruby's driveway. Saw the dark house with the huge lake right behind it.

Someone could swim ashore...hide in the reeds, then behind the trees in her yard.

He got out when she did. Reached for the box of puppies.

"What are you doing?" she asked, stopping at the front of his truck on her way to the sidewalk leading up to her front door.

"Based on the poison information you provided, and on some evidence found at the scene tonight, Glen Steele determined that the puppies were being poisoned when you pulled up to my house. That it's likely all the puppies, and Jasmine, too, would have died if you hadn't arrived when you did. This guy's for real, Ruby, and he's escalating."

"And you're afraid to go home?"

How could a woman's scrunched-up face look so cute to him in that moment?

"Hell no. I'm uncomfortable leaving you home alone, especially arriving this late, until we know more."

The set of her chin didn't budge. "What on earth does the time matter? If I'd come home earlier, I'd still be here now, this late."

Right. If she'd arrived home alone, and someone had been watching...

He had to get himself together. Focus.

"I'd still like to stay," he said quietly. How could he protect her if he wasn't there?

"I don't want to be rude, Sebastian, but you are not staying here. I'm going inside. Alone. And I'll have someone bring me out in the morning to get my SUV. I appreciate your concern. I know we're both a bit off-kilter. I'm glad we're going to be friends through all of this. And there's no way I'm risking more intimate moments with you right now. Good night."

He stood there and watched as she turned, walked slowly, steadily, up to her door, went inside and shut the door behind her. He watched until he saw lights come on.

And then he drove around a bit and checked back.

Once. Twice.

Thinking about her. About the baby she was carrying.

Needing a battle plan.

Finding no ready answers.

Sometime after one, he caught a glimpse of himself from the outside looking in. A guy in a truck, driving the same roads, watching a house, when he needed to be getting three puppies back to their mother, checking everything over, setting his alarm for two-hour intervals and stretching out on a mat in the medical building that had been invaded by a would-be killer that night.

The police were on the case. Ruby was a Colton, a member of the family that owned half the town—they'd definitely be watching over her. Robert would have already seen to that.

She wasn't telling anyone he was the father of the baby yet. She hadn't even been to the doctor to confirm that things were in place to progress normally.

He had some time to figure it all out.

RUBY CALLED FOR an obstetrician appointment in Connors as soon as she was up and showered Friday morning. And was lucky enough to grab a canceled appointment. She'd intended to catch a ride out to Crosswinds to get her vehicle, but there'd been a text from Sebastian saying he'd had it delivered. When she checked him on it, she found the SUV locked in her driveway.

She had the keys.

He must have had it towed.

Which couldn't have been cheap.

When she started to wonder how he'd explained the choice to the truck driver, she shook her head and pushed the thought away. Didn't matter to her what someone else had said to another. She had her vehicle.

The forty-five-minute drive to the medical complex where she'd been going since she was a kid calmed her.

She was taking action. Gathering information. From there, she could determine her next step. And the one after that.

She was taking control of her life, rather than letting life control her.

She was getting away from Owl Creek, shrapnel in Oscar, poisoned puppies, a shot-out windshield, the secret-boyfriend drama created by her sisters… and Sebastian Cross. For the morning, she could just breathe.

And she did so fairly well, remaining calm and in charge of her life, right up until she was lying on the table for the ultrasound her doctor had just ordered. The procedure had been part of the canceled appointment Ruby had snagged, and the timing was right.

Wasn't it great how that all worked out? Saved Ruby a trip back.

Except that she wasn't mentally prepared. Not for the procedure—she'd have worn pants that were easier to slide down to her pelvic bone to make room for the Doppler to travel in the gel. And she wasn't ready to be face-to-face with the screen that would make the inconceivable a medical reality to her.

Internally, Dr. Evelyn had said, everything looked perfect.

Things that were supposed to be changing inside of her were doing so right on target and as well as she liked to see them.

According to the doctor, she was most definitely pregnant.

Ruby still couldn't grasp the concept in terms of herself. The past twenty-four hours were like an out-of-body experience.

She felt the gel. Heard the technician explain things she already knew. Ultrasound was ultrasound, whether you were using it to diagnose human bodies or animal ones.

Frozen, lying stiffly, her arms tense at her side, her fingers clenched into fists, she stared at the ceiling as the procedure began.

Concentrated on the sensation of cold jelly spreading over her stomach. The there and then. Not the what-would-be.

Tried not to hear the deafening lack of sound as the technician's silence permeated the room.

Find the fetus. Measure. Determine that everything was normal. She listed the woman's duties as far as she could think through them.

A muffled thump sounded in the room. Again and again. Rhythmically. Booming through every wave in Ruby's eardrum. Faster than she normally heard.

But it was undeniable just the same. Her head turned of its own accord. Her gaze landed on the grayscale image on screen and she couldn't look away.

There it was.

She saw it immediately. Analyzed every inch of material on the screen. Knew exactly what she was looking at. And diagnosing.

Her. Alone. By herself.

The uterus looked great. The fetus. Perfectly positioned. And that sound, muffled and seemingly so loud…

"We have a heartbeat," the technician said, pleasure in her tone.

Stating the obvious.

And Ruby burst into tears.

Chapter Eight

Sebastian checked on the puppies several times that day, finding irony in the fact that he was tending to babies he owned when he'd never be a father to his own child.

The child couldn't know about their biological connection. Sebastian could be a friend to Ruby and nothing more.

But he could assist Ruby in any way possible. He'd already spoken with his financial advisor, who was setting up a trust fund for the child that Ruby was carrying.

In her name.

And by noon, he was convincing himself that it would all be okay. When problems arose—as they always did—he and Ruby would work them out, with her having the final say.

If he didn't take ownership over the situation, he'd be okay.

What he did intend to get to the bottom of was the escalating vandalism on his property.

Three puppies had almost died.

He wasn't going to sit back and wait for more to happen. He needed answers, even if he had to find them himself.

Calling Glen Steele, he asked for a full rundown of what the police had found the night before, what they made of the evidence and what more he could do to assist.

They'd found a partial smudge of a footprint not far outside a window in the medical building. The window facing the kennels had shrubbery beneath it, which made the footprint unusual. They'd also found some freshly fallen greenery. The window had been found unlocked and had been opened recently, with no obvious signs of a break-in.

Which made no sense to him. The windows, most particularly in the medical building, were always kept locked.

The poison had been administered, they believed, through puppy treats. A tainted one was found several feet from the building, on the way down to the lake.

To that end, Sebastian arranged to have surveillance cameras installed along the shore of his land by nightfall. He wasn't sure what good they'd do, since the culprit had managed to avoid all cameras around the kennels and medical building, but it was worth trying. He threw away all the dog food on the premises and ordered new options to be delivered by feeding time that night.

But he didn't figure that that would make any difference, either, as the puppy treat found in the grass was not anything he'd had on site.

Clearly, his place was being targeted. For what reason, no one knew. The police weren't completely ruling out Ruby as a target, either. Though they were less worried that the attacks had anything to do with her, they noted that she'd been present during the last two of them.

They had acknowledged that perhaps her presence, her arrival at his house the evening before, had prevented the rest of the puppies, and possibly Jasmine, from being poisoned as well.

Her arrival. She hadn't been at his house to see to the puppies. She'd seen the puppies only because she'd walked out on him when he'd been such a jerk to her.

She'd been there to tell him about the baby.

It was no mistake that he'd been in the throes of a nightmare. Fate intervening, showing him why he couldn't be a father, before he found out he'd biologically created a human being.

Still didn't explain his emotional overreaction to Wade's news the day before. His friend had questioned him before the nightmare. After his session with Malcolm and Elise, Sebastian had been feeling good.

But because he'd thought Ruby had had a boyfriend when she'd had sex with him, he'd suddenly felt sucker-punched.

Come at her like a pubescent boy.

At a time when she'd needed him to be a support.

It was just more proof to him that he was best with dogs as his family, not people. His parents, a high-profile thoracic surgeon and a well-known philanthropist, had been gone more than they'd been home when he was growing up. That, coupled with the summers he spent away from his school friends in Boise and being made to stay at the remote cabin at Owl Creek with a nanny, meant that he'd pretty much been a loner his whole life. Not unhappy. At all. He'd always been treated with care and respect. He'd loved Owl Creek. And had had every advantage in Boise, too. He'd had Jerry. The spaniel had been his constant. Winter. Summer. Boise. Owl Creek. Always home. In his room every night.

Until the year he'd graduated from high school. And then he'd joined the Marines, where he'd been a member of another family.

Several times that day he thought about calling Ruby. Felt compelled to do so. But knew the desire was driven by his own selfishness, not with her best interests in mind.

Just as his insistence that he was going to stay with her

the previous night had been. It would have made him feel better to be there protecting her from whatever boogeyman might appear out of the ether. In making the choice, he hadn't considered how having him there in her space would have made her feel.

Maybe growing up the only child of wealthy parents had made him a spoiled brat.

He didn't give in to any of his instincts to drive into town and check on Ruby, either. He'd texted her Friday night, just asking how she was.

Saw her text back: Fine. And let it go.

And on Saturday, he got back to dedicating himself to work that helped others survive traumatic situations. Jaxon Walker, a new handler, had arrived in Boise the night before, was driving to Owl Creek Saturday morning to check into a hotel in town. He would be heading out to Crosswinds to meet Echo, the two-year-old male search-and-rescue shepherd that Sebastian had been training for him. Jaxon, a detective with the Buffalo, New York, police had been referred to Sebastian, and if all went well, Crosswinds could be training another dozen dogs through Jaxon and his contacts.

As Sebastian headed to the kennel to prepare for the first session between Jaxon and Echo, he got a thrill considering the potential successful searches, with the future lives saved by his dogs. Similar to the way he'd felt the first time he'd put on his Marine uniform, knowing that he was willing to give his life to fight for his country's safety and freedom.

Protecting and saving lives—those were his callings. And they were good ones. He just had to make sure that he didn't let his enthusiasm to care for others overstep onto Ruby's rights to live her own way.

Even while he spent the rest of his life doing what he could to protect her and the child she was carrying.

Not an easy task he'd set for himself, but one he was up to, he was sure. Easy had never been his way.

As it turned out, Jaxon Walker, clearly as eager as Sebastian to get their association started, showed up more than half an hour early. Sebastian hadn't even gone in to spend his usual few minutes with Echo yet.

Energized by the other man's enthusiasm, he invited Jaxon into the kennel with him, and gave the man a general spiel about the work they did, pointing out various training areas. He was still several yards from Echo's kennel when he heard whining and crashing up against a kennel door.

Instantly alarmed, his mind immediately going to Jasmine and her puppies, Sebastian called for help and had everyone on site checking every kennel for signs of a distressed dog.

He headed straight toward Echo, was relieved to see the dog standing and wagging his tail at his door. Still a few feet away, noting the dog's empty water bowl, he made a mental note to talk to Bryony—his youngest employee, at twenty—who'd been in charge of watering that day.

And then, as Echo started to whine and jump up at her door, he frowned.

"Down," he said firmly. "Echo, sit." Basic commands the dog had followed without fail since his eleventh week of life.

When Echo continued to ecstatically greet his approaching visitors, a sense of foreboding came over Sebastian. Something was wrong.

Very, very wrong.

His hunch played out in the worst possible scenario over the next twenty minutes—which was as long as Jaxon Walker hung around Crosswinds.

Echo, once out of his kennel, ran around uncontrollably. Sniffing. Digging. But not on cue, and not at anything that mattered.

The dog wouldn't come. Jumped up on Sebastian for treats. And ran off playing with another dog in training.

Jaxon, obviously disgusted, told Sebastian that he was not only taking Crosswinds off his list, but was also going to spread the word to other law enforcement as well, and strode out.

It was the single most awful moment of Sebastian's career with Crosswinds.

And he did what he had to do.

He called Ruby.

WHEN SHE SAW Sebastian's number come up on her phone, Ruby almost didn't answer. His text the night before had been...nice.

Welcome, even.

And enough.

Other than her clients and patients and employees, she didn't want to see anyone—most particularly not him.

So much so that she'd done nothing to stop the spread of her sister's secret-boyfriend saga. Or the amateur detective work her family was engaged in to find her out.

Let them spin their wheels, waste their time and fail, she thought.

At least it would keep them off her back for a couple of days. Time for her to come to terms with the fact that her world had been irrevocably changed...forever.

To accept that she wasn't going to be living the life she'd planned.

And to figure out why her heart was so protective of, so

incredibly caring about, a tiny floating mass she absolutely hadn't ever wanted.

She was trying to wrap her mind around the fact that she was going to be a mother. That in roughly seven months' time, she'd be dealing with breast feeding every two hours, diaper changes and...

The phone had quit ringing.

But it started up again.

"Hello?" Sitting at her desk, trying to get her breath back from the gulp she'd just taken, Ruby figured it was better to answer a call then have the man on her doorstep.

If indeed, he had any intention of coming anywhere near her once he'd had the time to process her news.

"Ruby?" His voice had an unsettled tone. If he was just making an assuage-the-guilt call, she'd put an end to that immediately.

"What do you need, Sebastian?" she asked in her calmest, most professional voice.

"You."

Her heart leaped. To the ceiling. Stuck there.

"Out here," he said, loosening her emotions from their elated state, crashing them to the ground.

It had to be hormones, she thought briefly, before she sat upright. "What's wrong?"

She should have known, should have sensed...

"It's Echo. He's out of his head. Won't follow commands, won't..."

He'd had Echo's handler, some bigwig cop from Buffalo, coming in that day. "I'm on my way," she told him, her bag already over her shoulder before she dropped her phone into it.

Letting her receptionist know that she was out on a call,

she made it to Crosswinds in seven minutes. Pulled up next to the kennels and headed straight for Echo's caged room, before noticing the confusion out on one of the training courses.

Echo, running and playing with another dog, Lucky, who'd been in training for months.

Lucky, bless his heart, was sitting at attention, on command, while Sebastian and his other trainer, Della Winslow, were trying to corral the shepherd.

"Hey, Dr. Colton, I was just in Echo's kennel, filling her water again—it was empty and I'd just filled it a couple of hours ago. She'd thrown up in the back of it, behind her bed, and I found this in it…" Bryony, in jeans and cowboy boots, held up a couple of pieces of dark paper, and Ruby's heart sank.

After thanking the kennel assistant, she grabbed a handful of dog treats and ran out to Sebastian and Della, slowing as she neared the door to the training area, where they had Echo at least semi contained.

Barely glancing at either of the humans, she held out the treats, calling to the wild dog. Whether it was the new voice in her immediate vicinity or the word *treat*, Echo, looking toward Ruby's outstretched hand, stopped long enough for Sebastian to get hold of the dog's collar and Della snapped on a leash.

Within minutes, Ruby had the dog in the medical building, with Sebastian beside her, holding Echo steady while she listened to the dog's heart rate. She administered activated charcoal and waited in the building while Sebastian turned the dog over to Della and the others to watch over her for the next several hours.

As soon as he returned, Ruby held out her hand. "Bryony

found this in Echo's kennel," she said, handing him the crumpled and stained pieces of paper she'd brought back with her.

"Dark chocolate?" He looked from the paper to her. "A fifteen-ounce package?"

"We have to assume he ate it all," she told him, finally, for the first time, meeting his eyes. "It could kill him, Sebastian. I don't think it will. He's young. His heartbeat is rapid, but not alarmingly so. He vomited afterward, so that's a good sign. Hopefully the activated charcoal was introduced soon enough to counteract the theobromine and caffeine in his system."

He nodded. Held her gaze. And it was like he was talking to her. Out loud. She heard his frustration. His worry. His pain.

And his anger, too.

Still watching her, he pulled out his phone and dialed Glen Steele.

"We've got the type of chocolate, the amount purchased—we have to be able to get something off from this, even if we have to go to every store in town ourselves," he said after hanging up with the detective's assertion that he was on his way out.

At first, thinking his *we* meant him and her, Ruby's heart swelled. With him. For him.

And then she realized that he'd been using a generic *we* to encompass everyone working on the case.

"I'm going to stay a while," she told him then. Because she didn't want to leave. Not him. Not Echo.

She didn't want to sit home by herself on a Saturday night, knowing that she was taking on the biggest challenge of her life and would be doing it all alone.

"If he does go into cardiac arrest, the ten minutes it would take me to get here could be a matter of his life or death."

From chocolate.

Sebastian didn't argue. Because he wanted her there? Felt a sense that she should be there, with him, as she did? Or because he was too distracted to argue? She didn't know.

"It could just be one of your employees brought it to work and…"

"No food in the kennels, ever," he said.

She hadn't been sold on the theory, anyway. Who'd drop a fifteen-ounce bar of chocolate and not notice? Or carry one in their pocket while they were working? It wasn't like a bar that size would fit in a normal pocket.

"I'm guessing he got a hold of it, that it was given to him sometime before daylight," Ruby said then, needing to help him. To fill the silence that was growing too deep. "It can take hours for a dog to react…"

"Before anyone got here," Sebastian said. "Every single attack has been in the dark. I just don't get it. What is this guy trying to prove?"

"You said the police think he's trying to sabotage Crosswinds for some reason. To run you out of business."

"It's one theory." He was watching her again. Really watching. Her eyes, her face, down her body and back to her eyes. "And it makes a certain kind of sense. This thing with Echo definitely cost me today—and who knows for how long into the future." He told her about the detective's parting remark regarding spreading the word among other police departments to take Crosswinds off their list. "Who am I hurting out here?"

Her heart lurched at the tone in his voice. And she took a step forward.

"Don't let him get to you, Sebastian. Don't let him win. He made a mistake, giving Echo the whole bar, paper and all. Maybe you're right and the police will be able to find him through its purchase. And even if they can't, he left behind tangible evidence this time."

He nodded. "Thank God for you," he told her then. "He hits and you swoop in and save us, three times now."

Because he'd called her, yes. At least two of the three times. The puppies two nights before—well, that had been... not him calling her.

She'd been there for an entirely different reason.

And she and Sebastian were going to have to talk more about that.

But not yet. Not with Detective Steele on his way.

"I didn't save you today," she said. "You still lost Jaxon, but, if you'll allow me to, I can call him while he's still here in town. I can explain from a medical perspective why the dog was acting as he was."

Shaking his head, Sebastian pulled out his phone. "That's something I can do myself," he told her, and walked out of the building.

Because that's how he worked. Doing everything he could possibly do by himself.

Just like her.

Independent loners. Both of them.

Which didn't bode well for the baby they'd created.

Chapter Nine

Jaxon Walker agreed to another trip out to Crosswinds. He'd already driven back to Boise, hoping to catch an earlier flight out, but said he'd check into a hotel instead and let Sebastian know when he'd be in Owl Creek the next day. While Sebastian had been adamant about keeping the attacks against his business out of the news and away from his clients, he'd told the detective what had been going on, and instead of losing a client, he seemed to have gained another law-enforcement person with a mind to discuss the case and the motive.

All anyone could think of was that someone needed revenge against him. Or, as Jaxon had pointed out in their phone conversation, perhaps against his mom or dad. The property upon which he'd built Crosswinds had been in his family for generations. It was all that was left of his parents' estate. Sebastian had used a chunk of his inheritance to renovate the cabin and build Crosswinds, as well as to support himself until he'd grown the company into the elite training facility it was. The business was lucrative. And he'd invested well himself. Had more money than he'd ever spend. No one but his financial advisor knew that. He didn't care about spending the money. He needed the security.

Maybe, until he'd made a success out of Crosswinds, no

one had known there was anything left of Sebastian's parents to go after.

It was the most workable theory Sebastian had heard. And when he'd shared it with Ruby after the police left, she'd agreed with him.

"Your father was a doctor, so maybe there's someone who lost a loved one he couldn't save—a kid who's now grown, who maybe had a hard life after their parent died." It made sense. Better sense than anything else he'd heard to date.

At Jaxon's suggestion, the police were already broadening their search into his parents' lives. For all Sebastian knew, one or the other of them had had an affair and there was some illegitimate child who was jealous that Sebastian had everything. Maybe it was someone who had just, in recent months, discovered their heritage through one of the popular DNA-testing organizations.

The thought was out there. He recognized that.

And yet...the uncertainty lingered.

He stood in the kennel with Ruby, watching Echo, who'd calmed dramatically and whose heart rate Ruby had just pronounced a little high, still, but within normal range. Sebastian felt a twinge of resentment when his phone rang.

Because...what? He wanted a minute alone with the woman he'd already determined he didn't want to be personally alone with?

The call took all of thirty seconds. Phone still in hand after he hang up, Sebastian told Ruby, "James Greenaway just quit." One of his three part-timers, James had been cleaning out the kennels. "He said that three interviews with the police was enough. He didn't do anything wrong, but they're treating him like a suspect. He wants to be done."

Sebastian could have argued, tried to reason with James,

talk him back to work, but he hadn't. He didn't blame the kid. And hoped that James had nothing to do with the attacks. He'd hired him right out of high school. Had had hopes of moving him up to assistant trainer in another year or so.

Still standing there in the dimly lit structure that housed the dogs' separate living quarters, Sebastian called Steele one more time to report James's resignation.

"It's probably going to make the police look at him harder," Ruby said as he disconnected that call. She still didn't seem to be in any great hurry to leave.

He nodded, not liking the feeling of helplessness that had been pervading his life over the past weeks. First Oscar's gunshot injury, then Ruby's windshield, the puppies, and Echo...

A baby.

"How exactly does putting you out of business, if this is what the guy's trying to do, help him any? You still own the land. And five lakefront acres with the newly remodeled, enlarged and updated home..."

"Unless he's just bitter and trying to make me suffer as he has." Before killing him? And filing for a possible inheritance? The only way that worked was if there was another biological child...

He stared at Ruby.

"What?"

"I set up a trust for...the child. It's in your name, so you can use the money however you see fit without having to go through any hoops."

"I don't need your money, Sebastian." In her jeans, tennis shoes and long-sleeved short black shirt, she stood up to him. Didn't back away.

And he said, "It's done, Ruby. You can choose to use it

or not, and whatever is there when the child turns eighteen will belong to them." But something else had just occurred to him.

"On Monday, I'm going to be drawing up a will." He'd write it yet that night. Sign it. In case something happened to him over the weekend. "Everything I have will go to the child in the event of my death."

Her frown, the rush of emotion in her gaze, held him captive. "Don't talk like that," she said. "This guy…they're going to stop him."

He nodded. Wasn't fearing for his life.

He was just figuring out how to be a father to a child he couldn't live with or raise.

SHE HAD TO get out. Get away from Sebastian's magnetism. His conscientious heart.

He wasn't offering to be an active father to her child. She wouldn't accept if he had been.

So why did his distance, and yet his immediate help with money and wills—legal, lawyerly things—hurt?

He was the only person in the world other than herself who knew that he was her baby's father. The only one who could share that with her.

And he was thinking about money and wills.

She understood.

Admired him.

And had to hold back tears because…his actions left her feeling utterly alone. In a building filled with him. And dogs.

How could she possibly feel bereft surrounded by any of her beloved four-legged beings?

"I need to get back," she said, maintaining her calm as she started for the door. She was not going to make a scene. Or

give Sebastian any reason to doubt that she could be pregnant with his child while remaining friends and maintaining a healthy working relationship.

At the door, she smiled at Della, who was coming into
the kennel, and when the trainer spoke to Sebastian, Ruby
just kept on walking.

With all the outside lights still on in the training areas,
she could make her way on her own as though the sunshine
still lit her way.

One foot in front of other.

To her waiting SUV. Paid for. In her name. Her property.
Hers. And, soon to have a car seat in it, would be the baby's
main mode of transporation, too.

The little flip-flop in her heart at the thought was…nice.

Realizing that her vehicle looked a little lopsided was not
nice, however. Hurrying, wanting to get out of there before
Sebastian came to find her—or, maybe worse, didn't—Ruby
looked at the back driver-side tire with a sinking sensation
that went far beyond having a flat.

The tires were less than a year old. Still under warranty.

Didn't mean she hadn't punctured one. Driven over a nail.
It happened.

But that it would go flat right now? Another injury to her
vehicle at Sebastian's? After dark?

She knew what he was going to think, even before she
called him.

Truth was, she was having a hard time not going there
herself.

Their vandal had struck again.

But to what purpose? And how? The lights had been on.

Around the kennels. Not behind her car. And not down
by the lake.

"It's just a flat," she told Sebastian when he came jogging over from the kennels.

"Steele has officers coming back out just to check the area," he told her. "And for now, you need to stay away from Crosswinds."

"Don't be ridiculous, Sebastian. This one is probably not even an attack. Why just do one tire?" And only her car?

"I don't know why." His tone held the frustration she could read on his expression as he bent to the tire, shining his phone light all around it, following with his hand. "I don't know why any of this is happening. But I do agree that one flat tire seems to be a bit of a de-escalation. Why risk getting caught for one tire?"

Unless the perpetrator had been interrupted again. Like with the puppies.

From his squatting position, he came back with, "How could anyone have known that Echo was the one dog that would cost me the most, today of all days?" He looked up at her and then added, "I can't find anything. Not a nail, or an obvious cut." Moving around to the back, he opened the hatch and the flooring to access the spare tire.

"You don't have to change that," Ruby said quickly. "I'll call…"

"Are you serious?" The look he gave her was long and hard. "I know how to change a tire. And would do so for anyone who got a flat on my land."

With a nod, she silently acknowledged her overreaction, with a note to keep a better watch on herself.

"You don't think Echo was just a random choice," she said then. Sebastian had a real issue going on. One that involved both of them. One they could actually talk about.

"Do you?"

She didn't. The handler in town, the potential for so many more clients… "But how would anyone know that?"

He hauled out the tire, set it standing up right next to him, holding it with his jean-clad knee. And met her gaze. "I know, right?"

Only someone who knew…

"You think James is doing this? But why?"

"Maybe not doing it, but he could have been passing on information. Even unknowingly. Just talking about work…"

She loved that he was trying to think the best of his young, ex-employee. And wasn't so sure that James couldn't be behind the vandalism. "His dad died in Afghanistan, did you know that?"

He nodded. "We talked it about it once."

"Maybe he's jealous that you came back. That you're building something great here, and helping other veterans better their lives, when he's struggling to make ends meet."

He shook his head, then said, "Maybe, but it doesn't make sense. I've been paying his community college tuition."

She hadn't known that. Flooded with warmth to know that he'd do such a thing. And remembered the baby she was carrying.

One who wouldn't have a father, but would have Sebastian paying college tuition.

"I went to the doctor yesterday." She didn't plan the words. They just fell out. And when she heard them out in the open, she started to panic. She didn't have answers yet. Didn't want to talk to him again until she had herself firmly settled wherever she was going to land with her new life. "There was a cancellation," she said, starting to babble. "A woman who'd also had an ultrasound scheduled, so I was able to get it all over with in one quick visit."

There. It was done. Time to move on. "What do you need

me to do there?" she asked, pointing toward the spare tire he was still holding. When he didn't answer, she looked up at him. The struggle in his gaze grabbed her.

"I can just send someone to get the vehicle in the morning," she said inanely. "Catch a ride home with Della."

"Do I ask what you found out? How it went?" He seemed stupefied. Frozen.

"I don't know." She barely got the words out.

"I feel like I need to know."

Her heart soared for the second it took her to get a hold of it. "Then I guess you should ask."

She didn't offer the answer. He had to need it badly enough to seek it.

Instead of asking, he set about changing her tire. Like a madman in a race to save his life. Bolts flew out, tire off, tire on, bolts back in. All without a noticeable breath.

Tool loaded back in her spare-tire compartment. Floorboard replaced.

He finally spoke. "Steele asked that you leave the tire, for now. As possible evidence. Just in case."

She nodded. "Thank you." She didn't look his way as, hugging her satchel to her side, she reached for the driver's-side handle.

"Is everything okay?"

Freezing with one foot on the floor of the car, the other still on the ground, she faced the windshield, not Sebastian, and said, "Yes."

She moved to sit down, but stopped again as he asked, "What did the doctor say?"

She'd told him to ask. Implied that she'd answer. "About what?"

"Everything."

Ruby took her foot back out of the car, but left the door

open, leaned herself against the frame and part of the seat. Ready to fall in. To get away.

"I'm eight weeks along, everything looks perfect—her word, not mine. She said I needed to start prenatal vitamins, and that she'd see me in a month." She left out the part where she'd said Ruby might experience some fatigue, and to get enough rest. Those were both on her.

"And the ultrasound?"

Ruby stared at him. "We're really going to do this?"

His expression didn't harden, really, but it grew less tentative. He crossed his arms. "You said to ask."

"Why are you?"

With a shrug, Sebastian met her gaze, his face half-shadowed by the bright lights on one side of him and darkness on the other. "I have no idea," he said, sounding like the words had been wrung out of him.

And once again, her heart relented. "If you're feeling guilty, Sebastian, don't. This isn't on you. My choice. I don't need a man to complete me. I'm as independent as you are. I don't know why this happened. The odds are so completely against it. We only did it one night. It was my first time in years, and we used condoms. The chances are minuscule and yet..."

She heard herself. Grew instantly self-conscious that she was babbling again, and finally said, "I'm okay doing this alone."

"I don't think it's guilt that's pushing me to know."

Oh. She stared at him, her mouth suddenly dry as her heart pounded. Not in any way that felt good. "What then?" she asked.

When he shrugged, shook his head again, she wanted to sit down, shut the door in his face and gun it out of there.

Which made about as much sense as him just shaking his head at the important answers.

"How was the ultrasound?"

A *fine* came to mind first. Succinct. Followed by a dramatic exit. She waited herself out. "It was amazing," she said, finally telling him the truth. "I look at those films all the time, and so seeing, not only a human one, but my own body, with that tiny orb of life in my own uterus..."

Her throat clogged up with tears and she had to stop. Swallowed. Blinked. Took a deep breath. Needed to show him how strong she was. How capable.

And then she looked at his face, the set chin, unsmiling mouth, eyes wide...and glistening.

"I heard the heartbeat," she told him. Felt her own chin trembling and sat down. "That was it," she concluded, all business, a doctor in her own right. Her own field. "Thanks again for changing my tire," she said, then shut the door, started her vehicle, pulled away and...

Left him standing there.

Unmoving.

The first glance in the rearview mirror was a mistake.

The second one, curiosity.

The third, just plain not smart.

If she lived twenty lifetimes, she was never going to forget the sight of that big mountain man, the father of her baby, standing all alone.

Chapter Ten

A razor-thin spike was found in Ruby's tire. A matching piece had been retrieved from the ground nearby. While there was a small chance that she'd brought the spike in with her, the bigger probability was that the shard had been put in her normal parking spot on the chance that she'd drive over it.

Not a life-threatening event. Not even a potentially dangerous one. At most, she'd have had a slow leak, rather than the more rapid one that had transpired.

Sebastian wanted to believe the flat tire on Saturday night was just a fluke. But his gut was telling him otherwise. No one but Ruby parked next to the medical building.

She parked there every single time she was at Crosswinds.

Her windshield being shot out, and a tire flattened, definitely seemed to him to have both been done on purpose. Aimed at Ruby.

Other things—the puppies, Echo, the complaints, Oscar—were clearly meant to hurt him. Or, at least, Crosswinds.

And on three of those occurrences, Ruby had saved the day.

Her windshield had been shot out after she'd saved Oscar.

Then the tire flattened after the puppies were poisoned. And her unexpected arrival that evening had most likely prevented the rest of the puppies and Jasmine from also being poisoned.

He didn't want to find out what would happen to her if she returned to Crosswinds after saving Echo. Most particularly after Jaxon Walker paid for the dog and made arrangements for a couple of more weekend training sessions before taking Echo back to New York.

Maybe the perpetrator didn't know that yet, but Sebastian had to figure he would.

By the following Thursday, Sebastian had received three calls through Jaxon Walker's referrals, resulting in at least one sale. And every time something good happened for Crosswinds, he got more tense. Wondering if his stalker, as he was beginning to think of the vandal, would somehow find out and make him pay.

Or, God forbid, go after Ruby again.

The police had followed leads and were watching young James and checking out his associates. But so far, nothing had clicked. The chocolate bar that had poisoned Echo, their most concrete lead, was sold in every tourist shop in town, in hotel gift shops and in the local grocery store, too.

The biggest issue on Sebastian's mind was getting the mystery solved, the threats stopped, before word of Ruby's pregnancy got around. They hadn't spoken since she'd driven away Saturday evening, but he'd texted her every day. Asked how she was feeling. If she'd had any more light-headedness. How her work was going. And she'd responded promptly.

Almost as if they'd made an agreement that it would work that way.

He could go about his life knowing that she was working normal hours, eating well and feeling fine.

But he needed to speak with her. He didn't want any mention of the baby or pregnancy in writing that could be seen, hacked, or looked up by law-enforcement officials. Was he paranoid? Hell, yes.

It was all going to come out. She'd start to show. Her family wouldn't rest until they knew who the father was.

And Sebastian wasn't going to hide from his responsibility, either.

But she wasn't showing yet.

And had sworn her sisters to secrecy.

Dialing her on Thursday afternoon, her early day at the clinic, he half expected his call to go to voice mail. Was pleasantly surprised when he heard her pick up.

"I won't keep you long," he began. "I'd just like to suggest that as long as you aren't showing, as long as we can keep the situation under wraps, I'd rest a lot easier if we could do so."

Her pause made his gut clench.

"Ruby?" he asked when no response was forthcoming after several seconds of dead air.

"I don't intend to tell anyone you're the father, Sebastian, so you can rest easy." Her tone was not friendly.

"It's not that," he quickly clarified, while feeling kind of offended at the same time. Though, to be fair to her, he'd made it quite clear that he wasn't going to be a father to the child. "I've been working with Steele, walking every inch of my property, watching cameras, going over names and faces of people I don't even remember having ever met, getting a daily rundown of James's activities, and everyone he speaks to publicly at least, to see if we can put together any pieces. Until we find something, I'd feel a whole lot better if no one knew you were pregnant."

Silence met him again. It occurred to him that maybe they should have had the conversation in person. "So far, there's no definitive sign of my father having an affair, but I allowed Detective Steele to search all my parents' past financial records and there are suspicious local hotel bills. None of them close to any hospital where my dad might have been dealing with an emergency. There'd always been corresponding restaurant bills. And, in many, if not most of the instances, my mother's credit card showed up in use across town. There are hotel bills for her, too. So maybe they just both had meetings, dinners where they might be drinking, and made mutual decisions to get rooms. Could also be that they were both having affairs, but I know for certain she wasn't pregnant because she had to have a hysterectomy after I was born..."

He paused to breathe. And to check his phone to see that there was still an active connection to Ruby's.

"Who was home with you when both of your parents were gone?" The question hit him from left field. Who cared? It was so long ago.

"By the time I was twelve, no one. Not in Boise." He'd been plenty big enough to take care of himself. "At the cabin they always hired someone, to keep house and cook as much as anything else. And in Boise, when I was younger, I think at least one or the other of them always came home at some point. There was always someone there when I woke up in the morning." It had all seemed normal to him. He'd had Jerry.

Even when his parents had been out, one of them had always phoned at bedtime.

He'd been fine. Blessed, in a lot of ways. He'd learned independence. Self-sufficiency. Responsibility.

He'd also become a loner.

And if he'd had his way, he'd have had parents who wanted

to be at home with him, not out living their lives even though it meant leaving him alone.

Now his own kid was going to grow up with an absentee parent.

He was getting way off track.

"We've been lucky that the attacks have either been misses or uneventful up to this point," he told her, rushing to wipe away any images he might have just planted in her brain. Needing to get them out of his mind.

"But this guy has been at this more than two months. And if you take the anonymous complaints into account, it's been closer to four. There's no reason to believe that he's done. Other than your flat tire, Steele and his team believe that the attacks are escalating. If this guy is going to all this trouble to hurt Crosswinds, to get back at me, can you imagine what he'd do if he knew that you were carrying my child?"

He hadn't meant to put it quite that way.

"I just think, due to your association with me, it would be safer if no one knew you were pregnant," he said, finishing with the only thing he'd really needed to say.

"You're afraid that, if this person gets desperate, the baby could be a target."

It sounded fanciful when she spoke his fear aloud. But... "Yes."

"I agree."

At first, he thought he hadn't heard her right. But then she continued, "Hannah and Frannie have been driving me crazy, but I've warned them that they're going to lose me if they say anything before I'm ready. For their silence, I'm having to put up with one or the other of them bringing me at least one meal a day and sharing it with me. They want to see me eat. And, you know, one owns a café and the other a catering business, so there you go."

She sounded as though the love of her siblings was a huge hassle. But he heard other undertones in her voice, too.

"It's nice being spoiled a little bit, huh?" he asked softly.

To which she said, "Good night, Sebastian," and hung up.

Leaving him with a smile on his face.

RUBY WAS STILL asleep at 5:30 Friday morning when her phone rang. Recognizing the number as the Crosswinds kennel line, she picked up immediately.

"Ruby? Della, here. Sebastian took Elise out night training last night and isn't back yet. I just arrived to find the kennel flooded. The sprinkler system won't shut off. All the dogs are partially submerged. I have no idea for how long. They're all responding to me, but…"

Already out of bed and throwing off her nightshirt, Ruby said, "Get them to the medical building, cover the floor with cloth, mats, anything. I'm on my way…" Then she dropped the phone and got herself out the door. They'd been having unusually warm weather, in the fifties and sixties, but it still got down below freezing at night.

As soon as she was in the SUV, she voice-dialed Crosswinds, instructing Della to get the blow dryers used for grooming and, on the low, not hot, setting, dry the dogs as quickly as she could, starting with the puppies. Bryony was there, helping, and Sebastian, Della told her, was still out of cell range.

She drove as fast as she felt she could safely drive. That early in the morning, with dawn not even a promise on the horizon yet, she had the road mostly to herself. And when she noticed a car coming up behind her, just leaving town with her, and keeping pace, she allowed herself to put a little more pressure on the gas. While dogs weren't in as much danger of immediate physical distress as people were in such situations, they were still at risk. And the dogs she was on her way to save would go on to save human lives.

The car behind her was gaining on her, so she sped up more. The sooner she got to the dogs, the better. But when the other vehicle still stayed on her tail at twenty miles over the speed limit, she slowed down instead, hating the time lost, but wanting to let whoever it was pass. For all she knew they were on their way to a human medical emergency.

She watched impatiently as the headlights moved to the passing lane, checked out of habit to make sure nothing was coming from the opposite direction that could crash with it and almost didn't see when the vehicle, another SUV, based on its size, started to cross back over the line. Putting on her brakes, she swerved, keeping the wheel turned hard to the right, and managed to do a complete circle in the shoulder, and get herself safely back on the road in time to see the other vehicle's taillights rush off in the distance.

Thankful that everyone was okay, hoping the other party made it safely to their destination, she slowed down to signal her own turn.

Racing up Cross Drive, she had a moment's unease, seeing herself hurrying to the rescue again, after another bad thing happened at Sebastian's training center. Assuring herself—hoping—she was just overreacting to the near miss on the road, she still cautiously parked directly in front of the medical building. In view of all cameras, and anyone out and about at Crosswinds. Once inside, she forgot about her vehicle completely as she quickly looked in enough mouths, saw enough pale gums, to know she had an emergency situation. Instructing Della in how to assist, she prepared, and began to administer, warm intravenous liquids to the dogs from smallest to largest, puppies first. Took temperatures of the ones showing sluggishness, and warmed water bottles to pack around the ones waiting for treatment, with layers between the bottles and the dog's skin.

By the time Sebastian called in, she'd taken the temperatures of every dog on the premises, and Della reported to him that every one of them showed some sign of hypothermia. Echo and a few of the larger dogs were warming just with the water bottles. Ruby was just finishing up the last of the IVs. She'd been monitoring heart rates and felt that every one of the dogs, including the new puppies, was going to be fine.

But only because Della had come in early. And thought to call Ruby immediately.

She couldn't be certain that the faulty sprinkler system was due to what Sebastian now called his stalker. But as she assessed the damage, looking at all the dogs that could easily have been lost, that possibility loomed larger inside her. It gave the early morning emergency an additional sense of dread.

Detective Steele arrived before Sebastian did and quickly drew the same conclusion that Ruby had. He stopped by the kennel briefly to say that the attacker had likely struck again. The locked box controlling the thermostat in the kennel had been cracked. It was possible the unknown subject had turned up the heat high enough to trigger the sprinkler system, but more likely that he held some kind of lighter up to a sprinkler head, and then only used the thermostat to turn off the heat. They'd know more once they got inside the computerized thermostat.

Sebastian, the lines under his eyes making him look worn out, burst into the medical building minutes after Steele headed back to the kennels. "They're okay," she said at his first frantic look around the room. Della had gone with the detective, to give him access to the office attached to the kennel by a bricked hallway.

The big mountain man nodded, but walked from dog to dog, starting with the puppies, squatting down in front of each one, feeling feet and tails, calling all the newborns "little one" and each of the adult dogs by name. Asking how they were doing.

Ruby watched with a lump in her throat.

Hating what was happening to Sebastian.

His animals were his family. His only family. He placed every one of them carefully. Like a parent sending his children off to college. He followed up with them all after they'd found their permanent partners as well.

For a brief second, watching him give his all to his dogs, she was swamped by a wave of jealousy. Because her own child wouldn't get the benefit of Sebastian's undying attention or unconditional love.

The thought passed and by the time she left the medical building late that morning, helping to transition the dogs back to their kennels, she and Sebastian were working seamlessly together again, exactly as they had for the past several years.

Walking out of the kennel with him to get some lunch, she was feeling better than she had since before Oscar was hurt. Seeing a way for her and Sebastian to be friends, to take on challenges, and work through them together.

They were passing her car, on the way up to his house, when he stopped. "What's that?" he asked, pointing to a clod stuck in one of her wheels. And then, walking closer, they could see the dirt stuck in her bumper, too.

"That's from the three-sixty I made in the mud this morning," she told him, hoping again that the party who'd been more in a hurry than she'd been, had made it to wherever they were going safely. As they started walking again, she told him about the incident.

"He was probably drunk," Sebastian said. "You should have called the police."

If she'd had any inkling that the vehicle was out of control, she definitely would have. The person had almost run into her, had effectively run her off the road. Why hadn't she considered alcoholism for the excessive speed?

Filled with panic for a second, she worried that her failure to alert police might have gotten someone killed. But she slowed down her thoughts to go back over the morning's incident more carefully.

"There was no sign of any lack of control," she said aloud. Checking herself. "The vehicle stayed steady in the lane the entire time it was behind me," she recalled slowly. "I kept watching it because I was going so fast and it was clearly coming up on me. Not like someone who was racing, just like...someone—" catching up to her "—in a hurry."

She'd been in a rush. Had she transferred her own tension-inducing motive to the other car?

Before she could answer her own question, Sebastian was on the phone, talking to Glen Steele again, relating what Ruby had just told him.

"He's on his way over here," Sebastian told her, hanging up. "He wants to speak with you, and he wants to see your vehicle before you drive it again."

She nodded. Kind of glad at the moment that the morning's odd event was getting looked at again.

And hating the shadowed look that once again marred Sebastian's face.

Chapter Eleven

Leaving Della and Bryony with the dogs, Sebastian insisted on following Ruby back to Owl Creek after Steele was done with her. The detective had not only taken photos of her car, but he'd also taken the dirt clumps, too, in case that could help prove how she was forced off the road.

Ruby thought his following her home was overkill. He'd received the message loud and clear. From the looks she'd sent him, and from her repeated words, too.

He'd just nodded. And climbed back into his truck. He'd been out half the night. Had to get back to the dogs. He felt like a sitting duck, just waiting for the next bullet to hit.

He had to talk to Ruby.

And he'd wanted her off his property the second Steele had said she was free to go.

They'd had grilled-cheese sandwiches at his place while they'd been waiting for the detective. She was going home to shower and change before heading into work for her afternoon and early evening appointments.

He didn't like that, either, but knew that he had no say on that one.

Just like he wasn't packing up and taking his dogs and

going into hiding, he couldn't expect Ruby to curl up under her couch and quit living.

Steele had stressed that if the perpetrator wanted Ruby gone, he'd had plenty of opportunities to try to make that happen. Same went for Sebastian. It continued to appear as though someone was out to sabotage his business.

To what end, he had no idea.

He was considering finding other boarding for his dogs until the stalker had been caught. He'd already, at Steele's suggestion, hired three full-time, armed and bonded security officers from Boise to patrol the kennels at night. Two patrolling outside. One inside with the dogs.

The sprinkler system would be reset and ready to go by dinnertime.

The kennel was going to be kept locked, day and night, with only Crosswinds employees and security allowed inside.

And Ruby was to be nowhere on the premises.

She waved at him as she pulled into her driveway, as though she thought he'd just drift off into the wind.

He pulled into her driveway behind her, instead. She'd opened the garage door, and he was standing inside the garage when she got out of her car.

"Sebastian, what are you doing?"

Glancing around, he said, "Can we go inside for a second? We probably don't want anyone to see us having a fight." He just put it right out there.

And with one look at him over her shoulder, she led him inside.

"What's going on?" she asked, the second her door was shut. The garage led into a laundry room, and she didn't lead him out of it. Instead, with her satchel still on her shoulder, she faced him down right there by the washer.

"You are not to step foot on Crosswinds again," he said, every bit of frustration inside him seeming to roll out with the words. "If you do, I'm going to press charges for trespassing."

Okay, that was more than he'd intended. But the woman and her independence and her refusal to let him help her and the baby inside her...were upending him a little.

"I know I can't dictate your actions and I have no say in where you go or what you do, but I do have a say on my own property."

To his utter astonishment, he saw tears brim her eyes. What the hell?

With a nod, she turned to head into the kitchen, telling him to let himself out.

"Wait," he called behind her, following her to the kitchen door, but going no farther. He wasn't invading her home unless she invited him in. "Ruby..."

She turned then, no sign of the tears, but her gaze was filled with something worse than disappointment. Sadness, maybe. Accompanied by resolution.

"It's okay, Sebastian. You have to do what you have to do. I knew the baby was going to be a problem for you. And you were quite clear that you couldn't be a part of their life. It stands to reason that, since right now the two of us, the baby and I, are one, you can't have me in your life as well."

What the...? He took a step. Stopped. "Ruby," he called softly. "I'm doing this so you and the baby will be safe..."

With another nod, she met his gaze, looking sadder than he'd ever seen a woman look. Or that's how it felt to him. "I know. You're afraid you'll have an episode and one of us will get hurt..."

Well, that. But... "That's why I'm never going to marry

or have a family, but…you, and the child, will always be welcome to call on me anytime, day or night." He told her something he hadn't yet come to terms with on his own. And yet the words rang with such truth, he accepted them fully. "I hope we'll stay in contact," he continued, working things out as he went along. Feeling…freer for having said them.

And then, before things got rocky, said, "This no-trespassing thing…it's only until whoever is after Crosswinds is caught. This *person*," he growled, "obviously knows who you are, and knows that every time he tries to create a situation that hurts me, you're there, fixing things. You heard Steele say it almost seemed as though the perp lay in wait this morning, watching to see if you'd head out to Crosswinds, and was out on the road, ready to stop you from saving the dogs."

Sebastian had barely been able to remain standing there in calm conversation when the detective had let that piece of information drop.

"We don't know that for sure," Ruby responded, finally speaking, taking a step closer to him. But when he looked her in the eye, she glanced away. As though the theory made sense to her, too.

"You'd already figured that out on your own," he challenged her.

When she glanced up again, she met his gaze and nodded.

He took a step. Stopped. "May I come in?"

"Of course." The tone of voice, like there'd never be a question of his welcome, sent warmth through parts of him that felt like they might just freeze to death.

Walking up to her, he took her hands in his. "I'd die if anything happened to you because of me," he told her, letting honesty guide him. He had nothing else left but raw truth. "And now, with the child, and these attacks…how do I fight the unknown? It's like I'm this tense bundle of potential screwup with no power to do anything about any of it. Except this. I can forbid you from coming to Crosswinds, until we know it's safe."

She smiled then. A wide, slow, warm smile.

And Sebastian figured he'd won the round in a battle that was never going to end.

RUBY HAD A call from Detective Steele while she was in an appointment that afternoon. And listened to his message as soon as she was free.

Police had found evidence of a large vehicle parked in some brush behind leafy trees, about a mile outside of Owl Creek, on the road to Crosswinds. The vehicle had been facing to pull out toward the dog-training facility. They could tell by tire tread and track depth that the vehicle had to be at least a full-size SUV. Which was exactly what she'd thought it to be.

There was nothing on traffic cams in town to show anyone in an SUV driving from town toward Sebastian's after the bars closed. And no traffic cams a mile out of town.

She hadn't even finished the message when a new call coming in interrupted the voice mail. Seeing Fletcher's name pop up, she answered immediately.

"I'll be in Boise by eight," he announced as soon as he told her hello. "By the time I rent a car, that should put me at your place by around eleven."

"What?" she asked, dropping down to her desk chair, with a glance at her watch. She had two more exam rooms with patients waiting.

"Didn't Steele tell you? I've taken a leave here and I'm

heading to town to help Steele figure out what in the hell's going on there. You could have been killed today."

Her heart fluttered with love and gratitude at the same time it tightened with tension. She didn't need her family overreacting. Or thinking she couldn't take care of herself.

In her current circumstances, she needed as much time apart from all of them as she could get.

"I didn't hear his full message," she uttered inanely. "I was listening to it when you called. And you most definitely don't need to fly home for this."

"I'm already at the airport," he said. "Finding criminals is what I do, sis. One of my own is being attacked—no way I'm not going to be there."

The tone of voice, and the words, stopped any other protest she might have made. Because she knew it would be pointless.

"Do Mom and Dad know you're coming?"

"Not yet. I was planning to bunk with you tonight. I'd like to hear everything you can remember, about all of it, in your own words. Tonight. Without anyone else interrupting. That way, I hit the ground running tomorrow. I'll move in with Mom and Dad tomorrow night."

She nodded. Realized he couldn't see her. And said, "I'll have the coffee on," before she remembered that the smell of the stuff made her nauseous.

She'd stop and pick up some beer for him instead. Or fix him some tea.

And then get him the heck out of her house before he figured out that she wasn't drinking alcohol, or caffeine, and threw up if she smelled coffee.

Detective that he was, Fletcher would figure out her secret and then all hell truly would break loose.

CALL HIM OVER-THE-TOP, but Sebastian was bunking out at the kennels Friday night. He sent the third security officer outside with the other two. One was watching the road frontage. Another patrolling along the lake.

And the third had the buildings.

He was on a cot with a sleeping bag, with Oscar's bed beside him, right in the middle of the kennel building. Or he would be. He'd also brought in lawn furniture, including a small table, and sat, sipping a beer and reading a book about prenatal care on his tablet.

If he was going to protect, support, he had to know the dangers. He'd expected to struggle, had bought the six-pack to relax him through it. But, still on his first beer, he was more fascinated than agitated. There were possible malfunctions, to be sure, but Ruby's age and physical condition allayed most of the concerns.

The birthing process he was familiar with, having birthed many puppies over the years. He wouldn't be there, of course, but...

His phone interrupted the thought.

Ruby.

"Something wrong?" he asked, picking up in the middle of the first ring. She didn't randomly call him. Ever.

"Why would something be wrong?"

He could come up with dozens of reasons, both stalker- and pregnancy-related. "No reason."

"I'm just finishing up here at the clinic and wanted to check in on the dogs." Which he should have figured from the get-go.

"I just did rounds half an hour ago," he told her. "All gums look healthy and pink. Everyone's eating, responding to stimuli, and the puppies' temperatures are all normal." She'd left a thorough list with Della.

"Thank goodness. I'm so glad to hear that." She sounded glad. Genuinely happy, in fact. Which gave him pleasure, too.

"So, what did you have for dinner tonight?" he asked—a personal question that would never have occurred to him to ask until she got pregnant. She'd told him earlier that it was Hannah's turn to provide the daily meal and she was bringing Lucy along to the clinic to share it with her.

"Grilled chicken salad with, I think, every vegetable known to man in it. And pudding for dessert. I need my dairy, after all." He heard the note of sarcasm in her tone—and pictured her smiling.

"I picked up takeout when I went in for some beer."

"I had a juice box. Lucy said she got to share one of hers with me."

Her five-year-old niece. He'd met the little girl several times. She was a cutie. He'd never, ever considered what a child of his own would look like.

Until that second.

"Have you heard from Detective Steele?" she asked then, sounding a whole lot more tentative. In light of their earlier conversation in her kitchen, he suspected.

"About the fresh tire tracks hidden in brush and trees a mile outside of town?" He'd been right to ban her from his property. He was not going to back down on that one.

"Yeah. Did he tell you about Fletcher, too?"

Sebastian's brow raised. "No."

"He took a leave of absence and is flying in to help Steele. He lands later tonight and will be staying at my place until morning, when he's moving to my parents' place."

"He heard about your road incident today."

"Yeah. Steele called him. After the windshield thing, I haven't told my family about any of the stuff at Crosswinds. But apparently Fletcher, one detective to another, had asked to be notified if there were any further actions against me. Steele didn't think the flat tire qualified, but this morning's run off the road did."

"You don't sound happy about his arrival."

"I don't need my big brother disrupting his entire life over something the local police can handle. Something that I dealt with quite fine this morning, I might add."

He'd stopped to look at the tire tracks in the dirt not far from his place. Could retrace her three-sixty. Standing there alone in the dirt, he'd been angry as hell that it had happened, frustrated that he couldn't stop the jerk from getting near her again, and impressed, too, at her driving skills. He'd been thankful she'd kept herself alive.

Not something he wanted her to have to be doing. Ever again.

"Fletcher's a decorated detective, Ruby. Him and Steele working together—they're going to catch this jerk. The sooner that happens, the better."

Her pause gave him pause, until she offered, "As you said, he's a great detective. And… I have secrets I don't want my family to know about yet."

Ahh. Sebastian finally caught up to her. With a screech. Knocking his palm against his head.

"If you feel like you need to tell them—"

"I don't," she interrupted before he'd figured out how to finish the statement.

She had every right to tell her family anything she wanted them to know. He needed a plan to weather the backlash.

Once a Marine, Always a Marine. War in Afghanistan, raising search-and-rescue dogs, a stalker, an unexpected pregnancy. He needed the best training he could get, the ammunition and the battle plan.

"I need some time to myself. To figure out what I want and need, regarding the future, before I have a dozen people telling me what's best."

He couldn't imagine the tension in that particular situation.

"I guess that's where I'm lucky," he told her, glancing around at his own family. Reaching down to pet Oscar, who rose immediately and nudged his hand. "I have listening and support, but no advice givers."

Hearing the words aloud, he didn't feel that lucky, and said, "Advice can be good, you know. Different perspectives sometimes show you something you didn't think of yourself."

"I'm all for advice," she said with a chuckle. "But with five siblings, four cousins and two parents and an uncle all coming at you at once, it's hard to hear any one piece of advice."

For a second, he envied her. *Hard.* "You also have five siblings, four cousins, two parents and an uncle who have your back," he said softly.

Hence, her big-brother detective taking a leave of absence to find whoever was putting his sister's life at risk.

"It's kind of funny," she said, her words coming back softly. "You and me, two totally independent people, who live alone because we want to, who dedicate ourselves to our careers, which both happen to revolve around animals, and yet we come from completely opposite backgrounds."

"I guess it just goes to show you that no matter the upbringing, we are who we are."

"Yeah, as long as we can find ourselves..."

Or until life threw you a curveball you weren't sure you could catch.

"I'm sorry, Ruby. So sorry."

"Sorry?" Her tone stronger. "For what?"

"I'll get backlash, a hell of a lot of it from your family, I imagine, once they know I'm the father of this unplanned pregnancy. I expect there's a good chance I'm going to lose my closest friend over it. But my life is still going to be just me. Independent. Heading up a family of dogs. While your whole future has just changed course. It's not right."

"It's my choice."

"What?" She'd chosen to... Wait, had he...?

"To have the baby is my choice," she told him. "To keep it is my choice. If nature were different and you were the one carrying the embryo we created, the choice would be yours. And you'd make the one that suited you best."

True. "It still doesn't seem right."

"Then maybe you need to do more thinking," she told him. "I've learned that if something doesn't feel right, I'm probably not where I need to be, or doing what I need to do, or with who I need to be with."

"You live a second life as a shrink?" he asked, with a friendly chuckle he hadn't heard in a long while. Hadn't realized he'd lost the ability to just relax and converse.

"No one is preventing you from being a father to this child, Sebastian," she said then, as though he hadn't just lightened the moment. "A lot of fathers don't live with their children, many don't ever have them for overnight stays, but they're still important entities in their children's lives. They're present for the choices, the big events, for some smaller moments. For giving advice..."

Sneaky, the way she'd brought that advice bit back to him.

In new light.

He took a sip of beer. Made note that he wasn't jumping up out of his chair and moving on to whatever he could find that needed to be done.

"I'm not asking, Sebastian. I fully understand if this isn't your choice. I don't blame you. I won't hold it against you. I just..."

"I'm not hating the idea," he said. And then quickly added, "I'm also not seeing it yet. Can we...revisit what this might look like?"

"Anytime you're ready."

He wasn't there yet. But he wanted to be.

Which scared him way more than any stalker ever would.

Chapter Twelve

Ruby's late-night interview with her big brother was nice. Really nice. Fletcher's questions, the way he led into them, opened her mind to a little more detail. Nothing that identified a suspect, or a motive, but Fletcher seemed pleased with the result.

More than that, he'd treated her like an equal, someone fully capable of taking care of herself. The relief was palpable.

The validation was more needed than she'd known.

And it all came crashing down the next morning, when Hannah burst into her office even before she'd seen her first patient.

"This is it, Ruby." Her shoulder-length dark blond hair flew around her and her green eyes shot daggers. "I just heard that Fletcher's in town to help the police figure out who ran you off the road yesterday?" When Hannah's voice rose a notch, Ruby got up and closed her office door.

Her office was secluded, down a hallway from the rest of the clinic, but there was no way she wanted anyone hearing the conversation.

"You shouldn't be here," she told her next younger sister,

standing by the door, arms crossed against her white doctor's coat. "I wouldn't burst in on one of your catering events."

"Not even if my life was in danger and you knew I was hiding information that could lead to my intended killer?"

"No one is trying to kill me."

"Fletcher wouldn't be here if he didn't think otherwise."

"I think he's just trying to make certain that it doesn't get to that point," Ruby said, leaning her backside against her desk. "The police are pretty certain that I've only been targeted because I'm at Crosswinds. I'm not going back there until this is cleared up."

Hannah's mouth stayed closed. The fire brimming in her sister's eyes spoke for her. She met her gaze to gaze. Had fought the battle many times over the years. Intended to win.

And then, Hannah said, "The police, and Fletcher, don't know that you're hiding a man for some reason. And that you're carrying his baby." Her sister kept her voice low.

That was the only credit Ruby could give her.

"Let it go, Hannah." The warning was implicit in her tone.

When Hannah looked down, Ruby filled with remorse, but didn't back off from her position. "It's going to be okay," she said.

Hannah's eyes glistened when she looked back up. "I know. Because if you aren't going to tell, I have to, Ruby. I can't shake the idea that some guy might want you gone because he doesn't want it known that you're pregnant with his child. I don't care if he's married, or famous, or whatever reason you have for keeping him secret. It's not worth your life…"

Ruby started to speak, but Hannah cut her off. "I'd never be able to live with myself if I stayed silent and this guy got to you."

Sitting down, Ruby took a deep breath. Hannah's valid claim was changing her tactics. But not her decision. "He's not going to get to me, Hannah." She met her sister's gaze, held on steadily.

"So…" Hannah closed in, perching on the edge of Ruby's desk, closer to her. "You admit that there is a *he*."

"No." Ruby crossed her hands at her waist, needing her calm to be the only thing that showed. "I'm not in any kind of a relationship. I told you that from the beginning."

"You're not still going to try to convince me that you aren't pregnant, are you? Because when I tell the family, you're going to have to lie to them, too, and then when you start showing, everyone's going to know you lied to their faces."

She got the message.

Hannah was hurt that she was lying to *her*.

And she'd made her point.

"I am pregnant," she said aloud, shocked at the fissure that passed through as she heard her own words. Not an entirely unpleasant experience. "But I still need you to keep it a secret for now, Hannah." Her tone was no longer commanding. "Please. Just until we figure out what's going on here. I don't want whoever is behind these attacks to know about the baby. I don't want to give this jerk more bait."

Hannah's head shake put knots in Ruby's stomach, as did her sister's words when she said, "I can't keep that promise anymore. There's something not right about this guy. So you aren't in a relationship anymore. It's clear that two months ago, you were having sex with him. And this is the kind of motive you read in the news all the time."

Always-practical Hannah.

But her sister had known her own share of heartache.

Which she'd taken on the chin. And grown up out of the ashes to make a great life for herself and her daughter.

Ruby met Hannah's gaze again. "I know the father is not behind this, Hannah. I am as positive of that as I am that Lucy is your daughter."

She was that serious. Hannah seemed to be considering Ruby's words, giving them weight, but then she shook her head. "Maybe he wants you back. He's doing this to scare you back into his arms."

"I know him, Hannah. And he knows about the baby." The words came because they had to. "But we aren't in love. Neither of us want to get married. Him even more than me and you know how much I've always cherished my space alone at home." She couldn't tell Hannah that the father was being stalked and both Ruby and the father feared that if anyone knew he had a child on the way, that child could be in danger. But she had to get her sister's promise of silence. "Please," she said then. "Just give Fletcher a few days to work on these attacks. As soon as the person is caught, I'll tell Mom and Dad myself."

"And the father...he's okay with that?"

"He's not thrilled by the idea. After all, we're the Coltons, you know?"

Hannah's answering nod, the look on her face, held total commiseration at that point. And Ruby said, "But he knows it's the right thing to do. And I get the feeling he's going to insist on it once this violent behavior is solved."

"So he knows about the attacks?"

"Yes."

Hannah nodded again. She didn't look like she was ready to be done yet, though. "So why won't you at least tell me who he is?"

"Because we need some time to figure out how our parenting situation is going to work. Time without anyone else even knowing that we're going to be sharing a child." She met her sister's gaze head-on. Hannah knew all about the trials and tribulations of parenthood. "I'm going to retain full custody," she added. Something else Hannah would understand, being a single mother herself.

Hannah's face softened then, and she headed toward the door. But turned when she reached it. "By the way, Mom wanted me to remind you about Uncle Buck's birthday party next week. It's going to be at the ranch instead of in town because so many people accepted invitations. Mom asked me to cater it."

Ruby wasn't in a partying mood. Most particularly when one family member or another was bound to bring her a glass of her favorite wine and wonder why she wasn't sipping from it. But she nodded. Congratulated Hannah on the job offer.

And wondered, but didn't ask, if Sebastian Cross had been on the guest list.

And if so, had his name been on the acceptance list as well?

SEBASTIAN HAD A visit from Fletcher Colton on Saturday. Watching the broad-shouldered man walking toward the training pen, seeing his dark hair, worn a little long, he was struck by the fact that Fletcher's niece or nephew was going to be Sebastian's biological child. Would the baby have blond hair like Sebastian and Ruby? Or darker hair like Fletcher and Wade? He and Ruby both had green eyes. Wade's were blue.

He had no idea what eye color the rest of the Coltons had. Including Fletcher.

Until the man got closer.

Green.

Sebastian was probably going to have a green-eyed kid.

Giving a "sit" command to the Labrador he'd been training, Sebastian held out a hand to his long-time friend's older brother.

Finding himself fighting a load of guilt, unable to shake the fact that he was the father of the man's younger sister's unplanned baby. If Fletcher knew...

When Wade found out...

Glen Steele, as the lead on the Crosswinds case, had called to let Sebastian know that Fletcher would be coming out. The Utah detective had been deputized by the Owl Creek Police Department in order to officially help find Ruby's attacker.

Being the father of the unborn child who could be in jeopardy with any further attacks, as well as the owner of the property involved and the friend of the woman who'd been put at risk, Sebastian kenneled the Lab and walked Fletcher around the property, pointing out every place an attack had happened. Fletcher pulled out crime-scene photos and Sebastian walked the other man through every one of them.

Gave him a full tour of the kennels. Introduced Ruby's brother to every one of his ten adult dogs. Including Fancy, the two-month-old shepherd mix Sebastian had determined had the scent skills to be trained for search-and-rescue. "I've got a few people who foster potential trainees for me," he told the man. "Ruby's friend Kiki Shelton and her grandfather, Jim, have agreed to take Fancy."

There, he'd put Ruby on the table.

Gotten the fact out there that Sebastian was indirectly responsible for Fletcher's presence in town.

As the two headed down to walk the shoreline, where,

Steele was certain, the unknown assailant had been accessing Sebastian's land, Fletcher said, "This nastiness aside, you've saved my sister's life, man."

Sebastian pulled on his beard at that thought. If the man only knew...

When he knew...

"That woman had always had more of an affinity with animals than with people," Fletcher continued. "Probably had something to do with the way we grew up—has she told you about that?"

Indirectly. There'd been too many opinions, he knew that.

"You know that our mom's a twin, right?" the detective asked, his mind seemingly only half on the words he was saying as he perused every inch of land upon which they walked, while keeping an eye on the horizon, and occasionally turning to look back toward the house and other buildings, too.

"I didn't know that," Sebastian said. He'd been a summer pal of Fletcher's younger brother. They'd fished. Challenged each other to dive off docks into the lake. They'd shared freedom from parents—they hadn't sat around and talked about them.

Partially because Sebastian didn't do that with anyone. Or hadn't, until recently. With Ruby.

When a guy didn't want to share, he didn't put himself in a position to have sharing expected of him.

"Her name is Jessie. She was Uncle Buck's wife."

That was news. "The woman who ran off and left him with four kids to raise?" You didn't live in Owl Creek without knowing some of the history.

Buck and Robert Colton were brothers. Buck went off to the army, leaving Robert to take over the family's hardware store in town. Buck came back, sold his share of the store to Robert and used the profits to buy Colton Ranch. Then Robert saw Owl Creek's potential to grow into a tourist area and spent his profits buying land cheap and purchasing buildings in town under market value. When the market turned around, he'd amassed a small fortune of land and rentals.

And that hardware store now served as the lobby for Colton Properties, though Robert had left a lot of the shelving and the register in place for posterity's sake. He'd added two additional floors, still with the redbrick facade, but all decked out with modern offices and the best of technology. A newcomer couldn't miss the place. Other than the town hall, it was the tallest building in Owl Creek.

And Fletcher had been about to tell him something about Ruby's upbringing that had made her better with dogs than with people. He could argue that point, no matter what reasoning Fletcher gave. Ruby most definitely worked her magic on people as well as dogs. He had personal testimony to confirm that.

But he had no intention whatsoever of sharing. So he didn't ask any of the questions he suddenly had.

Fletcher had stopped to take a couple of photos with his cell phone. Of the house, and then, of the lake. From midyard.

"I think Mom always felt guilty, her sister leaving Uncle Buck that way, and with Dad traveling so much, she'd cart us six kids over to the ranch, to help Buck out with his kids and things around the house. We'd spend nights there, with Mom tending to all ten of us at once."

Sounded chaotic. Somewhat fascinating.

Why hadn't Wade ever said anything about that?

Or had he, and Sebastian hadn't thought it a big enough deal to remember?

He hadn't known Ruby well back then.

Hadn't been making a baby with her.

"Rubes, being the middle child in our family, and the same age as Uncle Buck's youngest, Lizzie, kind of got lost in the shuffle, I think. Or just figured the dogs were less trouble than putting up with the rest of us."

Sebastian figured he should feel guilty about listening to Ruby's older brother profiling her, but he was too interested to stop the man.

"We all saw veterinary science as the perfect choice for her," the detective jumped ahead before Sebastian was ready to leave the past behind. "Problem was, that's all she wanted. Worked seven days a week, on call twenty-four hours. She was starting to show signs of burnout until she began working at Crosswinds so much. Volunteering with your PTSD program gave her something she'd obviously been missing. She's more relaxed. Has hired a couple more doctors for her clinic, and, from what Mom and the girls tell me, she's taking complete days off, and sometimes whole weekends."

Like the weekend, two months before, when they'd dealt with Oscar, and then made a baby together?

Fletcher wasn't going to be thanking Sebastian, or thinking he'd saved anything, once he knew the truth. And to that end...

"I've got an idea to try and draw this stalker out," he said. He'd come up with the plan the night before. Lying on his cot, awake in the middle of the night, thinking about Ruby's near miss on the road the morning before.

He intended not only to draw out the fiend who was trying to ruin him, but also to keep the unknown assailant busy at Crosswinds, where Ruby absolutely would not be.

"I'm going to run a huge ad campaign for Crosswinds. I've

already contacted a marketing firm my mother worked with in Boise. They'd offered to help before, but I'm already at capacity and don't need the publicity. Anyway, a film crew will be out from a local station in Boise to film what we do, interview me, that kind of thing. The crew will be made aware of the situation and will all be privy to the danger before accepting the job. They'll be provided bodyguards. We'll be doing other videos as well, paying social-media influencers to air them. I've got an ample supply of photos and some videos of our dogs out in the field. We'll be asking for permission to use those and include them in the campaign." They'd almost reached the shore. He just kept talking. "To begin, though, the firm is going to hit Owl Creek hard, with news that the marketing firm is honoring me and my parents for a lifetime of service to our communities. They wanted to do that when my parents died, but I needed my privacy."

He cringed at the idea, but to draw out the stalker, trap whoever it was and end the threat of violence…he'd do whatever it took.

"They'll get posters designed and printed, with the idea to put them up on trees on public property coming in and out of town, not involving any individuals or businesses. The plan is there. Ready to roll. I just want police buy-in before I give the final go-ahead."

They'd reached the shore. Stopping, Fletcher turned to Sebastian. "You're taking the offensive, egging him on, rather than waiting for him to strike again."

"And again," Sebastian said, nodding. "I've got three armed security officers here at night. I can bring in a day shift as well. And will work around the clock, if I have to, to keep running things here without staff, if it comes to that. I started out alone. I can do it again."

"You can afford all of this?"

Sebastian shrugged. "I'd spend my last dime if that's what it took to put an end to the reign of terror. This individual went after Ruby," he said, unable to keep the boiling anger out of his tone.

Fletcher studied him. Sebastian, holding the other man's gaze straight on, was up for it and then some.

"Let me talk to Steele," Fletcher said then. "While a bit more elaborate than I'd like, I think we can work with what you're planning. We'll need to assign extra officers to the case and I don't know what kind of staff he has on hand. And maybe we hold off for a few days. Steele's been looking at those hotel bills your father charged. He's got some leads on a woman who was also known to be there. And she later had a kid. A boy. Let us get a look at him."

Sebastian fell back against the tree behind him. Leaned there.

He'd been right? He had a half brother?

Who'd pushed Ruby off the road and could have killed her? And the child?

"Sorry, man," Fletcher said then. "Steele led me to believe you kind of figured your father had been having an affair."

Right. Fletcher would have no idea that he'd been thinking about Ruby at the hands of a deranged guy who resented Sebastian so much he had to take him down.

"I threw it out as a possibility," he said, straightening. "I never suspected it before now. I'm an only kid. The idea of a half sibling…"

"I've got five siblings, and the idea of a half sibling out there somewhere would throw me for one, too. Wrapping your mind around that one…hell, you gotta see your parents, your whole life different…" Fletcher was walking again.

Clearly trying to put a witness, and a friend of his brother's, at ease.

Sebastian would be at ease when the stalker was locked behind bars.

When he knew Ruby and the child were safe.

Until then, he was at war.

Chapter Thirteen

Ruby awoke Sunday morning to a text-message notification.

Thinking it was Sebastian, who'd been the last one to text her the night before, just to ask how she was doing, she rolled over and picked up her phone.

A smile on her face.

Not a horrible way to wake up.

The man got her. He not only accepted her right to make her own life choices, but he also understood her independence. Her need to be a single decision maker.

Not part of a twosome.

Lying on her back against the pillows, giving her stomach a chance to wake up before she started whirling it around, she held up the phone and tapped the text icon.

STAY AWAY.

Two words. All caps.

And her heart was pounding.

Sitting up, she pushed Fletcher's speed dial. Nodded when her brother told her to stay put. And away from windows.

With him on the phone, she walked to the bathroom attached to her bedroom. And when he hung up, she tapped Sebastian's icon.

He wasn't the police. Or part of the investigation.

But he was her partner, of sorts, on the new route her life was taking. If something happened to her, to the child she was carrying, he'd lose his own biological offspring.

"I just thought you should know, because Crosswinds is involved, that I got an eerie text a few minutes ago. Fletcher's on his way over."

Dawn was barely breaking on Sunday morning. He was probably still in bed.

"I'm on my way to Connors. Elise is bleeding. I've got a tourniquet on her, but I think she might have slit a vein—"

"Connors?" she interrupted, her text message an issue for later. "You bring her here, Sebastian. If it's a vein, she might not make it to Connors."

"I'm not involving you or the clinic…"

"Bring her to my house," she said. "I have my kit here. And anything else I need, someone can get for me." She was pulling on jeans and a sweatshirt as she spoke. And, as she heard a car outside and peeked out, added, "Fletcher's here. Bring her to me, Sebastian," she said, hanging up.

She wasn't going to argue with him. Elise might not have that much time.

Ruby already had a sheet in hand as she gave her phone to her brother and went straight to the kitchen table, covering it.

"Sebastian's on his way with an emergency," she told him. "One of his dogs, whose handler is arriving this week to pick her up."

Frowning, Fletcher, whose hair was standing up at the back, in a bedtime cowlick, didn't say a word as he asked for her phone's password and then typed it in.

She ran for her bag, then laid out supplies.

Fletcher came closer. "I don't like this."

"I don't, either," she told him. "But it's the best I can do. He said a vein's been cut. Depending on which one, she could bleed to death before I can help her. She might need a transfusion..."

"The text, Ruby. I don't like the text."

Right. Fine. Neither did she. "You figure that out, I'll work on this," she told him, thinking of the girl she'd birthed two years before. Of all the hours of training Sebastian and Della—and her cousin Malcolm, too—had put Elise through. The golden retriever had shown more promise, from the beginning, than any of Sebastian's other dogs. She was going to a group of mountain rangers who lost lives every year when they couldn't find missing people in time.

"A dog is hurt and right afterward you get a text telling you to stay away?"

The thought had crossed her mind.

"We don't know that the two are connected," she told him. "If Elise got cut digging, I'm saying the chances are slim. But in any event, I *am* staying away. And ultimately, this guy is after Crosswinds for some reason, not me. Or Sebastian, either. If he was a murderer, why not just take out Sebastian and be done with it?" She was busy arranging, running a silent checklist through her mind. Preparing an IV. Antibiotic. Getting sutures ready. "This isn't just a dog I'm hoping to save here, although I'd do the same if it were. This animal is going to save human lives. It's her calling. And I'm not going to have people die because I got a text message."

Her text notification sounded again. She glanced at Fletcher, who was watching her screen.

"Sebastian's here," he said, and headed toward the door to the garage.

She heard the double garage door open. Listened while her brother told Sebastian to pull in. Counted seconds while she heard the truck's engine shut off and the garage door close.

And counted more as the men carried the injured dog into her.

"She's conscious," she breathed with relief. She showered the girl with praise, with reassurance, even while her heart thudded at the sight of the blood-soaked bandage around Elise's left ankle. "There's blood on her right foot, too," she said, taking a brief glance, seeing cuts, as she unwrapped the gauze around the dog's left front leg.

"Sebastian, stay at her head, comfort her. Fletcher, keep tight pressure right here." She moved her brother's fingers about an inch above the gauze.

And five minutes later, they were all breathing huge sighs of relief. Sebastian's quick thinking and the tourniquet had made the injury less catastrophic. "It's the cephalic vein," she told the two men, relieved to find that only the superficial vein had been nicked.

It took a while longer to dig small pieces of glass out of several cuts and incisions on Elise's lower front legs. She was still assessing damage, tending to immediate medical concerns, when Fletcher told Sebastian about the text Ruby had received that morning, finishing with, "I need to know what happened."

With a swift hard look to Ruby, and a new frown marring his brow, Sebastian said, "She's due to leave us this week. I was running her through all the courses one last time, in the dark, just to be sure I felt she was completely ready. Instead of hitting the spot where I'd buried her scent, she stopped on a hill and began digging frantically. Next thing I know she's spurting blood..."

Fletcher, who'd been dismissed from pressure application a few minutes before, pulled out his phone. Tapped. And then said, "Get a team out to Crosswinds." Talking to Sebastian, her brother received and relayed exact location coordinates to, she assumed, Glen Steele, and then hung up.

"Aren't you going to join them?" she asked Fletcher, adding a second, and final, stitch to another left-foot wound.

"You received a direct warning to stay away, Ruby. I don't think the guy cares about geography at the moment. He wanted you to stay away from the dog."

"Because every time he strikes, you save the day," Sebastian added through clenched teeth.

They didn't even know yet if the two were connected, which she pointed out, only to have two strong male voices come back on her at once.

Ruby felt ganged up on.

And...loved, too.

THE TEXT WARNING to Ruby had come from a burner phone. Off a local tower. No surprises there. But frustrating as hell.

Once again, Sebastian had to call an elite client and explain that his dog had been attacked, and would not be ready for delivery as soon as expected. Thankfully, he was dealing with law enforcement, and once they knew the details, they were not only willing to wait for Elise's cuts to heal, but were also offering suggestions to catch the fiend who'd deliberately harm dogs.

And a third piece of great news—Ruby found no muscular damage to the dog at all. If a small piece of glass hadn't pierced Elise's vein, her wounds would have been mostly superficial. Not that he gave his stalker any credit for that one.

The police had quickly located the spot where Elise had been digging and Fletcher had left to check it out, asking Sebastian to stay with Ruby until they knew more.

The hole Elise had dug was on an incline, coming up from the shore of the river. The land was fenced as part of a training course, and didn't appear to be obviously breached, but someone could have climbed the fence. The enclosure was made to keep young, eager dogs inside, not to keep humans out.

Steele had found pieces of steak with shards of glass embedded in them, buried just inches underground in three different locations along the incline. All out of range of cameras.

Clearly planted there.

And not for a good purpose.

Whoever was after him was smart. Watchful. And vigilant.

And, as Fletcher had pointed out on one of his calls to Sebastian, the subject seemed to have a lot of time on their hands. Or, as the visiting detective had suggested, the stalker worked second shift and Sebastian was the man's current after-work activity.

Ruby's brother had another interesting theory. That the person they were after had a place along the lake. Possibly even in view of Sebastian's property. The police were checking rentals. Not a small task, considering the tourist mecca Owl Creek had become.

Fletcher, in going over the case files the night before, had found another possible suspect as well. He'd been looking for anyone who'd had a history with both Sebastian *and* Ruby. There'd been a man a few years back who'd claimed to be a veteran in need of a PTSD dog—part of the volunteer portion of Sebastian's outfit. Veterans received trained dogs for free. The guy had lied about his military service. He'd never served his country and had no medical records to show he'd received any treatment, or even had a consultation for the stress disorder.

Ruby had been the one to raise doubts in the beginning. She hadn't liked the way the man related to the dog they'd been about to give him. There'd been no bond at all. More like someone who was going to turn around and sell the dog for a nice profit.

His name was David Pierce. Sebastian remembered him. According to police, the guy's last known address was the county jail, dated a few years before. He'd been in for a misdemeanor swindling charge of some sort. Meaning it had to have involved less than a thousand dollars. He'd disappeared upon his release.

Moved out of state.

Fletcher was attempting to find out where.

Sebastian was sitting at Ruby's kitchen table, his truck still in her garage, relating the gist of the most recent telephone conversation he'd had with her brother. Ruby was going over the dog's paws with a bright light, a magnifying glass and tweezers, looking for small shards of glass she might have missed.

It was her third time doing so—giving Elise breaks in between—and she was still finding little glints that turned out to be more shards.

"I remember him, too," Ruby said slowly, as though her mind was only half on her words. "The guy gave me the creeps. The way he didn't even seem to see dogs as living beings. He never looked any of them in the eye. As I recall, he didn't even talk to them."

Listening to her, Sebastian smiled. In some ways, the woman was his twin. Who else judged people by whether or not they spoke to dogs? Or looked them in the eye, as opposed to just looking at them?

"I like Fletcher," Sebastian said then, the other man's integrity pushing at him. Hard.

"Yeah." Ruby rubbed an alcohol-soaked pad on the paw she'd just been picking, and, praising Elise, helped the dog down. "I kind of like him, too," she said then, returning to her conversation with Sebastian.

Sebastian dropped to the floor with Elise, petting the girl, and said, "I'm thinking we should let him know about the baby."

He'd spent a good bit of time soul-searching after his meeting with Fletcher the day before. "When something doesn't feel right, it means you're in the wrong place, or with the wrong people, or doing the wrong thing," he said, paraphrasing her words to him during their Friday-night phone conversation. "It doesn't feel right to me that he doesn't know that when this guy goes after you, it's not just your life that's in jeopardy."

"Would it make any difference to his policing?"

It would not. The answer was a no-brainer. Fletcher would protect his sister's life with everything he had. Period.

"It could change how he thinks about me," Sebastian said, feeling a bit less proud of himself in that moment. "When he finds out…knowing that I knew…"

When had he ever made choices based on others' opinions of him?

But then, he'd never had his own biological kid's potential aunts and uncles swarming in the background, either.

"It doesn't make you any less trustworthy." Ruby's tone held the confidence that made a lot of people just nod their heads and do as she said.

It wasn't the tone that got him. It was the fact that she'd known what he'd been thinking. Or how he'd been feeling.

Which, strangely enough, brightened his mood some. "Just as a heads-up, which one of your three brothers is most likely to come looking for me with a baseball bat when they find out?" he asked, sending her a raised-brow look. With the beginnings of a grin.

There they were, with a stalker, threats, Elise hurt...and talking things over with her made the burden seem lighter.

"I'm guessing Wade," she told him, her tone holding no humor at all. "He won't hit you with it, though."

He'd already known that part. He and Wade had taken care of proving their physical superiority over each other as kids. Both had won some and lost some.

"He's not at his best right now," Ruby said, and Sebastian nodded.

"I tried to talk to him, but he's not ready," he told her.

"Plus, you guys have been close since you were kids. I'm guessing he's going to take our situation a little more personally than the rest."

"Because we aren't getting married."

"Yeah. I can see him taking offense that you don't think I'm good enough for you."

His hand on Elise's back paused. "You don't think that do you?"

"Do *you* think I think you aren't good enough for me?"

She didn't look at him. Didn't even slow her cleaning and disposing of the supplies she'd just used.

And he knocked off another reason to feel bad from his list. Ruby didn't want marriage any more than he did. He'd have thought the relief at that one would be palpable.

Finishing up with her supplies at the table, Ruby dropped down to the floor on the other side of the retriever. Elise wagged her tail, looking none the worse for wear.

Because, once again Ruby had saved Sebastian's day.

When he needed to be the one who saved hers.

Chapter Fourteen

With Fletcher home, Jenny Colton had insisted on having Sunday afternoon dinner with all her kids at the table. There was no way Ruby had been able to get out of going. Everyone was worried about her, and they needed to see that she was fine.

Her dad and oldest brother, Chase, who was vice president at Colton Properties, talked business. Fletcher and Wade took the boat out for a while. Her mom and two younger sisters talked cooking and food and coffee drinks. And Ruby played with Lucy.

She'd been worried that Hannah or Frannie would blow her secret somehow, even by trying to talk to her alone and being overheard, but neither one of them sought her out. Jenny had been too busy helping to plan the food for Buck's birthday celebration and both of her sisters were deeply involved with that. Apparently, Frannie was providing a full bar of coffee drinks to go along with dessert.

Sebastian had taken Elise and gone home shortly after noon. Della had been planning to train, but with the police there, she had fed the dogs and worked inside the kennel instead. And from what Fletcher told her at dinner, Sebastian had decided not to do any more training until he had some-one out to check every inch of the other courses.

Fletcher insisted on having Colton Veterinary Clinic in-spected as well. He brought in a K-9 officer, which Ruby saw as total overkill, but she had to admit she felt safer going into work Monday morning knowing that the place had been checked for any booby traps.

She wasn't so much afraid of being physically hurt. But living with the constant threat of criminal activity disrupt-ing daily life and hurting dogs was taking its toll on her. She could only imagine what it was doing to Sebastian.

And she figured that the stalker had intended the emo-tional distress as much as anything physical he'd done.

Which meant, she thought, that the unknown assailant was after Sebastian, not her.

Sebastian had asked her to text when she got home Sun-day night. She did, hoping that he'd call. He just texted back instead.

And she figured that was just as well.

He thanked her for letting him know and telling her that Elise had been out in the exercise yard several times and was doing just fine. He kept things on a less personal level.

More their usual style.

Other than the vein bleed, the retriever's wounds had all been fairly superficial. Because Sebastian had been out there to stop the dog from digging any further for the blood-cov-ered meat she'd found.

Fletcher had let her know quietly after dinner that the blood on the meat had tested as human.

But as gruesome a warning as that sounded, he, Steele and Sebastian all figured it was the sign of a thorough stalker, someone who knew that human blood would be most likely to attract a search-and-rescue animal, not a warning of more human bloodshed to come.

They were testing the blood for a DNA match, though. Hoping that they'd have a lead on the assailant within a few days.

That blood could be the mistake they'd been waiting for.

And before she could fully begin to plan the next phase of her life, she needed the stalker caught. Overkill, maybe, but she was growing more and more adamant that she didn't want the person to know that she was carrying a baby. And most particularly did not want him even suspecting that it could be Sebastian's.

Still, having been with her whole family, in her parents' home, playing with Lucy... She couldn't help thinking how the family dinner would look next time Fletcher came home. If he waited for his next yearly vacation. There'd be a play-pen, a car seat. She'd be breast-feeding. Changing diapers. And holding a baby. Her mom would be taking charge of the infant, holding baby cheeks up to her own and talking that sweet talk again...

Elation welled in her, mixing with panic. And other things, too. Excitement. And an odd combination of sadness and re-gret that she didn't understand.

Which had led her to wanting to hear Sebastian's voice. To talk to him. Telling herself she yearned for him in particular because he was the only one who knew her full secret. Who had an idea of what her future looked like.

But Monday morning, as she left for work, seeing the empty place in her garage where his truck had been parked the morning before, she realized that it was a good thing she and Sebastian hadn't talked the night before. With emo-tions running abnormally high, they could lead themselves into a place neither one of them would want to be when the dust settled.

And the last thing she wanted to do was trap a man into being there for her.

But it wasn't just her who'd need him. Ruby might be the only visible occupant of her vehicle, but she wasn't the only living human there. She wasn't alone anymore.

Ever. Not even for a second.

And while her child would grow up, and apart from her, that new life forming inside her would always be a part of her.

The concept was mind-boggling.

Every aspect of her life was going to change.

Driving along the lake through her hometown, Ruby started to see the businesses differently, too, just as she had her parents' house the night before. The Tides, the high-end restaurant located on the lakefront, was rented out frequently for weddings and special occasions. Jenny had thrown a party for Ruby on the large open patio there when she'd graduated from veterinary school.

Would Ruby be arranging a high-school graduation party in that same space in eighteen years?

And Tap Out Brewery, with its local brews. She'd had some good times there, eating pub food with friends back before they'd all gone their own ways and her work had become her life. The place turned into more of a party venue after 8:00 p.m. Would she be driving by to make certain her teenager wasn't getting sucked into drinking underage?

As the muscles in her stomach tightened with tension, she passed Hutch's diner. And relaxed some. Hutch had always only made breakfast, but it was the best. She'd been going there since she was a kid. Hutch had been gone for four years, but his wife, Sharon, still ran the place, with the help of their son, Billy.

And maybe Ruby's child would one day join her at the clinic. Just like Chase had joined Robert at Colton Properties. And Wade and Malcolm both worked with Uncle Buck at Colton Ranch.

She'd love that. To have her own little one grow up to love animals, to want to care for them with her. And even after her.

There was a sense of permanence in the thought. Of continuity. For years she'd been pushed by the sense that if she didn't work hard all the time, her clinic wouldn't survive. The idea that it could possibly thrive even after she was no longer there was…nice.

Coming up to the newest addition on Main Street, she pulled over in front of the long, narrow three-story brick building and turned off the SUV. Frannie's bookstore and café, Book Mark It, wasn't open yet, but her sister had offered the night before to have tea ready for Ruby on her way to work if she wanted to stop.

Frannie hadn't said, but it would be decaffeinated. Because… Frannie knew.

And while Ruby could make her own morning beverage at work, and normally would have just to save the time, she went inside to see her little sister, instead.

SEBASTIAN WASN'T WAITING on Ruby's brother, or anyone else, to start his lure-the-stalker-out campaign. He'd wait to involve anything in Owl Creek, but the filming, and interviewing was going to begin on Monday. And the first segment would air in Boise later that week. He'd called

Andy, Bryony and Della to let them know they needn't come into work.

Not Monday, for sure. And, if they chose, they could take off until the Crosswinds attacker was caught. He couldn't require people to risk their lives.

Della refused to take any time off. And she brought her own two-year-old search-and-rescue black Lab, Charlie, with her when she arrived in time on Monday to help Sebastian with the feedings and kennel cleanings.

Neither of them ended up doing much of either as Bryony and Andy showed up, too, telling Sebastian they'd work extra hours to make up for James's absence.

His crew wasn't just there to make money. They cared about the Crosswinds mission, they told him, in an impromptu little meeting in the kennel that morning. They loved the dogs.

And maybe they cared about him, too, he thought, as, fueled with energy, he left them to their tasks and took Oscar home for a PTSD session.

He'd been working with the dog since Ruby had first suggested that Oscar could be cross-trained. He'd figured trying couldn't hurt.

If it worked, he could add cross-training to the list of Crosswinds services.

The film crew and cohost interviewer weren't due until afternoon, when it would be warmest outside.

Sitting at the table, Sebastian started bumping one heel up and down on the floor. Two seconds, and Oscar was there, nudging his knee.

"Good boy!" He gave the dog a treat. And repeated the process.

He'd noticed that the heel bump was something he did

when he was starting to get tense. He'd always taken the movement as a rhythmic reminder to himself to relax. But if he could teach Oscar to cue him when it started, the dog's distraction and loving attention might calm him before the tension escalated.

He knew the ropes. Had been training PTSD dogs for a few years. It was different when he was working with his dog. For himself. The thought created a curious level of anxiety.

Except that...he wasn't just doing it for himself. What if he was around his kid sometime, fell asleep and had a flipping nightmare?

If Oscar was there, if he was trained to nudge Sebastian when signs of a nightmare began, there'd be an added level of safety for the kid.

Not that he planned to have the kid around and fall asleep. He wasn't a family guy. Just the thought of not having his space to himself created a level of anxiety.

But the thought of not helping Ruby? Of not being a part of his own child's life? At first, he'd gone there automatically. Had made the logical choice. But as he'd lain in bed at night, and went about his tasks during the day, as he faced the fact that Ruby could be hurt, and that his child would, too...

Oscar nudged him.

Hard.

And he relaxed. "Good boy!" he said, giving the dog a treat. Oscar had the calming skill down. Far better than Sebastian did, apparently.

He moved on to simulate a moaning sound that he knew commonly accompanied nightmares. Ruby had told him he was moaning. Showing Oscar a treat, and moaning, and giving the dog the treat.

Oscar, who'd already mastered search-and-rescue training, caught on quickly. A couple of more moans and the dog was nudging for treats.

Figuring he'd move on to serotonin-level change, getting up to retrieve hormones that would simulate the smell, Sebastian stopped when his phone beeped a text message.

He hadn't yet heard from Ruby. She'd said she'd text when she got to work. Just so he'd know she was there.

More eager than he should have been to hear from Crosswinds's veterinarian, he grabbed his phone off the table.

YOU CARE MORE ABOUT DOGS THAN YOU DO PEOPLE

The phone number was blocked.

Tapping the newest icon on his speed dial, Sebastian got Fletcher on the first ring.

He hadn't even started his campaign and the guy was escalating.

Hitting out at him and not Ruby. Because he thought Ruby had minded his command and stayed away the morning before?

"Bring it on," Sebastian said aloud, standing. "Come at me and we'll get this done."

Facing the danger on his own, by himself, he wasn't afraid. He was trained.

THE DAY FLEW BY. Other than breaks for proper nutrition to go along with her horse-pill-size vitamins, Ruby moved efficiently from appointment to appointment, enjoying her time with each client and patient, answering questions, advising, giving lots of hugs and getting plenty of nose kisses, too. Until late afternoon, the day was the kind she liked best—all well checks. And everyone checked out well. She never scheduled surgeries on Mondays unless there was an emergency.

She was just getting ready to sit at her desk and make notes in her charting system when she got a call from the reception desk telling her that a dog injured in a car accident was on the way in. A runaway beagle had been hit on Main Street.

Three hours later, tired, but filled with satisfaction, with the sense that she was living her best life, she headed home. The beagle had lost part of an ear, and one kidney. He might walk with a slight limp, but he should fully recover and live a normal life. Barney's elderly owners had both been in tears when she'd led them back to see the boy before going home for the night.

Maria would be spending the night at the clinic and would call Ruby if anything changed with Barney before morning.

Figuring her family should be proud of her—in prior days Ruby would have spent the night on the couch in her office and sent her technician home—Ruby was looking forward to some of Hannah's homemade vegetable soup as she pulled into the nighttime traffic. Filled with tourists all year round, Owl Creek was always a happening place during the evening hours as people came in from days of boating, fishing, skiing, or climbing and were looking for evening entertainment.

The Tides was booming, as was the brewery. She figured the nightclub just outside of town would be, too. But not for Ruby. None of it sounded good to her. Her sister had made up several individual containers of her soup for freezing and had gifted Ruby, and the rest of the family, with them the night before. Ruby was having part of her share for dinner.

And maybe she'd hear from Sebastian. More than just

a text message. He'd had a marketing crew in that afternoon, she knew. But she hadn't talked to him or heard from Fletcher or Detective Steele all day.

Didn't mean nothing had happened. Only that it hadn't directly involved her.

She didn't like not knowing.

So why didn't she ask? Who said she had to wait to hear? And if she wanted to talk to Sebastian, why didn't she?

Filled with self-righteous energy, she gave the voice command to call Sebastian. And grinned in the darkness of her car's interior when he picked up on the first ring.

"Have you eaten?" she asked without preamble.

"Nope. Just coming in from the kennels for the night." He'd had a long day. She wanted to hear about it. As a volunteer in his program. Her Dr. Colton persona wanted a rundown on her patients, too.

"You like vegetable soup?" she asked before she could get ahold of herself and change her mind. She was carrying his child. He wanted to be involved. They were friends. And she wanted to see him.

"I do."

"You want to come over?"

"Of course."

"I'm not there yet. I had an emergency come in at the end of my day. Spent three hours in surgery."

What in the hell was she doing? Sharing her day with him like they were a couple or something. She always went home alone after work. Long days and not so long. Grueling and easy. Her, alone. It's how she wanted it.

"I'm leaving now," Sebastian said.

Starting to doubt herself, she almost canceled the invitation she'd just issued, but he'd hung up. Too much was changing. Too fast.

She wasn't a woman who ever had a man over after work.

Or ever.

Her home was her haven.

It was soon going to have a new human being living in it full-time.

Sebastian was an offshoot of that little person.

And a big man with an appetite to match. Her servings of vegetable soup weren't going to be enough to satisfy the mountain man who'd been working all day and hadn't had dinner. She turned into the grocery store, then ran in and grabbed a loaf of freshly baked Italian bread from the bakery and a precut vegetable tray from the deli. Paid at self-checkout and was back at her car within minutes. Her little house, right on the lake, was only another couple of minutes away and he had ten to get to town.

She'd left her nightshirt on the kitchen counter, to remind herself to do a load of laundry when she got home. And hadn't put away the rest of the supplies she'd used for Elise the day before, either, which she needed to do to set the table for dinner.

For that matter, she hadn't emptied the dishwasher.

She had not thought the evening's events through.

She wasn't a woman who could just entertain a man on a moment's notice.

"He's not a man. He's Sebastian," she said aloud as she rounded the curve to her little lakefront home. Heard the absurdity of the statement, considering the fact that his manly part had very much changed her life, and…

Lights shone to the left of her. Blinding her in her rearview mirror.

Sebastian?

Already?

The vehicle wasn't behind her.

What the...?

It was there, up to her bumper, beside her, going to hit her...

Ruby swerved. Had no shoulder to turn on. And came to an abrupt stop in the ditch.

Heart pounding, she sat for a second. "I'm fine," she said aloud, checking to make certain her assertion was correct. The airbag hadn't deployed. She hadn't hit the steering wheel. She'd felt her seat belt, but hadn't been bruised.

Glancing in her mirrors, she unbuckled herself with shaking hands. All was dark around her. The vehicle had sped on past. She could see lights shining from homes down from hers. Their little access road didn't get a lot of traffic.

Taking a deep breath, she tried to calm herself. She needed to get home. But the nose of her SUV was stuck in dirt. And with the small but sharp incline she'd headed down, there was no way she could back up.

She'd have to walk. Or wait for Sebastian. Opening her door, she pulled out her phone to call him so he didn't miss her and drive on past. She couldn't stop shaking, missing his speed dial on the first attempt and...

She screamed as arms came around her from behind. Pulling up under her armpits. She saw black gloves. "No!" She got a word into the second scream.

"I've been told that land is mine," a male voice said softly into her ear. "I will have it. God says animals are here to serve man, not for man to serve them. It's blasphemy."

Scared, trembling, unable to breathe, she flung her head

back as hard as she could, hitting her assailant in the face. He released her and pushed away, and she fell to the ground.

Lights came around the corner. She had a flash of the man's face. His bloody nose. Then he turned and ran off through the trees.

Gasping for air, trembling, Ruby crawled to her tire. Pulled herself up.

Saw Sebastian.

And started to cry.

Chapter Fifteen

Leaving Ruby's SUV nose-down in the ditch, Sebastian picked her up, cradled in his arms, grabbed her satchel and rushed them both to his truck.

"I'm fine," she said, but the way she laid her head against his chest, pushing into him, showed him the lie in her words.

He dropped her satchel to pull open the passenger door. Set her on the seat, pushed the button to ease it back, strapped her in and set her satchel on the floor of his truck as though he'd been through save-your-child's-mother basic training.

He just moved. On instinct.

Got himself in the driver's seat the same way. No thought. No feeling. Just do.

As soon as the truck was on, and headed back to Main Street, he voice-called Fletcher Colton, telling the detective in a few succinct words what he'd come upon, giving a description of the back of the fleeing man, which was all he'd seen, and let him know the direction in which the man had gone.

Fletcher had questions, spat out in the same manner.

He answered every one of them.

Including that he had Ruby and was taking her to be examined.

By the time he hung up, he was already heading toward the highway.

"I don't need to be examined." She was raising her seat as she said the words. "He didn't hurt me, Sebastian. He just scared the air out of me."

"I saw you on the ground." Emotion hit then. Hard. Full of anger. He'd find the man. And show him why he should never have touched Ruby Colton.

"I head-butted him," she said, sounding more like the woman he'd known since childhood. Controlled. Self-sufficient.

She'd been crying when he'd picked her up. It was a sight that was going to haunt him.

"I think I broke his nose." She sounded as though she might be bragging a little. "I know I made him bleed."

Sebastian's grip tightened on the wheel. "How do you know that?"

"I saw the blood coming out of his nose."

"You saw his face."

"Yeah, in your headlight as you came up the road. I think that's what made him run off." He heard the fear in her tone at the last remark. She shuddered.

And he gritted his teeth against the need powering through him to go hunt the guy down. Right then. Himself.

Because getting Ruby to the emergency room was more important.

"If you hadn't come—"

"You'd have been fine," he interrupted. He had to believe those words.

"I should talk to Fletcher," she said then, as though just coming into a full awareness of the situation. "Turn around. I'm fine, really. We need to get back so I can talk to the police. And I have to get my car out of the ditch. I have to be in early to check on Barney. And I have appointments starting at eight."

"You're pregnant, Ruby. Your SUV obviously hit the ditch with some force. And if you were close enough to head-butt the guy with enough force to land you on the ground, I have to assume he had some kind of hold on you, and then let you go in a way that caused you to fall."

She wouldn't have deliberately lain down for the guy. Sebastian would bet his life on that one.

She was fully dressed. Her clothes weren't torn. He'd just been on the phone with her ten minutes before he'd come upon her...

The man hadn't had a chance to...

He owed fate his life for sparing her...

Thoughts flew. Started and stopped.

"Fletcher and Steele will have people out casing the area. I had enough of a description for them to apprehend him if they find him soon. We need to get you checked out to make certain the baby is okay. That's more important than a police report," he told her.

They just needed the baby to be okay.

He repeated the words to himself. And then again.

Until he realized just how much he had invested in the small being growing inside Ruby. Not just his biology, but the heart and soul of him.

He wasn't going to be a father. But he'd fathered a child.

And would give up his life for that tiny being, too.

SHE AND THE baby were both fine. Ruby had known they were, and yet, when the doctor came into her Connors emergency-room cubicle and told her so, she'd been flooded with relief, anyway.

There'd been no doubt, since she'd found out she was pregnant, that she was going to have the child. That moment alone with the doctor, waiting on the precipice of knowing what the ultrasound had revealed, she'd been shown just how much she wanted the baby. How deeply she already loved it.

The worried look on Sebastian's face when she approached him in the waiting room touched her heart, too.

He cared.

And that mattered.

"All good," she said, unable to stop the smile that spread on her face.

Or to stop the flip-flop her heart gave when he smiled back.

Reliving the near kidnapping, trembling, as she stepped out into the dark, she stopped her hand from sneaking around his elbow, forcing herself to keep her distance as she walked with him back to the truck.

They were friends.

Not lovers.

As she reminded herself on the forty-five-minute drive back to Owl Creek—Sebastian was all business, and there was no reason for her feelings to be hurt by that fact.

Her emotions were on overload.

She was not only hormonal due to pregnancy, but she'd also been through a near abduction. Sebastian was the guy who'd happened by to clean up the mess.

She'd be on top of the fear by morning. And would have the rest of her heart back in line by then as well. With all the upheaval she'd experienced growing up, she knew she could count on herself to be strong and step away from the drama.

As soon as they were in the truck, Sebastian started filling her in on news from Fletcher.

There'd been no sign of a man between five-ten and six feet in dark pants, a dark, long-sleeved hoodie and dark shoes anywhere in the woods or neighborhood surrounding Ruby's house. Officers canvassed houses and businesses on Main Street, too, but no one remembered seeing a man with that description.

They were requesting private security footage, both in the neighborhood and from businesses along Main Street, to go through.

"He had dark hair," Ruby said, when Sebastian paused for breath. "And he was white." She remembered his hands coming up from her sides, as his arms slid under her armpits, and shuddered again.

Glancing at her, his chin seemed to tighten, but in the darkness of the truck, she couldn't be sure.

"They found an SUV, Ruby," he said, his tone like a sergeant, reporting to the masses. She knew the tone. From Fletcher and Wade, too.

Wasn't overly fond of it.

But being one who sometimes had to be the bearer of bad news at work, she completely understood it.

"It fits the description you gave from Friday morning. It was abandoned in the woods across from your house."

"He ran me off the road," she said, as it occurred to her that Sebastian hadn't known that part. She'd been in panic mode when the father of her child had arrived. Was still trying to comprehend that she'd nearly been taken against her will.

Shivering, she wanted the memory, the horrifying sensations involved with it, to go away. Forever.

"Just like Friday morning…"

But that night she'd been in the ditch. "I wasn't able to turn out of it," she said slowly, reliving those moments, with darkness looming larger than the lights on the dash, the lights in the homes along the lake. "I sat in the ditch," she remembered. "Trying to figure out what had just happened. Deciding what to do. I was just getting out of the SUV, to flag you down, when…"

He'd grabbed her.

She was cold. Needed a warm blanket. Forced herself to think.

"My phone," she said. "I was calling you…"

He glanced her way again. Maybe it was her imagination, but he seemed pleased by those last words.

And in times of crisis, a little fantasy to get her through didn't hurt, did it?

"FLETCHER'S MEETING US at your house." Sebastian repeated something he'd told Ruby on the way to the truck in the hospital parking lot.

She didn't respond. He wasn't sure how much she'd processed of anything he'd been telling her.

"He talked to me," she said softly, her entire body shaking, as though warding off a chill. He reached to the dash, turned up the heat in the truck. Kept his eye on his driving, and glanced at her, too. Back and forth. The road. Her. The road. Her.

She'd hadn't mentioned hearing a voice.

Was she imagining things?

It was only a couple of hours since she'd been attacked, and he knew what trauma-induced panic could do...

"It just came to me, the sound of his voice in my ear." She hugged her arms, her voice sounding almost childlike.

"What did he say?" Sebastian asked softly. With as much kindness as he had inside him.

"'I've been told that land is mine, I will have it. God says animals are here to serve man, not for man to serve them. It's blasphemy.'" The words rolled off her tongue with no intonation whatsoever. "It was him, Sebastian. Your stalker. The SUV, yeah, but those words. It was him." As she looked his way and continued talking, her tone rose, panic lacing every syllable.

And Sebastian pressed his foot on the pedal all the way to the floor.

He had to get her back to Fletcher.

And needed to hold on to her.

No way was he leaving her to drown in the panic all alone.

He knew how that felt.

And she was there because of him.

RUBY REFUSED TO go to her parents' house. Or to the police station. At ten o'clock at night, her big brother could come to her house.

She had to go home.

To be where she was the boss of the land.

She heard Sebastian relay the information to Fletcher while they were still ten minutes outside of Owl Creek.

"He doesn't think it's a good idea for you to go back to that neighborhood right now," Sebastian told her, hanging up.

"That's exactly why I *have* to go back," she retorted. "I won't let this fiend turn my home into a haunted house. Besides, if he was going to do something to me at home, he'd simply have waited until I got there," she added. "I was three houses down. If nothing else, he could have waited for me to pull into the garage and slipped inside..." Her voice trailed off as another wave of panic hit.

Sebastian shot a quick look at her. And then said, "I think you're probably right about that."

He almost sounded relieved.

"I guess it's better that tonight's...episode relates to my work at Crosswinds, rather than just that I'm unlucky enough to be the target of a second madman." Dear God, let that have meant that he wouldn't have forced himself on her.

No. She wasn't going to borrow trouble.

She had enough real boogeymen chasing her mind at the moment.

As they passed the sign announcing the turn-off for Owl Creek in two miles, Sebastian blurted out, "We have to tell Fletcher about the baby. I've been trying to figure out a way to get your cooperation on this one, and I know it's not what you want or what would be easiest for you. I get that you don't need your family breathing down on you any more than they already are, or will soon be, but I'm not backing down on this one. Not anymore."

When he finished, finally giving her a chance to get a word in, she said, "I know." And then added, "But we don't have to tell anyone that you're the father."

He'd pulled to a stop at the bottom of the highway exit ramp. They had the road to themselves, and when he glanced over at her, he didn't seem to be all that concerned about turning into town. "Are you ashamed to tell them it's me?"

"No!" She'd screamed the word once before that night. Her throat still stung from the sounds she'd made. That second time, it wasn't filled with panic. But with exclamation. "No," she said again, more calmly. "I'm thinking of you, Sebastian."

"Then you don't know me all that well." He faced forward.

"What does that mean?" She could see the set of his chin in the darkness but little else. Avoiding the strong desire to unbuckle and touch that chin—it wasn't anything she'd know how to pull off casually—she continued into the silence, "Talk to me, please," she said, in her more professional tone.

"I'm a man of honor. I don't shirk my duties. And I won't have anyone in your family thinking that I do."

She wished she hadn't asked. Her heart fell as she heard the words.

It wasn't about her.

Or their baby.

It was about Once a Marine, Always a Marine. Wade's explanation anytime she told him he was getting on her nerves with his need to fight for and defend everyone in their family anytime he was home on leave.

With a nod, she accepted his explanation and waited for him to take her home.

Chapter Sixteen

Are you ashamed to tell them it's me? Where in the hell had that come from? If ever there was a man completely out of his element, it was Sebastian.

Fighting the enemy, he knew what to do every time. Whether that enemy was a terrorist in another land, or one in his own backyard, antagonizing his dogs. And his veterinarian.

But finding out that the night his friend had taken pity on him, he'd made her pregnant? In spite of the precautions they'd taken…

How did a confirmed bachelor go about figuring out how to deal with that? Most particularly in a small town that, along with his dogs, was the only family he had left?

She'd gone cold when he'd overreacted to her very sweet offer to keep his name out of her baby confession that evening. He'd have apologized if he hadn't thought it would make matters worse. If for no other reason than because they'd almost reached her house and had no time left to talk about it.

Her SUV was already back in the driveway, with her brother's right beside it. Fletcher climbed out as Sebastian pulled up out front. Half expecting Ruby to wish him good-night before she exited his vehicle, he was aware as she climbed down from the truck and then stood there, as though waiting for him to finish rounding the front of the vehicle.

No way he wasn't going to be present for the coming conversation. Just felt irrationally good that she'd seemed to take his presence for granted.

After giving his sister a thorough once-over glance, Fletcher took a seat at Ruby's kitchen table—still strewn with supplies from her attention to Elise the morning before—and announced that while Steele was running command on the officers out on the street, Fletcher would be recording the interview with Ruby.

Sebastian sat diagonally across from the detective and Ruby sat next to Sebastian. He didn't make anything of it.

The ten-minute conversation was straightforward. Ruby told her brother everything she'd told Sebastian in the truck. Adding more description to the man's face. With the light's glare she hadn't been able to tell an age, but she'd seen no age lines. He'd had facial hair, but no beard or mustache. Just stubble. Light-colored, not dark, like his hair. She agreed to sit with a sketch artist Fletcher was calling in from Boise in the morning.

Then Fletcher turned off the recording, putting his phone down on the table instead of back into his pocket.

Glancing between the two of him. The detective's frown, the uneasy look in his eyes, had Sebastian looking at Ruby. Gearing up to take the brunt of whatever was coming.

She seemed to be holding up fine. Hands folded on the table, tone strong. It was as though the attack had never happened.

"First, it's pretty clear to everyone that this guy tonight is the same one we've already been hunting," Fletcher started in. "The SUV they found tonight just yards from where Ruby was attacked fits the description she gave Friday morning and then again this evening." Fletcher looked at both of them. "The vehicle was stolen last Thursday from a big-box store in Connors…"

"Which means we've just lost our best chance at getting him," Sebastian guessed. "He's changing vehicles. Driving stolen ones."

"It looks that way. Which would explain why we haven't been able to find the same vehicle leaving town on all the nights there's been attacks at Crosswinds."

His enemy was a canny one.

"He's been told that the land is his," Fletcher said, glancing between him and Ruby, but settling on Sebastian. "We have to assume this means the land upon which Crosswinds is sitting. Which brings us back to the possibility that your father had a child outside of his marriage to your mother. From Ruby's description, he sounds younger as opposed to not—that would fit, too."

Sebastian nodded. He'd also gone straight to the idea of a love child after Ruby had told him what the guy had said.

"But this…" Fletcher referred to the notes he'd also been taking on a yellow pad. "'God says that animals are there to serve men…and not for men to serve…'"

"Has to refer to the kennels," Sebastian mused. "Until James quit, there were five of us there, pretty much every day, taking care of the dogs."

"And Ruby most definitely fits the role of serving animals," Fletcher continued, glancing back at his sister.

Sebastian felt her stiffen beside him. She was no longer shaking. Whether it was because she had her fear under con-

trol, or just enough determination to remain strong in front
of her brother, he couldn't be sure.

Suspected it was the latter.

The woman had certainly perfected the guise of being
a rock on the outside. Growing up as she had, he couldn't
blame her.

"He's after you, too, Ruby. And judging by his behavior,
it would appear that he's no longer satisfied just going after
the dogs and issuing warnings. Tonight's episode shows us
that he's escalating. They found rope in the car. He wasn't
going to just warn you and let you go."

She nodded, surprising Sebastian. And scaring him. Ruby
rarely just acquiesced and that was the second time that
night. First one being when he insisted on telling her brother
about the baby.

But then, looking from Sebastian to her brother, she asked,
"What possible reason would he have for kidnapping me? I
volunteer at Crosswinds—I don't own it. I get that I've an-
gered him. That my work has systematically undone pretty
much every attempt he's made to put Crosswinds out of business, but what does he gain by taking me? There are three
other veterinarians in my office alone…"

Sebastian glanced at Fletcher, who said, "How many do
you think will be eager to service those dogs, knowing that
they could end up like you? Or how do you think it will look
in the news? 'Crosswinds veterinarian kidnapped…'"

She shook her head. "I can't believe someone would re-
sort to such tactics…"

"He would if he was experiencing some kind of psychotic
break." Sebastian issued the explanation softly, while inside,
every fighting instinct he had was at the ready. "Assuming
he's a result of this affair of my dad's they think they've dis-

covered at this point…he's grown up on the outside look-ing in. Even if he didn't know that my dad was his father, he'd have grown up without knowing his real father. Some-how he finds out, either he's always known, or maybe his mother told him after Dad died. She could easily have known about the Owl Creek property. Maybe even told the kid he deserved to have it. For all I know some lawyer told him it was his. From what Ruby said, he seemed to have no doubt that what he'd been told was true. And yet, he gets here and finds out that I'm firmly ensconced. The only known heir, the only legal heir and running an elite training business on what he thinks is his land. Then you come along—" Sebas-tian looked at Ruby "—and thwart every attempt he makes to get me to tuck my tail and go."

"He hasn't done enough homework if he thinks you'd ever do that," Ruby said, her words more of a statement of fact than praise. His heart lifted a bit at the words, anyway.

"I see where you're going with this," Fletcher added then, his gaze toward Sebastian assessing. "You could be hitting it exactly right. Ruby's in his way. He's getting more and more desperate, maybe becoming more unhinged, and just sees her as someone he has to get out of the way. Which makes him even more dangerous. He's still thinking clearly enough to create all these issues without ever being seen or coming close to getting caught. He's wearing gloves, so leaving no prints. Other than the rope, there was nothing else in the car."

At her sudden intake of air, Sebastian sent her brother a look. Ruby was strong. She wasn't inhuman.

"I'm sorry," Fletcher said, then added, "But not com-pletely. You can't stay here, Ruby. I don't care how much you argue. He clearly knows where you live."

Relieved that he wasn't the one bringing up the matter

he'd been planning to discuss with her as soon as they were through with Fletcher, Sebastian said, "Your parents have state-of-the-art security. You'd be much safer there."

If her brother hadn't been sitting there, he'd have mentioned the baby. Even if she survived another attack, the baby might not get that lucky. If the man had hit her harder, if the seat belt jerked tighter across her belly, if the airbag had deployed...

He started to sweat again...as he had pretty much the entire time he'd sat in the hospital waiting room that evening. She had to see the sense in not staying home alone until the unknown man was caught. "You saw his face," he added. "He's going to know you can identify him."

"Which brings a whole new level of desperation to his thinking," Fletcher said.

"Did someone check the ground for blood splatter?" Ruby asked. "Or my hair? Maybe I got some of his DNA on me when I hit him with the back of my head."

Sebastian's tension increased. He needed her on her parents' property. Safely locked in. Not sitting here trying to solve the crime. But while Fletcher called Steele to check the dirt in the area of the attempted kidnapping for blood, Sebastian turned on his phone light and studied the back of Ruby's hair. It was tucked up in her usual messy bun.

"I hit him with the bun," she said then. He grabbed some paper towel off the rack in the kitchen and pulled out her scrunchie. He saw no sign of blood but gathered the plastic bag she told him was in the drawer, inserted the hair band and paper towel and handed it over to Fletcher when the other man completed his call.

"If your shampoo has peroxide in it, and many of them do, that will most likely falsify any result for blood testing,"

Fletcher said. But he added that they'd test the few hairs attached to the scrunchie, just in case.

And he asked Ruby for her clothes. Again, just in case.

While she went to change, Sebastian looked at Fletcher. "She didn't say she'd go."

The detective nodded. "If I have to, I'll stay here myself, but I'd rather meet up with Steele, compare notes, see what we can find on the few new leads we have. We know the guy was in Connors on Thursday. Maybe surveillance tapes from there can give us something."

"She can't stay here," Sebastian said. Almost bursting with the need to know that Ruby would be in a safe place.

"I can hear you," she said, joining the two and handing Fletcher a bag with her work clothes inside. She'd put on jeans and a sweatshirt. Sebastian hoped that meant she was planning to go out again that night. To her parents' house.

Ruby looked at him. A long, meaningful glance.

Gut knotting, he sat back down when she did.

"What's up?" Fletcher asked.

"I'm pregnant."

If Sebastian hadn't been so involved, so disturbed with worry and his inability to control Ruby's every move so that he could keep her safe, he might have felt a small bit of amusement from the way the detective's jaw seemed to drop down to the table.

"You don't have to look that astonished, Fletch. I have had sex now and then on occasion."

Her brother coughed. Glanced at Sebastian, as though looking to him for some kind of guy way to handle the moment. "Pregnant?" Fletcher said then.

Flipping back his chair with force the detective stood. "By

who? For how long?" And then, turning a complete circle, he asked, "Tonight...is everything okay?"

"We're both fine," Ruby told him.

And that's when Sebastian jumped up. It was either that or grab the woman and hold her close and out of danger, her and his child, for the rest of his natural life.

RUBY DIDN'T WANT a whole drawn-out thing. She'd had a long day. A horrible evening. And wanted her brother's piercing stare—and the knowledge that he was going home to their parents' house—gone.

She needed some peace. Time to recover. To relax, if she could. To think.

Standing, with her arms crossed, she said, "The father's a friend. A good one. The baby is the result of one night that was filled with tension, just like this one. We used protection. It didn't work. I was shocked when I first found out. I'm already in love with the child. Intend to raise it on my own, my choice, and Hannah and Lizzie know, but no one else does, and I really need you to keep this quiet." She finished the spiel she'd been working on, mostly subconsciously, for the past week, then added, "I've got enough on my plate at the moment."

"You have to tell Mom and Dad," Fletcher replied. "You're going to be staying with them."

The baby was one of the reasons she'd been fighting with herself to stay home. There was no way she could live with her mother, a nurse, and not have Jenny figure out something. The first time Ruby smelled coffee and threw up would do it.

"And how good a friend is this guy if he's letting you take this on all alone?" Fletcher's tone was sharp, but faded at the end. He glanced at Sebastian. "A night filled with tension just like this one." Fletcher repeated her words. And then added, "He's not leaving you to take this on all alone, is he?" The question was meant for Ruby, but her brother hadn't moved since he'd locked eyes with Sebastian.

"No, he is not," Sebastian answered for her. He wasn't moving, either.

The two men were like… She didn't know what—opposing forces that didn't ever back down or lose. And the last thing she needed at the moment.

When Fletcher said, "Okay," and took a step back, Ruby was the one standing with her mouth open. "And now that I know the full detail—" he very clearly meant just one "—I understand why we need to keep this quiet. We absolutely do not want this guy getting any idea that there's another heir in the making."

Ruby cringed and looked away, fearing Sebastian's reaction to the casually dropped phrase, until she felt his hand on her shoulder. "I do agree that your parents should know, though," he said, increasing the tension he'd just deescalated with his touch. "She can't stay there without them being aware…"

"Hello, I'm right here," she said, frowning at both of them. But deep inside, where she didn't want to look at the moment, she knew they were right.

But… "I'll make a deal with you," she said. "I stay here tonight. One of you stay with me. And tomorrow we go to Mom and Dad's. And we tell them about the baby. I just don't have it tonight to deal with them. Not on top of everything else. Please."

"I'll stay," both men said at once.

Ruby glanced at Sebastian, making her choice clear.

And Fletcher let himself out.

Chapter Seventeen

Sebastian heard the door close as Ruby's brother departed. He didn't watch the man go. He couldn't take his gaze from Ruby. The past few minutes, the entire evening, had been so fraught with tension, and being alone with the slimly built, green-eyed woman, with her long golden blond hair, was doing things to him that weren't right.

Not given the circumstances.

Those being that he was her friend.

And nothing more.

In dress pants and doctor's coat, makeup fresh and hair shiny clean, or in jeans and a sweatshirt after a near kid-napping, she was a vixen, luring him into space he knew he could not occupy.

"How about some of that vegetable soup?" Ruby broke the spell, turning away, toward the kitchen. She mentioned a grocery bag that, last she knew, had been on the front passenger seat of her SUV, and he gladly went to retrieve it for her. To breathe the nippy fresh night air, which cooled his body, but not his mind. Outside, he was a soldier, checking every inch of Ruby's small property, knowing that he was on duty for the rest of the night.

So thinking, he called the night security team manning

Crosswinds, had them coax Oscar through his doggy door and lock him in the big kennel room with that officer for the night. He didn't want the boy letting himself out in the middle of the night in the event of an intruder. Sebastian had been closing off Oscar's personal entryway into the house every night before bedtime.

By the time he returned inside, Ruby had the soup heated. He cut bread while she unwrapped the veggie tray and set the table.

Growing up, he'd been the one to set the table. Until he'd deemed the chore not manly enough and then been assigned to do the dishes every night after dinner.

Then he'd learned to cook and was the one who'd prepared dinner. More often than not, he'd eaten it alone. With his plate on his mother's expensive side table, he'd sit on the couch with Jerry right next to him, watch what he wanted on television, or play video games, taking bites as it suited him.

Good memories of easier times.

Much easier than being part of an intimate twosome preparing a meal in the smallest kitchen he'd ever done any food service in.

Ruby talked while she worked. Telling him about Barney, the dog who'd been hit by a car that evening, causing her to stay late at work. Which gave him pause.

Their attacker couldn't have hit the dog on purpose, could he? To keep Ruby late? So that he could attack, as always, at night?

The theory was far-fetched, he silently acknowledged. But he texted Fletcher, anyway, suggesting that they contact the dog's owners and get a rundown of the incident. If it *was* their guy, maybe there was surveillance-camera footage…

Figuring it would be too rude to eat standing at the kitchen counter, which was what he'd have felt more comfortable doing, Sebastian sat across from Ruby, as she indicated which place was his. He put his napkin in his lap as his parents had taught him. And wiped after every spoonful of soup inevitably left drops on his beard.

He'd been on more dates than he could count. Had spent full weekends in the company of whatever woman he'd been seeing. He had never, not even once, been self-conscious sharing a meal with any of them.

Or with Ruby, either, in the past.

He'd never been having a child with any of them.

"This is good," he said, motioning toward the soup.

Ruby nodded. Looked at him, and said, "It's weird, though, isn't it?"

"The soup?" He knew that wasn't what she'd meant. Was not eager for the conversation that was coming. Her brother knew she was pregnant and Sebastian was the father of her child.

Her parents were going to know in less than twenty-four hours.

"We've never even been on a date," she said then. "I've never had a man in my home for a meal, either," she added. Took another bite, almost as though glad for the distraction.

He knew he was. Helped himself to a celery stick and another piece of bread, too. And did what he'd been trained to do—march into battle, not run from it.

"Tell me how you want to play this," he said. "If you want everyone to think we've been secretly dating, or that we were dating and broke up—whatever you need to tell them, give it to me and I'll back you up. One hundred percent. You have family to answer to—I don't. So whatever you need our story to be, that's what it will be."

Ruby took a bite. Then glanced at him, her gaze soft. "I've been sitting here trying to figure out how to tell them that we aren't a couple, aren't in love, have never dated, and are having a baby," she said, her tone as gentle as her look. "And you're right—we don't owe anyone our intimate truths. We just give them what works for us, while staying within boundaries of the truth." Her sudden smile, like she'd solved the problems of the world, pulled an answering smile from Sebastian.

The woman had a way with him that no one else had ever had.

He prayed that it didn't turn out to be what killed him.

"WE'VE BEEN TOGETHER a lot these past months, with my volunteering at Crosswinds. One thing led to another, and now we're having a baby." With Sebastian sitting across from her in her small dining room, late at night, smiling that way, the words just rolled off Ruby's tongue.

Funny how what had seemed impossible was easy, when shared with a friend. A caring, yet different perspective, that didn't try to force one particular way down her throat.

"Whether we're dating or not isn't anyone's business. We're friends. We know that, in whatever fashion you choose, you're going to be involved in the child's life. So we present ourselves as friendly with each other, sharing a child. Done. End of what they need to know."

She liked it. A lot. Felt a bit easier inside. Took a bite of bread. Enjoyed the homemade, feel-good taste.

"And when your father asks me when the wedding's going to be?"

Chewed bread stuck in her throat. She washed it down with the decaffeinated iced tea she'd served them both.

"We haven't set a date?" she asked, but was only half-serious. He was right. Their situation was bigger than she was making it out to be.

"We're adults, Sebastian," she told him then. "We simply tell him that at this time we aren't planning on getting married. I'll tell him when I tell them that I'm pregnant."

"He's still going to come to me," he said. "I'm not complaining here. Or trying to get you to do anything. I know your father well enough and have heard way more stories from Wade over the years to know that he's traditional. He cares about how he and his family look to others. Appearances matter to him more than, say, being close to your mother. And while he loves you all very much, he's not beyond a little ruthlessness if that's what it takes to make the world what he thinks it should be."

Setting her spoon in her not quite empty bowl, Ruby stared at him. Not sure whether she was angry with him for...what? His honesty? Because he'd been spot on.

But no one was perfect, and Robert Colton was her father. She should defend him.

So why wasn't she?

"He's going to try to force me, somehow, to convince you to marry me."

Force—no, her father wouldn't go that far. But he did wield a lot of power. And had the gift of persuasion down pat.

Robert was also traditional enough, old-fashioned enough, to think that a man could still sweeten a pot enough to get a woman to marry him.

As though being alone was not the better choice.

Enough. Enough. Enough. Enough was enough.

"How about if you come with me in the morning? We tell them together, and I make it very clear to my father that it is my choice not to marry and that there is nothing you can do, say or offer that would make me change my mind?"

She respected Robert. She didn't agree with him a lot of the time. And had no problem standing up to him. Most particularly when it came to the way he took her mother for granted.

He, in return, gave her space and supported her endeavors, even while he had her brothers keeping an eagle eye over her.

And did so himself as well.

Ready to pick up the pieces in case she failed.

At least, that was her take on their relationship. She couldn't speak for any of her siblings.

Sebastian held his bowl up to his mouth to scoop out the last bite. Set the bowl down. Wiped his mouth. And, hands on the table, very quietly said, "I don't need you to handle your father on my behalf, Ruby. Not now. Not ever. I will talk to him man-to-man. I'm asking how you want our story to be so that I have your back."

She blinked. Wasn't sure what to say. Except... "I didn't mean to offend you."

"I'm not offended." He gave an easy shrug. "But I'm also not having you bear the brunt of awkwardness due to our situation. I was fifty percent of the creation, and I will carry fifty percent of the burden." He stopped. Held her gaze, and then said, "There are obvious things that you have to do, like actually giving birth to the child, giving them a home, but I can handle all of the child's financial details, rather than a fifty-fifty split like the law generally requires. And anything else, as yet unknown, you're going to need from me along the way. Right now, I'll be standing right beside you as your parents find out about the baby, and later, when the town does."

Tears pooled in her eyes. She didn't mean them to. Hadn't known they were coming. Didn't know why they were there.

But she knew why Sebastian suddenly leaned over and ran a thumb softly along her cheekbone. It wasn't a gesture of love. Or even of affection.

He'd simply been wiping away the moisture on her face.

APPARENTLY, HE INTENDED to reveal his future plans to himself in spurts without thinking ahead.

Sebastian hadn't considered the town, his employees, or anyone but Ruby's family finding out about the baby. Just hadn't gotten that far.

But there he was. Standing by her through all of it.

And feeling completely right about doing so.

"How do we do this?" Ruby asked, turning to him in the kitchen as she stood at the sink rinsing soup bowls. As soon as he'd seen her tears, and attempted to wipe them, she'd jumped up and grabbed their dishes and spoons.

He'd gathered up the rest of the meal and had been silently seeing to storing it.

When she leaned back against the sink, he took a rest against the opposite counter, facing her. "I don't know," he said. "I guess we just do it."

How did they give answers to questions they didn't yet know?

Or explain what they hadn't yet figured out for themselves.

"One step at a time," he added, because that was what he knew. You assessed the enemy, or the problem, you figured out your end goal. And you took the first step toward reaching that goal. Sometimes the step was face-to-face meetings to reach a satisfactory conclusion for all involved. Sometimes mediation was necessary. And if all else failed, you fought.

Ruby's nod lessened some of the tightening in his gut. "For now, it's just my parents. And we tell them..." When her voice faded off, she was still looking at him, and Sebastian got all tight inside again.

"What?" he asked.

"How do you feel about the baby?"

Not the step he was expecting. "I'm not sure what you mean," he said, anyway. "I'd die for it, if that's what you're asking."

Her lips trembled on their way to a small smile. "That pretty much covers it," she said. And then added, "Are you angry?"

"No." Straight up.

"Sad?"

"No."

She nodded. He was relieved he'd passed her test.

"Happy?"

Of course not. The words were there. Didn't come out. "I'm not happy that it's creating such havoc for you," he told her honestly.

"And for you."

He shook his head. "The only havoc in my life where the child is concerned is this damned Crosswinds stalker and keeping the two of you safe until he's caught. And what telling your parents is going to do to you." Truth.

"Are you happy there's going to be another Cross, your flesh and blood, coming into the world?"

"Yes."

Oh. Well then. He was happy about the baby. He'd arrived in a new place. Because she'd known him well enough to know how to get him there.

She grinned at him.

And he grinned back.

THAT GRIN.

Not sure what to do with herself now that they'd eaten and the kitchen was clean, Ruby continued to lean against the counter, facing Sebastian. Wanting to get lost in his smile.

Just for a little bit.

She had a two-bedroom home, but only one of them held a bed.

Fletcher had said the couch was really comfortable.

But the night she'd spent at Sebastian's, he'd shared his bed with her. She wouldn't mind having him in hers. It wasn't like they hadn't done it before.

Or would have repercussions...

Feeling heat rise up inside her, she halted the thoughts. Prayed Sebastian hadn't gotten any hint of what she'd been thinking.

"I'm thinking we tell my parents the truth," she blurted. "That we're happy about the baby. That we are both independent people who never want to get married. And that we're going to be raising the child together."

As soon as she heard the word *raising* come out of her mouth, she froze. Stared at him.

He was nodding. His expression...calm. Easy. "I'm good with that."

He *was*?

He didn't just want to be a help to her, he wanted to be involved in raising his child?

"Why do you look so surprised?" he asked. "I told you I'd go with whatever story you needed to tell."

Story. Her heart sank.

Chapter Eighteen

Ruby, still standing against the sink, heard Sebastian say he was going out to do one more perimeter check.

Nodding, she went to get a sheet, pillow and blanket for the couch.

Having a furious conversation with herself as she did so. What in the hell was she doing? Building some kind of fantasy where Sebastian was a fully engaged, participating father to her baby? Was that what she was really hoping? That they were going to engage in shared parenting? That he'd be by her side, figuratively if not physically, for the tough moments?

Telling herself she was perfectly fine doing it alone... Had she been lying?

By the time she was in the living room, dropping the pillow on top of the bedding she'd just tucked in, she'd calmed some.

She hadn't been lying. She really could see herself mothering the child alone. Knew that she'd be fine. Happy. That she'd be a good mother.

"I was wondering," Sebastian said, coming back in through the kitchen. "Maybe we could..."

He stopped. Stared at the couch.

As if to put the bow on her handiwork, she dropped a sealed toothbrush and paste packet on the pillow. "I collect them from hotels," she said inanely. "When they're complimentary, I bring them home…"

Her words dropped off. And she asked, "Maybe we could…what?"

He looked at the couch. "You're ready to get some rest," he said. "I'm sorry, I should have realized…with all you've been through tonight, and being pregnant…" He shook his head. "I guess I'm going to need some practice at the support role."

"Maybe we could…what?" She repeated her question. And then, as though it made some kind of statement, she sat down in the middle of the bed she'd just made for him.

With a shrug, he sat down beside her. Leaving a few feet between them. "I was thinking we could talk about what the future might look at in terms of my role. But I wasn't thinking about your long day with the late emergency, the ordeal, you needing to get up in the morning and being pregnant."

"I'm fine," she said, feeling much better now that he was sitting there, talking to her. "Tired, but not ready to sleep just yet."

"I was thinking about talking to your parents. Maybe it would be easier if we started to talk about it all. You know. Just between us."

His voice, the look in his eyes, the shaggy dark blond hair… Those muscles…everywhere… Ruby liked every bit of it. A lot.

She particularly liked the *just between us*. Her life was overflowing with people, with family. But to be a part of something that belonged to no one but her and one other person—her and Sebastian…

The flood of warmth that the moment invoked in her was brand-new.

And like the seed he'd let loose inside her to make her pregnant, Ruby had a feeling that Sebastian had once again altered the course of her future.

She just had no idea where his road led.

And that scared her more than the attempted kidnapping had.

THE EXPRESSIONS CROSSING Ruby's face were like a jigsaw puzzle. Sebastian watched them all, but wasn't sure how to put them together.

Or how to answer the question she posed in the midst of them.

"What kind of involvement do you want?" The medical-professional tone she'd adopted each time they'd reached this conversation in the past was absent.

He'd have done better with its presence. With veneers stripped away, all he had was "I have no idea."

"Would you want to know if the baby got sick?"

"Of course."

"To the point of a call in the middle of the night?"

"Absolutely." What did any of that have to do with their future, though? He wasn't getting it. "I already told you, I'm always here to support you, every step of the way."

"Say the child likes soccer. Would you want to be at games?"

He hadn't thought that far ahead. In terms of his own wants. But… "If we could work that out, sure." Who wouldn't enjoy that?

She shook her head. "What's there to work out? You're there or you aren't."

And it hit him. The problem.

"Who do we tell the kid I am?" As soon as he asked the question, he wanted to take it back. He didn't allow insecurities.

And most definitely did not take on anything that he couldn't handle full out.

Ruby's frown sent his turmoil into tornado mode. "I don't get it," she said.

"If this baby knows that I'm the father, then why am I not being a father?" He had the questions, but no answers.

Only…more sweat. More discomfort.

Mouth open, Ruby stared at him for long seconds. Too long. Way, way too long. "You intend to tell my family, and the town, that you're the father of my child, but you didn't think the child would know?"

"It's a baby," he said weakly. Hating his lack of attention to detail. His failure to have all the answers.

Or any at all.

The child was going to grow.

Would look up to those in their life for example.

He'd had a thoracic surgeon to model himself after. A man who'd spent a good deal of his adult life in operating rooms saving lives—and in his spare time, had taught others how to do so.

And Sebastian's kid?

He looked straight at her. "You really want your child to have me as a role model? The ex-Marine who had a panic attack when his dog was shot and in the midst of it, had sex with the angel who'd appeared to save him and got her pregnant?"

He didn't.

RUBY'S DAY MELTED off from her as she sat there in the aftermath of Sebastian's painfully honest question. Heart open, she felt the compassion, the caring, emerge from her and pour outward, toward him. In an effort to flood him with it.

Used to allowing herself to give her whole heart to the animals she cared for, to all the dogs in her life, she wasn't quite sure what to do with herself.

How to act.

Who to be.

"Maybe you need to hire a different writer for your story," she said softly. Talking because the words were there and she had no other ideas present. "Maybe the example is one of a friendship between two loners, there for each other without question in time of need, and fate steps in and gives them both a human being to love as their own."

Intensity shone from his sharp blue eyes. Pulling more words out of her. "In that story it wasn't just the ex-Marine who got the woman pregnant. She needed something from him that night, too, which he so tenderly and unselfishly gave, and she was equally responsible for what happened."

For a man who wasn't moving at all, Sebastian managed to bathe the room in emotion. So much that she had to start swimming or drown.

"Now might not be the best time to say this, or maybe it's the exact right time, I don't know, but I need to rest, Sebastian…"

Of course. He stood, blinked, and it was as though he turned off the faucet and sucked all the fluid out of the room. "I'll just…"

"What?" she asked him, feeling a strange kind of power as she sat there looking up at the strong mountain of a man. "I'm sitting on your bed. There's not much you can do."

Her words were almost a challenge as, empowered by the knowledge that her friend and co-parent had a whole lot of him hidden inside.

And had shown her a huge chunk.

Crossing his arms on that massive chest, he stared her down.

When she didn't do anything but stare back, he said, "Finish what you were going to say."

"What I got that night... I could use another dose. I'm finding that I don't want to go to bed without it."

He started, his head jerking back sharply, maybe in horror. But at her eye level, he had a different response. "Are you actually sitting there telling me you want to have sex with me tonight?" he asked.

She was saying far more than that.

She'd already given him too much. More than she'd ever given anyone.

Which scared her.

So for starters... "I'm not much in a position to have it with anyone else now, am I?" She had to be strong.

To keep her wits about her.

"No, I guess not, so, if that's what you want, then, of course..."

No way. Uh-uh.

"Is that what you want?"

"This isn't about me."

There. That bothered her.

"So it's not a good thing when you're in need, and I help, but it's okay if I'm in need and you help."

He sat back down. "We aren't talking about sex here, are we?"

She looked him in the eye. "Yes." And said, "On a practical level, I was mishandled by a man tonight. I'd like to have a pleasant male-female physical experience to replace the repulsion my skin is feeling. On another similarly practical level, I think you and I did sex remarkably well, and it makes sense for two friends who understand and respect each other, friends who don't ever want to marry, to be able to share physical pleasure with each other. And there's the third aspect, which I've already mentioned... The awkwardness of me having sex with another man when I'm pregnant with your child..."

She was losing control of the situation. She could feel it.

And see it in his expression, too. The shift in power.

Teetering on just letting go, Ruby pulled herself back. Something much larger than winning and losing, than staying strong and maintaining independence, hovered around them.

We aren't talking about sex here, are we...?

"And no," she said, giving him the deeper answer to his question. "The friendship you gave so tenderly, so unselfishly that night... I need it again, Sebastian. Tonight, at least. As you said, it's been a rough day..."

She hadn't finished speaking when Sebastian reached for her, sliding his arms under her knees and back, just as he had earlier that evening.

But this time when he carried her, it wasn't to drop her alone in a car seat.

Or to deposit her anywhere.

He strode to her room, sat and then lay down with her on her bed.

Never letting her go.

For the night only, she knew.

As his lips came down on hers, and she closed her eyes,

opening her mouth to welcome him, her last conscious thought was a reminder to herself.

It was only for the night.

SEBASTIAN WAS AT his best Monday night. Holding Ruby in his arms, pleasing her, letting go and consciously allowing himself to take what she had to give him, energized him in a whole new way. She strengthened him, even as they wore each other out.

He entered her differently, too. Slowly. Reverently. Aware that in another space inside her, his child was growing into life.

He was a part of the two of them.

They were a part of him.

What it would all end up looking like, what it meant in a real-world sense, he had no idea. He didn't ask. For those hours in her bed, he just lived.

After she fell asleep, he allowed himself the light doze that came with living in a battle zone. He slept, but always aware that he was protecting precious cargo.

And yet, he rested better than he had in a long while.

Which was a good thing, he realized, when, just after six, Fletcher called to say that both Robert and Jenny wanted a meeting with Ruby at seven that morning, in the kitchen of the family home.

"You see how he played that?" Ruby asked, in her work clothes, as she sat beside him in his truck. He'd showered, brushed his teeth, turned his underwear inside out. He had nothing but the jeans, button-down shirt and dirty socks from the day before.

"Telling your parents that you had to talk to them?" Sebastian asked, admiring the detective's grit where his sister was concerned. Ruby was not easy to love when it came to worrying about her.

Not that he loved her.

He was in the unique position of being a friend who'd made a baby with her who also happened to own a business being targeted, with her getting caught in the crossfire. He could see how it would be hard to also love her when she was so independent and mostly refused to let people tell her what to do.

As a friend, and co-loner—as she'd sort of called them in her little story from the night before—he admired her independence and spunk. Understood it, even.

Better to go down on your own terms than to live a life that wasn't right for you.

As long as you didn't get closed-minded and forget that you weren't always right. As long as you always sought the evidence and looked at it with an eye to finding truth.

He'd known Ruby Colton, peripherally, since she was a kid. "Did you know that you used to irritate the hell out of Wade, always asking questions about everything, wanting to know how he knew something, verifying facts?" he asked as they drew closer to Hollister Hills, the affluent neighborhood of mansions where her parents lived in the five-bedroom, three-bath lake home Jenny had designed.

He knew Jenny was behind the home choices because Ruby had mentioned the dark green that colored every building at Crosswinds the night they'd tended to Oscar. She preferred his color to the gray wood and dark gray trim of her parents' lovely home…and figured she was the only person on earth who didn't find the exquisite beauty in the grayness.

He pulled to a stop at a light. Looked over when she didn't

answer his Wade question. Figured he'd stepped in his own crap again. But wasn't sure how to get out of it.

"Does it irritate you?" she finally asked. Not at all what he'd expected.

"It comforts me." The truth fell out with his relief. "You get the facts, rather than let yourself be swayed, and because you're open to the truth, you make good decisions."

Relief dissipated as he heard his own words. And saw the surprised look on her face.

Thankfully, the light turned green, and he didn't have to keep staring into that expression.

"I think that's the nicest thing anyone has ever said to me." Her words settled over him. Gave him added confidence as he prepared to square up with her father.

"And for the record," she continued, "of course, I knew. You think Wade would be irritated and not let it be known? Ad nauseam?" Sebastian heard the words and heard the note of deep compassion in her tone, too.

And was envious.

Not because he wanted her affection toward Wade for himself. Or in any way begrudged all her siblings her love. But because, in the end, no matter what happened between the two of them, she'd always have her family.

And he'd always be without one.

Chapter Nineteen

Ruby had made a deliberate choice in accepting Sebastian's offer of a ride to her folks' place. Her SUV was drivable. He'd be taking her back to it in time for her to get to work.

She'd ridden with him because it meant she could leave with him. If things went bad—and she gave a fifty-fifty on that—she didn't want to send Sebastian off alone without a chance to talk about things.

And thinking of which…

"Do we need to talk about last night?"

He'd already been in the shower when she'd woken up alone in her bed that morning.

"We didn't talk about it last time."

"Right." But had it been the right way to handle it?

"Do you need to talk about it?" His question surprised her. She'd thought they were done.

"No, unless you're regretting it." He'd been so distant. But then, he'd had the call from Fletcher before they'd even seen each other that morning.

He turned into her parents' neighborhood. "No regrets here."

"Good."

"It was good, wasn't it?" He didn't take his eyes off the road, but he seemed to be playing with a grin.

"Very." She didn't even try to rein in her smile.

Until he pulled into her parents' place. Then she shoved his teasing words into her private thoughts.

"You ready for this?" she asked, as she walked beside Sebastian up to the door.

His shrug, his easy stride, was so... Sebastian. He was who he was, no apologies. But no airs, either. She'd always liked that about him.

Figured his parents had done something right in that they'd raised a man filled with quiet self-confidence.

Real confidence. Not bravado.

Ruby had gained her own confidence through sheer determination and hard work. She'd had to prove to herself who she was. What she was made of.

And refused to revert back to being the girl who always had to please her parents as she walked into their home with a quick knock and headed straight to the kitchen. Sebastian had been in the home before, with Wade. For some reason, the idea was a comfort.

Taking his hand would have been a greater one.

She purposefully did not do so. She had to stand on her own two feet.

Her parents both rose as they stepped into the room, Jenny rushing forward, grabbing for Ruby's hands, looking her over with concern, checking her over, as she said how worried she'd been. While Robert, who joined them as well, kept up appearances in his welcome to Sebastian. Not expressing the surprise that he had to be experiencing.

Over her mother's shoulder, Ruby saw the coffee cups on

the table—along with her father's Irish cream liqueur—and stopped short.

"This isn't exactly how I wanted to go about this, but can you please remove the coffee cups from the table?" she asked, not wanting to chance another step closer.

Frowning, Jenny studied her harder, like a nurse studied a patient, and then did as asked, taking her cup to the kitchen island before motioning Ruby and Sebastian to seats. Robert, retrieving his cup, stood with it at the island, then began sipping. "What's going on?" he asked in the commanding tone that had been giving Ruby security, and intimidating her, since childhood.

"I'm pregnant," she told them both. Just dropped it out there. "The smell of coffee makes me throw up." She could have worded it better.

Jenny stared at her, her mouth hanging open. "You're pregnant?" Shock was evident in her tone. Concern. And possibly a slight bit of pleasure, too. It was no secret that Jenny Colton, who'd basically raised ten children and only had one grandchild, wanted more.

Robert, cup frozen halfway to his mouth, bellowed, "You're what?"

"She's pregnant, sir." Sebastian's calm words made it sound like a piece of good news. "And I'm the father."

In that moment, going up against her parents with her, he was her child's father, but he was much more than that. He was her hero.

THERE WERE SOME tense moments, but overall, "That went well," Sebastian said as he and Ruby headed down the walk toward his truck.

As predicted, Robert had asked about marriage, a wedding. Ruby had preempted Sebastian's ready reply with a version of what she'd said the night before about them being happy about the baby, independent people who never wanted to marry, and raising the child together.

"It went amazing," she said, grinning at him over her shoulder. She'd been leading the way all morning. He'd been fine to have her do so. Knew better than to help her climb up into the truck, but he did stand by the door and closed it behind her.

"That's the first time in my life I had someone sharing my situation as I faced off with my parents," she said, still grinning at him as he climbed into the driver's side.

"You had five siblings," he reminded her. "Surely there were times when you all banded together to further a cause." He'd always envisioned Wade and his brothers and sisters that way.

"Not really, no," she told him. "What just happened there, Mom and Dad meeting us together, that's not the norm. I'd have a session with Dad, or a session with Mom. They weren't close, you know. Didn't present a united front for us kids. The only time I can remember having the attention of both of them was when I announced that I was buying my house."

How being a member of a family with six kids and two parents could sound lonely, he didn't know. But right then, it did.

"My folks were gone a lot of the time, pursuing their separate professional interests, but when they were home at the same time, when there was some big decision or announcement to make in my life, they always presented it together. We'd talk things out, the three of us. All three opinions on the table, being heard." Something he'd taken for granted until just that moment.

"Not here," Ruby said, nodding toward the gorgeous lake-front home with walls of windows providing beautiful views of the water. "Maybe because there were so many of us…so much going on. But Mom and Dad… Sometimes I wonder how they ever made six babies. They're more like strangers in the same house, or business partners, than lovers."

Sebastian glanced over at her as he put the truck in Reverse. Had he just seen a glimpse of why Ruby preferred to live alone?

Not that the *why* mattered. She preferred it. He preferred it. And that made them a good team.

A team. He and Ruby Colton. A baby-having team.

Surprised at how much he liked the idea, he glanced at the other member of his unusual partnership. "I agree with them that I'd worry less if you weren't going in to work, but with the security you have there, and being right in the middle of town, and this guy only hitting at night so far, you're probably fine to go."

"There's a lot of security at Mom and Dad's and I see the sense in staying there at night, especially with Fletcher there, but it's right on the lake, Sebastian, and this guy…the way he got to the dogs—it really does sound like he approached from the lake. I figure I'm safer at work than alone out at their place all day."

He liked that they could talk to each other. Be honest. Maybe the future really was going to work as well as they'd just led her parents to believe it would.

He wanted it to.

And believed that she did, too.

"You sure don't let your father intimidate you any," he

told her. "Telling him that he had no room to talk about you still working full-time while you're pregnant—did he really have a minor stroke four years ago?"

"Yes, he did. Doctors had been after him for years about the sallowness of his skin, the pouch. Years of working all hours, being on the road for a week at a time, hard living, eating red meat every day, the whiskey he consumes, those daily cigars... They took their toll."

"And he hasn't given any of it up?" Sebastian clarified what Ruby had hollered at her father when he'd tried to put his foot down with her. He'd seen the Irish cream whiskey on the counter.

"Nope."

"I'm surprised, with your mother being a nurse, she doesn't have something to say about that."

"I think she gave up trying years ago. As you noticed, he doesn't listen to her much."

"I like her," Sebastian said, feeling generous with his emotions. He'd been welcomed back to the Colton home, been invited for dinner every night that Ruby was going to be staying there, and had been told to come and go, treat the house as his own, for the duration as well. Robert had stopped short of saying he was welcome to spend the night, but in the end, the real-estate magnate had been gracious.

And, Sebastian thought, sincere.

The man might be hardheaded, but he knew when to capitulate. Both qualities necessary to build a small hardware store into an empire that owned half of Owl Creek and still be well thought of in the town he'd taken over.

"Mom's the best," Ruby said. "She's wealthy enough to travel the world and she's still here, looking after all of us, and Uncle Buck, and doing some private nursing, too. She just sometimes wants different things for me than I do."

"I'm guessing our kid will want differently from us as well." The statement just came off his tongue. He'd been in the role, being the dad, for her parents, sharing everything with her and...

He had to go. Get back to Crosswinds. To Oscar and the rest of his dogs. To his employees. He couldn't expect, or allow, Della and the others to carry his weight.

He couldn't leave Ruby alone at her house. He'd agreed, in front of her parents, to wait while she packed. He'd do it even if he hadn't agreed. He also thought he should follow her to the clinic to make sure she made it okay.

And then he had to go.

They were getting in too deep. Sleeping together. Spending the night together. Visiting her parents together. He'd even been invited to her uncle's birthday party.

He'd accepted the invitation. Had actually wanted to go. With her.

Like a real date.

He was letting the vague description of their future that they'd delivered to her parents lure him into a place he didn't belong.

Ruby didn't want to marry any more than he did. Watching her parents together, he kind of understood that—though, of course, all unions weren't like that. Still, she'd spent the first eighteen years of her life surrounded by a plethora of needs all vying for attention. Still had to brace herself against all the lovingly offered, but still intrusive, interference in her life.

She needed her independence. He'd just watched her go up against Robert Colton to defend it.

And Sebastian needed his, too. For different reasons, but the result was the same. She'd pegged it the night before. He was a loner.

Which made them perfect for each other.

As long as he kept his distance.

He'd been doing it for thirty-two years with complete success.

No reason to think he couldn't get it done for the rest of his life.

With his thoughts firmly back in line, Sebastian waited comfortably in his truck, parked outside Ruby's house while she packed.

He helped her carry her things to the back of her SUV.

Followed her to work.

And went home.

Where he belonged.

Alone.

OVER THE NEXT couple of days, Ruby watched her back constantly. She didn't go anywhere alone, other than to drive to work, and wasn't at the clinic by herself, either. Until the kidnapper was caught, she was his prisoner.

She missed Sebastian like crazy. Which made no sense to her. He was in touch. Making sure she was okay. Asking if she needed anything.

It wasn't the same as the two of them alone together taking care of his dogs. Or eating soup. She wasn't safe at Crosswinds. And he wasn't coming into town.

He had a handler coming in from out west and, apparently, a load of work to go through, video to view and approve for the marketing campaign he was launching to try to lure out his stalker.

She heard more about his plans from her brother than she'd ever heard from Sebastian. With Ruby's attempted kidnapping, the Owl Creek police were planning to do all they could to help with Sebastian's plan, including having extra patrols in the area, both on land and on the lake.

The city had agreed on Tuesday to allow posters to be hung and distributed, too, advertising the celebration for Sebastian and his parents in Boise later in the month, with tickets available to attend the black-tie event. She'd heard from Fletcher that the honor was a real one. Sebastian had turned it down in the past.

Her brother talked as though she knew all about it. He'd just been reiterating details in terms of the investigation. Fletcher seemed to think she was going to the event.

Sebastian had never even mentioned it to her, let alone invited her to accompany him.

Because they weren't a couple. They were just friends who'd made a baby and were dealing with the situation as best they could.

Which was exactly how she wanted it.

Except that…she didn't.

She didn't blame him for withdrawing from her after spending time with her parents. She had a tendency to do the same after even a normal day at home.

And Sebastian's time with the Coltons had been anything but that. Their daughter was in danger because of someone stalking his business. And she was pregnant by him.

He'd handled the whole thing like a pro.

He didn't need her lying in bed panicking about him needing some space.

So on Tuesday night, she turned over and went to sleep. On Wednesday night, too. But she dreamed of him.

Of them together.

And woke up with growing discomfort regarding the future.

The time she and Sebastian had spent alone together over the past couple of weeks, the personal conversations, even when they got intense, eating together, touching…she craved more.

And yet…she loved her little house. Needed a place where she didn't have to fight to have her way. Her psyche relied on the peace she found there.

The baby was going to change a lot of that. Starting with no full night's sleep for a while. But she'd still have the final say in the house. Still be paying the bills. Making the choices. She'd still be in control.

Lying in her bed at her parents in the wee hours of Thursday morning, she remembered being out of control a couple of nights before, in her bed, with Sebastian.

Her thoughts flowed freely in the dark, and for a while there, she entertained the idea of a lifetime of out-of-control moments.

With desire pooling at dangerously high levels, she finally slid from beneath the sheets to wake herself up and find her reality, and was suddenly beset with the strangest feeling. Like someone was watching her.

Her gaze went immediately to the corners of her room. There were no cameras there. She knew that. But after days of living with the need for surveillance to keep herself safe, she sensed the presence of cameras everywhere.

Watching them.

Watching her.

Was that a twinkling out on the lake? The nighttime view

from the lovely wall of windows across from her bed was generally dark. She blinked.

Had a spotlight just flashed across her wall?

She waited for it to come again. Some kind of talisman for a lost boat, she told herself. Or surveillance out on the lake.

Closing her eyes, she stood against the wall on the side of the window, hiding behind the curtains, and tried to picture what she'd seen in her blink. Had there really been a flash of light?

Not liking the darkness behind her eyes, she peered out at the lake again. Where was the small light she'd seen moments before? Had it been a boat?

Someone night fishing?

Or a lonely person locked in a private hell of their own smoking a cigarette on a dock?

She was tired. Exhausted. From lack of restful sleep, but more from all the uncertainty in a life that had been carefully planned to avoid all chance of surprise.

A streak of white spread across the water. The moon came out from behind clouds. She recognized it. Welcomed it, even, in its normalcy.

For all she knew, she'd seen the moon's glow in her mind's eye as she'd blinked, and not a flash on her wall at all.

So, thinking, she went back to bed, pulled the covers up to her chin and forced herself to breathe deeply, to replay an old TV show rerun in her mind over and over until it bored her to sleep.

The boogeyman was not going to win.

Chapter Twenty

Sebastian woke up before dawn on Friday morning to the sound of his text message notification. *Ruby*. Phone in hand before he'd fully opened his eyes, his heart pounded as he pushed to open the app. This early, it couldn't be good.

It was a text, not a call, so not an immediate trauma. He was just reassuring himself as the message popped up on screen.

THE LAND IS MINE GOD SAYS PRIDE COMETH BEFORE THE FALL AND YOU ARE ABOUT TO FALL BIG FOR YOUR PRIDEFUL WAYS

He read, and read again. Calming even as adrenaline pumped through his veins. The two previous texts, one to Ruby and one to him, had come from burner phones. Pinging from the Owl Creek tower. Whether the man was in town only in the dark hours, or full-time, no one knew, but it was likely he was close by.

After texting Fletcher, Sebastian was out of bed and into jeans, a flannel shirt and cowboy boots by the time he had a response. Ruby's brother was on his way out. Commercials had run on the local television station the previous day and were scheduled throughout the weekend, talking about Crosswinds, featuring photos of people who'd been saved by Sebastian's search-and-rescue dogs. One had a testimonial from a veteran who was able to take up life again thanks to a PTSD dog. Posters about the dinner honoring Sebastian and his parents were up all over town.

They'd pushed the guy's button another notch. His current text, all caps like the previous two, was less to the point. It was longer, more preachy, like someone who'd reached a stage of rambling thoughts.

If they were lucky, they'd have him in cuffs in the next hour.

And Ruby had to stay home.

He didn't even try to get an agreement through text. He dialed her cell phone.

And felt a twinge of fear when he heard her voice. If anything happened to her...

"He's on the move," Sebastian said, not even attempting to tone down his tension. "Fletcher's on his way out. The plan is working. And I'm going to beg if I have to, but please stay out of sight today, Ruby. Please."

The long pause on the line didn't bode well. Antsy to get outside, Sebastian stood in his kitchen, ready to remain in that spot for as long as it took.

"I've egged him on," he said. "I've purposely pushed him over the edge. Please let us get this done without giving him a chance to get to you."

"Okay."

Knees suddenly weakened, Sebastian said, "Did you just say *okay*?"

"Yes. What you say makes sense. I'll ask Wade to come

spend the day with me, at least until we get the all clear," she told him.

And Sebastian actually smiled. He was going to get his guy. And until he did, Ruby would be protected by the best of the best.

The woman knew him well. Knew how to deliver exactly what he needed. Just as he hoped he was able to do for her.

"Thank you."

"Anytime," she said, but the word wasn't issued lightly. There was a message there.

He just wasn't ready to hear it yet.

RUBY TRIED TO go back to sleep. But the more she forced herself to lie still, the less sleepy she felt. Her stomach was in knots, and as they grew tighter, they started to swirl, too. Not wanting to wake her parents, she made a quick stop at the bathroom, and headed down to the kitchen for saltine crackers.

Her brother had left a light on during his hurried departure. She worried for him. And for Sebastian. Told herself over and over again that Steele and his men would be there, too. They were all well-trained.

Many against one.

But the one knew who and where they were, while they were against a phantom.

"Ruby? You okay, sweetie?"

Jenny, a few gray streaks in her dark blond hair, came into the room, her pajama pants and long-sleeved T-shirt top showing the body of the slim, fit woman.

"I'm fine, Mom. You don't need to be up at this hour."

"I heard Fletcher leave."

Because, of course, Jenny was on call in her home, for her children, 24/7.

Would Ruby ever be able to be half the mother her own mom was?

The thought almost tipped her stomach over the edge. She took a bite of the cracker she'd just pulled out of the wrap.

"You want to talk about it?"

"About what? Morning sickness?"

"If that's what's on your mind."

The shrewd look her mother gave her reminded Ruby that she was alone because she chose to be. Jenny was always available.

Having a seat on the kitchen stool, she asked, "How did you do it? All those kids. Social functions with Dad. Taking over for Jessie when she ran off, mothering her kids, too, and still having your own career?"

Jenny poured two glasses of milk, put one on the island in front of Ruby and kept the other in her hand as she perched on the stool next to her. With a shrug, looking at her milk, she said, "Love."

What? Ruby frowned. "Love," she repeated.

"I loved your father, wanted to spend my life with him, so I married him. Our love gave us six kids. When each one of you were born, I fell in love in a way I'd never imagined. You start to feel it when you get pregnant, but once that baby is out of you and you're holding this tiny little human...it's like a wand waves over you, sprinkling you with gold that doesn't ever get lost. No matter what happens, you just know that as long as your child is alive, you have the jackpot. Not in money. But in love. It's the love jackpot."

Her mother had never been a wordy woman. Transfixed, Ruby homed in on the glow in Jenny's eyes. "Way more than money has ever done, the love I was blessed with for each of you kids has carried me through every tired day, every sleepless night, every chore and every tear. And with poor Buck… I loved my sister. I was happy when they married. And I loved their kids. Love is what does it, Ruby. In the end, it's all that really matters."

And was it love that kept Jenny with Robert? Despite the chill in their mutual treatment of each other? Deep down, did her mother get strength from spending her life with the man she'd fallen in love with all those years ago?

Jenny didn't say. Ruby was afraid to ask. Not sure she wanted to hear the answer, either way.

"Do you love Sebastian?" Jenny's gaze wasn't judgmental. But it was direct. And filled with compassion.

Ruby shook her head. But couldn't get the word *no* to rise up through her throat. "I don't know," she told her mother. What was love?

She loved her entire family. Deeply. But didn't want to spend her life with any of them, in the same house, forever.

"He makes you feel things you've never felt before."

Was Jenny guessing? Or telling? Did her mother, in all her wisdom, see something Ruby was missing?

"Doesn't mean it's love."

"No." Jenny's head tilted to the side a bit, and then straightened. "But if it is, fighting it is a losing cause, sweetie. Love comes through the heart, not the mind, and there's nothing your mind can do to stop it from coming."

Ruby wasn't sure she'd gained any clarity in thought, or even in understanding, but as she took a sip of the milk her mom had poured for her, her stomach settled some. And her heart felt stronger.

She might not get all of life's choices right.

But she'd make them.

And be able to live with them.

SEBASTIAN SAW THE brief trail of sparks in the air and Fletcher had yet to make it to his place. After calling the security company on site until daybreak, he'd grabbed his gun, jumped in his four-wheeler and sped out to the kennel. Dialed 911 to report a fire, and then Fletcher, as he drove, then circled the big building housing his dogs and turned his vehicle toward the lake.

He could see the blaze already, an acre away. After jumping out of the off-roader, he grabbed a shovel out of the back and started to dig. Some of his land was going to burn. He'd likely lose some trees. But he was not losing any buildings.

Sweating in the early morning chill, he dug eighteen inches wide, and then down to mineral soil, his only illumination coming from the vehicle's headlights. One man, by himself, he might make enough of a difference to at least divert the flames. Della, Bryony and Adam should be on their way to get the dogs up to his house. And to be prepared to vacate the premises altogether if necessary. Fletcher had said he'd make that call.

And police were heading toward him by lake, as well. They'd be looking at both sides of the shore for the detonator. He'd told Fletcher the flare had not come from his land.

He'd only dug about a yard before he started to see the flames coming toward him, far faster than a grass fire in the spring should have done.

Like it was following some kind of accelerant...

Heart pounding, shovel in hand, he ran toward the flame, stopping half an acre away to check the ground in line with it. And with the light from his phone, saw the primer cord lying in the unmowed mange.

He shoved his phone in his pocket with one hand, raising his shovel high with the other, and with both hands and arms fully engaged, slammed the tip of the blade into the line, again and again, so angry he felt as though he could have ripped the thing in half with his bare hands. He wouldn't be able to stop the fire. But if he could prevent the speedy projectile to his buildings...

He would prevent it.

The fire was coming toward him. More rapidly than he'd assessed. Bearing down. He slammed the shovel again and again, watched the flames continue to speed at him.

He slammed the shovel. Jumped on it. And felt a snap.

Digging with his bare hands, he took hold of one end of the line in both hands, the end leading toward the building, and, pulling so hard his muscles stung, he ran toward the lake. He didn't have time to get to the buildings, to the end of the line, but if he could get his section far enough away from the fire...

He heard sirens. Didn't turn to look. He just kept running.

For his dogs. For Crosswinds. For all of the people who'd yet to become lost and needed to be found. For the veterans who'd sacrificed all for country and come back broken. For Ruby.

For his little baby.

The human yet to be born that was as much a part of him as he'd been a part of his father.

RUBY HEARD FROM Fletcher while she and Jenny were still sitting in the kitchen. Her brother needed her to phone Della to get to Crosswinds and move the dogs. He'd said that Sebastian wanted his trainer to call in Bryony and Adam, too.

Ruby made those last two phone calls instead, letting Della concentrate on getting dressed and out to Sebastian's place.

And then she stood.

"Where are you going?"

"To Crosswinds," she said. "I have to help. The dogs will be panicked. They know me. And I can tranquilize anyone who might try to run. I can treat any if the fire…" Her words broke off as she reached the stairs.

"You can't go out there, Ruby. You're a target. Think of the baby."

The baby.

She stopped, one foot on the stairs.

Why hadn't she thought of the baby?

She'd been thinking about the dogs.

Thinking.

Not feeling.

And as she sat on the bottom step, calling one of the veterinarians on her staff and asking her to head out to Crosswinds, she had an inclination that she'd just been given a lesson in what her mother had been talking about.

Love came from the heart, not the mind.

She was smart. Learned. And she trusted her mind.

Her life was cerebral by choice.

But if she was going to make it as a mother, she had to let her heart take the reins.

No matter how scary that might be.

SOMEONE WAS WATCHING HIM. Sebastian slowed to a walk, still heading toward the river with the highly flammable line in his hand, but took in the area around him as though he was back in Afghanistan, in the desert during the night, expecting an attack at any moment, from any direction.

A leaf fluttered down out of a tree, and he stopped.

If the enemy was in the tree, he'd be dead in seconds. His gun would do him no good when he didn't know where to aim. He could shoot into the tree and hope.

The enemy could shoot right at him and win.

He was in the open. The other was not.

And it hit him. The line.

Resuming his trek to the lake, he veered on a diagonal. Threw the rope up over a branch and shot it all in one move.

The tree lit up in an instant blaze.

Giving Sebastian a view of wide eyes filled with horror, just before a skinny male body hurled down at him. The fiend had the advantage of gravity. Sebastian had the superior height, weight, muscular build and a trained warrior's mind filled with intent.

Taking the brunt of the man's weight with a severe blow to his chest, he dropped his gun, grabbed hold with both arms and rolled, while the fire blazed right above them.

He had to get to his gun before his assailant did. The enemy may have been skinny, but he was a wild man, kicking and throwing punches, hurling his body around, reaching toward Sebastian's gun.

The smaller hand got there first, grabbed hold, and just as he was raising his arm, Sebastian's hand slammed down on the man's wrist, lifting it again, and slamming it down, until the gun was free. With complete focus and clear thought, he grabbed his gun and pushed into the attempted kidnapper's chest, pulling back the hammer all in one move.

He heard voices in the distance. Had flashing lights in his peripheral vision. All just distant background.

"Who are you?"

"Your brother, come to save you from your sins…" The voice came out strong and solid. Deep, as though the man was channeling a sacred tone.

With a hand at the chest of the man's hooded sweatshirt, right next to the barrel of his handgun, Sebastian pulled up and slammed the man back down.

"Your name," he growled, feeling nothing but a need to take the man down. But he couldn't let go until he knew the truth.

"Leon."

"Who's your father?"

"God is my father and you are a sinner, worshipping animals instead of God. This land is…"

"Sebastian!" Fletcher's voice sounded from outside Sebastian's sphere, cutting off his prisoner's tirade. "Hold on, man," Fletcher said, running up to them. Aware of other feet starting to circle them, Sebastian felt a hand at his back. "I've got this, brother," Fletcher said, more softly.

Brother.

One on the ground beneath his gun.

And one who would never be his, not even in law.

With a knee on the man's chest, holding him down, he kept the gun firmly pointed, but handed it to Fletcher Colton. Nodding at Glen Steele and other officers as he stood, Sebastian turned his back on the man on the ground, the half brother he'd never known, and walked away.

He didn't look back.

His job was done.

Ruby was safe. The child she carried was safe.

His only living relative in the world was being taken into custody.

He had to get back to his dogs. To make sure everyone was okay.

They needed him.

And he needed them, too.

Chapter Twenty-One

Sebastian wasn't picking up. Ruby had tried several times that day. He texted each time, to make certain she was okay, but didn't engage any further, even by text.

Fletcher had called shortly after dawn to let her know that since she didn't need Wade's protection, their brother was going to be at Crosswinds, helping to clear out fire debris with other townspeople.

An impromptu volunteer service for a member of their community family. Her brother had thought she'd already heard from Sebastian.

For some reason she didn't want to think about, she'd let her detective brother go on thinking she knew what was going on. And had called Sebastian.

And received a text asking if she was okay. Her *fine*, followed by a question to him, went unanswered.

Jenny had ended up being the one to tell her that her kidnapper was behind bars. She'd heard from Chase, who'd heard from Robert after Glen Steele had called him at work to let him know that his daughter was safe.

She'd heard all about Sebastian's heroic actions, trapping the kidnapper in a tree, and then fighting him physically to subdue him until police arrived.

And she knew that the man who'd tried to ruin him was his half brother.

Sebastian Cross had family after all.

He had to be taking it hard. To find out he had a living relative, only to have the man be a criminal who'd attempted to kidnap the mother of his baby, and could have killed the baby, too.

A brother who'd tried to kill several of his dogs. More than once.

A man with evil inside him. One who wanted to take, not give. To steal, not earn.

Saddest part was, if the man had simply approached Sebastian, she'd bet her life savings that Sebastian would have gladly shared the land with his younger sibling.

Instead, on their first meeting, he'd held a cocked gun to the man's chest until law enforcement arrived.

Ruby moved back home. After only a short time away, the place seemed like a long-lost friend to her. She walked through it. Absorbing the peace she'd created through color choice and beautiful objects. She showered. And, instead of having to call off, she went to work.

At lunch, she drove herself to the police station next to the fire station at the west end of Main Street and was shown to a room to identify the man who'd attacked her.

He'd seemed smaller to her at the station, but Fletcher said that wasn't unusual, given that he'd grabbed her from behind. He'd have seemed like a big specter at her back that night. The man, according to her brother, was incredibly strong. If she hadn't head-butted him, much worse things could have happened.

She'd reminded him that she'd been well trained through

a myriad of self-defense classes. Her brother had helped her find the best ones.

She'd had a glimpse of the man's face on Monday night. In the dark, with headlights shining. The only thing she'd recognized, the only thing she'd really seen, other than the dark blue hoodie that he'd apparently been arrested in, had been the wild, glazed look in his eyes.

It was still there. Even sitting alone in a police interrogation room.

Fletcher offered to take her to lunch after the ID procedure was over. She'd been afraid she'd throw it up, so she went back to work and had an apple. And later some crackers and an orange. Thanking the fates that her sisters weren't there to see what she was consuming. Or rather, how much she wasn't.

By late afternoon, when she'd seen her last scheduled client and her most recent call to Sebastian went to voice mail, she signed herself out. Exchanging her white doctor's coat for a dark purple fleece coat, over light purple scrubs, she grabbed her satchel, climbed in her SUV and headed straight out to Crosswinds.

Being busy was one thing. Ghosting her was not okay. He got a point for keeping in touch to ensure she was well.

And dozens of them for the trauma, the emotional tension, the life-changing news of the past weeks. Things she mentally relived during the ten-minute drive out to his place.

The points in his favor were catapulted by him finding out that the love-child theory he and others had tossed around had become deadly reality.

Her frustration with him had pretty much dissipated by the time she pulled onto Cross Road. Along with any self-righteous anger that might have been mixed in there.

When she saw the land, by the lake, the charred remains of some trees and the blackened ground, she felt tears prick the backs of her eyes. She had no idea which tree might have been the one that Sebastian had lit afire himself. From what she'd been told, the police had run their prisoner away from the burning embers and a fire crew had taken their place, but that didn't mean they'd managed to put out the fire before the tree had burned to the ground.

Needing something to be normal, she pulled into her usual parking space, relieved that it could be hers again. That their attacker was safely, and quite firmly, from what she understood, in custody. The man was in chains and was assigned a twenty-four-hour watch. Not for his own good, but the peace of mind of all those who'd sought him. And for those who'd suffered at his hands.

There'd be no worry of escape.

Because she was there, she peeked into the medical building, but had already heard from her colleague, who'd returned to the clinic, that no dogs were injured in the morning's attack. The building was empty. From there she walked up to Sebastian's house. He'd been up since well before dawn. Had, from what she'd heard, trained that day. And had helped with fire cleanup, too.

Oscar greeted her at the door. As did Turbine, a dog leaving them that week to be adopted by a female veteran pilot whose plane had been shot down. She'd managed to land the plane safely, to get her and her crew out, but had been taken hostage overnight before her rescue.

"Where is he, boys?" she asked softly, stooping to pet them both as she looked around.

"I'm right here."

Rounding the corner into the kitchen, she almost wept

as she saw Sebastian, in jeans and a checked, long-sleeved shirt and tennis shoes, standing at the stove, stirring a big wok, with his three other burners filled with huge saucepans.

He was okay. He'd come through the day and was either making himself a freezer's worth of meals, or was cooking for a very large gathering.

"Can I help?" she asked, walking over to look in his pots.

"I'm almost done," he told her. A nonanswer that she took as a *no*. He'd barely glanced her way. It could have been because he was clearly quite occupied, but she didn't think so.

"Is this it, then? We're done?"

"Now's not the time, Ruby." She got that, but her emotions wouldn't settle with the logic. The man had to be suffering. And even if he wasn't, he'd been distant since long before the day's activities. Ever since they'd been to her parents' house, to be exact.

"When is the time?" she asked, taking a seat at the kitchen table, quite sure that if she waited for an invitation she'd be standing until she grew tired and left.

"I can't make you be a part of my life, Sebastian. I wouldn't even want to. But I'm not going away until you tell me that our friendship is over, and you want no part of the baby's life."

She'd been through a hell of a lot, too. It would be a long time before she drove down her own road and didn't avoid looking at the ditch where her SUV ended up. Didn't shudder with the memory of those arms coming up behind her.

Sebastian just stirred. Browning what had to be several pounds of what smelled like—judging by the meat packages she could see in the trash—minced chicken.

"You having a party of some kind?" she asked then, getting frustrated with him again. And maybe a little panicked.

She could do the baby thing alone. She didn't doubt that for a second.

But the thought of not having Sebastian in her world, understanding the loner parts of her no one else got, was more than a little unsettling.

"I'm making dog food," he told her. "They've been through a hellish two months, continued to work hard, and so for the next few days, they're going to eat like the kings and queens, princesses and princes, that they are."

She teared up. Quickly blinked away the moisture. Asked about the recipe he was using.

And found out it was one of hers, posted on her website.

She should have known from glancing in his pans. The chicken. The rice. Mixed vegetables, also minced.

Perhaps she wasn't doing as well as she'd thought she was. Maybe not any better than he was. Just different. She was reaching out...to him. Only to him.

Needing him to be wrapped in compassion.

As she'd been that morning.

Her mind froze as she reached a new place. The major difference between her and Sebastian. He'd known it already. She put pieces together as thoughts and memories of conversations tumbled on top of each other. She'd never known a single day of her life without her family in her background.

Being surrounded by people who cared even when she didn't think she wanted them there. Having a mother who'd get up in the middle of the night, pour her a glass of milk and sit on a stool with her.

She was a loner by choice, always knowing she had her family.

Sebastian was a loner because...he was alone. Maybe even more so, having just held a gun to his newfound little brother's chest. Having just had confirmation that the man who'd fathered him, the man who'd taught him what family was, had had a separate son somewhere else.

Seeing the big can of dog nutrients on the counter—the brand she recommended, something she should have noticed walking in the door, something she *would* have noticed if she'd been as together as she'd thought she was—she picked it up, grabbed the scoop she needed and started dropping scoops into the rice Sebastian had just drained.

"You brought Turbine in with you," she said as he dumped the ingredients of his pots into two huge bowls, handed her a big metal spoon and took another for himself.

His silence was hard to take. But she did it. Stirred right alongside him.

If he didn't want to talk about why he'd opted to take home his best-trained PTSD dog for the night, that was his choice. Still didn't change the fact that he'd done so.

Or that she knew why.

Sometimes, that's what friends did. They knew and just stirred food in a bowl.

Being a friend, a daughter, a sister, a cousin, a parent—none of it was going to be easy all the time. Jenny was a living testimony to that.

And yet, if Ruby ever wanted to emulate another woman, ever wanted to hope she'd one day be as shining an example as any one woman she'd ever met, heard of, or read about, it would be her mother.

Jenny got up every single day to tend to those she loved. No matter what.

Those she loved…

Ruby looked at the tall, broad, bearded man standing next

to her and could no longer deny what Jenny Colton had already seen in her daughter.

She loved him.

THEY'D USED THE four-wheeler to cart the containers of dog food down to the kennels, filling bowls and putting the rest in the refrigerator. And then, feeling as though he owed her a good turn, Sebastian offered Ruby a homemade chicken-salad sandwich.

He'd saved the cooked chicken and she cut up grapes while he diced onion and celery. He made the dressing from scratch. She spooned it over their mixture. Sitting at his kitchen table with glasses of milk, they consumed the entire bowl. She'd had hers on crackers. He'd had three sandwiches.

He hadn't eaten all day.

Hadn't been hungry.

He figured she was sitting there needing more from him than chicken salad. And he was just waiting for her to leave.

She was safe.

He'd captured her kidnapper.

And cooked.

He'd done what he was trained to do.

What he could do.

They cleaned up the kitchen together. And she still didn't pick up her satchel to go. As he hung the dish towel on the oven-door handle, Sebastian was trying to figure out the best way to tell her he needed to call it a night.

And said, "He didn't look anything like me."

"I didn't think so, either."

Ruby leaned back against the sink, reminding him of the night at her house. The night of the attempted kidnapping.

The night they'd talked about the future.

The night they'd had sex.

The night that everything had flown out of control.

And... *I didn't think so, either?*

"You saw him?"

"Fletcher had me go to the station at lunchtime to identify him."

"Why didn't I know that?" He, of all people, should have been told. The woman carrying his child, facing her kidnapper? His half brother. "I should have been there."

"You didn't answer my call."

Since it was part of the case, Fletcher should have let him know. "You could have texted the information."

"You could have answered your phone."

Swallowing, he met her gaze, full on, for the first time since he'd driven her away from her parents' house on Tuesday morning.

It felt like coming home. Shock waves went through his system.

The start of an episode? The panic after the attack was done? Turbine wasn't indicating, yet.

"Were you able to give the ID?" He belonged next to her, supporting her as she stared through the glass at the man who'd attacked her.

"He matches the description I gave that night. Today, all I could remember for certain was that glassy, wild look in his eyes. Your headlights were bright, and every time I think of those seconds, it's those eyes that get me."

And, selfish ass that Sebastian had been, he hadn't answered her repeated calls that day. Thinking that she was checking up on him.

And that he couldn't encourage her to expect more from him than he'd be able to deliver. After they'd left her parents, he'd been talking as if the two of them would be parents, together, to the child they'd created. He'd had to take a break from the situation to get himself in check. The idea of disappointing her, which those comments had set him up to do, was worse than any PTSD nightmare.

"I'm sorry I didn't answer my phone. I will always do my best in the future to answer any call that comes in from you."

She smiled then.

And he hoped he'd redeemed himself a little.

Chapter Twenty-Two

"Fletcher says he's not talking." Ruby stayed by the sink, just leaning there, a friend in conversation before heading out. Wanting Sebastian to know that he wasn't alone in his suffering. That even if they didn't talk about it all, she was aware.

And cared.

Something she'd learned from her mother just that morning. And through the rest of her life, too, she supposed. She'd just been too set in her own thinking to realize what else had been there.

"He told me he's my brother."

She'd heard that, too. Could only imagine the shock that must have reverberated through Sebastian in that second. But according to her brother, who'd been watching from afar as he ran to the scene, Sebastian hadn't so much as twitched the entire time he had the younger man on the ground.

"I'm sorry it turned out this way."

"Sorry that your child is related to an unhinged criminal?"

"Stop it, Sebastian."

"Stop what? Speaking the truth? You're the Coltons. Your reputations matter."

"Stop putting thoughts in my head. That man is not a reflection on you. He never even met you. There's no way you could have had any influence on him, or, for that matter, him on you. He was deserted by your father, not raised by him. And he had a different mother."

"Who's dead," Sebastian said. "Fletcher said they'd tracked down the woman my father was meeting with in that hotel. She died a couple of years after their last visit."

"And she had a son."

"Yes."

"Is your father listed on the birth record?"

"No. And the rest was sealed. He was adopted out after his mother died."

"I wonder if your father even knew about him?"

He shrugged. "Leon knew about me..."

Leon. Her kidnapper had a name. She swallowed. "He must have found your connection through one of the DNA companies...or maybe his mother left him something that his adoptive parents gave him when he turned eighteen. Maybe they knew all along..." She was there for him. Not to get herself worked up again.

Her part was done. The ordeal was over.

Sebastian's chin jutted, but otherwise he gave no reaction to her words. Because he didn't care how Leon had found him? Or because he was just that good at hiding the turmoil inside him?

He rubbed at the beard on his chin as he said, "Fletcher said the only question he's answered, period, is when they asked him who his father was. He just keeps saying God is his father now. And that God will save him because he's righteous." With a shake of his head, Sebastian ended with, "When he told me he was my brother, he said he'd come to save me from my sins. Which, apparently, have to do with worshipping animals..."

"He needs help," Ruby said then, glad that the threat was done. Fearing that Sebastian would be a long time in healing from the ordeal.

TURBINE, WHO'D BEEN lying on the floor, stood and moved to Sebastian's side, nudging his hand. Sebastian pet the dog as he said, "He needs a good lawyer. And I'm thinking about paying for it." His gaze challenged her.

Ruby just kept looking at Sebastian's hand on the dog's head. Petting, just lying there, petting again. And Turbine, leaning up against him.

The dog was working.

Sebastian's stress level had just raised.

She looked at him. "You think I'm going to have a problem with that," she guessed, glancing at the dog again, and then met Sebastian's gaze.

"Seems like a traitorous thing to do, from your point of view," he said then. "Paying for the defense of the man who's terrorized your life."

Yet he was going to do it, anyway. "So why are you?" Her tone was neutral. She wasn't sure how she felt.

"My reasons are twofold." As soon as he started talking, she knew he'd given the matter enough thought. He'd already made his decision. And was worried about her.

Just as she'd worried about her family's reactions when she'd known she was going to do something they wouldn't like.

Their opinion mattered because she cared about them.

Sebastian cared about her.

Ruby's heart softened, and filled.

"First," Sebastian continued, "I want to make sure that he has the best defense first time out so that when they put him away, he stays there." His words were clearly stated. His expression unflinching. "And second, I grew up with my father's love and all the financial benefits I'd ever need. He's been denied the love, but I can still see that money that morally should have been shared with him, benefits him."

Which just confirmed what she'd already figured. If Leon had just gone to Sebastian, his older half brother would have given him part of the land.

Just as Sebastian would always be there for her child. Sharing what he had. In any way he could.

She felt her expression lighten as her heart did.

He frowned. "Why are you smiling? I thought you'd be upset."

"I'm happy that you're the father of this child," she said, holding her still-flat belly.

And looked him straight in the eye so he'd know she meant every word.

SHE WAS HAPPY *he was the father of her child?*

Sebastian didn't doubt Ruby. He just didn't get it.

Why couldn't she see that he wasn't great father material? He lived a far-from-traditional life.

When he was alone in that life, Sebastian was good. He liked himself and the life he'd built. Around Ruby, all he could seem to think about were the areas where he was lacking.

Which made no sense to him. He'd never been a poor-me guy. Not when he'd watched his friend die. Not when his parents had been killed.

He'd suffered. But others had suffered far more.

"We aren't getting married. Aren't moving in together. The child is going to grow up in a single-parent home..."

"But this baby is going to be loved and protected and given opportunities to succeed," Ruby said. "I'm seeing it more clearly now," she continued. "In a way, Leon did us a favor, showing us what matters most. It's not the license or where our bedrooms are, or how many adults are in the house when a child goes to sleep at night. It's having someone there, having people to turn to, to be able to count on, to believe in you, support you, help you grow and you do all of that, Sebastian. All the time."

If he wasn't careful, she was going to have him believing he could celebrate his child's birth without guilt. Without feeling like a failure.

Without doubting his every move.

"We're human beings, not cookie cutters," she said then. "We're not all meant to be the same, feel the same, want the same. But we are all deserving and needing of love."

Throat tight, he had to restrain himself from reaching out to her, pulling her into his arms and spending the night showing her how very much he valued her.

"And you know what I need right now?" she asked.

"What?" He wasn't afraid to ask. She knew his limitations. Respected them. And, best of all, had her own set of rules by which she insisted on living her life.

She was as stubborn as he was.

"I need to put these past weeks behind me. To feel no fear. To have some hours in the darkness where only pleasure and happiness exist."

She wanted to go to bed with him.

If ever there had been a woman made for him, Ruby was it.

And… "I can't risk it, Ruby, not tonight. After what happened out there today, I'm like a time bomb here, ticking off until I have a panic attack, or go to sleep and transport myself to hell."

"You have Turbine and Oscar here. They'll be in the room with us. And if I have to jump out of bed, then I do."

"I can't risk hurting you." And it wasn't only the results of PTSD that scared him. He was a loner. He didn't answer his phone every time it rang. Or enjoy being surrounded by people all the time.

"There are some hurts that are worse than physical ones," she told him. "That cut deeper."

He was between a rock and a hard place. Needing to please her. Wanting her to please him. And trying to prevent a future of failure.

He didn't walk into losing battles.

"I need to know that you won't suffer because of me."

"Then invite me to spend the night with you."

She wasn't backing down. He couldn't, either.

"I've spent the past several nights in stark fear, Sebastian. Lying awake, reliving it all. And the only thing that takes away the ugliness is thoughts of you. Please, even if you don't touch me, just let me stay and get a good night's rest."

It was like she was reading his mind. Facing the night ahead alone—with visions of his half brother's wild eyes glaring up at him, with the internal fight to accept that he *had* a half brother, that his whole life with his father had somehow been a lie—he needed more than Oscar.

He needed human conversation to sort out the chaos inside him.

Ultimately, he needed to support her and their child.

He'd made the promise.

And he was not going to fail.

"Just for tonight," he told her, and, opening his arms, grabbed her close as she fell against him.

HIS TOUCH WAS URGENT. Needy. Giving. Tender. And for a few hours, Ruby let herself believe that as she gave him her love, he gave his back.

She didn't weave fantasies about living together. Or marriage.

Her entire being was geared toward avoiding both.

But as she was lying beside Sebastian, fully satiated, wanting to know that she'd be in his bed again sometimes, she needed more than they'd agreed to share.

As exhausted as he had to have been, he wasn't sleeping, either.

"Fear's an insidious thing," she dropped softly between them. With the dogs at the end of the extra large king-size bed, she drew from their silent support. "It's the root of PTSD and panic attacks. And stops us from reaching higher, trying for more."

"You're talking about us."

Turning, the sheet up under her armpits, she looked at his head on the pillow next to her. His ear was facing her. She studied the half of his face she could see.

"I'm talking about all of it," she said. "There has to be a balance. The dangers we run from, and the ones we take on because if we don't, we lose too much."

He didn't agree. But he didn't argue, either.

"And sometimes," she continued, "you manage them."

"I need to know what, in particular, you're hoping to manage."

She did, too. Wasn't quite there yet. But since he was listening, seemed to be open to consideration, she reached inside herself and found, "Like tomorrow night, for instance. Uncle Buck's birthday. It's going to be a pretty big affair. Lots of people we both know. And there's no longer any reason to keep my pregnancy a secret, or to not announce you as the father..."

She started out bigger than she'd meant to go, or even wanted.

He hadn't left the bed.

"I'm not suggesting any kind of formal announcement," she quickly added, for her own sake as much as his. "But maybe we attend together. Not holding hands, or arm in arm, just...together. And when I start to show and news of the baby gets around—which, with my family, it will—we just continue appearing together on occasion. We show the world who we are. Friends who enjoy each other's company and are going to be raising a baby to whom they are both parents."

The announcement—too much. The plan she's just laid out...not enough.

"We've both spent our adult lives carving out the existences we've wanted. We've established ourselves as the people we want to be. We're strong-minded enough to carry this off. There's no reason why we have to define ourselves or explain to anyone. We just continue to be who we are."

Except that she was deeply afraid that she was changing. Fear again.

"You make it sound easy."

Yeah. But they both knew it wouldn't be.

Still... "What's the alternative? We live in a small town. We work together. Even if you decided not to have anything to do with me, you're never going to abandon your child, Sebastian."

The reality was right there. Both of them knew it. "We're

in control of how this goes, is all I'm saying," she finished, as much for herself as for him.

"I'm never going to decide not to have anything to do with you." He turned his head then, looking at her. "You've become a part of me."

Her heart flooded and she blinked back tears. Reached out and touched his face, running a finger along the lines under his eyes. "You've become a part of me, too."

He kissed her. Long and full.

She kissed him back, pouring herself into the silent communication.

And for that night, it was enough.

Chapter Twenty-Three

Before Ruby left early Saturday morning, she'd asked Sebastian if he'd be at her uncle Buck's birthday party that night. Looking in her eyes, he gave her the only answer that he could get out, telling her he'd be there. And felt good about doing so when he saw the brief flash of relief, and then the pleasure in her eyes.

The Coltons were her family, so technically, they were her problem, not his. But this child was going to be a Colton. And he'd impregnated a Colton. He couldn't leave her standing by herself, period, let alone in a very public crowd.

His father had always told him that he gave his all to everything, which meant that he'd succeed at whatever he tried. Certainly, his time in the Marines had played out that way right up until his friend had died instead of him. And Crosswinds put truth to his dad's words.

And, he supposed, Ruby did, too. Leave it up to him to impregnate a woman whose father owned half the town. Could sic the entire town on him for what he'd done.

He fed the dogs. Got some training in. Cleaned up a bit more residue from the fire. Thanked his employees again for all their support over the past couple of months. Giving every one of them generous bonus checks for having done so.

And he tried not to think about the evening's event at Colton Ranch. His gut knew he didn't want to go. His mind knew it, too.

A new tension related to Ruby pushed at his back all day, calling him to the ranch. To be there to stand beside the mother of his child.

More, to support his very, very good friend.

Friend.

There would be baby talk now that everyone who knew also knew there was no longer any reason to keep the baby a secret. Sebastian realized he couldn't show up at Buck's place without telling his lifelong very good friend of a different nature.

Wade.

By two that afternoon, he'd been unable to fight off the emotions over which he kept such tight control. After calling Ruby to let her know what he was doing, to give her a chance to voice disapproval, he then drove over to Colton Ranch and told Wade that he was having a child with Wade's younger sister.

As talks between them went, it could have gone better. Compared to sparring they'd done in the past, it hadn't been so bad.

Once Wade knew his father and mother had been told, and that all hell hadn't broken loose, he could hardly try to condemn Sebastian himself. And when he called Ruby, to hear from her that she was happy with the way things were turning out, Wade held out his hand to Sebastian and congratulated him on becoming a father.

That was when Sebastian should have felt a lightening inside him. Relief, certainly. And satisfaction with the reassurance that he and Ruby really were going to pull off the parenting thing without having to change their lifestyles all that much.

It was what they both wanted. And it was working.

The stalker had been caught.

Life was good again.

So why didn't his step feel any lighter?

The question hit him again early that evening as Hannah Colton came up to congratulate him. "I was scared to death for her when she wouldn't say who the father was, but when I found out it was you... I'm happy for both of you."

He smiled. Glanced at Ruby, who was in conversation with a couple from town he knew only peripherally, and then forgot the moment for a bit as he was pulled into conversation with Malcolm.

The evening wore on, and he and Ruby gravitated to each other more and more, as they stood together and received congratulations for news that had spread as quickly as he'd figured it would. But he was left more and more unsettled.

People were accepting. Excited. Seemingly truly happy for them. Showing no misgivings over their unusual arrangement—friends living apart and having a child. Even when he wasn't with Ruby, people came up to Sebastian and offered words of encouragement and advice. He couldn't have scripted it any better. But felt more deflated than not.

Those who knew about the crimes at Crosswinds, and Ruby's near kidnapping, were congratulating them both on a successful conclusion to a very bad situation.

It was obvious to Sebastian that people cared.

That he was one of them. A couple even mentioned his parents, saying they used to come into their shop every summer, saying how proud they'd been of Sebastian. And how much they'd have loved having a grandchild.

The words left him feeling gratified. And strangely empty, too.

Because the investigation was still ongoing until the perpetrator was formally charged, the police weren't yet releasing any information on the suspect. No one knew, yet, that Sebastian had a half brother.

Until nightfall, people mingled outside with an open bar and live music. Tables were set up in a barn with food in warming trays, buffet style. Balloons and banners gave the party a festive air. A mammoth cake sat in the middle of a table surrounded by small plates, napkins and forks.

Sebastian was glad he'd come. Most particularly when he was with Ruby. The woman had a way of lighting up the space around her. And not just because she was a Colton or owned the town's veterinary clinic. She was unique and strong and...

Jenny Colton brushed by him carrying a large birthday present toward the front of the room, where a microphone had been set up. Robert, across the room, was holding court with a group of five or six people circled around him.

"Here, Mrs. Colton, let me help you with that," Sebastian jumped in, then carried the package, and caught Ruby watching him. She smiled.

He smiled back.

And wanted more.

Jenny, Buck and Robert were the first to go through the food line. And had gone in that order. When Jenny sat at Buck's table to eat, and Robert headed over to a table on the other side of the barn with a group of people in line with him, Sebastian found himself thinking about his own parents. How, even during major social events, they'd always eaten together. And had a dance together, too.

Had his mother known about the affair?

Been hurt by it?

He and Ruby went through the food line together. He hadn't asked her to wait for him. Wasn't sure she had. But he liked them there. Doing that.

Even the fact that he'd noticed such a thing didn't make sense to him.

He was just leaning down to point out the vegetable soup to Ruby—more of what they'd shared at her house, he knew, because her sister Hannah had catered the event—when there was a commotion at the far side of the room.

Chairs pushing back. A collective gasp.

"Call 911!" Shouts came one after the other.

And beside him, Ruby dropped her plate.

"It's my father!" she cried, and ran off toward the crowd gathering around.

FOR THE REST of her life Ruby would be grateful to Sebastian for his quiet presence during the couple of hours that followed her father's collapse. The big mountain man insisted on driving her to the hospital in Connors, where the ambulance was taking her father.

Once she'd seen that her brothers and sisters were traveling together in one vehicle, she'd gratefully climbed up with Sebastian. All that collective fear together in one vehicle would be too much for her.

Buck and Jenny, who'd both been at Robert's side almost as soon as he'd passed out, had ridden together in the ambulance.

Her cousins, with hugs, concern and pleas to be kept informed, had stayed back at the ranch to see off the guests and clean up, as best they could.

He's alive. Sebastian's words as they'd pulled out behind the ambulance came back to Ruby again and again while they waited to hear any news at all.

Buck and Jenny were inside the emergency room cubicle, where they'd first taken Robert. The rest of them sat in various chairs in the waiting room. Hannah called her sitter to let her know she might need her overnight. And she then sat holding hands with Lizzie, their heads bent together as they talked softly.

Wade was by himself, reading a magazine. Chase kept checking at the desk for news. And Fletcher was scrolling on his phone.

Ruby sat with Sebastian, not touching, but so glad he was there. After an hour passed with no real news, other than that Robert had not yet regained consciousness, but was breathing on his own, and tests were being run, Ruby reluctantly told Sebastian, "You don't have to stay. I can catch a ride home with either Mom and Buck, or the crew." She motioned toward her various siblings scattered about.

And yet, all together, too.

When Sebastian said he was fine right where he was, she didn't question him. Or offer again. She found herself more calm—frightened, but not panicked—with him sitting next to her.

SEBASTIAN FELT AS relieved as if he'd been sitting vigil over his own family member when Jenny finally came out to tell her children that their father had suffered another stroke, but that he'd regained consciousness a couple of times and was holding steady.

The slim blond woman was clearly concerned—for her children as well as their father.

"Buck and I are both going to stay the night with him," she said then. "The doctor said each of you can come in for a minute, but that's it. They'll be moving him to a room and you can all come up tomorrow," she said, even glancing at Sebastian as she did so.

As though, because he'd fathered a Colton child, he was one of them.

He nodded at Ruby's mother, touched her shoulder as she passed and made a silent promise to her to watch over Ruby. Wanting to tell her that Robert would pull through just as he had four years before.

Like Sebastian, or Robert, had the ability to control fate.

He waited outside the emergency-room door as the siblings went in three at a time, to give their dad love, and was moved when Ruby, who came out first, looked to him as soon as she exited the door.

"I need to stop by Mom and Dad's," she said as they wished her siblings good-night and headed out into the night. "Mom wants me to pack a few things, including her pills, to bring up in the morning."

All business. Keeping a stiff upper lip. That was his Ruby.

He knew now, though, that underneath, she was as scared as the rest of them. He'd seen the chinks in her armor that no one else ever saw. With the exception, he suspected, of Jenny.

"I left my SUV there, anyway," she continued without a pause as they approached his truck. "I went over to help Mom load up decorations this afternoon, and rode to the party with her. Dad came straight from the office."

Sebastian wanted to just nod, keep his mouth shut. But said, "I can drive out to let Oscar out and put him in the kennel and meet you back at your place if you'd like." He didn't want her to be alone. Didn't think she wanted to be alone.

And since she didn't have a husband or boyfriend to call on, a friend was the next best thing.

He tried to wrap it all up nice and clean, but knew that he needed to be with her. To share the anguish with her, just as she'd sat with him through his own on a couple of occasions.

If ever a panic attack or nightmare could be better than another. Those two times with Ruby would qualify.

She hadn't given him a response and as he pulled out of the parking lot, he saw her wiping at her eyes. He stopped.

She glanced at him. Nodded.

And gave him the saddest smile he'd ever seen.

RUBY WANTED MORE.

Seeing her father in that hospital bed, knowing he could have easily died that night, could still die, had brought it all home to her.

Life didn't come with a single guarantee, other than that it would, at some point, end. Robert wasn't the perfect husband. He'd been an absentee father much of the time. But he loved them all. Had gone to battle for every one of them when they'd needed it growing up. Had always provided well, both in advice and monetary advantages.

"I just realized something tonight," she said aloud. "My dad, he's lived his whole life big. If not for his over-the-top dreams, maybe over-the-top energy, his need to always reach for more…we probably wouldn't even still all be together. He'd be running the hardware store with Uncle Buck. There'd be no ranch. No Colton Properties. Owl Creek would be the small town with no industry that it had always been. Maybe even be dwindling into nothing, if not for my father's vision of it as a tourist town. Us kids, if we'd been lucky enough to afford a college education, would have had to move elsewhere to get good-paying professional jobs. I sure would have had to. At least as far as Connors. If I'd even been lucky enough to get to go to veterinary school. Without the example I had, to dream big, to reach for what I wanted, I might not even have considered the possibility that I could be a vet..."

She was rambling. She knew it. Had to do it, anyway.

And wasn't the least bit worried about it, either. Sometime in the past weeks, or maybe slowly, over a period of years, Sebastian had become her safe place.

She wasn't looking at him. Stared at the road ahead of them, the headlights on pavement in a sea of darkness.

"I think that once I reached that dream, becoming a vet, I quit reaching," she said then. "I do good work, that I love, that completes me, and I go home where I feel peaceful. But, you know, there'll be plenty of time for peace when I pass on to the next life, right?"

Sebastian glanced at her. "If you want to do more with your life, you absolutely should," he agreed.

"If you spend your life avoiding turmoil, if you don't take risks, then you miss out on the possibility that you could have it all, instead of settling for peace."

It was all becoming clear, there in the darkness.

"What more do you want?"

She wanted him. As a husband. A lover. A boyfriend. The father to her child. A housemate. Or, if all he could give her was friendship, she'd grab at that for all she was worth.

"I want love," she told him, remembering what Jenny had said the other day in the kitchen. "I want love," she repeated, almost to herself, with total conviction. "And if that means my siblings drive me up the wall, then, oh, well. What goes up, has to come down, right? I want this baby. I want to be the best mother I can possibly be. It's going to be messy and unpredictable, but I want it, Sebastian. More than that, I think I need it."

His hands were gripping the steering wheel so tightly she could see the whites of his knuckles in the dash lights.

"I want you, too," she told him then. Taking the biggest risk of all. "However we work it out, so it's good for both of us, I want you."

Chapter Twenty-Four

Sebastian had no words. His friend was in pain. Pouring her heart out. And he had no words. He'd known the time would come.

Her father had just collapsed and was in the hospital. Could yet die. She was pregnant with Sebastian's child. She'd been nearly abducted that week. Had IDd her kidnapper the day before.

And she wanted him.

Say something, dammit.

"I'll be here for you, for as long as you want me to be." More than he'd ever said to anyone.

And, he was sure, not nearly enough.

"I know."

She didn't sound like she was settling.

But like she knew better than to ask for anything more.

"It's not enough, is it?"

When she didn't answer right away, his gut sank. They shouldn't be having the conversation right then. They'd been through so much. Were both tired. She had to be worried sick about Robert.

Should probably be with the siblings who shared her agony as acutely.

But…he knew what it felt like to lose a parent. "No matter what happens, you'll get through it, Ruby," he told her then. "If you risk and fail, or risk and get an entirely different result than you planned… If you need your father's advice someday and he's not there to give it…you'll get through. You'll learn. And you'll grow. And you'll have a future in front of you, too." He'd found words. Maybe not the right ones, but they were better than a deafening, potentially hurtful, silence.

"If one thing doesn't work, you'll take another risk. You're as determined as I am to chart your own course, and I can promise you that what I'm saying is true. When my folks died, I was lost. I sat in our home in Boise, knowing that I was the only family left within those walls, and felt like I was through. I was having nightmares, and panic attacks, and couldn't see a future. I came to Owl Creek just to get away from those walls. The cabin was mine, no one would come looking for me there, or visit, like they were in Boise. And look at me now," he said, not in a bragging way, but in an attempt to give her hope where he'd just snatched it away. "I've got Crosswinds, a career that I love, a town that is peripheral family to me, a baby on the way…and I've got you."

He bit off the last bit quickly. They'd reached Owl Creek. Would soon be at her parents' home.

"You've got me, too," he said then, restless, frustrated as hell. Filling with tension that he knew he couldn't assuage.

Pulling into the Colton community of Hollister Hills, he slowed the truck. "It's not enough, is it?" he asked again, when he knew the timing wasn't right.

Because he knew, too, that she'd needed to have the conversation. Which was why she'd brought it up.

Once again, she didn't answer.

So Sebastian did what he said he'd do. He pulled into her

parents' drive. Dropping her off as she'd asked him to do. "Do you still want me to come over tonight?"

She nodded, jumped down, put her satchel on her shoulder and turned back to him. "You'll always be enough, Sebastian. You are who you are, and I want you in my life. I need your friendship. There just might be someone else, too. Sometime down the road."

With that, she shut the passenger door and walked, head high, with steady steps up to the Colton mansion front door.

He waited until she was inside, wishing he'd said differently. More.

But didn't know what he'd add.

Backing out of the driveway, he headed out to tend to Oscar.

She wanted him with her that night.

And so he would be.

SHE WASN'T GOING to let herself cry. Her father was probably going to be just fine. He'd survived his last stroke without any adverse effects. The same could happen again.

He'd just been to the doctor, she reminded herself, comforted herself. His tests had come back no worse than previously.

Yes, according to Jenny, Robert's doctor had continued with grave warnings in the event that Robert didn't change his habits, but the man was only fifty-nine.

And other than the effects of his hard living he was in good health.

And the rest of it?

She was out of danger, thank God!

As she climbed the stairs up to her mother's room, to collect the things on the list Jenny had texted to her, she made herself focus on the good in her life.

Thoughts of Sebastian's words, the deep honesty in them, as he'd told her about coming home from Afghanistan, having to leave the Marines early, to deal with his parents' tragic and unexpected deaths.

The Sebastian she'd always known never spoke of such things.

And the picture he'd painted—a man all alone, suffering from what was probably, at that time, acute PTSD, to have pulled himself up and out and built Crosswinds from the ground up, who spent his life giving to other veterans, and training dogs to save lives of those who've gone missing... She'd fallen in love with a good man.

She wasn't sorry about that. Nor was she sorry she was having his baby. To the contrary, she felt honored to be the mother of Sebastian Cross's child.

And she wanted more. She wanted love.

Maybe Sebastian loved her and just couldn't tell her.

But she wanted marriage, too.

She was, after all, Robert Colton's daughter. She wasn't going to settle for peace and quiet. She was going to risk failure to try to have it all.

To live big, as her dad did.

She'd reached Jenny's room. Found the overnight zipper bag right where her mother had told her it would be. Didn't recognize the black leather satchel, but saw it as something her mother would use. There was a change of underwear inside already, so she crossed that off her mother's list.

She wondered where Jenny had been overnight. As far as she knew, her mom hadn't left town in over a year.

Sitting on her mother's bed for a moment, she remembered

a night when she'd awoken with a nightmare and crawled in bed with her mother. Jenny had wrapped her arms around little Ruby and she'd fallen back to sleep safe and secure.

She'd grown up in a home filled with chaos, but she'd been well loved. Had never doubted that.

It was that assurance, more than anything else, that she wanted to give her child. Whatever she had to do to accomplish the mammoth feat.

She took her time packing.

The pants and blouse were right where Jenny had said they'd be. The hospital was providing a toothbrush and paste for the night, but Jenny wanted her own in the morning, just in case she had to stay another night.

Her mom's hormone pills were in the cabinet.

And she added the few makeup items and the hairbrush Jenny had requested.

If Sebastian hadn't been coming over, she'd have driven the bag back that night. To sit with Jenny as her mother had been there for her so many times in her life. But Uncle Buck was with Jenny, and maybe it was best for the two of them to have some time alone with Robert. They'd all grown up together right there in Owl Creek.

Had gone to high school together.

Where, of course, Robert had been quarterback on the high-school football team.

Her dad was a competitor. A fighter. He was going to be fine.

With the bag on her shoulder, she wandered into Robert's room next door.

Separate rooms.

When had that happened?

After Lizzie was born?

Or had it been that way from the beginning?

Looking around, noticing the burned butt of a cigar in the ashtray on the nightstand by her father's bed, Ruby frowned, trying to remember how old she'd been when they'd lived in a house big enough for her parents to have separate rooms.

And then frowned again as she smelled something.

It was familiar.

And she didn't like it.

Heart pounding, she opened her father's nightstand drawer. Was she really searching her father's things for drugs? Of the illegal variety?

She'd been around marijuana in college. Had strongly disliked the sickly sweet smell.

It was illegal for any use in Idaho.

Or maybe it was just cut grass she was smelling. Leaving the drawers, she went to her father's open closet door, thinking maybe he'd been golfing earlier that day.

A Saturday in late April, made perfect sense to her…

"And now, my pretty, I've got you!" The familiar male voice reverberated through her brain, through the clothes in her father's closet, as a gloved hand reached out from between them and grabbed her wrist.

SEBASTIAN TOOK HIS time getting back to Crosswinds. It was late. Traffic was nonexistent. The night was peaceful. And he wanted to give Ruby time to get home and have a minute in her own space.

It was an act of selflessness.

What he wanted to do was turn around and follow her home.

Just to be by her side.

Life had spiraled in so many directions. For both of them.

The two of them together was the constant. Through all of it.

The attacks were on Crosswinds, and her.

The baby was equal parts of both of them.

He had a half brother. Her father had a stroke.

For years, they'd been living peaceful, productive lives. Side by side, through her brother, and then through work, but separate. And suddenly, they implode together. It was like fate was out to force them together.

The last thought triggered a self-deprecating grunt. He was so tired he was getting punchy.

Oscar greeted him with happy whines and a wagging body when he walked in the door. He fed the boy, and found a sense of rightness within himself, too.

Dogs were another thing he and Ruby had in common. A deep understanding of the relationship between canines and humans. Of the bond that existed between them.

"You want to go for a ride?" he asked Oscar then. He'd take the dog to Ruby's with him. Oscar would bridge the gap of need between them.

She'd told him once that she'd love to have a dog of her own, but just couldn't subject a precious canine to a life spent mostly alone. He'd suggested she take the dog to work with her every day. She'd seemed open to the idea. And then Oscar had been shot and he and Ruby had slept together and they'd quit talking like friends.

Grabbing food for the dog for the morning, and a clean pair of underwear and his toothbrush, Sebastian was just bagging his items to head out the door when his phone rang.

He'd only left Ruby a brief fifteen minutes before…

His entire being stopped flowing as he saw Steele's name come up. Close to midnight?

"What?" he answered.

"Working late here, and heard you were in Connors with the Coltons, so figured it wasn't too late to call," the detective began.

Get on with it. Sebastian kept his impatience to himself. Holding the phone to his ear with his shoulder, he shoved his things between paper handles, motioned for Oscar, and was heading out the door as Steele said, "A report just came through from Boise. Your father wasn't having an affair. The woman he was seeing was a patient. She didn't have health insurance and couldn't afford a hospital stay. He paid for her hotel and treated her there, on and off for a couple of years. When she got pregnant, he told her it would likely kill her to have the baby. She opted to have it, anyway. And when she died, the child was adopted out."

"Leon."

"That's what we thought because we thought he was your brother, but we haven't been able to confirm that. It's what we were after when we had Boise checking on the woman. We still haven't been able to positively ID this guy. He's got no driver's license, his prints aren't in the system. We've sent out DNA samples but haven't heard back."

Sebastian's mind was ticking. His father hadn't had an affair. He had to tell Ruby. And... "If he's not my brother, why does he think the land is his?"

"We're still working on that. He's not talking. Just keeps saying God is his father. And spitting out renditions of bible verse that aren't accurate. Our theory right now is that he did some amateur checking and somehow thinks you're his brother."

The young man sounded delusional.

"Has his attorney been in to see him?"

"Today. Of course, I have no idea what was said."

Right. And knowing the kid was in good hands—hands Sebastian would continue to pay for now that he'd started—he could walk away.

And he did.

RUBY SCREAMED, "NO-O-O-O!" burst out of her as the man in the closet held a vise grip on her wrist. She kicked her elbow out like a chicken wing, striking him under his chin, and twisted her arm with a purposeful jerk as she did so.

In the split second that his grasp loosened, she was free. Slamming the closet door, she ran for the room's exit, pushing the lock in the knob as she shut that, too.

The lock wouldn't hold. The door was solid wood, and the jambs were standard, attached to trim wood. Her attacker was strong. She had two minutes, max.

Too late, she identified the stench.

The smell of the man who'd grabbed her from behind in the dark.

He'd been smoking dope before he attacked her.

Her kidnapper wasn't in jail.

He was right there in her parents' house. Like he'd been lying in wait. Watching all of them. Had he followed her to the hospital, and back?

He'd smelled like pot the night of the attempted abduction. How could she have forgotten that?

How he had gotten out of jail, and how long it would be before anyone knew, she had no idea. Just knew she had a baby to protect.

She had to stay alive.

She'd left her purse downstairs. Had to get to her phone.

Her parents, like so many, no longer had a landline. Thoughts flew as she moved down the hall.

Seconds later, she passed the bedroom she'd recently used and was turning toward the stairs when she heard the loud crack of wood behind her.

Her attacker was already free, just around the corner.

She'd never make it down the stairs in time.

Instead, she slipped behind the door in the bathroom, prayed that he'd run past her toward the stairs.

Her heart thumped. Pressed against the wall behind the door, she could hear the beat in her head, feel the ends of every nerve. She could hardly breathe, but had to keep thinking.

To keep focused.

She was alone. Had to save herself.

She knew the house. The fiend after her did not.

How long would it be until Fletcher got home?

Her brother had a gun in his room. Fletcher was wearing his personal gun in town, and had showed her the nine-millimeter, for her use if she needed it to stay alive, the first night she'd stayed with him and her parents.

She was going to need it to stay alive.

Doors banged against walls down the hall, followed by seconds of silence. The kidnapper searching rooms? He was coming closer. If he banged her door, she'd be dead.

Turning her cheek to the wall, she prayed for all she was worth. And saw the sink. The cupboard under it was empty. She'd stored her toiletries there.

Hearing another door slam, figuring she had seconds while the intruder was in the guest room, she used those seconds to crawl inside the small cupboard, scrunching up, with her head tilted to avoid the drain.

The door just outside her space slammed.

If he opened the cupboard, found her, she had one shot. A kick straight to the groin, or she was done.

She had to wait for him to open the door. To be that close, facing the cupboard, or she wouldn't have a shot at incapacitating him.

She could hear the man's heavy breathing.

Could feel his incensed desire to lay his hands on her.

And held her breath.

Chapter Twenty-Five

Sebastian wasn't even up Cross Road before he voice-dialed Ruby to tell her about Steele's call. Her kidnapper wasn't his brother.

Though, logically, he'd known the relationship wasn't his fault—wasn't a reflection on him, as Ruby had pointed out—the relief was palpable. Coursing through him with a newness of life. His child was not going to have an uncle in prison for heinous crimes against the child's mother.

Expecting her to pick up on the first ring, as she generally did lately, he waited impatiently through the second.

And then the third.

After the night she'd had, he was antsy to give her some good news.

By the fourth ring, Sebastian was fully focused.

The young man in jail sounded delusional. Was quoting bible verses wrong. He must have done his amateur sleuthing incorrectly to have come to the conclusion that Sebastian was his brother.

Even with desperation driving escalated behavior, the man in jail did not resemble a stalker shrewd enough to elude investigators, leaving no clues at all, for more than two months.

A kid spouting religious rhetoric. Like the kidnapper had

spewed to Ruby the night of her attempted abduction, and to him via text, and with a clever plan to torch his place that fit the man's method of operation. Calling him brother. Maybe he was overreacting.

It would be way too much of a coincidence, some kid just happening to torch his place after he'd initiated a campaign to squeeze out the stalking kidnapper.

And it hit him.

With cold certainty.

A man who'd been pushed past his limit, who'd been forced out of his carefully calculated plans, might hire someone to be in one place, while he would lie in wait for what he'd obviously determined was the root of all of his problems. Ruby.

Why the guy wanted his land, why he thought Crosswinds belonged to him, he had no idea. And at the moment, didn't care.

Calling Steele back, Sebastian told the man to get to Ruby's house, while he broke all speed limits to get there himself.

She thought she heard her phone ringing.

Would it draw her attacker down the stairs?

What about the security system?

Where was Fletcher?

Her kidnapper had shoved the bathroom door against the wall. And then...nothing.

Had he left?

Was he standing there? Staring at the cupboard?

Had she left a trail?

Did he know she was in there?

Chest tight, she couldn't breathe. Hurt everywhere.

And…she heard the screech of rings against metal just feet away as he pushed aside the shower curtain.

He was going to find her.

Sebastian had just reached the outskirts of Owl Creek when his phone rang again. Steele.

"She's not at her house."

The words sparked a fear in him that he couldn't contain. Gunning his engine, he spit out the words: "Her parents." And, turning his wheel sharply to the left, screeching his tires, he told Oscar to hang on as he entered the private neighborhood of mansions.

Feeling sick, ready to kill or die, he saw Ruby's SUV still in the drive of her parents' home. And saw the light on upstairs.

"Please, God, let her be in Jenny's room, taking her time collecting things. Needing to be close to her mother."

Comforted himself with the thought of the security system.

He dialed her again as he pulled up the drive, stopping right behind her vehicle. Told Oscar to stay and was already heading up the walk as he heard the ring of the connected call. He could see her satchel through the window. On an ottoman not far from the front door.

And knew with dead certainty that something was wrong. Very wrong.

With her father in the emergency room, Ruby would not let her phone go unanswered unless she had no other choice.

Not knowing if she'd fallen, was hurt, or if his worst suspicions were true and the man in jail was not their stalker, and the kidnapper had Ruby, he picked up a rock and broke the front window, using his shirted arm to swipe away enough glass to get inside.

Gun out, he surveyed the space, looking for… *Oh, God, not blood.*

"Ruby!" The call was a cry from the heart.

Then he saw curtains blowing through an open window in the back of the house.

And went into full battle mode.

She might already be gone.

He had to check the house first.

Maybe he wasn't too late.

Maybe there would be a clue to who had her, where he'd taken her.

He'd quickly canvassed the downstairs, was heading upstairs when he heard what sounded like wood slamming against a wall.

Gun pointed, ready to take out the fiend with one bullet to the head, he took the stairs three at a time, heard a grunt. Fear made adrenaline race through him as he rounded the corner.

"You…" A man's voice.

He swung around. Saw a jean-clad backside and shot.

The wall at the end of the hall.

It was enough to make the man stand upright for the split second it took Sebastian to shove the barrel of his gun to the back of the intruder's head. "Move and you're dead."

RUBY SAW BLOOD drip to the hallway floor. And didn't move.
Move and you're dead.

She'd heard Sebastian's voice but could only see the intruder.

And blood.

After looking in the bath, her kidnapper had left the bathroom. Ruby had breathed a full breath. She'd heard the door slam against the wall. And then nothing.

Until she'd heard Sebastian call her name.

Tears had flooded her eyes. She'd bit her lip to keep from making a sound.

And had heard her kidnapper as he whispered, "I know where you are. You're going to come out of there nice and slow…"

He was going to use her as a human shield. She just knew.

Would hold her up and make Sebastian let them walk away.

The cupboard had opened.

She'd kicked, but the evil man had been ready for her, keeping himself back far enough to ward off any self-defensive blow. Her foot landed on his shin.

Painful, but not debilitating.

That's when she'd seen the gun. Held low, in one hand, it was pointed straight at her. Still.

Did Sebastian know? He was behind the man. Could he see the gun?

Did she warn him?

Hoping that Sebastian was a quicker shot than the man who'd been eluding police for more than two months?

The kidnapper had escaped chains and jail.

Her parents' security system…

She was going to die, right there in front of Sebastian…

"Turn around slowly." Sebastian's controlled, commanding tone brought more tears. If his voice was the last one she heard, she'd take it with her forever.

Staring unblinkingly at the intruder's feet, she waited for them to move.

They didn't.

She was still staring at a gun barrel.

She was going to die.

Sebastian would never know his baby.

Never give himself another chance to have a family of his own.

If he didn't know about the gun, he'd never forgive himself when Ruby got shot.

Her only chance was to take a chance.

The gun was two feet away.

She'd get one move. And it had to be quicker than a trigger pull.

She'd positioned herself to kick out and up. If she could knock the gun...

A quick movement, and the feet in front of her suddenly twisted away. "Drop the gun, you..." Sebastian's curse words sounded. She waited for the sound of another shot.

Heard... Was that Fletcher?

And Detective Steele?

"We've got this..."

"Ruby..."

Sebastian's voice. Warm. Worried.

She wanted to tell him she was fine.

But she lay there, curled up, her back to the wall, a drain in front of her face, her arms cradling her baby, and couldn't move.

SHE WAS SHAKING. But breathing. Reaching a steady hand in, Sebastian felt for a pulse. It was rapid, but strong.

Her gaze didn't seem to be focusing.

Fear struck through him again. "Ruby?"

When that beautiful, deep green-eyed gaze moved to

him, he felt tears prick his eyes. He hadn't cried since Jerry had died.

While everything inside of him wanted to rip the vanity apart and lift her up against him, never to let her go, he remained on his haunches, holding her gaze. "Are you hurt?"

If the man had…

She was fully dressed in the same red jeans and black pullover sweater she'd had on all night.

"No."

She still didn't move.

And he understood. The chaos right outside the bathroom door. The sounds of police voices, sirens in the distance. He shut the door.

Flipped on the bathroom light.

And met her gaze again, immediately.

"You want to come out now?"

She shook her head. "Not until he's gone."

"Ruby!" Fletcher's voice sounded panicked, followed by a strong knock on the door.

Standing, Sebastian opened the door.

"Her vitals are fine. She's scared to death. Stay with her," he said, taking the stairs down two at a time, and racing for his truck.

"Come on, boy," he said, slapping his thigh and racing back toward the house. The blue-hooded man was in cuffs, being led out of the house. Sebastian didn't look at him. Just slapped his thigh again and took the stairs back up, with Oscar keeping pace beside him.

"It's okay, sis, it's over." Sebastian heard Fletcher's voice.

And when there was no reply, he tapped the detective on the shoulder and motioned for him to make room. Seeing Oscar, Fletcher stood.

It took strength for Sebastian to stand back and let Oscar rescue the mother of his child. He watched as the dog put a paw on Ruby's leg, and then moved closer, laying his front paws in as much of her lap as he could get to.

But when he saw her hand move to Oscar's head, and then slowly start to pet the dog, he knew she was going to be okay.

And dropped to his knees with relief.

Chapter Twenty-Six

Ruby had no need for medical attention. An EMT on scene checked her out, but she'd have refused to head back to the ER in Connors even if it had been recommended.

Standing in her parents' front yard, looking at the crime-scene tape, the flashing lights, she could only think of one place she wanted to be.

"Take me home with you," she said to Sebastian, her hand on Oscar's head. "Please."

Her brother was going to be at the police station for a while. If she didn't detest the fiend who'd been terrorizing them for months, she'd have felt sorry for him. Fletcher was not going to leave the man alone until he had every answer he wanted out of him.

He'd do it legally. But her brother would not give up.

He'd also said he was going to head up to the hospital in the morning to speak with their parents. Or at least Jenny, if Robert wasn't well enough to hear what had happened.

Steele agreed to put off that particular notification for the night.

By morning, they should have answers to give Jenny—like how the kidnapper got past the security system—along with the bad news that her beautiful home was a crime scene.

Or even, who the kidnapper was. In the meantime, officers were going to secure the house for the night. Tape cardboard to windows and assign a watch so the place didn't get vandalized.

It wasn't until she and Sebastian were in the truck, on their way out to Crosswinds—Oscar sitting in the back seat with his head popping over the back of the seat—that Ruby remembered the blood.

"Did you crack him with the butt of the gun?" she asked. She'd heard his report to Steele and Fletcher, right after she'd given her own without Sebastian present.

They'd both been told to stay close in case they'd need to come in for further questioning in the morning.

"Nope. No way I was risking any chance that man has any cause to come after me again. I played it fully by the book."

She glanced at him. "I saw blood drip on the floor."

When Sebastian pulled up his red-checked flannel sleeve, showing her the gash on his forearm, she gasped. "Why didn't you have the EMT look at that?" she asked him. "It needs attention, Sebastian."

"And I have someone perfectly capable of taking care of it, if that's the case," he said, adding, "Right here in the truck with me." He glanced over at her. "I needed to get you out of there."

Yeah. Even just five minutes down the road, she was feeling better. Breathing easier. Her chest felt lighter.

"I think it's just surface," he said then, sounding calm. But she saw those white knuckles on the steering wheel.

In his own way, Sebastian was as agitated as she was. And she thought of something she'd just heard.

"Leon isn't your brother." He had to be feeling good about that.

He nodded. Gave her nothing more on the subject.

And then they were pulling into Crosswinds. She insisted on a stop at the medical building so she could check out his arm—cut from breaking the front window glass in her parents' home. She found herself picking out a couple of shards—remembering when she'd been similarly engaged treating Elise not so long before—and could hardly comprehend that it was really over.

She'd thought it was. Trusted it was.

But it hadn't been.

Sebastian didn't need stitches. She'd have insisted on a trip into Connors if he had. She patched him up with butterfly strips and looked up at him, to see if he was satisfied, only to catch him staring at her with the most intent look in his eyes.

An expression she didn't recognize.

And couldn't look away.

He didn't say anything. Just looked at her.

And then lowered his lips to hers. Showing her what he was feeling.

Because that was who he was and what he had to give.

And when she'd needed him, he was there.

He'd saved her life. Not once, but twice.

Maybe she wasn't meant to get married. Maybe a good friend, hopefully occasional lover and co-parent was all she was ever going to have.

Because she wasn't going to walk away from Sebastian. Ever.

There was no one else on earth whose presence made her world okay. No one else who seemed to take the same comfort from her own nearness.

So what he had to give was going to have to be enough.

LYING IN HIS bed with Ruby that night, Sebastian watched the expressions chase themselves across her face. Frowns. Looks of pain.

No smiles.

He'd dozed some. Had definitely rested, with her body lightly touching his. He'd refused to allow himself deep sleep. After all the trauma of the past few days—culminating that night when he'd seen the gun in the kidnapper's hands and had thought, for a split second, that he could very well lose Ruby and the baby—there'd been too much chance of a nightmare.

He'd been surprised at just how relaxed he'd been, from the moment they stripped down to their underwear and crawled in bed together.

There'd been no sex. She'd given him no hint at all that she wanted it. And he'd had no inclination for it, either.

They'd been through too much to put themselves through any more emotional upheaval. Even ecstasy.

But as dawn neared, he wished he'd made love to her. To have that be her last moments before sleeping, to chase away the demons that seemed to be haunting her in her sleep.

To have a pleasant memory be the first thing on her mind when she woke up.

And right then, in that moment, lying there watching her, focusing solely on her, he knew. And bent down to kiss her.

Her lips moved beneath his before her eyes opened.

And then she was lying there staring up at him, completely open. No filters.

It was a second that would be locked in his memory for life. The thing he would be striving to achieve for the rest of his days.

"Marry me," he said then. So easily.

She blinked. And when her eyes opened again, the smart, assessing, closed-off woman he knew was staring back at him.

"Don't, Sebastian."

Absolutely the furthest reaction he'd expected to get.

"Don't what?"

"All of it—just don't." She slid from the bed.

And he followed right behind her. "I thought you'd changed your mind, that you wanted to get married some-day," he said as she pulled a flannel shirt out of his closet and slid her arms into it on the way to the kitchen.

He wasn't going to panic. He was going to be there. Period.

Turning, she stopped him in his tracks. "I want you," she said. "The real you. Not someone who gives me what I want when it doesn't fit. That's a recipe for failure."

Something she'd been afraid of her whole life, he realized. Thinking of all her questions, always. Needing to know. To be sure. To limit…

And he took a deep breath.

"Last night, when I saw his gun…"

She hissed in a breath, but he didn't stop. "I knew I could lose you. And that if I did, the light in my life would go out. You are my constant, Ruby. And… I saved your life. I was able to protect you, in spite of myself. You said not too long ago that there are dangers we run from and those we choose to manage. I'm asking you to take on the potential danger of living with a man with PTSD. I've started training Oscar. Our awareness of the situation, the potential triggers and a dog trained to stop me before I escalate out of control could be how we manage that. And when our child is young, I'm never left alone all night, or at least, I never go to sleep, without another adult present, just in case. I know your stubbornness, your strength, and know that if I'm ever out of control when you're there, the first thing you'll do is see to our child."

She was shaking her head. Not smiling.

He didn't get it.

"I love you, Sebastian," she told him, as if she'd said the words many times before. "And right now, I need you to take me home. To get a shower and head to Connors to see my mom and dad. And you need to feed dogs and train..."

"Della's going to cover Crosswinds for me," he told her. "I texted her last night when you were in seeing your father." And then, with his newly opened heart shattering a bit, he said, "I'm fine to take you home. I'd like it better if you'd let me get a quick shower, first. And then I can come to the hospital with you. Just in case."

He left that "in case" hanging there. Just in case there were questions about Ruby's near kidnapping the night before. Or, just in case Robert wasn't doing as well as expected. She could take her pick. Both were there.

And when she nodded, saying, "I'll feed Oscar while you're showering," his heart started to piece itself back together again.

THE MAN ALREADY owned her heart. There was no reason for him to give up his own path to walk hers. As badly as Ruby had wanted to throw caution to the wind, reach for what she most wanted and suggest that she and Sebastian go to the courthouse that day to complete marriage paperwork, she couldn't.

Maybe she'd never be a person like her father. One who could just take what he wanted, create what he needed by hard work, dedication and sheer force of will, and deal with the consequences later.

She was a woman who'd been too shut in, too cautious to dare to dream. But she was also one who needed to look for possible consequences and be prepared to deal with them in the event her reaching, her risk, brought them about.

And the consequences of marrying Sebastian, when he was so definitely not a marrying man, were too brutal to consider. She could lose him entirely.

She'd rather be his friend for life than his enemy.

Or, worse, his nothing at all.

An early morning proposal, out of the blue, after the night they'd had, preceded by the weeks they'd had… She'd have been nothing but selfish to accept.

But she kissed him when he came out of the shower. Deep. Long. Like a lifetime lover would do. Squeezed his arm before she got out of his truck at her folks' house and got into her own SUV. She waited for him to pull into her garage after her and walked with him into her house.

And smiled, an expression she felt to her soul, when he was waiting for her with breakfast made when she came out of her room. He pulled her into his arms then, kissing her as deeply as she'd kissed him earlier, and she started to rest a little easier inside.

They were going to find their way.

It might not be traditional. Or be exactly what she thought she wanted.

But in the end, what she wanted was him.

And if he wanted her as badly, they'd find a way to make it work.

Fletcher called just as they were getting ready to leave for the hospital. He was heading up after a shower, and asked that she wait to tell their parents what had happened until he got there.

A condition with which she was quite happy to comply.

She put him on speakerphone then, as he relayed what had transpired during the night. Sebastian drove, as they heard, together, that her kidnapper's name was Bob Thompson.

"I know that name," Sebastian said.

"His lawyer approached you six months ago with an offer to buy your five acres on the lake," Fletcher said. And Sebastian and Ruby frowned together.

"All of this is because Sebastian wouldn't sell his land?" she asked, incredulous. No matter how much research, how many questions asked, or how many foreseen risks she might have turned up on a land offer, she'd never, in a million years, have come up with such a potentially deadly consequence.

"Yes and no. Yes, if Sebastian had sold the land, the man wouldn't have gone after the two of you. But he'd have been living right here in Owl Creek and that would not have been good," Fletcher continued. And Ruby grew more and more incredulous, and horrified, too, as she listened. "He's an Ever After Church member, and claims that God told him that the property belonged to the church. That God wanted the land for a new church."

"I've never even heard of the Ever After Church," she said, glancing at Sebastian, who shook his head.

"Neither had we. Supposedly it was founded by some guy named Markus Acker. But this is where it really gets weird. This guy, Thompson, has a record. He ran an illegal gambling ring for years without getting caught. And when he was apprehended, he made a deal to turn in some of his clients who were mobsters to stay out of jail. Apparently, the second chance turned his life around, he found religion and has dedicated his life to the service of Ever After Church, claiming it saved him. To the point that he was willing to risk going back to jail to follow what he claims are God's edicts. He's been living in plain sight, staying at a cabin on the lake. Dressed in expensive clothes. Golfing. The blue hoodie was for his nighttime persona. Using a rowboat along the shore in the dark to access Crosswinds. He's a smart guy. Too smart for his own good. He was able to hack into the Wi-Fi on Mom and Dad's security system so if it went off, it dialed his number instead of the security company or police. He'd done that the day after the kidnapping, when you started staying there. He'd been following you ever since."

Ruby had no words.

Sebastian's were off-color. And pretty much expressed her own feelings. Shivering, she put her hand on the console between them, and he laced his big, warm fingers through hers.

"He's still claiming that we're all sinners and that God will make us pay," Fletcher said.

Consequences again. The thought hit Ruby. They were everywhere, those things that happened due to choices made. She was never going to be able to control them all.

And she sure as hell didn't want to try and end up losing sight of reality, as Bob Thompson surely had.

"What about Leon?" Sebastian's question brought her back to the moment at hand. And the man at her side. One who'd asked her to marry him when marriage hadn't even been a dot on his radar. And who'd been rejected by her.

"When he saw Thompson in handcuffs, being led by his open door..."

"Your suggestion, I'm sure," Ruby butt in.

"Yeah, well, when Leon saw Thompson, and knew that he'd been arrested, he was only too happy to tell us that

Thompson had been a visiting minister at his church on and off, and had approached Leon, saying he'd had a vision, that God had chosen Leon to do a hard part of His work..."

"He duped the kid into setting my place on fire," Sebastian said. "But what about saying I was his brother?"

"This kid believes that all people on earth are brothers and sisters, per his bible readings. His last name's Connolly. Turns out his dad's in prison. His mom abandoned him. He's been in and out of foster homes his whole life. Some of them abusive. And, in high school, landed in the home of a couple of zealots, who took him to a small, very strict church. He'd been looking for something to believe in, someone to believe, his whole life, and he thought he'd found his family. His home."

There it was again. Family.

Home. She placed her other hand over her stomach. Cradled her tiny but growing baby.

"And hey, sis, you'll be the first in the family to know—I've been offered lead detective here in Owl Creek. And I've accepted. I'm moving home!"

Ruby burst out with enthusiasm without even thinking about how it would be with one more sibling watching her. Giving her their opinion of her life choices. Butting in. Instead, she let herself be happy to have someone she loved back home.

And after they hung up, she asked Sebastian to pull into a mountain park not far from Connors.

He stopped in a small, deserted lot by a hiking trail. "What's up?" he asked, turning to run a finger through a few strands of hair that had fallen out of her always loose bun.

"Why did you ask me to marry you? Full-out honesty here, Sebastian..." she said, her tone filled with warning.

Though she couldn't have told him to save her life what the consequences would be if he didn't comply.

Because the heart knew what it knew.

And was strong enough to deal with the consequences.

"Because I realized something last night on my way back to Owl Creek," he told her, looking her straight in the eye, his fingers remaining in her hair. "You and I—we're a constant. When life flew out of control for both of us, others were involved, in the picture, helping, but you and I were my constant. Us. Together. I'm good alone. I'm better with you. And I think you're better with me, too."

Her eyes flooded with tears. Her lips were trembling so much, her throat so tight, she couldn't speak.

"I love you, Ruby Colton. As much as I'm going to love that kid you're carrying. I don't want to go to bed at night without you, wondering about you. Or wake up in the morning thinking of you, when I could be lying there with you. This morning, it was all…just there. The battle I'd been fighting, to be independent and live alone… Maybe I was just afraid of losing love again. Maybe I was just plain uninformed. But I lost the battle, Ruby. I don't need to fight it anymore."

She swallowed. Tried to speak. And when she couldn't, she threw her body over the console, her top half landing against Sebastian, and her butt on the hard cover between their seats. It wasn't a well-thought-out plan. Or elegant.

It didn't work well.

And she didn't care.

Because it got her where she most needed to be. Her body in the arms of the man she loved. And her arms around the human who needed her just as badly.

He lowered his lips as she raised hers. And in that kiss, she found her future.

It wouldn't be perfect.

There'd be hardship and pain along the way.

Their child would grow up to disagree with them, go out into the world and take their own risks. And if they had more than one...then they'd all eventually go and there would be even more risks.

She had to take them.

When they both finally came up for air—only because they couldn't go any further to assuage their physical needs on the driver's seat of his truck—she whispered, "Ask me again."

"Marry me," he said, and this time she smiled.

He hadn't asked the first time.

He'd commanded.

If she'd heard that, she'd have understood.

Because she knew Sebastian Cross. He hadn't been commanding her. He'd just been that sure of his own personal course going forward. And that's all she'd needed to know.

"Marry me," she said back, in just as forceful a tone.

And this time, when they kissed, they did so around the smiles on their lips.

* * * * *

COMING SOON!

We really hope you enjoyed reading this book.
If you're looking for more romance
be sure to head to the shops when
new books are available on

Thursday 15th February

To see which titles are coming soon, please visit

millsandboon.co.uk/nextmonth